A SECOND
HELPING

Also by Beverly Jenkins

Contemporary

BRING ON THE BLESSINGS
DEADLY SEXY
SEXY/DANGEROUS
BLACK LACE
THE EDGE OF DAWN
THE EDGE OF MIDNIGHT

Historical

CAPTURED
JEWEL
WILD SWEET LOVE
WINDS OF A STORM
SOMETHING LIKE LOVE
A CHANCE AT LOVE
BEFORE THE DAWN
ALWAYS AND FOREVER
THE TAMING OF JESSI ROSE
THROUGH THE STORM
TOPAZ
INDIGO
VIVID
NIGHT SONG

A SECOND HELPING

A BLESSINGS NOVEL

Beverly Jenkins

AVON

An Imprint of HarperCollins*Publishers*

HarperCollins books may be purchased for educational, business, or sales promotional use. For information please write: Special Markets Department, HarperCollins Publishers, 10 East 53rd Street, New York, NY 10022.

FIRST AVON PAPERBACK EDITION PUBLISHED 2010.

Designed by Diahann Sturge

Library of Congress Cataloging-in-Publication Data
Jenkins, Beverly, 1951–
   A second helping : a blessings novel / by Beverly Jenkins.
      p. cm.
   ISBN 978-0-06-154781-2 (pbk.)
      1. Kansas—Fiction. 2. City and town life—Fiction. 3. African Americans—Fiction.
I. Title.
PS3560.E4795S43 2010
813'.54—dc22

                                              2009036258

10 11 12 13 14   OV/RRD   10 9 8 7 6 5 4 3 2 1

To foster parents and adoptive parents everywhere.

PROLOGUE

Get in the car!" Jack James snarled at his sixteen-year-old son, Eli. Snarling was better than cursing and yelling though both were justifiable when you get a call from the LAPD in the middle of the night telling you your kid has been picked up for joyriding in a stolen car.

Eli plopped down into the seat and slammed the door.

Jack gritted out, "You've been gone for four days! Do you know how worried I've been? You're lucky the car owner didn't press charges."

A surly silence was followed by "I'm not moving to Kansas with you. I don't care what you say."

"Then you go into foster care until you're eighteen."

"What!"

"You heard me. It's either Kansas or foster care. Legally, you're not old enough to be on your own, and if you think I'm kidding, the papers are in the glove box. I'm done trying to make you do right, Eli."

Jack, a widower, didn't know his son anymore. Since Eva's death, two years ago, Eli had become increasingly distant and angry. His grades were on life support, his attitude surly as the ocean in winter, and his contempt for his surviving parent obvious. Jack remembered the day Eli was born; how tiny he was in his little blue blanket and how perfect. He'd held his child in his arms and thought about what a blessed future their family would have, and it had been that until the day Eva was diagnosed with a particularly aggressive form of breast cancer. She'd fought for her life with all the strength, humor, and faith she possessed, but it hadn't been enough.

And so here he sat, furious at that same perfect child; furious, tired, and heartbroken. "I love you, Eli, but I'm going to Kansas to take this teaching position. If you don't want to, fine. We can go back inside and you can wait for Child Protective Services to come pick you up. Like I said, paperwork's ready to go."

"I hate you, you know."

"I do. I also know that you're hurting and angry about losing Mom, but did it ever occur to you that I might be feeling the same way? I loved her too," Jack whispered.

Startled, Eli looked over, but Jack ignored him and started up the car instead.

CHAPTER
1

Eleven-year-old Amari Steele looked down at the food on his plate. He guessed the yellow stuff on the left was eggs, and he knew a muffin when he saw one, but this other stuff, it looked like spinach. Who ate spinach for breakfast? "What's this supposed to be again, Dad?"

Trenton July, the mayor of Henry Adams, looked up from his own plate and into the skeptical eyes of his foster son. In truth, Trent didn't have a clue. "Not sure."

Bing Shepard, one of the town's elders, leaned over from the booth behind them and drawled, "French cuisine."

Amari moved his plate away, grumbling, "Doesn't she know we're in Kansas? I came here for waffles."

The *she* in question was the new cook at the town's recently rebuilt and refurbished diner, the Dog and Cow, aka the Dog. Her name was Florene Maxwell. She was a culinary student at the community college, but as far as the local residents were concerned, she couldn't cook a lick.

Trent looked around the diner. The place was as packed

as it was supposed to be on a Saturday morning but if all
the plates being sent back to the kitchen were any indica-
tion, no one was pleased with Florene or her cuisine.

She'd taken over the kitchen this past Monday, and proceeded to serve up not the pork chops, chicken, rice, and
other familiar fare on the menu when Rocky, the previous cook, reigned in the kitchen, but an ever-increasing
array of strange dishes no one could pronounce, let alone
cared to eat, like itty-bitty potatoes set on sprigs of green
twigs, multicolored spats of pureed root vegetables that had
to have come out of baby food jars, and portions of meat so
small they wouldn't have fed a cat.

And she had the nerve to be snippy. Earlier in the week,
when Trent asked why there were no pork chops, chicken
breasts, or anything else on the new menu real people wanted
to eat, her response had been a haughty "Because this is my
kitchen and if you don't like the changes eat somewhere
else."

Well now.

Because the town's owner and fairy godmother, Bernadine Brown, who usually handled the town's problems,
had flown off to Barcelona on Monday morning to hang out
with her girlfriends, the disgruntled residents had no one
to take their complaints to but Trent and his father, Malachi, the owner of the diner. Malachi and Florene had been
going round and round about the food. The only reason
she hadn't been fired the very first day was that Malachi
wanted to wait for Bernadine to return. It was his hope
that she'd be able to talk some sense into the girl.

In the meantime, Henry Adams was a small town. Population, seventy, give or take a few, and folks had small-town values. As a result they'd bent over backward to be kind and welcoming to Florene. For the first few days nobody overtly complained about the unpronounceable dishes or the teeny-tiny portions, but spinach for Saturday breakfast instead of waffles and pancakes? They were done.

Amari pushed his plate farther away. "May I be excused? I want to go home and get my bike."

Trent asked, "Why?"

"So I can ride over to Tamar's. I want waffles."

Trent chuckled. "Me too. How about I drive?" Tamar was Trent's grandmother. She knew grandsons like him and growing boys like Amari needed their Saturday morning waffles, so Trent paid their bill and with a wave good-bye to the rest of the grumbling diners, he and Amari made their exit.

Driving the road to Tamar's, Trent glanced over at the boy beside him riding shotgun. Amari "Flash" Steele. He was born in Detroit and given the nickname Flash for his lightning-fast ability to steal cars. Amari was wise beyond his years. One would think that a child who'd spent the majority of his young life moving between foster homes would be distant or empty inside. Not Amari. Beneath the street smarts and swagger beat a heart of gold. The kid also had a charismatic charm bordering on the magical.

Trent's eyes drifted back to his driving and the expanse of plowed Kansas fields that stretched to the horizon and lined both sides of the gravel road they were traveling on. Being a father had always been a dream of his, but after two failed marriages and marking his fortieth birthday, he'd all but given up hope. Then Bernadine Brown entered the town's life, bringing with her a bunch of blessings, and five needy foster children she wanted the Henry Adams community to help raise: fifteen-year-old Crystal Chambers; thirteen-year-old Preston Mays; eleven-year-old Amari; and Mississippi-born and -raised Devon Watkins and little mute Zoey Raymond, who were eight and seven respectively.

Trent chose Amari to foster, and so far it had been a good fit. Initially he'd questioned the decision once it became clear that Amari asked questions 24/7, 365. The kid was smart as a whip and curious as the proverbial cat in spite of being academically behind. Now, thanks to local schoolteacher Marie Jefferson, his grades were improving and the questions continued to flow like the Mississippi.

"When's Ms. Bernadine coming back?"

"Sometime tomorrow night, if they make all of their connections."

Bernadine was traveling with her foster daughter, Crystal, and Lily Fontaine, the town's COO and Trent's lady. Lord, he missed Lily. Back in the mid-eighties, they'd been high school sweethearts, but after graduation their relationship crashed and burned. She came back to town last summer and they'd reconnected, so now Trent had Amari and Lily, and life was sweet.

There was nothing sweet going on between Crystal and Amari, however. When the kids first came to live in Henry Adams, they'd been strangers, all hailing from different parts of the country, and Crys and Amari had gotten along like warring nations. The one time they did see eye to eye, half the town ended up in court, including Trent and his father, Malachi, because Amari had "borrowed" Mal's truck to help Crystal run away so she could track down her birth mother, Nikki. Luckily the caper had been cut short by the local sheriff, but the judge placed Henry Adams's unique foster child program on probation for one year; a probation that would end in the fall as long as there were no more Stupid Kid Tricks in the interim.

"When Ms. Bernadine gets back, first thing I want her to do is fire that dumb cook," Amari groused. "Even I know you don't serve people spinach for breakfast."

The smiling Trent agreed.

When they reached Tamar's, the two got out. The freshly painted green house with its wide wraparound porch had been home to the July family since the late nineteenth century. Its first residents had been Trent's great-great-great-grandmother, Olivia Sterling July, and her husband, Neil July. Olivia had been the Henry Adams mayor and Neil the eldest of the train-robbing, bank-robbing, always-wanted-by-the-law July family. Trent swept his eyes up over the grand old structure, noting the white gingerbread trim and the rusted rooster weather vane Tamar refused to replace. Both his grandmother and his father had been born inside; he himself had grown up within its sheltering walls, and now, thanks to the repairs and remodeling courtesy of Bernadine and her town revitalization efforts, it would stand tall for generations to come.

Tamar must have heard his truck's approach because she stepped outside just as they reached the porch's bottom step.

"Well, good morning. What are you two up to?"

"Will you make us waffles?" Amari pleaded.

Tamar, dressed in her signature caftan robes of black

and green, long silver hair flowing like a river, looked first at the boy she'd agreed to raise as her great-grandson and then over to her grandson Trent. "Why me?"

Amari answered, "Because that crazy girl perpetrating as a cook gave us spinach!"

Tamar kept a straight face. "Thought you liked spinach?"

"Not for breakfast. Please, Tamar, you make the best waffles in Kansas. Please?"

"Sucking up, are you?"

"Oh, most def."

Ignoring Amari's patented megawatt smile, or at least trying to, she moved her attention to Trent. "I suppose you want waffles too?"

"Yes, ma'am."

She eyed them both for a long, silent moment, then sighed. "May as well. If I don't feed you now, you'll just be back here begging later on." She reentered the house.

A pleased Amari did a Tiger Woods fist pump. An amused Trent followed him up the steps and inside.

Trent and Amari had just dug in when Bing Shepard and his housemate, Clay Dobbs, walked into the kitchen. "Got enough to feed two more?"

Tamar looked up from the griddle. "I take it you all didn't want spinach for breakfast either?"

"Don't get us started," Bing muttered, taking a seat at the table. "When does Bernadine get back so she can fix this?"

Clay sat too. "Hopefully before dinner, because if I have to look at another fancy-shmancy plate I'm going to shoot myself. Why can't we just have plain old American food?"

Tamar used a fork to transfer a waffle from the griddle to a plate. She handed it to Bing. "I had a run-in with Miss Florene earlier this week. Told her if she put some of that attitude into her cooking she might be able to whip up something folks might want to eat."

"Amen," Bing cracked.

"Have you talked to her about the menu?" Clay asked Trent.

Trent looked up from his plate of golden brown waffles swimming in butter and maple syrup and wiped his mouth with his napkin. "I did. Blew me off. Said she only answers to Ms. Brown."

Amari cracked, "She keep cooking that mess she calls food and Ms. Bernadine might give her an answer she may not like. Tamar, can I have some more, please?"

Bing laughed. "For that piece of wisdom, I think he should get two."

And when Tamar placed two more waffles on his plate, Amari grinned over at his dad. "I love being a July."

Trent forked up more waffles and grinned in response. "It does have its perks."

That night, lying in his bed in the dark, Amari thought back on that conversation. Being a July did have its perks. Not only did he get to eat Tamar's great cooking, he got family: from his dad, to the O.G.—his nickname for Malachi—to Tamar. He'd never had family before. Some social workers made believe that being in a foster home was just as good as having real family, and maybe it was that way for some kids, but it had never been like that for him. For him, foster care had been something to survive; something to get through until time came to move to another home where he'd have to do the same thing all over again. Admittedly some had been okay, like the first foster mother he remembered, old Mrs. Crandall, who'd taken him in at age five, because one, she had a good heart, and two, the money she received from the state for his care helped supplement her tiny Social Security check. She'd taken him to church, on trips to the zoo, and hadn't demanded much except that he sit and watch cartoons and old movies with her. She died when he was eight, and he had to move again, and this time, to hell.

Her name was Willie Lee Oxford. Crackhead. How she managed to get a foster care license was beyond him. The only things he remembered clearly were her screaming at him and the four other kids in the house, the daily whippings, and that he was hungry all day every day because every penny in the household went to feeding her habit. Six months into his sentence she was busted for prostitution and the state took him and the other kids back. Just before he came to Henry Adams, he saw her on a street corner in Detroit. He'd been looking for a car to steal and she'd been working. She recognized him immediately and asked him for a dollar. When he told her he didn't have any money, she cussed him out, in between yelling to anybody who would listen that he used to pee in the bed.

But now he was in Kansas with a real family. No bullshit, no screaming, no crackheads. For the first time in his life he was sleeping on a mattress that wasn't secondhand and full of stains. He had a brand-new bike, clothes the right size, purchased specifically for him. None of that Salvation Army, Goodwill stuff. He even had his own bedroom that he didn't have to share. Yeah, Henry Adams was out in the middle of nowhere, but to tell the truth, Amari didn't care. He liked the people, the town, and he definitely liked his family. The last two words made him smile. Being a July did have its perks, and because of that, he'd come to a decision. He wanted to be a real July and he planned to talk to Ms. Bernadine about it, right after he convinced her to fire the new cook. Satisfied, he turned over and drifted off to sleep.

In the dream, Amari was driving. The speedometer on the black Carrera convertible hovered at 120 and he was chilling behind the wheel, sounds blasting. The smooth two-lane road twisted through the desert-looking landscape like something out of a TV commercial. It felt real as hell, even though it couldn't be. For one, he hadn't seen any other cars, and two, according to the GPS he was heading west, but the sun was setting behind him. He had no idea what that was about, or where he might be heading, but it felt good to be rolling again. He looked to his right and saw a big brown hawk with black-flecked feathers riding shotgun. It was standing in the seat, facing forward, keen eyes focused on the road ahead. For some reason, that didn't strike Amari as odd. He just smiled and turned his attention back to the wheel.

Seated in the snow-white interior of her personal jet, the very tired Bernadine Brown looked out at the starry night. She'd had way too much fun in Barcelona at the Bottom Women's Society annual convention and she had the weariness to prove it. Not only had the event been an over-the-top, five-star affair, she'd gotten to show off the beautiful city to two of the most important people in her new life: her fifteen-year-old foster daughter, Crystal, who'd spent the entire time being blown away by everything from the food to the architecture, and Lily Fontaine, Bernadine's friend and administrative right hand.

Now she couldn't wait to get home and sleep in her own bed. Who'd've ever thought a woman with all her wealth would find happiness in a town so small it wasn't even on most maps? She certainly wouldn't have. When she divorced her oil executive husband, Leo, four years ago because of his cheating, her divorce settlement had been an eye-popping $275 million. Having been married to Leo for over thirty years, she'd already owned everything monetarily a woman could ask for. However, having been raised in the church, she knew that when much is given, much is expected, so after the divorce she asked God to send her a purpose for all the excess wealth. That purpose turned out to be the financially destitute town of Henry Adams, Kansas. She saw a news report about it being for sale on eBay, so she purchased it. Lock, stock, and barrel. Best investment she'd ever made. Not only had she gotten the unique opportunity to rebuild a historic Black township founded in the 1880s, but she'd found peace and family there as well.

She glanced over at Crystal, who was fast asleep in a seat across the aisle. Crys could be a handful. Having been a ward of the state since the age of seven, it was a wonder she wasn't more so. In the world of social work, Crystal Chambers was a survivor. Tough on the outside, gentle as a newborn kitten on the inside. In spite of the horrid blond extensions she insisted on wearing, she'd stolen Bernadine's heart. The two of them had been family almost nine months now, and Bernadine couldn't imagine life without her hip-hop princess.

In a seat behind Crystal, Lily Fontaine was asleep too. Divorced in her early twenties, she was now a forty-something single mom of a son who'd recently graduated from college. Lily had grown up in Henry Adams, but had lived most of her adult life in Atlanta. Last summer she'd come back to town for her godmother's birthday and wound up being hired by Bernadine to help with the Henry Adams revitalization, becoming a foster parent to eight-year-old Devon Watkins, and finding love again with her old sweetheart, the town's mayor, Trent July. Bernadine loved Lily Fontaine like a sister and couldn't imagine life without her either.

Thinking about home made Bernadine wonder how things had gone in the week they'd been away on vacation. She hoped the new cook, Florene Maxwell, was getting along okay at the Dog and Cow. In its heyday, the town's diner had been a hub of the community. Now that it had been razed and rebuilt, Bernadine wanted it to reclaim its place and she wanted it to be run well. Thoughts of the diner inevitably led to its owner, devilishly handsome Malachi July. There was a definite attraction between her and Malachi, but she was choosing not to go there for myriad reasons, mostly because her ex-husband, Leo, had broken her heart and she was not in the mood to have it happen again, but Malachi was as tempting as a hot fudge sundae.

Turning her thoughts away from Malachi, she wondered about the town's other foster children and their parents. They'd all taken off for spring vacation too, and were due to return over the next couple days, undoubtedly filled with tales of all the fun they'd had. Maybe not thirteen-year-old Preston Mays, though. He and his foster parents, Barrett and Sheila Payne, had flown to Florida to a reunion of Barrett's old marine regiment. She hoped Preston had a chance to see something besides uniformed men and women saluting each other all day.

"We've been given clearance to land, Ms. Brown." The lyrical Jamaican voice coming through the jet's speakers and interrupting her musings belonged to the pilot, Katie Skye.

"Okay, babe," Bernadine replied. "Take us down."

The voices roused Lily and Crystal from their sleep and they looked over at Bernadine with smiles. Moments later they were on the ground.

It was midnight when Nathan, the driver of the hired Town Car, turned into their small subdivision. The street-lights acted as beacons in the cold April darkness, softly illuminating the sub's five houses and the last of the winter's snow.

"So glad to be home," Lily said, stretching her tired arms and shoulders as the car stopped in front of her house.

"Me too," Crystal added, yawning. "But it's cold." Hugging herself and shivering, she whined playfully, "I want to go back to Spain, Ms. Bernadine."

"Tell me about it," Bernadine replied. When they walked out of the airport, the cold air had been like a slap in the face. Since the end of March folks around town kept assuring her that spring was on the way, but she didn't believe them.

"Cold or not, I'm still glad to be home," Lily said. "Can't wait to see my Devon tomorrow."

"What time are they due in?" Bernadine asked as the driver got out and went around to the trunk to unload Lily's luggage.

"Roni said around noon." Roni was Grammy Award–winning singer Veronica Moore Garland. She and her husband, Reggie, had taken their foster daughter, Zoey, and Lily's Devon to New York for the vacation week.

The driver carried Lily's suitcases to the porch, then returned to open the car's door so she could step out.

Once she did, she leaned back in to ask, "Are we working tomorrow?"

Bernadine drew back from the cold air swirling into the car's warm interior. "I am, but you go ahead and take the day off if you want."

"Okay, but Crystal, don't let her leave the house in the morning unless she gets a full night's sleep. You hear?"

Crys grinned. "Yes, ma'am."

Lily looked her boss in the eyes. "I know you, Bernadine Brown."

"Just close the door before you freeze us to death," Bernadine scolded with a laugh. "I'll see you later."

Lily waved and hurried up the steps. After sticking her key in the door, she waved once more before disappearing inside. As she closed the door behind her and turned on a lamp, the cordless phone in the living room rang. The illuminated number on the caller ID was a familiar one and caused her to smile. She picked up and asked, "What are you doing up so late?"

Trent replied softly, "Waiting for you. Saw your light. Welcome home."

"Thanks." Feeling like a teenager, she dropped onto the couch. "How are you?"

"Better now that I know you're back."

"That is such an old line, but it's working."

"Good."

"Missed you."

"Missed you too."

For a moment there was silence. Basking in the deep feelings they had for each other, no words were necessary.

"You must be tired," he told her, "so I won't keep you. Just wanted to hear your voice."

"Thanks for checking on me."

"Always. Get some sleep and I'll see you later."

"Night, Trenton," she whispered.

"Night, Lily Flower."

Lily held the phone against her heart and sighed like a woman in love. After replacing the phone in its cradle, she turned off the lamp and floated upstairs to her bedroom.

Next door, Bernadine climbed the steps to the porch and found a small yellow sticky note pressed to the door. Shivering in the cold, she pulled it free. Once she and Crys were inside, she dropped her purse in a chair and read the note. The wording made her shake her head.

"What's it say?" Crystal asked.

"'First thing. Fire the cook.'"

"Huh? Who's it from?"

"Amari."

Crystal rolled her eyes as only a teenage girl can. "No telling what that means. Boy's crazy."

Bernadine wouldn't call him crazy, but Amari did have a way about him that was uniquely his own. While she wondered if this meant something catastrophic had occurred between him and Florene, Crys declared, "Me, I'm going to my room. I'll see you when I get up."

She walked halfway to the staircase, then stopped and looked back. "Thanks for taking me to Spain, Ms. Bernadine. I'll never forget it."

The sincerity in her eyes and voice filled Bernadine's heart. "You're welcome, Crys. Sleep tight."

After her departure, Bernadine set the note down. As the silence echoed gently, she looked around at the familiar space that was her home. There was a sense of peace here; a sense of place that seemed to welcome her spirit and reaffirm that this was where she was supposed to be. It felt good to be back. At the moment, she was way too tired to investigate whatever Amari's note meant, and besides, he and Trent were probably asleep, so she turned out the lamps and climbed the stairs to her bedroom. His cryptic request would have to wait until the sun came up.

Leo Brown was tired too—tired of knocking around in his Bel Air mansion all alone. His latest, and soon to be ex-wife, number three, had stormed out a week ago, taking with her her parrots, her dogs, and the new Lexus he'd given her last fall, in hopes the fully pimped-out ride would entice her away from the pool boy she'd met in Boca Raton. Leo was fifty-seven years old, and had a potbellied, out-of-shape body to prove it. At his age, he couldn't hope to compete with the tanned and buffed

Stefan, or whatever the hell his name was. The Stefans of the world didn't need little blue pills to get it up either; they had youth on their side. James Brown once sang, "If it's all night, it's all right," but Leo hadn't been able to pull an all-nighter for over a decade now, and he was finding middle age very depressing.

The divorce from his first wife, Bernadine, should have gelded him financially, but her hotshot lawyers hadn't found all his income. There'd been more than enough millions hidden away to pamper wife number two, and after she left him, wife number three. Now, with the economy tight, and divorce number three staring him in the face, his money was in need of its own little blue pills.

Bernadine's pretty brown face floated across his mind's eye. Truthfully, messing around on her had been the dumbest thing he'd ever done, but back then, all he could think about was the excitement of it. Cheating on his marriage had made him feel more alive than he had in years, and now . . . ? Unlike the wives who followed her, Bernadine had loved him for himself, not his money, and he'd rewarded her by being unfaithful. He still remembered the day she walked into his office and found him bumping his secretary on the desk. The hurt reflected in her eyes was as clear to him now as it had been then. She'd looked devastated, shattered. He'd thrown away a good woman for a silly, weave-wearing tramp with fake nails and a tight body, who willingly accommodated his lust anytime, anywhere. At the time, he'd thought himself in heaven until he learned he wasn't the only man she was accommodating. Then heaven turned into hell.

So here he sat, getting ready to be served with divorce papers once again, and if the truth be told, he didn't really care. Since the day Bernadine divorced him, his life had been in the toilet. He'd heard she'd bought herself a town, of all things, and wondered how she was doing with that, but the real question was: If he begged her hard enough, would she take him back?

CHAPTER
2

Bernadine's alarm usually went off at 6:00 a.m. Rising early was a necessity with all the things she had to do every day, but this morning, she'd slept in until eight and it felt so good, she vowed to sleep in more often. Of course, she had no intentions of following through on that but liked thinking about it.

Downstairs, she put the coffeemaker to work and pulled open the door of the stainless steel fridge, then remembered she had emptied the interior before taking off for Barcelona, but to her surprise and delight, it had been refilled. Tamar probably. Grabbing a carton of eggs, she thought, *Yet another bonus of small-town living.* Where else but in a place like Henry Adams would your neighbors restock your fridge in anticipation of your return from vacation? Certainly not in any big city she'd ever lived in, and she'd lived in them all over the world.

She cracked eggs for omelets, put the carton back, and wondered if Crystal was still asleep. Just as she began

debating whether to go upstairs and check, her Black-
Berry went off. She picked it up. Looking at the familiar
number made her shake her head with muted amusement.
"Morning, Malachi."

"Welcome home. Did you enjoy Barcelona?"

She tried to tell herself that hearing his low-toned
chocolate voice didn't do things to her, but she was lying. "I
did, but it's good to be back. What's up with you?"

"Want to talk to you about the Dog. Lots of complaints."

"About what?"

"Florene, the new cook."

She sighed. "Amari left me a note about her."

"What's it say?"

" 'First thing. Fire the cook.' "

Malachi's laugh filled her ear. "That's my boy."

"When do you want to get together?"

"Bit early to be asking me loaded questions, don't you
think?" he tossed back in a humor-laden voice.

His flirting put heat in her cheeks. "I'm talking about
the cook at the Dog and Cow."

"Pity," he replied softly. "But how about we get together
anyway. I'm outside on your porch. Brought you breakfast."

Surprised, she walked to the front door and opened it.
There he stood, holding a plate wrapped in foil, and her
heart pounded like she was seventeen.

He inclined his head. "Your breakfast, ma'am." His dark
eyes sparkled with a mixture of mischief and temptation.

"Thank you." Taking the warm plate from his hand, she
discreetly drew in a calming breath and stepped back so he
could enter.

In the kitchen, he took a seat at the counter while she undid the foil and fought hard not to be affected by his silent scrutiny, but upon seeing three whole green beans sprinkled with almonds, balanced on what appeared to be risotto, nestled against four baby carrots, she turned to him and asked with confusion, "This is breakfast?"

"Welcome to the new culinary delights being served at the D&C."

She stared.

"We hired a bad imitation of Julia Child and the paying customers are ready to throw her into a pot of boiling grits."

Bernadine got herself a fork and dipped in. She took a few bites. "The green beans aren't bad. Risotto is great."

"But who eats green beans and almonds for breakfast?" he asked pointedly.

"You have a point. This is good, though."

He sighed.

"Okay, but I wouldn't mind having this for dinner."

He eyed her critically.

"I wouldn't," she told him as she tasted another small bite. "The girl can cook."

But she could tell Malachi wasn't buying when he said, "Tell that to the people who wanted pancakes and waffles Saturday morning and were served some kind of spinach instead."

"Spinach?" she asked dubiously.

"At least it looked like spinach. Nobody's real sure what it was."

"Did you ask her?"

"Yep. Told me if I had to ask, maybe I should sell the

place to somebody who did know. Almost fired her on the spot, but decided to see if you could get through to her. She also told folks that if they didn't like what was on the menu, to eat someplace else, because it was her kitchen."

"Really?"

"If I'm lying, I'm flying."

"Okay, we'll talk to her. I was just cracking some eggs. You want an omelet?"

"As long as it's made out of something I can pronounce."

Grinning, she went back to the fridge to get more eggs.

Like everyone else on the plains, Bernadine drove a pickup truck. A blue Ford F–150 she named Baby. Being a truck owner wasn't something she'd ever envisioned, but becoming a resident of Henry Adams had altered her thinking on a number of things. Take the lifestyle, for example. She was finding she enjoyed the slow life. The lack of pace encouraged a person to breathe and relax. Slowing down appeared to be helping her health as well. The checkup she'd had at her doctor's office before flying to Barcelona showed her blood pressure had dropped. All the walking she'd been doing with Lily on the rec center's outdoor track had decreased her sugar levels as well, which according to the doc made her less likely to contract the diabetes that killed her mother. Another blessing of small-town living: good health.

But what wasn't good for her health were what passed for roads in the rural community. She held on tightly to the steering wheel in response to all the potholes. The early spring's changeable weather made the dirt and gravel track freeze one minute and thaw the next, leaving behind a muddy, crater-filled mess. As she bumped along behind Malachi driving ahead of her in his '57 red Ford pickup, she gave thanks for the inventor of seat belts and prayed her teeth wouldn't rattle loose before they reached the D&C.

As they entered town proper the ride leveled off, and she sighed gratefully as they turned onto Main Street. She slowed as she drove past the new recreation center. It was a state-of-the-art, sand-colored beauty built low to the ground because they lived in Tornado Alley. It housed a movie theater, kitchen, exercise facilities, and rooms for groups to meet. She spotted a few familiar cars and dusty pickups in the lot. Pleased that things at the center seemed normal at least, she drove on.

Next up, and on the same side of the street, sat the new school. Schools gave small towns a sense of community, but Henry Adams hadn't had one in decades, so this one was going to be very special. It hadn't been named yet, but she hoped it would be in time for next Monday's grand opening and the arrival of the newly hired teacher, a man named Jack James.

They rolled past the old Henry Adams Hotel that had once been a town gem, and pulled into the newly paved parking lot of the D&C. Last summer when Bernadine got her first look at the diner, it had been a listing, tarp-covered dive. Its red leather booths had been patched with silver duct tape, the ceiling had holes, and only a few of the bare bulbs hanging from the rafters worked. Now it was new again and the interior had a sleek retro design. Its custom-made jukebox, refurbished red booths, and dark wood dining counter gave the place style again. The kitchen was top-of-the-line, chef-certified, and the diner had its own router, thus allowing the D&C to function as a wi-fi café as well.

Because it had once served as the hub of the community, everyone wanted it to become that again, but it wouldn't happen if folks had issues with the new chef and the chef with them. Oh, to be back in Barcelona with its warm weather and no problems, she thought wistfully. Bringing her mind back to the present, she focused on the empty interior of the D&C. It was Monday, ten in the morning. The place should have been bustling with locals and the workers from the town's various construction sites, but there wasn't a soul inside. She didn't even see the waitstaff.

"Where's everybody?"

Mal shrugged. "Probably taking her suggestion to eat somewhere else."

"That's not going to work."

"No kidding." She and Malachi also envisioned the diner as a profit-making establishment, but that wouldn't happen either if they couldn't put fannies in the booths. Although Malachi was the owner, she was the one paying the freight, including the salaries of the help until the place could pay for itself. With that in mind, she headed for the kitchen, hoping they could talk some sense into Florene so she wouldn't have to be replaced.

Florene was seated on a tall stool at one of the counters, writing on a pad. She was dressed in chef whites. Her light brown face appeared younger than her nineteen years and she had her auburn-tinted hair pulled back in a tail that she'd twisted into a bun. At their entrance she glanced up and set the pen aside.

"Welcome back, Ms. Brown. Did you have a good time in Spain?"

"I did. How are you?"

"I'd be better if the people around here wanted to eat something besides grits and pork chops," she declared, and glared at Malachi.

Bernadine ignored the bad attitude, for the moment. "I hear there's been a few bumps."

"Not from me. It's him and the rest of these country-time folk."

"Why are you serving green beans for breakfast?" Bernadine asked pleasantly.

"It's novel. Anybody can cook eggs. I want to be known as adventurous, eclectic—a chef that doesn't follow the trends."

"And there's nothing wrong with that," Bernadine explained as gently as she could. "But this is a diner in Kansas, Florene, not a bistro in L.A."

"So I should waste my skills?"

Bernadine sighed. Lord knew she didn't want to break the young woman's spirit. "Honey, there will be a time and a place for you and your skills. Right now you're in a community college culinary program and we need you to prepare what your diners want to eat. I don't mind you introducing new dishes. In fact, I'm encouraging you to do so. But on a Saturday morning, folks here want waffles, pancakes, and eggs."

"Then they want another chef."

Bernadine studied her for a moment. "Then you're quitting?"

"No. I want to be allowed to run *my* kitchen as I see fit."

"Then you're quitting," Mal said. "I'll send an e-mail to

your professor. You're a good cook and I'll tell her that, but you can't be hardheaded and work for me."

"But—"

"When you get *your* kitchen you can deal the deck," he added pointedly. "I'll put your last check in the mail. Thank you for your service to Henry Adams, Florene."

"You can't just fire me!"

But Bernadine wasn't about to spend the morning listening to a child whose opinion of herself was off the charts, so she said to Malachi, "Will you see to it that Florene gets all of her personal belongings?"

"Yep. Make sure she hands over my keys too," he added.

"Good." And with that said, Bernadine made her exit and added *Help find a new cook* to her mental list of things to do.

The locals called the short, squat, fire-red building where Bernadine worked the Power Plant. Although it had nothing to do with physical power like electricity or wind, it had everything to do with the fact that her office was housed inside. She was the town's engine, the conduit. Nothing happened in town she didn't have a hand in, and because she was the owner with the money to back it up, very few people stood in her way.

She pulled open the heavy metal door and went inside. Shaking off the shivers left by the cold April morning, she walked down the silent hall toward her office. Sunlight poured through the glass atrium roof overhead and through the sparkling clear windows that were partially submerged below ground. The light filled her path to her office and the large leaves of the healthy green plants lining the way.

Much of the flat-topped, circular building was underground. The design made the facility green and would
hopefully keep it from becoming a tornado snack.

The mayor's office was across the hall from her own. It
had been almost finished when she left for Barcelona. She
wondered if the work had been completed. Walking over,
she stuck her master key into the lock and stepped inside.

The carpet was covered by a tarp and there were large,
shrink-wrapped boxes stacked throughout the expansive,
white-walled suite. When Bernadine first came to Henry
Adams, she hadn't known a wall-bearing beam from a sump
pump, but now, after a year of rubbing elbows with con-
tractors and the like, she viewed the interior with knowl-
edgeable eyes. Wall plates for the electrical plugs were on.
The covers for the air and heat ducts were in place as well.
She took note of small details like the caulking on the windows, and that there were knobs on the doors. She hit a
light switch. On came the recessed lighting above her head
and a ceiling fan. Turning them off, she looked around the
space again. Unless there was a problem she couldn't see,
the place looked ready to be occupied.

On the other hand, Bernadine's suite of offices had
been the first one completed. The stylishly furnished outer
office, done in the earth colors she preferred, held chairs
and a few loveseats to accommodate folks waiting to see
her. The inner sanctum was where she worked.

Entering it now, she took one look at the mountain of
mail covering her desk and wanted to call Katie Skye, have
her refuel the jet and fly her back to Barcelona. She couldn't

believe how much mail there was. She was still eyeing the pile when her BlackBerry sounded. It was Lily.

"How much mail do you have?" Lily asked.

"Enough to start my own country."

Lily laughed softly. "You want me to come in and help?"

"No. One of us should get to enjoy the day. You wait for Devon and I'll get this mess sorted out."

"You sure? You're making me feel guilty."

"Good, then my work is done."

They both laughed, and Bernadine said, "I'll see you later. Let me know when everyone gets home."

"Okay. I—"

"Did you fire her?"

The interrupting voice made Bernadine look up to see Amari standing in the doorway. "Hold on a minute, Lily."

She said to him, "Don't you see me on the phone?"

He looked down at his shoes. "Sorry."

Bernadine spent a few more moments talking with Lily before ending the call. "Now, what can I do for you, Amari?" She stashed her Hermès bag in the bottom drawer of her desk and hung her coat on the coat tree nearby.

"First off, welcome home."

"Thank you."

"And second. Did you fire her?"

"No. She quit."

"I'll take it."

Bernadine hid her grin. "Anything else?"

"Yeah. How long do I have to wait before my dad can legally adopt me?"

She studied him for a moment. "Why?"

"I think I'm ready to be a July."

"Really?"

"Yep." There was pride all over his face.

"Have you and Trent discussed this?"

"Nope. Wanted to talk to you first, and then Tamar."

"I see. Well, talk to Tamar and then all of us will get together."

"Okay."

"Did you enjoy your vacation?"

"I did. Never went hunting or fishing before. Like the fishing part. Not the hunting. Seen enough shooting. Dad tried to tell me it was different, but the only difference seemed to be that the stuff dying wasn't shooting back."

Bernadine also hailed from Detroit. Granted, she and Amari had grown up at different times and the city had been safer during her residency, but she understood his aversion. "Trent was okay with you not wanting to hunt?"

"He was. You know, he's real cool. He's the kinda dad kids like me always imagine having, till you get too old, and realize it ain't never gonna happen."

The confession tugged at her heart. "But it has happened," she countered softly.

"Yeah, it has. Got me an O.G. too." In the vernacular of the kids of the day, O.G. stood for Original Gangster but Amari used it as a term of endearment. Trent often teased that O.G. stood for Old Geezer.

"And Tamar?"

"Tamar's pretty great too, unless you make her mad."

"Sometimes you don't get a second helping of life, Amari, but you have."

"I know. Barely had a first helping, so this ain't bad, at all."

She smiled. "I missed you."

He squirmed like an eleven-year-old male. "Ah, Ms. Bernadine."

"I did, Amari."

He looked her in the eyes and admitted, "Missed you too. Guess this is what family's about, huh?"

"Guess so."

Showing her his grin, he gave her a wave and left.

Chuckling, Bernadine started in on the mail.

As Amari climbed onto his bike and pedaled off to the rec to shoot some hoops, he wasn't sure what Tamar would think of his plans, but he knew her vote could make or break him. Even though she could be tough, he got the impression that she liked him. Hadn't she let him live after he stole Malachi's truck last summer? In fact, she hadn't said much at all about the incident. Which in a way sort of worried him because it would be just like her to be saving up the lecture so she could bring it up sometime in the future. All that aside, she was the most important person he needed to talk with about becoming a real, permanent member of the family, and there was no way getting around it. Without her approval, he might as well start packing for his next stop.

In Cleveland, Ohio, Ray Chambers was standing in line at Happy Hour Liquor to pay for a bottle of wine when an old acquaintance walked into the store. "Hey, Walt!" he called out. "That you?"

Walt Hurley stopped. When he recognized Ray, his face split into a wide grin. "Ray Chambers?"

Walt walked over and the two shared a quick grip. "Been a long time. You here visiting?"

"No. I'm back in town," Ray said, holding his place in line. "At least for a little while."

They spent a few moments catching up and then Ray asked, "When was the last time you saw Nikki?" She was Ray's ex and Walt's baby sister.

The people in line ahead of Ray moved up as customers paid for their purchases and departed.

"Not in a while, man," Walt answered, sadness in his voice. "That crack got her, and she wound up in the joint in Illinois. Got HIV too. My sister Jean went to see her a few months ago. Said she doubted Nikki would make it to the summer."

"That's rough. Sorry to hear it. She and I didn't get along at the end, but I wouldn't wish nothing like AIDS on her. That's too bad."

"Yeah, but she told Jean she was going to die happy because she got to see her daughter Crystal back in the fall."

"Crystal? My baby girl?"

"Yeah. Nikki told Jean that Crystal was set for life. Got some high-class, rich sister as her foster mother now."

"Really? Did Jean say where they lived? CPS took Crystal from me and Nikki when she was little. Haven't seen her since."

"Jean said something about Kansas."

"Kansas?"

By then Ray was at the cashier. He handed the kid

behind the glass a twenty, and asked for five Easy Picks for the big Lotto draw tomorrow night. He turned back to Walt. "You think if I called Jean she might be able to tell me something more? Be nice to see Crystal. Let her know her daddy's been thinking about her all these years."

Walt shrugged. "I don't know, man."

The clerk handed Ray his change, the bagged wine, and the Lotto tickets. Ray reached in his pocket and took out a business card. "Here, give her this."

Walt grinned. "Look at you. Business cards."

"Yeah. Own a cleaning company. Doing pretty good too."

"Okay. No guarantee she'll call you, though. You know how she felt about you when you and Nikki were together."

"Tell her I've changed. Go to church now and everything."

"You in church? Hell must be freezing over."

They laughed, and after another short talk about back in the day, they promised to stay in touch and parted ways.

As Ray headed up the street to his apartment, he smiled. So his daughter Crystal was living large. He liked the sound of that, and would like it even more once he found out where they were. Yeah, Ray had changed, but only because he'd grown too old to pimp. Life had reduced him to a gigolo and he trolled for victims in the Black churches where he had his pick of lonely, single Black females with good jobs eager to pay his bills in exchange for his affections. Yeah, he'd changed, but as in nature, a leopard never changes his spots.

CHAPTER
3

M ost of the mail on Bernadine's desk pertained to the new school. Before going on vacation, Lily had e-mailed some requests for info on textbooks and other educational equipment. Apparently word had spread because in response Bernadine was looking at enough unsolicited catalogs to supply a school district the size of New York City's. Some specialized in school uniforms, others featured desks. There were big fat ones devoted to science labs. Five had glossy pictures of gym equipment, and in another stack were piled the ones pertaining to textbooks and teacher supplies.

By the time she opened the catalogs selling school buses, her head was spinning. A knock on her open door caused her to look up. Mayor Trent July stood on the threshold. She could've kissed him for offering her a distraction. "God, I'm glad to see you. All this mail's about to give me a stroke."

Meeting her greeting with a smile reminiscent of his father, he took a look at her piled-high desk and cracked, "Welcome back."

"Yeah right," she tossed back in response to his obvious sarcasm, but her eyes were twinkling with amusement. "How are you?"

"I'm fine. Thanks for bringing my Lily home in one piece."

"Most welcome. She and Crystal had a great time. Have a seat and you can catch me up on what's been going on."

He eased down into one of her fancy chairs and made himself comfortable. "Dad said Florene quit?"

"Yes."

"In this economy, you don't want anybody to be without a job."

"True, but she wasn't a good fit for our needs. Told us she wanted the freedom to run her kitchen. Emphasis on the *her*."

"I'm sure you all set her straight."

"We tried to do it gently, but she made it hard."

"Do you have a replacement in mind?"

"I'd really like to give another student a chance, but after Florene, I'm a little gun-shy. What about this Rocky I keep hearing about? Folks keep telling me what a great cook she was."

"She was, but she's in Boston taking some truck mechanic courses."

"Truck mechanic?"

"Yeah. Her father used to own my garage. She grew up with a socket wrench in her hand. Working on big rigs is right up her alley. Haven't talked to her in a few weeks, but we do keep in touch. I can give her a call, if you want."

"Please." Bernadine had yet to meet the legendary Rocky, but the more stories she heard, the more her curiosity was piqued. "If she says no, I'll talk to Florene's professor about hiring another student."

"Hopefully one with a little less 'tude because we already have Crystal."

Bernadine grinned. "True."

"So what's with all the catalogs?"

"School stuff. Have you seen Marie today? I need to give them to her and let her head spin for a while. Also need to talk to her about the new teacher and when he's due to arrive."

"She and Genevieve are in Vegas."

Bernadine stared, dumbstruck. "Genevieve Curry went to Vegas?"

He chuckled and nodded. "Yep. They'll be back tomorrow."

Genevieve Curry had grown up with town schoolteacher Marie Jefferson, Clay Dobbs, and Malachi. She was quiet, reserved, and such a lady she still wore white cotton gloves to church. Her husband, Riley, disappeared last summer, along with his six-hundred-pound pet hog, Cletus, after Cletus caused the death of a human parasite named Morton Prell. All that aside, Genevieve being in Las Vegas was like finding the pope in a strip club, but the idea of it made Bernadine proud of her. "I hope she and Marie are having a good time."

"Me too. She's earned it after what Riley and Cletus put her through."

Bernadine agreed. Riley let Cletus move into the house, and it became so filthy the place had to be condemned and was razed. Now, because Genevieve had no home, she was temporarily living with Marie Jefferson and her mother, Agnes. "I wonder where they are?"

"Marie's got a favorite hotel—"

"No. Riley and Cletus."

He shrugged. "You'd think it'd be hard for Riley to hide a hog that big for this long, but they've been on the lam for going on eight months now, and so far, no word or sightings. Sheriff Dalton's warrant is still out on them, though," he added.

Bernadine shook her head. She'd had some real memorable experiences while living in Henry Adams, but the mess with Cletus and Riley and their involvement with Morton Prell's death had to be at the top of the list. As Amari said at the time, "Death by hog. That's wack."

"I see your office is done," she said, changing the subject.

"Yep. They finished the last of the interior details a few days ago."

"So, when are you moving in?"

He responded with a slight squirm that reminded her of Amari's, so she asked cautiously, "What's the matter?"

"I don't need an office, Bernadine."

"You're the mayor, Trent. Mayors have offices."

"I know—"

"But?"

"Why can't I do what I do from the garage?"

"Because you can't hold business meetings in the garage."

"Why not? It's worked okay up until now."

She sat back and eyed him.

He grinned. "Uh oh. Here it comes."

"Back in the day, when you and Tamar and the seniors ran things, meeting in the garage worked fine, but the town's too big now, or at least it will be. We're going to have new buildings to staff and maintain. We have construction projects going on, and we're doing business with partners from Hays to Miami. You can't be mayor in between fixing old cars."

He sighed.

"And if you tell me you want to quit, don't even try it. You're the duly elected mayor and your citizens need you."

"The guilt card. You need to quit hanging out with Tamar."

"I always run with the best."

"No appealing this to a higher court, I assume."

She gave him that look again.

He grinned and threw up his hands. "Okay, I surrender. Let me finish up a few things at the garage, and I'll move in after that."

Bernadine knew he was being purposefully vague, but she didn't call him on it. "That's fine. Did I mention the biggest benefit of all?"

"No."

"Lily. Her office is right next door."

"The dagger."

Bernadine enjoyed Trent's friendship. Were it not for his engineering background, last fall's initial construction season might have run less smoothly. For a moment she debated telling him about her earlier visit from Amari, but decided against it. Amari said he had some things to work out first. She'd let him tell Trent about his desire to become a full-fledged July when he felt ready. "If you need help unpacking or setting up, just let me know. Maybe I'll even ask Lily to help."

He got to his feet and shook his head. "You're hard on a man, Bernadine Brown."

"See you later, Mayor July."

Chuckling, he exited.

On his way back to the garage, Trent put in a call to Rocky. Her real name was Rochelle Dancer and she'd always had a special place in his heart. The failure of her less-than-a-month-long marriage had sent her to the East Coast to try and sort out her life, but he missed her friendship almost as much as he missed her cooking. The call to her cell phone went through, but he got her voice mail. After leaving her a message to get in touch, he ended the call.

Down in Texas, Eustasia Pennymaker looked at the beautiful bride and handsome groom, and felt as giddy as if this were her own wedding. Holding the video cam to her eye, she said, "Turn for Mama, Chocolate, I want to get the full effect of the veil. Let's show the folks why I sent all the way to Vienna for that lace."

Chocolate was a three-hundred-pound sow. She was dressed in a custom-made white silk gown complete with a lace-edged, two-foot train that matched the veil. Eustasia spent a few more minutes filming her baby, then turned the cam's lens on the groom, a six-hundred-pound hog named Cletus. Wearing Ray-Bans, he was outfitted in a black tux with a white insert and bow tie. When he stopped, seemingly to pose for her, Eustasia cooed, "You're a star, aren't you, big boy? Yes you are."

Eustasia had sent out a slew of wedding invitations for the event, mostly to local politicians and the state's biggest hog farmers, but this prewedding video was destined for the Internet. She was sure it would be a sensation. "Riley?" she called out. "Any guests arrive yet?"

He was standing up on the huge deck anchored to the back of her Texas-sized mansion.

"Not yet, honey bun."

She ran her eyes lovingly over the man she knew as Riley Baker. He was Cletus's owner, and had coordinated his outfit to match the hog's, even down to the Ray-Bans, which Eustasia found quite sexy. She'd met Riley and Cletus eight months ago in the parking lot of a McDonald's. After they moved in, Cletus took an instant liking to Chocolate and Chocolate to Cletus, so Eustasia knew it was going to be a match made in heaven. She and Riley were getting along like two hogs in a mud hole too. Life was good. She offered him up a wave and went back to shooting her video.

From his spot on the deck, Riley, whose real last name was Curry and not Baker, returned the wave and looked out at the crew of Mexican servants putting the finishing touches to what had to be the biggest bash he'd ever seen in his sixty-seven years of living. There were at least a hundred tables set out across the sprawling yard. Each wore a snow-white tablecloth draped with pink and brown silk ribbons. Chocolate's favorite colors, according to Eustasia. More pink and brown ribbons accented the white roses covering the pergola constructed especially for the grand occasion. The wedding ceremony would be conducted beneath it, so rows of chairs for the guests fanned out around it.

Meeting Eustasia at that McDonald's last fall had been a godsend. Who wouldn't want to live in a mansion owned by a big, beautiful, redheaded Texas millionairess who loved hogs as much as he? She'd provided them everything from clothing to feed, opening not only her home and her barns, but her bedroom for hanky-panky activities Riley hadn't concerned himself with in years, so his life was good too. Up to a point.

He hadn't told Eustasia his real last name, or that he and Cletus were on the run because of the death of Morton Prell, a nasty old extortionist Cletus killed in self-defense. After the incident, the county took Cletus away and locked him up in an outdoor pen with the intent of holding a hearing to determine Cletus's fate. Riley knew they were going to put Cletus down, so one night, before the county paperwork could come through, he broke Cletus out, put him in the bed of his old white pickup, and left town. They'd been on the lam since.

As a result, he didn't like the idea of Eustasia filming the wedding and putting it on the Internet. Had he known about it earlier he might have hidden the camcorder or "accidentally" dropped the thing, so it wouldn't work. Now, however, he could only watch and worry. He didn't know much about cyberspace but he did know that millions of people around the world flocked to it like a religion, and he was scared that one of those millions would be someone with ties to the Kansas law enforcement agencies. He and Cletus had had a great time spending the winter with Eustasia, but all this publicity meant it was time to move on.

He had no clear idea where they'd go next, but he'd been thinking about heading across the south, maybe to Florida.

He watched Eustasia greeting the first of the guests. His disappearance would break her heart, Chocolate's too, because she and Cletus seemed genuinely in love. However, recapture wasn't something he and Cletus could afford, so it was imperative that they not stay in one place too long. Continued flight was all they had.

Amari enjoyed the communal dinners Ms. Bernadine was always arranging, and this evening they'd gathered at Tamar's to welcome everyone home from vacation. Amari had been so happy to see Preston he'd grabbed him like they'd been separated for years. "Missed you, my man."

"Missed you too, dog. Looks like everybody's here," Preston said.

"Yep."

Ms. Lily was talking with Trent, Malachi, Bing, and Clay Dobbs. Preston's foster parents, Colonel Payne and his wife, Sheila, were on the far side of the room laughing at some story big-time singer Roni Garland was telling while her smiling husband, Dr. Reg, the town's pediatrician, looked on. Ms. Agnes was bending Ms. Bernadine's ear about lord only knew what. Ms. Agnes was still in her right mind but she was approaching ninety years old.

Amari asked, "You say hello to Crystal yet?"

"Nope."

"Me either. Guess we have to bite the bullet, huh?"

"I guess," Preston replied skeptically.

Crystal was seated on the couch with Zoey, the Garlands' seven-year-old mute foster daughter, and Devon Watkins, Zoey's best friend. Devon was decked out in yet another suit.

Preston shook his head at the little boy's formal attire. "When is he going to stop dressing like the president?"

Amari grinned and shrugged.

The two of them walked up just as Zoey was showing Crystal the new Barbie she'd gotten in New York. The doll was wearing all green, from the top of her fly hat to the bottom of her peep-toe heels.

"Zo, aren't you tired of all this green?" Crystal was asking her. "You really need to get a new color."

Zoey shook her head. Green was the color of her late mother's eyes, so it was her favorite. It was also the color of the Disney Princess tee she was wearing with her belted black jeans.

Crystal told her, "You're going to get so fixated, Ms. Bernadine's going to have to call in Dr. Phil."

Zoey smiled at Crystal's teasing and shrugged as if to say she didn't care.

Crystal handed the doll back. "Okay. Do you, girl, but I'll tell Ms. Bernadine to put Dr. Phil on speed dial, just in case."

The two girls grinned at each other.

Crystal looked up at Amari and Preston. "What do you two want?"

"We just came to say hey to Zoey and Devon. Excuse us for trying to be polite, your majesty."

"Beat it."

So they did.

Outside on the porch they took seats on the steps to wait to be called for dinner. Crystal all but forgotten, Amari asked, "So, what was it like being around all those marines?"

"Boring with a capital B," Preston grumbled. "I've never seen so many stiff-assed people, in or out of uniform, in my life. Women too. Except the one that kept trying to hit on the colonel."

"What?" Amari shouted.

"Keep your voice down," Preston warned, looking around hastily to make sure they hadn't been overheard by anyone inside. "Yeah. Some military nurse. She was acting like maybe she'd been the colonel's boo back in the day."

"Did Mrs. Payne check her?"

"Nope, but I could see the mad in her eyes."

"When was this?"

"First day we got there. There was a dinner that night. The nurse sat at our table. By the look on Mrs. Payne's face, I knew the nurse hadn't been invited to sit with us."

"Man."

"No kidding. All the nurse lady kept talking about was how much fun she and the colonel had while he was healing up from some wound he got during Desert Storm."

"Fun?"

"Yep. No telling what that meant, but the next day, Mrs. Payne rented a car and she and I went to Disney World for the duration. You ever been there?"

"Nope."

"It's great, man. Maybe we can get your dad and the O.G. to take just me and you sometime. It was off the hook."

But Amari was still mulling over the conversation about

Colonel and Mrs. Payne. He took a real interest in people, especially the ones he now called family, and the Paynes qualified as that. What part had this nurse played in the past lives of Preston's foster parents?

"Amari? You still on the planet?"

He looked up to see Preston standing. "Sorry, man. What?"

Preston smiled. "Tamar just called us. It's time to eat. Let's go."

"Okay. Right behind you."

During the renovation of Tamar's home last fall, one of the items on her wish list had been a larger dining room and kitchen. The wish had been granted, and now she had more than enough room to house everyone. Lily, like everyone else, was helping to set the tables. The adults were going to be seated at the big new one and the children were around the old one brought in from the kitchen. Of course, Crystal had issues with the seating.

"Why do I have to sit with the little kids?" she complained loud enough for everyone to hear.

Lily set a steaming bowl of mashed potatoes down on the kiddie table. "Because you keep whining like a little kid about where you're sitting."

Snickers from Amari and Preston instantly drew Crystal's ire, but she took her seat without another word and Lily went back to her job.

Once the tables were loaded down with food and everyone was seated, Tamar, reigning at the head of the grown folks table, quieted the room. "Devon, will you say grace, please?"

"Yes, ma'am."

The little eight-year-old ordained deacon stood. After everyone bowed their head, he began. "Heavenly Father, we thank you for this gathering and the bounty on our tables. Bless us with your love and guidance, and bless the hands that prepared this food. Please don't forget the poor and the people who give them hope. In your son Jesus' name, we pray. Amen."

Amens echoed in agreement.

Plates were filled, and as folks dug in, conversation resumed.

Lily surveyed this group of people she'd come to know and love. From the eldest to the youngest, they'd helped make her existence so much richer. Last year at this time, she'd been living in Atlanta. She'd just taken a corporate buyout, and although the money had given her the financial freedom she'd always craved, her so-called personal life had been nothing to celebrate. The man she'd been seeing was as boring as pond water, yet she'd considered marrying him. Thank God for Henry Adams and Bernadine Brown. The trip back to Henry Adams for her godmother Marie's birthday party last summer turned Lily's world upside down and inside out. Not only had she found purpose by working with Bernadine on revitalizing the town and fostering Devon, she'd rediscovered love with Trent July. As if knowing he was in her thoughts, he looked up from his plate and met her eyes. The wink he shot her made her grin.

She glanced across the table at Sheila Payne. Although Lily didn't know the colonel's wife as well as she did, say, Bernadine, the women in town had forged a bond in the

nine months they'd been neighbors, and it was plain to
see that all was not right with Sheila. She'd always been
somewhat reserved at these gatherings, but this evening
she looked withdrawn and sad. Her manner made Lily
wonder what was up. The colonel had never been the
most open person either, but he seemed himself and didn't
appear aware of his wife's mood. Lily had never been one
to meddle in other people's business, so she didn't plan on
asking Sheila for the 411, or on saying anything to Bernadine, but something about Sheila was definitely off.

Amari noticed it too, but unlike Lily, Amari knew the
reason. The sadness he saw in her eyes reminded him of the
look in Mrs. Curry's eyes when she lost her home because
of Mr. Curry's killer pig. Mrs. Curry had helped him a lot
with his reading in school last year and he'd been trying to
think of a special way to thank her that would also make
her feel better about all the mess in her life. So far he hadn't
come up with anything, but he knew he would, he just had
to keep thinking.

He looked across the room to Tamar. The idea of having
to face her was enough to make him break out into a sweat.
Right now, however, his biggest concern lay in finishing
the large bowl of homemade ice cream before him, so setting his worries aside, he concentrated on that.

Had Preston, Lily, or Amari asked her, Sheila Payne
would have told them they were all correct. Sheila was not
herself, and as she and Barrett drove home from the dinner
at Tamar's, the reason for her unhappiness could be laid at
the feet of Sheila's old nemesis, Martina "Marti" Nelson.
Barrett met the surgical nurse in a military hospital while

recuperating from a broken leg he'd sustained during Desert Storm and before anyone could say *Semper fi*, the two became lovers. Their affair lasted over a year. Although Sheila had known about the adulterous relationship early on, she'd had no idea what to do about it, or how to heal her hurt. A more confident woman like Lily or Bernadine might have confronted him, maybe even filed for divorce, but she hadn't done either. She was a marine wife and the daughter of a naval officer. Military women weren't supposed to complain. The corps had protocols for handling weapons and prisoners of war but nothing on handling adultery. Some of the other long-married military wives told her it was natural for a man his age to go sniffing around, and for her to sit tight, he'd come back to her eventually. They'd been right, but she hadn't been sure she'd wanted him to. Barrett was intelligent, strong, and knew everything under the sun about warfare but apparently nothing about the self-incrimination inherent in coming home nights smelling of Jergens, a brand of soap neither his household nor the military used, and that's how she'd known he was cheating.

Now, after so many years had passed, Sheila thought those old wounds had healed, but the moment Marti walked over to greet them at the reunion and hugged Barrett a few beats longer than friendship warranted, her hurt and pain flared like a match on gasoline.

"You've been awfully quiet since we got back," Barrett said, interrupting her musings. "You feeling okay?"

Staring out unseeingly at the landscape rolling past her window, she replied, "I'm fine. Just a little tired from the trip, I think."

"Are you sure?"

This time she turned to face him. "Positive."

"Doc Garland can take a look at you if you want."

"I'm okay." She had to admit, if she subtracted the affair, Barrett had been a good partner and provider. If only he loved her, even a tiny bit, she thought wistfully.

In response to her steady gaze, he asked softly, "What?"

Her answering smile was small, false. "Nothing." And she turned back to her vigil at the window.

When they reached home, Barrett stood silently watching while she took off her coat and hung it in the closet by the door.

Her voice barely ruffled the quiet surrounding them. "Since Preston is spending the night at Amari's, I'm going to head on up. Think I'll sleep in the guest room. These hot flashes have been giving me fits for the past couple nights. No sense in you not getting any sleep either."

Barrett studied his wife in an attempt to discern the truth behind the way she'd been acting lately. "I don't mind."

"I know, but I do. Hopefully my body will level off now that we're home."

Still assessing her, he nodded.

"Night, Barrett."

"Good night."

After she exited, Barrett went into the living room and turned on the TV. *SportsCenter* was just starting, but he muted the sound, sat back, and let his thoughts have their head. What was wrong with her? He knew she didn't really care for his unit reunions, but in the past she'd at least pretended interest. Not this time. The morning after the first night's dinner, she'd rented a car and she and Preston drove over to Orlando and spent the rest of the three days at Disney World. To his surprise he'd missed her. Not even Marti's flamboyant presence had filled the void. He was so accustomed to Sheila's 24/7 presence that the idea of missing her was something he seldom experienced. Even when deployed he didn't miss her, but this past week in Florida he had, especially while sleeping alone in the hotel's bed.

So, what was going on with her? he wondered again. Granted, Marti had been a bit drunk that first evening during dinner and her overt flirting had made for some embarrassing and awkward moments, but Sheila had handled it like the classy lady she always was, or so it seemed. Thinking back on Marti, Barrett couldn't believe he'd ever been attracted to someone so aggressive, yet at the time of their affair he'd thought her to be all the things Sheila was not—funny, risqué, tough. Their year-long affair had been very discreet, so he was sure Sheila never suspected. Or had she? The thought that she might know more than he assumed made him sit up straight. Had she known? Decades-old guilt burned his gut like the fires of Dante's hell. Surely her moodiness wasn't tied to his old affair with Marti? Convincing himself that he was seeing insurgents where there were none, he settled down and used the remote to bring up the sound.

CHAPTER
4

That following morning, after breakfast and Preston's departure, Trent said to Amari, "I'm heading to the office to start moving in. You want to come along and give me a hand?"

"Sure, but I need to talk to Tamar first. Do you think she's at the rec center yet?"

Trent checked his watch. It was eight-thirty. "Maybe. You want me to drop you off there?"

"Yeah, then I'll meet you at your office."

"Okay. You ready?" Trent picked up his keys. He had no idea why Amari needed to speak with Tamar but knew the boy was accustomed to handling his own business, so he didn't ask. He figured that if he needed to be informed, Tamar would let him know.

After stowing Amari's flashy blue bicycle in the bed of Trent's black truck, they headed to the center.

When they arrived, Trent eased the truck into a parking space. He could see Lily out on the outdoor track maintaining a slow, easy sprint and it took him back to high school, where they'd first met. He'd been on the boys' track team and she ran the hundred and the hurdles for the girls.

"You and Ms. Lily going to get married?"

Admiring her form, Trent shrugged in reply to Amari's question.

"You should."

Trent smiled. "I'm almost afraid to ask, but I'll bite. Why?"

" 'Cause she's hot."

"Go find Tamar. I'll see you later."

"She is."

"Get out of my truck, young man."

Amari was grinning. Trent too.

Amari watched Trent watching Lily gliding gracefully around the oval. "You should go say good morning to her."

"You offering courting advice now?"

"Only if you think you need it."

Trent's laughter filled the truck. "Out. Did you hear me?"

"Yes, sir."

Still watching Lily, Trent told Amari, "Saying good morning is a good idea though."

"See."

Trent cut the engine and opened his door. As he stepped out, Amari got out too, and retrieved his bike. For a moment a pleased Amari watched his dad approach the track and saw Lily slow to a stop and greet Trent with a smile. Deciding his dad now had things under control, Amari parked his bike in the stand by the front door and went inside.

Because it was so early, the building's interior was hushed. Although Amari enjoyed the place when it was filled with kids and seniors and all the noise of everything going on, he liked the quiet times like these too. Since Tamar and her crew usually hung out in the kitchen, he headed there first.

She was right where she was supposed to be and seated at the table having coffee with her running buddy, Ms. Agnes, the mother of schoolteacher Marie Jefferson.

"Good morning, Amari," the white-haired Agnes called out cheerily. "What brings you here so early? Have you had breakfast? There are some eggs and toast left."

"Yes, ma'am, I have, but thanks. I came to talk to Tamar about something."

Tamar looked at him over her cup. "Should I be afraid?" she asked.

"No, ma'am. Least I don't think so, but can we talk privately?"

She held his eyes for a long moment, then stood. "Sure. Agnes, I'll be back."

"I'll be here."

They went into the empty kiva-shaped theater that was one of the town's jewels. On Friday and Saturday nights, family movies were shown on the big floor-to-ceiling screen. They both took seats and Tamar asked, "So, what did you want to talk about?"

"What do I have to do to become a July?"

Her eyebrow raised.

Amari knew she could be tough and prickly, so he waited.

"You want to be a real July, as in being officially adopted and changing your name?"

"Yes, ma'am."

There were only a few things that Amari was scared of in this world and one of them happened to be the tall, silver-haired lady eyeing him now.

"Have you talked to Trent?"

"No. Thought I'd see how you felt about the idea first. Trying to be respectful, you know."

"Appreciate that."

As she continued to impale him with her black hawk-like stare, Amari tried not to squirm or more importantly shake in his seat.

"You sure about this?"

He nodded. "Very."

For a moment she said nothing, then finally, "Okay. In the old days, before a young man could become a warrior he had to go on a Spirit Quest."

That threw him. He swallowed. "Spirit Quest?"

"Yes."

"Will I have to do that?"

She nodded. "We don't let just any old body be a July, Amari. The Spirit has to find favor with you, and so do I."

He blinked.

"Can you raise a tent?"

He shook his head no.

"Own a hatchet?"

Another negative shake.

"Talk to Trent or Malachi. They'll help you."

That made him feel better. "Can they go with me too?"

"No. Mal would spend the whole time drinking Pepsi and telling you about his boudoir bimbos, and Trent has a town to run."

"But if nobody goes with me, how will I know what to do and where to go?"

"I didn't say you were going alone."

"Then who—" And as soon as those two words came out of his mouth, he knew, and he really started to shake inside. "You?" he whispered.

She nodded and smiled. "Talk to Trent about the stuff you'll need."

"So after the Spirit Quest will I be good?"

"Almost."

"Almost?" he echoed, cried.

"You have to do something that benefits Henry Adams. A tribute to the Duster Ancestors has to be offered too."

Deflated, Amari sighed. He knew from his school that the Dusters were the original Henry Adams settlers. They were actually called Exodusters because they came West during the Great Exodus of 1879. "What do I have to do to please them?"

"Something memorable that doesn't involve stealing cars and making the entire town go to court."

"Ouch," he replied.

She didn't smile. "It should be something folks will remember and that will be a benefit."

When he looked confused, she added, "Come by the house and we'll look through the old pictures. Maybe they'll give you some inspiration for your project."

"It's got to be a project—like a school thing?"

She stood.

Amari realized that becoming a July was going to be way more complicated than he'd imagined. "Okay, Tamar. I'll talk to Dad and the O.G. about the stuff I need for the quest. And I'll come see the pictures." Walking out of the theater, Amari felt like he had the weight of the world on his eleven-year-old shoulders.

Tamar waited for him to disappear before allowing herself to smile. In her heart, she knew he'd make a perfect July because he'd been sent to them by the Spirit. For the past few years, she'd despaired over the idea of her branch of the July line coming to an end once she, Mal, and Trent were gone, but now they had Amari, and he was a true July. Like her Seminole outlaw ancestors, he was smart, resourceful, and a bit on the dangerous side. His commitment to family was shown last fall when he tried to help Crystal by stealing Mal's truck. His actions might have been misguided but his heart was in the right place. More importantly, in the nine months he'd been in town, Tamar had come to care very much for the young carjacker and already thought of him as blood. She wasn't sure how his quest and project would turn out, but she knew without question that it wouldn't be boring.

Standing in the offices of the mayor's suite, Trent stared around at all the stuff piled everywhere. He spotted lamps, end tables, and in between the stacks and stacks of shrink-wrapped boxes that held lord knew what, he counted at least two leather recliners, both brown. Over by the windows was a large desk encased in thick layers of protective plastic. Beside it were three rolled-up rugs leaned up against the wall. Why did he need all this? The only reason he was mayor in the first place was that no one else wanted the job, and now running Henry Adams had become way more complicated. Being mayor presently involved having to deal with contracts, meetings, and budgets, when all he really wanted to do was come into the office for a couple of minutes each morning, open a few pieces of mail, and leave to go work on his cars.

Bernadine wasn't feeling that, however, and truthfully, neither was his adult side as it wisely pointed out that he was acting like a spoiled child. Mayors in towns all over America would love to be in the position Henry Adams found itself in, and who wouldn't with a take-no-prisoners fairy godmother like Bernadine sprinkling gold dust around. Because of her vision and big heart, Henry Adams no longer teetered on the precipice of extinction. What the Dusters began in 1879 remained alive and kicking due to her largesse, and in spite of his selfish protestations, he owed it to those original dreamers to ensure that the legacy lived on.

With that in mind, Trent shook off his bad mood and tackled the shrink-wrap with the blade of the box cutter in his hand.

It took him a good little while to free everything. A mountain of discarded shrink-wrap and plastic stood in a pile by the door. He was working on the boxes in the inner office when he heard, "Hey, Dad. You in here?"

Trent made his way back to the outer office just in time to see Amari battling the plastic Everest and slowly kicking his way through the mess like the Incredible Hulk. Trent smiled and wondered if Amari knew just how much fun it was for Trent to have him in his life. "Did you talk to Tamar?"

"Yep," he said before going quiet and looking around at the desk and chairs, loveseats, coffee tables and lamps. "I thought this was going to be your office. Looks more like Ms. Bernadine's living room."

"I know. The ladies who run this place went a little overboard, I'm thinking."

"I'm thinking you're right. Looks like all nice stuff, but they probably could have saved a whole lot of money just by going to Wal-Mart."

"I heard that," Bernadine called with a laugh from the threshold.

An embarrassed Amari dropped his head. "Sorry."

A smiling Trent came to his son's defense "He is right, Bernadine. This is a lot. Didn't you take a hit from the economy like everybody else?"

"Sure, but not so much that I have to furnish your place with stuff from the dollar store. If it's any consolation, Lily did the ordering, and girlfriend can squeeze a dollar until it screams, so I know she got everything at a good price."

That made Trent feel a bit better, and as he assessed the furniture with an engineer's eye, he had to admit, Lily had gotten some nice-looking pieces. From the lamps to the love seats to the desk, the lines of the designs were modern and clean. They flowed in a masculine way, strong yet not overpowering. "She has a good eye."

"Glad you approve," Lily said, walking into the office.

"I do." Approved of her as well, but he kept that to himself.

"I wasn't going to give you any excuse to stay away from this place, Trenton July. If you like it, you'll use it. I know you."

"Guilty as charged." Trent could see Amari grinning, so to give him something to do before he pointed out for the five hundredth time how hot Lily was, he said, "Amari, take the shrink-wrap and put it in the bed of my truck. I'll haul it to the dump later on."

"Sure, Dad."

"I'll help," Bernadine offered. "You two get started on setting up the place."

Lily looked critically at her boss's attire. She was wearing a pair of twelve-hundred-dollar, navy blue Jimmy Choos on her feet. Her trim size sixteen body was decked out in an original Dior designer suit, also navy. On her wrists there was enough gold to have her own hour-long show on QVC. "You aren't dressed for hauling plastic, Bernadine Brown."

Bernadine eyed her for a moment. "Do you want some time alone with the man or not, Lily Fontaine?"

Lily had the decency to look embarrassed.

Bernadine said, "I thought so. Let's go, Amari, so these lovebirds can get their bill and coo on."

"Their bill and what?"

"Just grab an armful and come on."

"Billincoo. What the he—" He froze at the disapproving look Trent shot his way. One of the first things Amari learned when he first came to town was no cussing. "I meant, what the *heck* is billincoo? Can't be an old-school R&B group, can it?"

Rolling her eyes, Bernadine told him, "No." Filling her arms with shrink-wrap, she gently pushed the still questioning Amari out the door.

"He is something," Lily said once she and Trent were alone.

Trent hooked his arms around her waist and looked down into her smiling face. "So are you."

Knowing they had only a couple of minutes before Bernadine and the Question Box returned, he leaned down and kissed her gently.

Lily returned the kiss, and when it ended she felt like a puddle of melted ice cream. "We need to go on a date. Preferably one inside a hotel room."

Grinning, he leaned back and raised an eyebrow. "Really?"

"Yep."

He chuckled. "Okay. I'll see what I can do."

Once all the plastic and shrink-wrap was removed, Bernadine, Lily, and Amari helped Trent set up the furniture. When most of that was accomplished, the women went back to their offices, leaving Trent and Amari alone to finish the rest.

"Can I talk to you about something, Dad?"

"Sure, shoot."

"The reason I wanted to see Tamar was to get her okay for me to ask you if I could be a real July."

Trent looked up from the prompts on the screen of his laptop that was loading software for his new printer and studied the boy for a long, silent moment before asking quietly, "You really want to be my son?"

"I do."

"I'm honored, Amari, because I want you to be my son too."

"Money!"

Trent had no idea that adding an eleven-year-old car thief to one's world could make life so sweet. "So what did Tamar say?"

"A bunch of stuff about a Spirit Quest. Do you have a hatchet?"

"Yep. Tent too."

"Good," he replied with relief in his voice. "Can you show me how to put up the tent?"

"Yes." Trent was still stuck on this remarkable young man wanting to be his son. "Did she say when you were going to do this?"

"No."

"Okay. We can ask her. She taking you?"

"Uh huh. She said you had a town to run and that the O.G. would spend the whole time talking about the honeys, so she'd go with me instead."

Trent knew that he was busy, but he would've taken the time off to do the quest. In fact, by all rights he should have been the one, but since she'd already staked her claim, he decided to let it go; he'd have a lifetime to bond with Amari, and besides, he loved Tamar too much to spend even a moment being mad at her. She was in the winter of her life and there was no telling how much longer she would be with them before leaving this plane to join the Ancestors.

"So you really want to be my son, even though I'm not going to let you get away with stuff like stealing cars or running game?"

That last part made Amari think back to the unique punishment he'd earned last summer for tricking Ms. Agnes into buying him and Preston adult-rated video games. "Yes."

"It's not always going to be fun being dad and son. Some days you're going to want to throw me under a combine."

"I know."

"And I'm going to push you hard to do your best in school. No getting around that either."

"I understand."

"With all that in mind, I'm going to ask you one more time. Do you still want to do this?"

"Yes, sir. I do."

"Then come here." Trent stood and held out his arms.

Amari closed the space between them and let himself be enfolded in the strong embrace of the man he very much wanted to grow up to be just like.

Above him, Trent held on tight and mentally prayed for all the blessings his son deserved after the life he'd been forced to lead since becoming a ward of the state. "You do your part and I'll do mine. We're both going to screw up from time to time, but that's okay."

Amari's chest got tight and his eyes began to burn. "Okay."

They stepped apart.

Trent held out his hand, and when Amari grasped it, Trent said, "I, Trenton July, take you, Amari July, as my son. In sickness and in health. In craziness and crisis. To love and guide, until we leave this life."

Amari replied solemnly, "I, Amari July, take you, Trent July, as my one and only dad. In health, and when you get old, to love and be guided by you, even when I want to throw you under a combine, until we leave this life."

As Amari looked up at Trent with that patented grin, all Trent could think was: *Now take that, Tamar,* but aloud he said, "I think this calls for ice cream. How about we sneak out and go to the rec and see if we can find some in the freezer."

"Good idea, and Dad?"

"Yeah?"

"Thanks."

"No problem."

"Oh. Do I still have to do the Spirit Quest thing?"

"Yep."

Amari sighed.

Trent grinned. "Sorry. It's tradition."

"Okay."

So they left the office and headed off to celebrate their new union with all the ice cream they could eat.

Over at Bernadine's house, Crystal stood on the porch and stared across the street at Preston seated on the steps of the Payne house. He looked dejected. His shoulders were slumped and he seemed to be staring at something only he could see. Interesting, she thought, and debated what she should do. The old Crystal would've shown him her hand and flounced back down on the porch's sofa to continue reading *Architectural Digest*, but she'd matured a lot in the last nine months, and by Henry Adams standards Preston was family. As the oldest kid it was her responsibility to play big sister so she left her porch to check him out.

"You okay, Brain?" He'd earned the nickname at school. The boy was scary smart. Even their teacher Ms. Marie thought so.

"Yeah."

Crystal didn't believe him so she folded her arms and waited for him to tell her the truth.

Her stance garnered a small smile and a shrug. "Just thinking."

"About what?"

He was quiet for a moment, as if he was weighing what to say. Finally he asked, "Is Ms. Bernadine home?"

"No, she's at the Power Plant."

"Then let's talk on your porch."

She nodded.

"Let me tell Mrs. Payne where I'm going. Be right back."

He went inside, and after his return they crossed the street.

They took seats, Crystal on the sofa, and he chose one of the chairs.

"So what's up?" she asked him.

He looked off into the distance for a quiet moment. "I think I'm going to be leaving."

That was so *not* what she wanted to hear. "Look. We all know what happened when I tried to run away."

"No, not like that. I think the Paynes aren't getting along and if they split up, we all know where that leaves me."

Crystal frowned. "What makes you think they're about to split?"

"She's real sad. It started at that stupid reunion the colonel dragged us to." Upon seeing the confusion on Crystal's face, he told her the same story he'd related to Amari the night at Tamar's.

When he finished, she asked, "You really think this woman was somebody the colonel used to kick it with?"

"The way she was acting? Big time."

"Damn."

"Exactly."

They both went silent for a few moments and then Crystal said, "Maybe they'll work it out."

He responded with a small shake of his head and then looked over into her eyes. "This is the first family I really wanted to hook up with. After a thousand wack foster placements, I'd started to hope. You know what I mean?"

"I do." Crystal knew exactly what he meant. She'd had the same sort of hope about her mom. It hadn't worked out.

Preston said, "So, that's what's going on with me."

"That's rough."

"As Amari says, 'No shit.'"

"Maybe Ms. Bernadine can help."

He shook his head. "No. Don't say anything to her, please. Let's just keep this between me, you, and Amari. Okay?"

Against her better, fifteen-year-old judgment, Crystal acquiesced. "Okay, I won't tell her. Promise."

"Thanks."

He stared off again and Crystal said quietly, "Brain?"

"Yeah?"

"It's gonna work out."

He nodded glumly, then stood. "I'm going home, get something to eat, and then run down Amari." Before leaving, however, he said sincerely, "Thanks for listening, Crystal."

"You're welcome. Just don't make it a habit."

Grinning, he headed home.

Crys watched him go. *Trouble in paradise.* She hated lying to Preston, but she planned to tell Ms. Bernadine about the Paynes just as soon as she came home because although she'd never tell him, Crystal was worried about him.

Having no idea what Crystal had in store, Bernadine concentrated on getting through the rest of the morning's tasks. She put in a call to Florene's professor, only to be told by the secretary that Malachi had contacted the office earlier. The résumés of potential replacements had been e-mailed to him an hour ago. A pleased Bernadine thanked the woman and ended the call. Crossing the D&C off her list, she turned back to her computer screen.

A few minutes later a knock on her open office door sounded. She looked up and saw Roni Garland.

"Got a minute?"

"As many as you need. Come on in. You want coffee?"

She shook her head. "Already had my morning three. Catch me around four this afternoon."

Bernadine truly enjoyed Roni's wit. "What can I do for you?"

"Haven't had a chance to tell you yet but we were mailed

the last of the paperwork for Zoey's adoption. Once we send it back, the court says it shouldn't take long."

"Good. You all have been perfect for her." The Garlands had first broached the subject about making Zoey legally theirs this past Christmas.

"It's been mutual. She's the reason I'm singing again."

Bernadine nodded. A few years ago, the estranged husband of one of Roni's backup singers had gone berserk with an automatic rifle during a concert. Roni left the blood-soaked stage that night and never sang again, until last summer. Now, to the delight of her fans like Bernadine, the multi Grammy Award–winning vocalist was presently hard at work on a new CD. "So how'd the recording session go while you all were in New York?"

"Laid a few tracks that I'm pleased with, but I spent most of the time taking the kids sightseeing. You should have seen their faces when they saw the Statue of Liberty." She laughed. "What was even better was the face of a man standing beside us when I started explaining to them that the statue was built in France and originally meant as an anti-slavery symbol. He almost choked to death."

Bernadine grinned. "Did he say anything to you?"

"Yeah. Tried to argue with me. Told me I was telling the kids lies. I told him to look it up. Then I gave him my producer's address so he'd know where to send me an apology."

Bernadine's shoulders shook with laughter. "You are something else."

"Best way to be. Anyway, back to the CD. I'll be flying back and forth to New York until we get it done, so the sooner we build the studio I want here, the better. I already know I'm not going to like missing Zoey."

The town's construction crew was hoping to make the recording studio a reality by midsummer. It and the other projects on Bernadine's build list for the year would begin in earnest just as soon as spring finished wrestling the weather away from Old Man Winter. Also due for construction this year was the health clinic Roni's husband, Reggie, wanted to open. Presently there were no doctors practicing in Henry Adams and his expertise was sorely needed. "Tell your hubby I need his wish list for the clinic by next week so that he and I can sit down with the architect."

"Will do. You know, after all the hustle and bustle of the Big Apple it's really really quiet here, and the silence feels good. Never thought I'd miss being in a teeny tiny place out in the middle of nowhere, but?" She shrugged.

"I'm glad to be home too. Missed this place a lot."

Roni stood. "Okay, Boss Lady, I'm going to head out so that you can keep turning the world. Take a breath every now and then, would you?"

"Yes, ma'am."

Roni made her exit.

Bernadine went back to work.

CHAPTER
5

Over at the Dog and Cow, Malachi was in his office taking another look at the résumés sent by the culinary college's secretary. Call him sexist, but he had no intentions of hiring another female. If Florene had been the pick of the female litter he wanted nothing to do with the runts. A few of the résumés had looked interesting. He picked up the phone on his desk and began to dial the first candidate's number when he heard, "Hey Mal."

The sight of Rocky Dancer standing in the doorway almost gave him a heart attack. "Oh my goodness!"

He jumped up and rushed over to give her a big hug.

She reciprocated, laughing, "Hey. Watch the back. Watch the back. I may need that spine."

He stepped away with a grin on his face. "You visiting, or back for good?"

She shrugged. "For good, looks like. Unless a better offer comes along."

"Your job's open if you want it."

"I think I do. Love what you've done with the place."

"Hallelujah!" And he hugged her again.

"Things been that bad?" she asked, laughing again.

"You just don't know. Have a seat and let me tell you a story."

So she did and he filled her in on everything from Bernadine Brown to Riley and Cletus to Florene.

"Lots been happening. How's Trent? Got a call from him but I was on my way here and didn't want to spoil the surprise by calling back and telling him I was coming."

"Could've knocked me over with a feather, seeing you standing there. Trent's fine. Lily's back."

She stilled. "Fabulous Fontaine? Why?"

Mal explained Lily's return to town and her role in the new and improved Henry Adams.

"So are she and Trent back together?"

He nodded.

"Not going to lie and say I'm happy for him. Never did like Fontaine, but hey, who am I to judge. He didn't mind me getting married, so I guess I can be nice."

"Good. Lily's done a lot of good here." He could tell by her cool eyes that she had issues with Lily being in Trent's life again, but he hoped her good side would eventually prevail over any jealously she might be harboring. "So, your marriage to Bob didn't work out?"

"Nope. When you walk in and find your husband wearing your underwear, it's time to go."

Mal's mouth dropped.

"I guess Trent didn't tell you."

"No," he replied in a voice filled with wonder.

"Well, now you know. So, if I'm coming back to work here, how about a tour?"

Mal was still stuck on the visual of her ex wearing her underwear and decided a tour might be just the thing to clear his boggled mind.

They spent the next little while walking around the D&C. She checked out the freezers, all the new appliances, and the new setup. "This place is sharp, Mal. You did a great job."

"It's all on Bernadine. She's responsible. Without her help, this place would still be a dive."

"It wasn't that bad."

"Yeah it was. So, when do you want to start?"

"In the morning, I guess."

"Then welcome back, Ms. Dancer. Place is all yours."

They went back to the office to discuss salary and vision.

Rocky said, "You know, if you want this place to eventually pay its own bills, how about we add a couple of big screens, do some theme nights—that sort of thing."

"I'm all for it, as long as we don't serve alcohol."

"I'm okay with that."

"Good, because I don't want anyone leaving my place and killing somebody on the way home. The only saving grace about my drunk years was that I never killed anybody."

They continued talking about their plans for the D&C but were interrupted by Clay standing in the doorway.

"Rocky! Is that you?"

She grinned. "It's me."

"Get over here," he said with a grin.

Hugs were exchanged, and Clay said, "Good to see you. I hope you're coming back to work here."

"That I am."

"Thank goodness. Now we can have food we can eat and recognize."

She chuckled.

Then he said, "Almost forgot what brought me in here. What's the deal on the limo out front?"

"What limo?"

"Come see for yourself."

A curious Mal and Rocky followed him out of the office.

Sure enough, parked outside was a gleaming black limousine. The tint on the car's windows prevented them from seeing whoever was inside.

Clay asked, "Who do you think it is?"

"No clue," Mal replied truthfully. "One of Bernadine's peeps, maybe? Music friend of Roni's?"

The driver got out first. Tall and White, he was wearing a crisp black uniform, complete with hat. He smoothly opened the passenger door, and out stepped a well-dressed Black man who appeared to be in his late fifties, early sixties. They watched as the stranger took a moment to look up and down the street. Considering the diner was the only building at this end of town, there wasn't much to see, but he seemed satisfied. After sharing a few words with the driver, he walked to the diner's entrance.

Once inside, he glanced around at the red and chrome interior and appeared impressed. Upon noticing Mal, Clay, and the lovely Rocky standing in the empty dining room, he came forward, smiling. "Morning. Can you tell me where I can find Bernadine Brown? Hope I'm in the right town." He directed a big grin Rocky's way, but was promptly ignored.

Mal checked him out. From his blue pin-striped suit and gold silk tie, to the handmade brown leather shoes, he stank of money. "And you are?"

"Not that it's any of your business, but the name's Leo. Leo Brown."

The ex. "Welcome to Henry Adams. Heard about you."

That seemed to catch him off guard. "Bernie telling tales out of school?"

"No. Just the truth."

His jaw tightened. "Just tell me where she is."

"Power Plant. Turn around, go back up the road. Circular building. Brick red. Can't miss it."

"Thanks," he grumbled, and strode out back to his ride.

"Wonder what he wants with Bernadine?" Clay asked.

Mal shrugged.

"You jealous?"

"You want the truth or the lie?"

The two old friends smiled.

Rocky said with surprise, "You didn't tell me you were hitting on Ms. Brown."

Clay said, "That's because he's batting a big fat zero. If he was a baseball player he'd be in the minors."

Mal lowered his head to hide his grin.

Rocky walked over and wrapped an arm around each of the waists. "You know, I really missed you two old players while I was gone."

"We missed you too," Mal said.

They each gave her a kiss on her cheek.

"Welcome back," Clay said. "Good to have you home."

And she replied, "As Dorothy said when she and Toto finally got back to Kansas. No place like it."

At the Power Plant, when Lily's voice came over the office intercom to announce the arrival of Leo Brown, Bernadine sat straight up in her chair. *"What!"*

Realizing he'd probably heard her response, Bernadine calmed herself, took in a breath, and replied as pleasantly as she could. "Let me finish this call," she lied. "I'll let you know when I'm done."

"Okay."

Before Bernadine could stop it, the memory of that day in his office flared to life and she was angry, hurt, and humiliated all over again. What in the world was he doing in Henry Adams! They hadn't spoken since the divorce. Was he dying? In trouble? She'd have to let him in before she could get answers, and lord knew she didn't want to. Running him over with Baby would be better, but she drew in another breath, and hit the intercom button again. "Send him in, please, Ms. Fontaine."

"Yes, Ms. Brown."

A few short seconds later, the man she'd fallen in love with at age nineteen and who'd broken her heart beyond repair at age fifty-two stood in her doorway. "Leo," she said, coolly, "how are you?" She didn't like him well enough to stand up and give him a proper greeting, but she did gesture for him to take a seat.

"Doing okay, Bern. Even better now that I see your face."

She gave him a fake smile. She'd always detested being called Bern but he'd insisted on using the masculine-sounding nickname anyway. "What can I do for you?"

"Just stopped by to see you. Been keeping up with you and your town through CNN and the Internet."

"You flew all the way here just to stop by?"

"Uh, no. I'm staying just outside Franklin consulting on a project for the company. And since I'll be here for a while, thought I'd drive over and see how you are."

"That's nice," she lied. "As you can see, I'm doing well. Town's keeping me busy, but it goes with the territory. How's the wife? You'll have to forgive me for not knowing her name."

"No problem. I'm divorced. Again."

"Sorry to hear that." Another lie. "Was this number two or three? I haven't been keeping up."

"Three. Kiara's her name."

"Ah." He'd always been a sharp dresser, but he'd put on some weight since she saw him last and the buttons on his silk coat were straining a bit. Possibly a result of having to eat all those Happy Meals his young wives probably preferred. *Stop it, Bernadine.*

"You think we could get some dinner sometime while I'm here?"

She didn't hesitate. "No."

"Oh, come on, Bern."

"No, Leo. Why would I want to do anything with you?"

"You always were hard on a brother."

"Only when deserved."

"Can we at least be friends?"

"Why?" she asked, taken aback at the outrageous proposal.

He shrugged. "Because we shared a lot of good years before . . ."

"Before you lost your mind, you mean?" she countered bitterly.

He had the decency to look embarrassed.

"You cheated on me, Leo. Me." *The one who really loved you,* she said inwardly, and thought about the old Mary Wells tune with that same title. "We're divorced. You made that happen, remember?"

He met her eyes. "I do, and I'd like to make it up to you if I could."

She shook her head. "You can't, and I won't apologize for how I feel."

"I understand, but I am sorry."

"So am I, Leo."

"Can I be frank?"

"Sure."

"I want you back."

"Excuse me?"

"I want you back. Cheating on you was the biggest mistake of my life. I realize that now."

"This wouldn't have anything to do with your latest PYT leaving you for a pool boy, would it?"

He went stock-still.

"I lied, Leo. I do keep up. It's in my best interest to do so." She sat back in her chair and folded her arms. "I also learned, belatedly, that you had a bunch of millions stashed offshore that you hid from my lawyers."

He took out a handkerchief and mopped at his suddenly damp brow. His hairline had marched back a few inches too since the divorce. "Look. I'm not going to lie. I treated you bad, and yes, Kiara left me, but I've been wanting you back for a long time."

She didn't believe that for a minute but she let him have the floor.

"I'm lonely, Bernadine. There, I admit it. You're the only woman who ever loved me for me."

"And you threw it in the trash," she reminded him softly.

He looked away for a long moment. "What if I promise it won't happen again?"

"Leo, you can promise to turn into Little Richard and it still won't matter. I'm not coming back. So unless you have some legitimate business to discuss, we're done here."

He sighed audibly. "What if I tell you I'm not giving up?"

"On what?"

He got to his feet. "On you, me. Us. I didn't get to be who I am by taking no for an answer."

"Did you hear me the first time?"

"I did, but we had a good marriage and we can have it again."

"If you come near me talking this nonsense again, I will slap you with a restraining order so hard, they'll feel it on Jupiter."

"I don't care. Not giving up. See you." He headed to the door.

"Leo!" she called angrily. "Leo!"

But he was gone.

She cursed.

Lily came in. "What's wrong?"

"I'm divorced from a crazy man, that's what's wrong."

In response to Lily's confusion Bernadine told her the story, and when she finished all Lily could say was "Wow."

Bernadine shook her head. "Why can't he go on with his life and let me do the same?"

"Because he doesn't have one?"

"Good answer."

"You know," Lily began, "if this were anyone else, I'd think it was kind of romantic, him wanting you back."

Bernadine speared her with a look.

"I said, if it was someone else. Remember I was the one who threw Winston's suitcases into the street when he tried to get me to move back to Atlanta." Winston was her old boyfriend and she'd wanted to choke him when they finally broke up.

"Leo's got a better chance of marrying George Bush than getting back with me."

"I hear you."

Lily studied the quiet anger in Bernadine's face. "It's lunchtime. Put the world down and let's go see what Tamar and Agnes are serving today."

Tamar and the seniors ran a small lunch operation out of the rec center's kitchen. The menu was limited to pre-packaged salads, sandwiches, and a soup of the day. All proceeds went into the center's general fund.

"You go on ahead. I'm not really hungry."

"You sure? Want me to bring you something back?"

"Yeah. A salad might be nice. I'll stash it in the fridge for later."

"Okay, but you sure you don't want to come?" Lily asked with concern. "Might take your mind off Leo."

"No. I'll be okay. You go on."

"Okay, I'll see you in about forty minutes then."

Once Lily was gone, Bernadine mentally reviewed Leo's visit. Had he lost his damn mind? No way was she becoming his wife again. She'd give her millions away to a crackhead first. But, if she were being truthful, seeing him had brought back the memories of not only his perfidy but the good times they'd had as well. He'd been her first and only boyfriend. Growing up, Black women with her build and coloring were rarely termed beautiful, yet he'd made her feel that way by surprising her with flowers and sending her cards. He did his best to make sure she knew how much he cared and how special he considered her to be. Then he began moving up the corporate ladder, and the more money he made, the more distant he became. The marriage had already died for her a good four years before she busted him with his secretary. So why in the world would he think she'd take him back? He was an executive with one of the big oil companies and she wondered if he'd been sniffing petroleum fumes. That was the only rational explanation she could come up with. The more she thought about him and his outrageous proposal, the angrier she became.

When Malachi July appeared at her door a short time later, the hot look she lanced through him caused him to raise his hands in mock defense. "I'm bearing food. Lily sent me. Please don't kill me, oh great queen."

She dropped her head and grinned. "I'm sorry. Come on in."

He put the packaged salad on her desk. "Lily told me you had a visitor."

"Lily's got a big mouth."

"She's just worried about you."

"I know. I wasn't serious. Sit, if you have time."

He chose a chair and took her up on the offer. "I saw him earlier." And he told her about the encounter with Leo at the Dog. "Lily said he wants you back?"

"Wanting and getting are two different universes."

"Good to know. I'm having enough trouble without adding him in the mix."

She smiled. "I'm not here for that, remember?"

"So you keep telling me. I'm patient though."

The lure of him floated around her like wood smoke; fragrant, wistful. "Thanks for the salad."

"I'm going to a picnic this Friday evening. Like to take you along as my guest."

"Who else is going?"

"Nobody. Be just you and me."

She chuckled. "It still gets cold in the evenings. We'll freeze."

"That's why I'm throwing it in my truck."

That left her speechless.

"So, do you want to go?"

"A picnic in a pickup truck?" she asked doubtfully.

"Sure, why not? Can't take you to the opera."

He had to be the most amazing man she'd ever met, and much to her own surprise she replied, "Okay. I'll go."

If he found her acceptance surprising, he hid it well. "Good. Pick you up Friday at seven. Your place."

"Should I bring anything?"

"Nope. Got everything covered. No fancy clothes though. This is a casual affair."

"Gotcha."

"Now, some even better news. I found a cook for the D&C."

"Already?"

"Yep. Rocky's back and she's agreed to take the job."

Bernadine wanted to shout with joy. "That is great news. When can she start?"

"In the morning."

"Does she like the new place?"

"Yeah. She also had some good money-making ideas that should help get you out from under the gun. Would you be willing to meet with her?"

"Of course. I'm looking forward to it."

"Thinking about making her manager. She's always run the place. May as well give her the title."

"Sounds good to me."

They spent a few more minutes talking about the salary he'd decided upon, and some other items related to the diner, like ordering a few big-screen plasmas so patrons could watch sports.

Bernadine liked the idea. There was nothing better than watching football on a big screen with a bunch of friends. "Get a couple of estimates and give them to Lily."

"Will do, and I'll let Rocky know you want to meet her."

Their business now done, he got to his feet. "Feeling better?"

She nodded. "Yes. Thanks. And thanks for the salad and the picnic invite."

"You're welcome. Just a few of the many services I provide."

Their eyes met and held. Bernadine found herself wondering what it might be like to have him in her life as more than a friend.

"See you later," he said softly.

"Bye, Mal."

Alone again, Bernadine opened her salad. She did feel better but she wondered if she'd been sniffing petroleum fumes too. She couldn't believe she was going to a picnic in a pickup truck. Who'd ever heard of such a thing?

Sheila Payne fed the lunch dishes into the dishwasher and turned it on. Preston had taken off for the rec and Barrett was seated at the kitchen table leafing through the latest issue of *Leather Neck* magazine. The melancholy she'd brought back from Florida continued to ride her and she had no idea how to make it go away. When she looked up, his eyes were on her, so she turned back to the sink and used the paper towel in her hand to finish wiping down the counter. In as cheery a voice as she could muster, she said to him, "I'm going over to the rec center and see if Tamar or Ms. Agnes need help with the lunch cleanup."

"Sheila, will you tell me what's wrong."

"I'm fine, Barrett."

"No, you aren't."

She sighed and said again, "I'm fine."

"I don't believe you. Was it the reunion? If you don't want to go next year, I'm okay with it."

She looked away and gave a tiny shake of her head. He'd never been a man sensitive to her moods, so she doubted he really wanted to know. More than likely, what he did want was for whatever was bothering her to disappear so that he could go back to the even-keeled, regimented life he preferred. Having to constantly ask after her was not something he was accustomed to. Maybe she should just blurt it out. It would probably make her feel better, but at what cost? She hadn't been raised to be confrontational and she worried about the effects of such disclosure on their marriage and their future with Preston.

"You don't have a fatal disease, do you?"

She gave him a genuine smile this time. "No, Barrett. I'm not dying." *Except maybe inside.*

He continued to assess her and she continued to avoid his eyes. Finally, as if he'd had enough, he got to his feet and walked over to where she stood.

"Tell me. Whatever it is. Please?"

Sheila thought about all the strength she'd noticed in women like Bernadine, Lily, and Roni and decided that maybe time had come to find her own. "Seeing Marti at the reunion reminded me of your affair with her, and it broke my heart all over again."

Her words seemed to rock him like a mortar blast. She actually thought he might fall over. "You wanted to know," she reminded him quietly. "Any response?"

When he continued to stare, apparently speechless, she

offered up a bittersweet smile. "I thought not. I'm going to the center. I'll be back in time to fix dinner."

Going to the closet to get her jacket, she could feel his eyes following her. She'd no idea whether they held anger, surprise, or remorse, because she didn't look back. Instead she put the jacket on and headed for the front door. He was still rooted in the kitchen when she left the house.

The rocked Barrett stood in the silence. He'd been so sure she hadn't known about his affair with Marti, yet there he stood. His heart was pounding and his body shook with both reaction and guilt. *She knew!* He had no idea what to do or say. Not that there was anything he could say to her; not after all these years. Having prided himself on being a man of honor, he was in reality an arrogant, hypocritical adulterer. Marti had been his only walk outside his marriage, but it didn't matter. *She knew!* Did she want a divorce? He prayed she didn't. Although their marriage lacked the fire and passion other married couples seemed to have, he and Sheila were comfortable with each other, or at least he thought they were. Now he wasn't sure how she felt, because over the years, he in his arrogance hadn't bothered to ask. He'd assumed she was content being his wife, but the earthshattering revelation she'd dropped just now contradicted that. *Lord.* He ran his hands across his face. All his life he'd been a man of action, but now he didn't know what to do.

When Amari looked up from his ice cream and saw Preston enter the cafeteria, he asked his dad, "If the Paynes split up, can Preston come live with us?"

"Who said the Paynes are splitting up?"

But by then Preston was on them and pulling up a chair and Trent was left with a bunch of unasked questions.

"Hey Mr. July; hey Amari." Preston saw the bowl of ice cream Amari was finishing. "Aw man, why didn't you call me to say you were getting ice cream?"

"Sorry. This was payment for helping Dad set up his new office."

Trent asked, "Have you had lunch, Preston?"

"Yes."

"Okay, then just tell the ladies to get you a bowl. Have them put it on my tab."

"Thanks!"

Trent rose to his feet. "Gotta get back to the office, guys. Drop by if you want to. See you later."

Trent patted Amari on the shoulder and departed.

Amari and Preston ate their ice cream but didn't talk much.

The place had gotten pretty crowded with locals and the men and women working the construction sites. They saw Mrs. Payne come in. She gave them a wave and disappeared in the kitchen.

Before Amari could comment, they heard, "When you two young men get done, I need you to start wiping down some of the empty tables, and take the trash to the Dumpster."

Both looked up at Tamar and replied in unison. "Yes, ma'am."

Once she moved away, Amari said, "Man. I can't wait until school starts back next week."

"Me too, so she can work somebody else to death."

After wiping down the tables and hauling the large garbage bags out to the big Dumpsters behind the building, they earned Tamar's thanks and made their escape.

They went outside in the chilly sunshine and sat on one of the picnic tables near the track. They were dressed for the weather in jackets with hoodies underneath, so the temperature wasn't an issue.

"Did Mrs. Payne look like she'd been crying when she came in?" Preston asked.

Amari nodded. "Yeah, she did."

"Reason one hundred and eighty-five why I hate the foster care system."

"What do you mean?"

"If the Paynes split up, I'm gone. The state will make me move to another home."

"Probably not. You're family, Brain. If the Paynes split up, Ms. Bernadine will figure out a way for you to stay here. Guaranteed."

"I don't know, man. I told Crystal—"

Amari's head spun sharply. "You talked to Crystal? About what?"

"What's been going on, and how I feel about it."

"You talked to her about your feelings? Are you on crack?"

Preston shrugged. "It was okay."

"Until she puts your business on YouTube."

"She promised not to tell Ms. Bernadine or anybody else what we talked about."

Amari was shaking his head. "Crystal is okay, but only up to a point. I didn't mind stealing O.G.'s truck for her last summer because she needed the help, but *I'd* have to be on crack before I told her anything personal."

"Well, talking to her made me feel better."

"Are you sure this was our Crystal? Blond weave? Lots of attitude?"

Preston grinned. "Same one."

"You're much braver than me, my man. Much braver." Amari let go of the humor and his manner turned serious. "You really that worried about this thing with the Paynes?"

"Yeah. It's my own fault though. It's what I get for thinking they'd be the ones to keep me forever."

"Hope can kill you."

"Got that right."

"Me, I'm stepping up."

"What do you mean?"

"I told Tamar and my dad that I want to be a full member of the family."

"What? Now who's lost his mind? Amari, we're foster kids. You know better than that. What did they say?"

"Dad was cool. Tamar said yes, almost."

"Almost?"

"I have to do something called a Spirit Quest."

"Like the kind the tribes took back in the day with the hallucinogenics?"

"The what?"

"The Native American version of what folks today call acid?"

Amari's eyes popped. "Acid? She didn't say anything about doing drugs!"

"That's just one way of going about it. I'm sure she's not going to make you do drugs. Least I hope not."

"You're scaring me, man."

"Sorry. So what did she say you had to do?"

"Get a hatchet and a tent, and that she's going to be the one doing the whole thing with me."

Preston asked doubtfully, "You sure being a July is going to be worth all this?"

"There's more. After I finish the spirit part, she wants me to do something to honor the town and the Dusters. She called it a project."

"Like in school?"

"Same thing I asked."

"Sounds like a lot."

"No shit." Amari sighed, then lay back on the table's top and looked up at the blue sky. "But Trent's the kind of dad kids like us always dream about."

"Wish I'd gotten him, although the colonel's not too bad for a military hard-ass. Sometimes."

"Exactly. Ms. Bernadine placed us right where we were supposed to be. Zoey got a musical family. You got the colonel because he likes to read and has a big brain like yours. Crystal got Ms. Bernadine so she could get taught some class."

Preston grinned.

"And I got the Julys because their ancestors were outlaws just like me." He sat up straight again and looked Preston in the eyes. "I know hoping is hard. We probably could write a book on all the reasons why it's bad for kids like us, but the Paynes are your rightful family. This is where we're supposed to be, Brain. Henry Adams, Kansas. Everything's going to work out."

"If you say so."

"And because I do, that makes it true. You got my back if I need you on this Spirit Quest?"

"Whenever. Wherever," Preston pledged with sincerity.

"Good."

CHAPTER
6

Out in Las Vegas, Genevieve Curry and her old friend Marie Jefferson were on their last day in town, and Gen felt as if she'd let Marie down by being such a stick in the mud. Genevieve's inner conscience kept her from playing the slots (it was gambling), checking out the shows (she didn't want to see naked young men), or hitting the bars (she was a teetotaler). And because Marie chose not to leave Genevieve behind and take off on her own, they'd spent most of the time sightseeing and lounging beside the hotel's massive indoor pool. She wanted to somehow make it up to Marie but had no idea how she might go about it. "Marie, I'm so sorry we didn't get to do any of the fun things you wanted to do."

Marie, wearing her signature cat eye glasses, had her suitcase open on the bed, packing for the flight home in the morning. She looked over the rhinestone rims at Genevieve's misery-filled face and waved her off. "No need to apologize, Gen. I had a lot of fun. I've been coming to Vegas for decades and had no idea they had such high-quality museums, or that you could sign on for a tour of the Hoover Dam. I should take you traveling with me more often."

"You mean that?"

"I do."

That made Genevieve feel better. "You're a true friend, Marie Jefferson. Without you these past few months, I would have been lost." And it was true. Riley and that murderous hog of his had altered her life forever. Her home was gone, and with it all the little keepsakes passed down to her by members of her family long dead, like her mother, aunts, and grandmothers. Then to be told by Bernadine's accountants that Riley had been systematically looting the annuities and investments left to her by her father made Genevieve realize she hadn't known her husband at all. Luckily he hadn't been able to get his greedy paws on everything in her portfolio, so there were ample resources available to start over, but she'd have to do it without her beloved heirlooms, and that hurt. "I should have married Clay."

Marie looked up.

"I should have, but I thought I was too good for a farm boy, didn't I?"

Marie kept her mouth shut.

"I believed Riley would take me places Clay would never be able to, like New York and Paris."

Seeing Marie's poker face, she paused. "Why aren't you saying anything?"

"Because I told you to pick Clay Dobbs forty years ago. No sense in me saying I told you so now. And with Clay you probably would have had those babies you always wanted."

Genevieve nodded solemnly. "Instead I had a six-hundred-pound hog shitting all over the place."

Marie fought hard to contain her laugh but lost.

"Life sure is strange, isn't it?"

"To quote the kids, 'True dat.'"

They had the room's wall-mounted, flat-screen television tuned to one of the twenty-four-hour news channels, but the sound was muted. Genevieve happened to glance over at it, and what she saw on the screen made her gasp. "Oh my word! Where's the remote? Turn it up!"

Marie grabbed the remote and complied.

The female announcer was showing the Viral Video of the Day, a wedding involving two hogs that had taken place somewhere in Texas. On screen was Genevieve's missing husband, Riley, standing beneath a rose-encrusted pergola. Walking down the aisle were Cletus and his bride, a sow named Chocolate.

Marie's jaw dropped.

Riley and Cletus were decked out in matching tuxedos and sunglasses. Chocolate was sporting an off-white gown with a lace train.

Genevieve's eyes flashed angrily.

According to the announcer, the short video was taken by the mother of the bride, a tall, redheaded woman named Pennymaker. She was on camera smiling with her hand tucked intimately into the crook of Riley's arm. The humorous news report ended with the watching audience being told that the hog wedding had been viewed by over a million people on the Internet.

Marie cut the sound. Outdone, she didn't know what to say.

Genevieve had no such problem. "Do you have Sheriff Dalton's number in your phone?"

Marie nodded.

"Call him. I wish to speak with him. And when I'm done, you and I are going down to the bar so I can get very very drunk."

Marie's eyes sparkled with amusement behind the glasses. "Yes, ma'am." She picked up her phone.

Riley and Cletus were ready to get on the move again. They were leaving Texas. Eustasia had gone up to Dallas for a few days to see her sister, thus presenting Riley with the perfect opportunity to vanish. Eustasia had called him last night to tell him she'd seen the video of the wedding on the news, and that at last count a million people had viewed it via the Internet. When he hung up he'd been worried to death that the video would bring law enforcement down on his head, so to eliminate that possibility, he and Cletus had to go.

Because her mansion was on hundreds of acres of land, he didn't have to worry about any neighbors seeing him leave. He'd also given the house servants and farmhands the day off, much to their surprise, so that no one would be able to report the time of his departure or the direction he'd taken.

He'd already placed his personal belongings in his old white pickup. Only thing left to do was to load Cletus in the bed and get on the road.

Problem was the hog wouldn't come. Riley had explained the plan to him that morning, and Cletus seemed to agree to the necessity of it, but now he was refusing to leave Chocolate's side.

"We can't take her, Cletus. I know she's your bride but she doesn't belong to me."

Cletus put his snout up and snuffled his displeasure.

"She can't go."

This went on for a while, then as if tired of arguing, Cletus sat down beside Chocolate in a huff.

Riley sighed. "Cletus. Please. We have to go. If the law finds us here they're going to turn us both into bacon."

But Cletus didn't appear to care.

"Dammit!" Riley swore. Eustasia was going to be distraught enough when she returned home to find him and Cletus missing, but realizing Chocolate had vanished too would send her into hysterics. And who was going to pay for all the food and other stuff the hogs would be needing? Riley still had a good portion of the money he'd taken out of Genevieve's account last fall, but it wouldn't last forever, especially with the price of gas. He couldn't leave Cletus behind, however. They were in this together. His only option was to surrender. "Okay," he said testily. "Bring her along. I'm going to be mad about this for the next couple days so don't expect me to be chummy."

Cletus stood. Chocolate followed suit. They slowly waddled up the ramp, and once they were secured in the hay-lined bed, Riley slammed the gate closed and got in under the steering wheel. The engine of the old truck groaned under the excess weight but there was nothing

Riley could do about it. Tight-lipped, he drove away from the pens and headed for the road.

Ray Chambers was also packing. Coming back to Cleveland had been a bad idea. His pigeon du jour, a woman in the congregation of a storefront church calling itself the Grapevine Tabernacle of the Good and Holy, had kicked it with him just long enough for him to learn that she wasn't the cardiologist she'd claimed to be, nor was she single. That shocking discovery occurred last night when her husband, a cop, came home and found Ray and his wife in the family bed. The cuts and bruises on Ray's face bore witness to the husband's claim of also being a former Golden Gloves champ. After treating Ray to a thorough ass kicking, the cop promised more of the same should their paths cross again, so rather than risk another round, Ray was leaving town.

His search for his daughter and her rich foster mother hadn't panned out much better. Because his parental rights had been severed by court order and because Crystal was still a minor, her files were locked up tighter than the thighs of a deacon's wife. He'd tried to contact Nikki in the Illinois prison, but was told by the switchboard that she was in medical isolation. Only immediate family members were allowed access, and no, ex-husbands didn't qualify. He'd had even less success with her sister, Jean. *Bitch*. She refused to give him any info on Crystal and warned if he called her again, she'd notify the police.

All in all, he was SOL. He cursed her and the cop again. Ray was a lover not a fighter, which was why when he was on top, he'd had bodyguards and a few crooked cops on his payroll to deal with the riffraff. Back then, he'd've paid somebody to take care of the champ and Jean too but it was a new day now, and the only power he had now amounted to grabbing his old suitcase and waiting for a city bus to take him to the Greyhound station. Once there he planned to buy a ticket to Kansas City, Kansas. It was one of the state's bigger cities, so he'd start his search for his daughter there.

Roni Garland tapped lightly on the door to her husband's study. She didn't like to disturb him when he was working but she needed to talk to him. "Reg, can I interrupt you for a hot minute."

"Sure."

She entered and found him seated behind his desk. It was covered with stacks of medical catalogs. "How's it going?"

He set aside an open catalog. "Pretty good. Almost done with my wish list for Bernadine. What's up with you?"

"Zoey's writing music, Reg."

Her face held so much concern, he paused for a moment before asking, "Is that a bad thing?"

"No, but it's scary. Look at these." She showed him some of the music. The lined pieces of notebook papers were covered with musical staffs and notes done in green marker.

"Baby, you know I don't know what I'm looking at."

Roni pointed to one. "This one is for strings." She placed another one in front of him. "This is for woodwinds. How can she know how to do this? It's like that movie we saw over Christmas. The one with Robin Williams? *August Rush*."

"That the one with the kid with the music in his head looking for his parents? The one you and Zoey cried through?"

She cut him a look. "Yes, that one. I know I taught her how to read music, but I didn't know she was doing all this."

"How'd you find out?"

"She just walked up to me a minute ago and handed them to me. There have to be at least fifty pieces of music here," she said with astonishment in her voice.

He smiled indulgently, "We knew she was special, Ron."

"Special yes, not possessed. This is like a musical remix of Chucky! And some of this is very dark. It's like, if thunder could make music or storms on the sea. This is not that light, sweet minuet stuff, this is like Beethoven reincarnated!"

Reg laughed. "Hold up. Take a breath."

"Reg, we have a certifiable prodigy on our hands and I have no idea what to do with her. I don't want to screw her up. And . . ."

He chuckled. "And, what?"

"She wants a violin."

"We can afford one, right?" he teased.

"Of course."

"Then what's wrong?" he asked gently.

Roni shook her head in an effort to clear her mind of all the emotion. "I'm just amazed, that's all. I'll order the violin. Since I can't play, I can't teach her, but knowing her, she'll probably just pick it up and start sawing away."

"Probably, and I wouldn't worry about screwing her up. She's getting lots of love. God will handle the fine print."

"You're right." She sighed, then flashed him a smile. "Thanks for talking me down."

"Any time."

She leaned down and kissed him softly. "You're the best."

"Because I'm married to the best."

Downstairs, Roni found Zoey and Devon sitting side-by-side on the bench of her baby grand. Zoey was scratching out notes on another sheet of lined paper.

"Zoey, this music you've written is fantastic. What do you want to do with it?"

She shrugged.

"Okay, then I'll put them in a folder so they don't get lost. What are you all doing?" She walked closer to get a better look at what Zoey was doing.

Devon explained, "Zoey's writing down the music for 'Onward Christian Soldiers.'"

That caught her by surprise. "Okay."

"We're going to sing it in church on Sunday."

"What church?"

"My church," he replied proudly. "I'm the pastor and Zoey's the musical director."

She smiled at that. "I used to play church when I was little too."

"This isn't play church, Ms. Roni. This is going to be a true house of the Lord."

Feeling herself about to climb back up on the roof, Roni took a breath and asked carefully, "Does Ms. Lily or Ms. Bernadine know about this?"

"No ma'am. They're too busy for me."

That tugged at her heart. "I see." She needed to talk with Lily. "And where will the service be?"

"We were going to ask if we can use this room so Zoey can play the piano."

He looked so sincere, what could she say but, "Sure, Devon. Dr. Garland and I would be honored. What time?"

"Ten o'clock. Will you sing?"

"Of course, if you want me to."

"We do. Don't we, Zoey?"

Zoey nodded enthusiastically.

Roni looked at the amazing pair and wondered if they were really angels in disguise. "You two go ahead with your practicing. I'm going to go find a folder for Zoey's music. Then I have to go to my closet and pick out a very special hat for Sunday service."

She placed a solemn kiss on the crown of each small head, then left them and walked into the kitchen. Wiping at her eyes, she picked up her phone and called Lily.

When Lily hung up the phone after her talk with Roni, she sat back in her chair and shook her head in amazement at the wonder that was Devon Watkins. He was starting his own church, to hell with her and Bernadine. Getting up, she walked across the hall to Bernadine's office.

"You busy?"

"Nope. What's up? Have a seat."

Lily told her about the conversation she'd had with Roni.

When she was done Bernadine shook her head just as Lily had done. "That boy. He's going to do his thing with or without us."

"Pretty much. Even asked Roni to sing."

"Amazing. I have been putting him off, I have to admit. I didn't know what to do about an eight-year-old boy wanting to be the town preacher. When I see him, I owe him an apology for not taking him as seriously as I should have."

"So do I. Are you going to the service?"

"Of course, and wearing one of my hats."

Lily smiled. "Good, me too. If you don't need me for anything earth-shaking, I'm going to go pick up Devon and take him home. He and I need to talk."

Bernadine nodded understandingly. "Think I'll head home too. I promised Crys she could call about her mom this afternoon and she's supposed to be cooking dinner."

"Crystal?"

"Yes, and I'm terrified, believe me. The girl has a mother lode of creativity beneath that ugly weave, so this week it's the Food Network."

"What's she cooking?"

"Too scared to ask."

Lily chuckled. "Good luck."

"Have Devon say a prayer."

Lily left to return to her office and Bernadine was just about to power down her computer when her phone sounded. It was Trent.

"Are you still in your office?" he asked.

"Yep."

"Okay. I'm going to send you a link I want you to check out. Lily still there?"

"Yes, I think so."

"She should see this too."

"Trent, what is this about?"

"Just watch the clip, then call me back."

The very puzzled Bernadine followed his instructions.

After calling Lily in, Bernadine went into her e-mail and clicked on the link he'd sent. When the YouTube video opened and began to play, the mouths of both women dropped to the floor.

"Oh my god!' Lily screamed. "That's Cletus, and there's Riley!"

"And both wearing shades, no less. Lord have mercy. Where did Trent get this?"

As they both watched Cletus and Chocolate move up the rose-strewn aisle to the sounds of a wedding march, Bernadine cracked, "And somebody spent a ton of money on that lace, girl. That is not a Wal-Mart buy."

Hands over her mouth, Lily stared. "I don't believe this."

"And we thought Leo's visit was going to be the Henry Adams highlight of the day."

The clip continued, showing next a man dressed as a preacher reading from what Bernadine hoped was a fake Bible. Then came a shot of Riley and a tall, red-haired woman. "They look happy," she tossed out sarcastically.

"Yeah they do," Lily responded tightly.

They shared a loaded look.

Bernadine picked up her phone. "Let's find out where this came from."

After getting the explanation, Lily left the office and went to pick up Devon.

On the ride home, she looked over at him sitting so solemnly in the seat beside her. He'd been awfully quiet since his return from New York and she wasn't sure what was going on with him. She assumed that some of it could be traced to how busy she'd been in the weeks leading up to vacation.

"Are you mad at me, Devon?"

"No, ma'am."

"You've been awfully quiet since you got back."

"I'm all right."

"Ms. Roni said you thought I was too busy for you."

He shrugged his thin shoulders.

"I want to apologize for making you think that, and for not taking you seriously about being the town preacher."

"That's okay."

"No it isn't."

For the first time he looked her way.

"It isn't," she said gently. "We're supposed to be family, and family should always have time for each other so they can do things together."

"Me and my grandma used to do things together."

Lily smiled. "What kind of things?"

"We worked in the garden. We went to church, and she always took me with her when she went to see Miss Eula to play her number."

Lily smiled again. So Grandma was as human as everyone else, after all. "I see. Is there anything special you'd like for us to do together?"

"I don't know. Can I think about it for a little while?"

"Of course."

He gave her a shy smile, and that made her feel better. The last thing Lily wanted was to bring Devon pain. Losing his grandmother had been hard for him and he didn't need her adding to it, even unconsciously. When the Garlands offered to take him along with them to New York, Lily hadn't hesitated. They loved him as much as she, and his bond with Zoey had always been a plus, but should she have declined? Should she force him to spend more time with her and less with them? She didn't have a clue. Bernadine was on the lookout for a full-time, on-site psychologist for the kids. Lily thought maybe the foster parents could use one too.

Before Bernadine could leave her office for home and dinner with Crystal, a woman she didn't know knocked on the open door. "Ms. Brown?"

"Yes."

"I'm Rocky Dancer. Thought I'd come by and introduce myself."

"Come in," Bernadine said cordially. "So glad to meet you and that you're back in Henry Adams."

"Thanks." She entered and took a seat.

Bernadine had had no idea the woman was drop-dead gorgeous. "Mal said you're going to start in the morning?"

"Yep. The place is pretty well stocked, so I may as well. Some of the stuff Florene ordered is going to have to be sent back or exchanged though. Can't use it. Not sure how you want to handle that."

"Just inventory what you want to send back and give the list to Lily. She'll take it from there."

"Lily Fontaine?"

"Yes. You know her?"

She nodded. "I was a few years behind her and Trent in school."

"Then you knew them when they were young and in love."

"Yeah. So, is his office here too?"

Bernadine sensed something not quite right. "Yes, he's across the hall."

But Bernadine didn't have to call him. He stuck his head into her office, and upon seeing Rocky, his face lit up like the Fourth of July. "Hey, girl," he said, and opened his arms wide.

She grinned and walked over and took the hug he offered.

"Good to see you."

"You too," she replied smiling. "How's life?"

"Not bad. Dad said you were back. For good?"

"I think so."

Bernadine noticed for the first time Amari and Preston standing beside Trent. Amari looked over at Bernadine and raised his eyebrow. She hid her chuckle behind a faked cough.

Taking matters into his own hands, Amari said, "Who's she, Dad?"

Trent backed out of the hug. "Amari and Preston, this is Rochelle Dancer."

"Hey, Amari and Preston. Call me Rocky. Everybody else does. Pleased to meet you. You all had just moved here when I left town last summer. How do you like it?"

Amari said, "I like it. Dad's cool and so's the O.G."

Rocky turned to Trent with confusion on her face.

"Mal," he replied.

She grinned. "Oh. Okay, I understand. How about you, Preston?"

Bernadine noted that Preston was looking at her as if he'd never seen a woman before. Rocky was both gorgeous and stacked, so Bernadine thought maybe he hadn't seen a woman quite like the Coke bottle–figured cook before.

Preston seemed to shake himself back to the present. "Uh, I like it here too."

"Good."

She turned to Bernadine. "Nice meeting you, Ms. Brown."

"Same here. Welcome back."

"Thanks."

Trent asked her, "Where're you heading?"

"Clay's outside. He's giving me a ride out to his place. He and Bing are going to let me rent my old room again for now."

Bernadine told her, "If you want a bit more privacy, there are a couple empty double-wides out on Tamar's land. The green one's going to be for the new teacher whenever he arrives, but the one with the blue front is yours for as long as you need it to be."

"That's nice of you. I'll check it out and let you know."

"Good."

"Okay. I'm gone. Trent, see you and your little guys later. Bye, Ms. Brown."

Everybody offered up good-byes and Rocky left to go grab her ride with Clay.

"Seems like a nice woman," Bernadine said to Trent.

"She is."

"Well, me, I'm heading home. Crystal is cooking dinner."

"You got 911 on your speed dial?" Amari asked. He looked to see if Preston thought that was funny but Preston was still looking at the doorway recently vacated by Rocky. "Brain. You still on the planet?"

Once again he shook himself. "What?" He then added, "Ms. Dancer is a very beautiful woman."

"And way too old for you," Amari pointed out.

Trent chuckled. "Come on, you two. We're on our way to the garage, Bernadine. See you in the morning."

She told them bye, and after they were gone, she stood there for a moment with Rocky Dancer on her mind. The cook hadn't seemed real pleased hearing Lily's name. Bernadine dearly hoped they hadn't let a snake into paradise, because personally, she was way too old to keep Lily from whipping somebody's butt.

Crystal's dinner turned out to be not half bad. Bernadine had been expecting something wild and outrageous; instead her young cook offered roast chicken seasoned with rosemary, glazed baby carrots, and Parmesan-topped, twice-baked potatoes. The chicken was dry, some of the carrots burnt, and the potatoes had small embedded chunks that could have baked longer, but overall the meal was okay.

"Thanks for dinner, Crys," Bernadine told her genuinely as they cleaned up the kitchen after the meal.

Crys was at the fridge placing plastic containers holding the leftovers inside. "Did you like it?"

"I did."

"Potatoes were still kinda raw and some of the carrots got burnt."

"Noticed that, but for a first-timer you did excellent."

"Good."

With the cleanup done and the dishwasher running, they left the kitchen.

Crystal turned to Bernadine. "I'm going to call the prison now and see if I can speak to my mom."

"Tell her hello for me and that she's in my prayers."

"Okay."

Bernadine walked into the living room and took a seat to watch the evening news. About halfway through, Crystal returned. Seeing the tears filling her eyes made Bernadine go still. "What's wrong?"

"She died this afternoon."

Bernadine went to her and held her tight.

"I didn't even get to know her," Crys whispered, then she broke down and her thin shoulders shook with emotion.

"I know, baby," Bernadine answered softly, stroking her back gently. "But you did get to see her and talk with her." Before being reunited at an Illinois prison last fall, mother and daughter hadn't seen each other since Crystal was seven.

Crystal replied through her tears, "I just wanted her to get well and come live with us so I could get to know her so she could get to know me."

"Life had a different plan, I guess." Bernadine's heart was breaking.

"Life sucks," she declared bitterly,

Bernadine could only agree. She'd been nineteen when diabetes took her mother and she'd cursed life too. She wanted to tell Crystal that one day the hurt and pain would lessen, but now was not the time. Now she needed to mourn.

So Bernadine held her for as long as she needed and when the grief loosened its grip a bit, Crystal drew out of the embrace and wiped at her eyes. "Even though I didn't know her, I'm going to miss her. Do you think she went to heaven?"

"I do. Bringing you into the world ensured her a place."

Crystal nodded as if that satisfied her. "The lady I talked to on the phone said the state's going to bury Nikki in a cemetery run by the prison because her family doesn't have the money."

The wrongness of that made Bernadine shake her head. "I can have someone take care of it if they want her body shipped home."

"She wants you to call her in the morning. Nikki had me down as next of kin, and you as my guardian."

"Okay. I'll call first thing. If her family has a funeral, do you want to go?"

She shook her head. "No. It'll just make it hurt worse."

"I understand, but you can change your mind if you want to."

"I won't."

Bernadine didn't press. She had no idea whether legally Crystal could have contact with Nikki's people or not, so

that was something else she'd need to look into if a funeral was indeed held, and if Crystal changed her mind
and wanted to attend. "Is there anything you want me to
do to help you through this?"

Another negative shake. "I'll be okay, I guess."

"You don't have to be tough, Crys. Death hurts, and
everybody gets a turn in the box sooner or later. There's
no shame in reaching out. If you need something or just
someone to listen, you have me and an entire town of folks
to pick from."

"I know." The tears began to stream down her face
again and Bernadine eased her foster daughter back into
her arms.

Crys hugged her tightly. "I just wished she'd lived."

"I do too." Bernadine kissed Crystal's tear-dampened
cheek. "You want to take a walk or something? We can put
in a DVD?"

"No. I think I'm going back up to my room and be by
myself for a while."

"That's fine."

Bernadine drew back and studied Crystal's face. "Your
mom loved you, Crys, very much. We both witnessed it
when we saw her last fall. Even with all the drama in her
life, you, she loved. Never forget that."

She received a small, almost imperceptible nod in response before Crystal turned and slowly exited the room.
When she was gone, Bernadine wiped away her remaining
tears, then said a prayer.

Upstairs in her room, Crystal looked up at the ceiling.
She told herself it was stupid to be doing all this crying but

she couldn't seem to stop. She'd had only one dream in her life—to find her mom and to get her off crack so they could live happily ever after. But when she saw Nikki at the prison, she knew that wasn't going to happen, especially after being told Nikki'd contracted AIDS, yet Crys hoped God would wave a magic wand and fix everything. Now, however, it was over. The life she was having with Ms. Bernadine was her real-deal life now. There'd be no going back. Not that she wanted to, Ms. Bernadine was awesome, but she wished things could have been different for Nikki and her somehow. The hurt inside welled up again like powerful waves rolling onto shore, so rather than fighting it, she turned over, put her face into her pillow, and cried.

It was 8:00 p.m. when Trent decided to call it quits for the evening. He'd been working in the garage on his old high school car, a black 1985 Chrysler New Yorker, aka Black Beauty. Amari and Preston had played assistants. Preston mostly sat and Amari mostly asked questions, but Trent enjoyed their company. Which was saying something because last year at this time, the only difference between Trent and a hermit was that Trent drove a truck. He'd moved back to Henry Adams on the heels of two bad marriages and a distaste for big-city living. The hermit's life became the life for him and he thought he was fine until he met Amari.

With the boys' help he carefully pulled the large tarp over the car's partially restored frame. Once it was in place, he sent Amari to the fridge for three juice boxes and they sat to enjoy the drinks.

"How old were you when you did your Spirit Quest, Dad?"

"Ten."

"Did you have to take—What are they called again, Brain?"

"Hallucinogenics."

Trent spit out his juice. Coughing, he wiped his mouth on the sleeve of his blue flannel shirt, eyeing the two suspiciously. "Who told you you'd be taking that?"

"Nobody. But Brain said sometimes the old tribes used something like it."

He studied them for a long moment. "Some did, but you won't be, so next question."

"Okay, then. What did you have to do?"

"Camp out on the prairie and wait for a sign."

"What kind of sign?"

"My sign."

"I don't get it."

"You will."

Amari didn't look as if he believed him.

"Everyone's sign is different, and your sign will give you your spirit name."

"What's yours?"

"That's private, and for the future, it's considered rude to ask someone that question."

"Oh."

"It's okay, you didn't know, but now you do."

Preston asked, "How long does the camping part last?"

"If nothing shows up after three days, you come home and wait another year."

"Another year?" Amari cried. "I want to be a July this year."

"Not having your name won't keep you from being a July, Amari."

"Tamar said I had to honor the Ancestors and that's what I'm going to do. She said the Julys don't just take any old body, Dad."

Trent didn't know whether to smile or get in his truck and drive to Tamar's and smack her upside her head, a move that would undoubtedly cost him his life, so he turned his mind back to saner realms.

"Why does she want me to have a hatchet?" Amari asked.

"For chopping firewood."

Amari's eyes lit up. "That sounds like fun."

"It is, in its own way. Just hope it doesn't rain. Nothing worse than being in a tent when it's pouring."

That seemed to deflate him a bit.

"So what are you going to do for the Henry Adams part of this?"

Amari shrugged. "Don't know. She wants me to look at the old pictures, said they might help."

"Okay, you know I'll help too." Trent could see that Tamar's tasks seemed to have given the sometimes cocky Amari pause, and that was a good thing.

They finished their drinks, then turned out the garage lights so they could head home. When they arrived Preston went into his house, and Trent and Amari entered theirs.

Trent hadn't forgotten the aborted conversation at lunch. "Now tell me about the Paynes and Preston."

So Amari repeated what Preston told him about the trip to Florida and his fears that he might have to leave town. "So if it happens, can he stay with us?"

"Definitely. Preston's a good kid."

"I think so too. So tell me about this Rocky."

"Nothing to tell," Trent said, picking up the remote and turning to TNT for the evening's ball game. "She's an old friend."

"Old friend or old *girl* friend?"

Trent met his eyes. Was there anything this boy didn't see? "Both, with emphasis on the word *old*."

"Don't mean to get in your business but just wanted to know."

"Satisfied?"

"Yes, sir. Going up to my room."

"Okay. Lights out by ten, and no texting. I get a bill like I got last month and you and Preston will be using carrier pigeons."

"Yes, sir."

After his departure Trent got comfortable and thought about the Paynes. Were they really having issues? He didn't know much about their marriage, but looking at it from the outside, things seemed to be okay. Preston seemed to think otherwise. Trent hoped that whatever was happening next door, they took Preston's future into consideration. The young man had been moved around enough.

As the game came on, he thought back on the day. It began with Amari's questions about him and Lily and ended with questions about him and Rocky. The boy made him tired. Trent was glad to have Rocky back in town, though.

Now folks could get some decent food at the D&C. He and Rock had had a unique relationship, but the intimate part ended when she married Bob. During the time she was on the East Coast, she and Trent had talked fairly regularly but they'd never discussed anything remotely flirtatious or sexual. With Bob, she'd hoped to find the true love she'd always wanted but instead wound up with a man who liked wearing her underwear. He shook his head with amusement at that. Maybe life would give her another shot. She was a very special lady and she deserved finding the happiness he'd found the second time around with Lily.

Later that night, Sheila Payne lay in bed in the guest room surrounded by the darkness. The melancholy mood had her in its grip again and she was at a loss as to how to fix herself, still. She'd noticed the concern in Preston's eyes when he came home from hanging out with Trent and Amari and she'd wanted to reassure him, but she didn't know what to say. Instead she'd given him a good-night hug, and he'd gone up to his room. Sheila didn't want the wake of her inner turmoil affecting him, but there was no way it wouldn't if she couldn't put herself back together. *Maybe I need to go away for a while.* But that would affect Preston too and she didn't want to jeopardize his status and possibly be the cause of him having to be sent to another home. That would hurt. She'd come to view him as her son and she wanted to be there for him and with him as he grew up and claimed his place in the world. That joy would be denied them both if they were no longer family.

Her thoughts slowly moved to Barrett. In her heart, she

didn't want to divorce him. Admittedly, knocking him off his high horse even if only temporarily felt good. Earlier, when she returned home to fix dinner, he'd had very little to say but spent the entire meal and the remainder of the evening quietly watching her as if searching for something; what, she wasn't sure—a way to apologize, a way to make things better. If he wanted to talk she was open, but it came to her suddenly that seeing Marti again, as painful and as maddening as it had been, constituted only a portion of the problem. And it was a large portion, but the bulk of what was going inside had to be laid in Sheila's own lap. She mulled that over for a few moments and began to sense the rightness in her conclusion. All the brooding she'd been doing for the past few days had her looking back at her life, and in that rearview mirror she saw a woman who'd been about service to everybody and everything except herself. She readily admitted that she had no idea who Sheila Payne was or what she stood for.

Something inside wanted to find out, however. She'd made Barrett move to Henry Adams so they could become foster parents in hopes of changing a life. Little did she know that the life needing change might be her own. Certain now that she'd finally gotten to the core of her ennui, she felt herself physically and mentally relax. Deciding she'd talk to Bernadine about all this in the morning, she closed her eyes, and for the first night in nearly a week, she slipped peacefully into sleep.

Ray Chambers got off the train in Kansas City, Missouri, along with the schoolteacher he'd sat next to during the ride

from Chicago. Her name was Anita something-or-other—
he didn't remember the last name, but it hadn't taken him
long to charm her. Middle-aged virgins were all alike. He'd
given her a heart-wrenching story about being one of the
thousands of newly unemployed autoworkers and traveling
the country looking for any work he could find. He'd been
polite too; hadn't wanted to spook her and now, because he
had no place to stay and had run out of money, he needed
to feed her the final bait. "Had a great time traveling with
you, Anita."

"I had a good time too."

"Let me make this call to my cousin and then I'll walk
you outside. Don't want anybody grabbing you, even if it is
daylight."

She smiled shyly. "Okay."

He'd told her on the train about this mythical cousin
who was supposed to be hooking him up with a place to
stay and a job interview. Pulling out his phone, he punched
in random numbers and held the nonworking device to
his ear. After a few seconds, he looked at her and asked
emotionally, "How can the number be disconnected? I just
talked to him before we left Chicago."

"Maybe you dialed the wrong number."

"Yeah, that's probably it." This time he made a show
of putting in the numbers slowly. He positioned the phone
against his ear again, and after a few seconds, shook his
head. "Same thing. Shoot," he added.

He snapped the face closed and stuck the phone back
into the pocket of his denim jacket. He sighed.

"Do you know where he lives?"

"No. Afraid not. Never visited him here before."

"How are you going to find him?"

"I don't know. Maybe I can find a cheap room some-where and wait it out."

"Why don't you come home with me? You can try him for the rest of the evening and if you don't find him, I have a guest room you can stay in for a couple days if you need to."

"I don't want to put you out. Besides, you don't even know me."

"You were very nice to me on the train, Walter Davis, and you impress me as being an honest man. I think I'll be okay."

"You sure?"

"Positive. Come on, my car's in a garage up the street."

As they left the train station and headed to the garage, the elated Ray Chambers shouted inwardly, *Bingo!*

That evening, she cooked him dinner. After a few glasses of wine, one thing led to another, and the next morning when Anita Baldwin woke up, he was gone, along with her car, credit cards, and the two hundred dollars she'd had in her purse.

Feeling good, Ray drove into Kansas City, Kansas, just as dawn was breaking. He'd emptied Anita's debit and credit cards of all their cash, then switched the plate on her BMW with another BMW he spotted parked behind a restaurant a few blocks away from her condo complex. He'd known from riding with her yesterday that the car had no theft protection system like LoJack, and with it being for-eign made there was no OnStar either. That being the case, he figured he could keep the ride for a few more days before he had to think about dumping it somewhere.

He didn't know the first thing about the GPS built into the dash. He figured he could probably fiddle with it until he figured it out but he didn't know if the police had a way to track it if he turned on, so he left it alone. Keeping an eye on his speed and remembering to use his signals so he wouldn't get pulled over, he drove around until he found a place to eat and used some of Anita's cash to buy himself breakfast.

After eating, he got directions to the main library from the restaurant waitress, and as in many urban areas, the homeless were lined up outside waiting for the library to open. There were also a few mothers with young children, and a couple of older kids with backpacks standing around too. Just as he walked up, a woman inside the big brick building appeared in the glass of the front door and undid the locks. He went in with the other early birds and walked up to one of the librarians behind the desk marked Reference.

The young blonde greeted him with a sunny smile. "Good morning. May I help you?"

"Yes. Can you show me how to look up something on the computer?"

"Is it something specific?"

"Yeah, my daughter has to do a school project on wealthy African-American women in Kansas. Any idea who I should start with?"

"Yes. Bernadine Brown. Not only is she one of the richest African-American women in Kansas, but in the country too. She lives upstate in a little town called Henry Adams. She's been all over the television. Can't believe you or your daughter haven't heard of her."

"I don't let my kids watch too much TV."

"Good for you."

Ray took a stab in the dark. "But I think I may have heard of Ms. Brown. Now, is she the one with the foster daughter?"

"Why yes. CNN has done quite a few reports on Ms. Brown and her fostering program. The clips are probably still on their Web site."

Holding on to his excitement, he asked, "Can you show me how to get a look at them?"

"Certainly."

A few minutes later, Ray was sitting in front of a screen watching replays of the news reports. That the Brown woman had enough bucks to buy a whole town left him amazed. There was a short interview with the foster kids she'd brought to the town, and there in the back sat his daughter, Crystal. Even with the tacky blond weave, she looked just like Nikki.

After thanking the woman, he left the library and drove to the nearest gas station. Once he filled the tank he purchased a map. Sitting in the car, he plotted out the route. It would take him a few days probably, but he had a gassed-up BMW, plenty of cash, and nothing but time. Laughing at how easy it had all been, he pushed one of Anita's jazz CDs into the player and headed north for Graham County.

CHAPTER
8

I t was 6:00 a.m. and still dark when Bernadine got up and dressed for work. Before leaving for her drive into town, she quietly opened the door to Crystal's bedroom and saw that she was asleep. Emotions flooded Bernadine and she debated spending the morning at home. However, she knew that even in her grief Crystal would only stand for so much coddling, so Bernadine decided to give the teen some space and closed the door soundlessly. She'd text her later in the day.

Bernadine swung by the Dog for breakfast and to get a firsthand look at how things were faring now that Rocky was running things. The place was packed. The college kids from the culinary program who were working as waitstaff were dressed in black tees and jeans and moving from table to table taking orders and topping off the coffee cups of the diners. She waved to a few familiar faces, like her construction foreman, Warren Kelly, and some of his workers. As she waited for the hostess to return and show her to a seat,

Malachi came out from the kitchen. Seeing her waiting he looked around the crowded place, spotted an empty booth, and beckoned her over.

"Thanks," she said to him as she sat.

"What can I get you?"

"Coffee to start. And so you'll know, Crystal's mom passed yesterday."

"Sorry to hear that. How's our princess doing?"

Bernadine shrugged. "As expected I guess. She took it pretty hard."

"Poor thing. Want me to pass the word around?"

"Would you, please? You'll see more people this morning than I will. Just want folks to put her in their prayers."

"Will do. Be right back with that coffee."

While she waited for his return, she looked around. The scent of food cooking was in the air, and the plates being set before the diners held real breakfast food like eggs, bacon, and pancakes. All in all, folks looked to be happy with Rocky's hand on the wheel and being served food they could recognize, and if they were happy, Bernadine was too.

Mal returned with a coffeepot and left her with one of the waitresses Bernadine knew to be named Kelly.

"Morning, Ms. Brown. Ms. Rocky hasn't set up a formal menu yet, so we're offering basics."

"Such as?"

"Eggs, grits, toast, bacon and sausage, oatmeal, waffles and pancakes."

"I'll have grits, toast, scrambled eggs, and one strip of bacon."

"Coming right up."

Her plate arrived a short while later and just as she was about to begin, a tall, black-haired White man with a George Clooney look about him, and a teenager who favored him so much they had to be father and son, entered the diner and stood by the sign that told people to "Wait to Be Seated." Both looked dead on their feet.

Mal cruised over to top off her coffee, and she asked him, "Do you know those two by the door?"

He looked over. "Nope. They look whipped. Let me go take care of them."

So while Bernadine watched and ate and purred in response to how good the food tasted, she went still when Mal escorted the man and teenager her way.

"This is Ms. Brown," Mal said by way of introduction.

The man stuck out his hand. "I'm Jack James, the new teacher, and this is my son, Eli."

She smiled with surprise and delight. "Welcome. How are you?"

"Dead. We just got in from L.A."

"Please, sit and join me."

They accepted her invitation and took the empty bench in her booth.

"How was the flight?"

"We drove," the son, Eli, told her. "Never want to see the inside of a U-Haul ever again."

At first Bernadine thought he was making a joke, but a closer look showed him to be quite serious, and quite angry if she was reading him correctly.

The dad simply said, "Eli's not real happy about moving, so excuse his rudeness."

"No problem. Being away from the familiar can be hard on kids. Not many of them like the unknown. Plus he's worn out."

Eli didn't appear to be paying the least bit of attention to either one of them, and she thought: *Well now.*

Mal returned with coffee for both newcomers, and when he was done, Kelly came over and took their order.

Once she departed, Jack took in the bustling eatery and said to Bernadine, "This is a nice place. Interesting name for a diner."

"Yes it is." She noted the sadness in his eyes even as he attempted to appear friendly and upbeat.

"Mr. July said Ms. Jefferson is in Vegas?"

"Yes. Should be back later today."

"She and I did the interview process on the phone, so we haven't met."

"She's a nice lady."

"Looking forward to meeting her. She told me the town just built a new school?"

"Yes, the grand opening will be in a few days, so you and Eli are right on time." She noted that Eli had his face turned toward the window. She wondered what the deal was on him.

She and Jack chitchatted while they waited for their food, and when it arrived steaming hot and smelling wonderful, the conversation between them continued in between bites. Eli ate but didn't say a word.

Once everyone finished the meal, Bernadine said to Jack, "I know you're probably tired, so let's get you and Eli situated. If you can stand to drive just a short distance more, I'll take you out to where you'll be living until we get your house built."

"Built?" Jack echoed.

"Yes. Didn't Marie tell you a residence came with the job?"

"Well, yeah, but she said it would be a trailer."

Eli's eyes went wide. "You made me leave L.A. so we could live in a trailer!"

People nearby couldn't help overhearing, and so stopped eating and glanced their way. Bernadine could see them assess Eli, and none appeared pleased. She didn't bother to explain the true housing situation to Eli, because one, he wasn't the adult, and two, she didn't care for his attitude. She took comfort in the fact that if he and his father stayed, Mr. Surly Teenager would be reined in before this was all over, even if everyone in town had to get involved. "You two ready?"

Jack shook his head wearily.

Eli stood, walked past them, and headed toward the door.

Jack said to her, "I'm really sorry about the way he's acting. Since my wife's death, he's been all mixed up."

"How long has she been gone?"

"Two years."

"My condolences, and no need to apologize. It'll be okay."

Mal was at the cash register when they reached the exit.

Jack reached into his pocket for his wallet, but Bernadine said, "My treat. You go on out to the truck. I'll be there in a minute."

"You're sure?"

"Positive."

"Thanks, Ms. Brown."

"No problem."

Apparently Mal had been watching the booth action too, because as he handed Bernadine her change, he said, "Tamar's gonna love him."

She chuckled. "Oh yeah."

On the drive, Jack looked over at his son's sullen, turned-away face. "You made a real nice first impression back there."

"They're paying you to be nice, not me."

"Do you know that if we lose this job we'll be living on the street until I find another? Which means there'll be no food, no cable, no nothing. Just a friendly reminder."

No response to that.

Driving the truck on the gravel road was a nightmare. Jack could feel each and every bump in the road and could only imagine what the ruts and holes were doing to the suspension of his old SUV being trailered on the back of the U-Haul. Luckily, they didn't have to go far. When Ms. Brown turned off the road and onto a narrow track that led to he had no idea where, he followed. A few moments later he spotted a large green Victorian house up ahead that had an old-fashioned porch on the front. Open prairie spread out around the house for as far as the eye could see.

"Where the hell are we now?" Eli grumbled.

Jack ignored him and slowed the truck to a halt beside Ms. Brown's cobalt blue Ford pickup. She motioned for him to stop where he was, so he did. They got out just as a tall, silver-haired Black woman stepped out the screened door and onto the porch.

"Morning, Bernadine. Who's that with you?"

"This is our new teacher, Jack James, and his son, Eli."

"Welcome," Tamar offered. "Pleased to meet you both. I'm Tamar July."

"Nice meeting you too, Ms. July," Jack James replied.

"Call me Tamar."

When the bored-looking Eli didn't offer any greeting at all, she speared him with a hawklike gaze.

"Are you mute?"

He blinked.

She asked him again, this time with a bit more bite, "Are you mute?"

He shook his head quickly.

"Again. Are you mute?"

"No."

"Good. Glad to hear it. In polite society, when you are introduced to someone, you respond with *Pleased to meet you*. It's what separates the civilized from the riffraff, so let's start this over."

Eli jumped, eyes widening slightly.

Bernadine shared a silent look with Jack.

Tamar slowly descended the steps, robes flowing. "I'm Tamar July. And you are?" As she closed the distance between them, Bernadine swore Eli looked like a rabbit about to take flight.

"Eli James," he replied, seemingly unable to look away from the tall, Seminole matriarch's powerful presence.

"Pleased to meet, you, Eli James."

He swallowed visibly. "Same here."

The wintry smile she gave him made Bernadine shiver, and she wasn't even the one in trouble.

"Welcome to Henry Adams, Eli."

"Thank you."

That done, Tamar turned to Bernadine. "So, what brings you out here?"

Bernadine heard Jack chuckle softly in response to his son being dressed down, and she smiled as well. To their right, Eli was viewing Tamar with a mixture of caution and apprehension. There was some fear in there too. "I'm here to get them settled into one of the trailers."

"Then have at it. If you all need anything, let me know. Nice meeting you, gentlemen."

"Same here," Jack responded.

She turned to Eli, who replied hastily, "Thank you, Tamar."

"You're welcome, Eli."

Walking back over to the porch, she climbed the steps and reentered the house.

Jack whispered lowly, "Wow."

Eli stared at the door.

Bernadine nodded. "She is something. Come on. The trailer's around back."

As they followed her, Jack noted that for once, Eli had nothing to say, and he decided that if Tamar was indicative of how life worked in Henry Adams, he was going to enjoy living there very much.

But Eli's silence didn't last long. Once Bernadine showed

them inside and departed with a smile and a promise to check on them later, he said in a cocky voice, "I thought the Pilgrims burned all the witches."

"Guess they missed one," Tamar cracked.

Both males jumped, Eli the highest. She was standing in the doorway of the trailer but they'd heard nothing to indicate her approach or presence. Jack honestly believed she'd materialized out of thin air. He took a look at Eli's horror-filled eyes and chuckled inwardly, *Oh yeah. I'm going to love this place.*

After letting Eli get a good long look at her, she smoothly turned her attention to Jack. "Bernadine forgot to tell you about the town meeting this evening. We're going to be naming the school, and you're both invited."

"I'd like that. Give us a chance to meet people. What time?"

"Seven at the Dog and Cow."

"We'll be there, won't we, Eli?"

He was still wide-eyed. "Uh, uh, yeah. Thank you, Tamar."

"You're welcome." Her dark eyes assessed him for another long moment. "What year are you in in school?"

"Junior this year."

"Good student?"

He glanced over at his father. "I used to be."

"Planning on college?"

"Yeah. Hope so."

"Good to know."

For Jack it was as if the whole world was holding its breath in anticipation of what might come next.

Eli was as stiff as the proverbial board.

When she resumed speaking, her tone held a smooth, easy pace but her smile was predatory. "We're real big on schooling here, Eli. We push our children to do their best, and when they express an interest in something, we adults try and help them out. You mentioned something earlier about witches. What was the question again?"

His eyes popped in reaction, and his thin, sixteen-year-old body began to quiver.

"I remember now. You said you thought the Pilgrims had burned all the witches. Interesting topic for a report, I think. How about you, Mr. James?"

Jack wouldn't have disagreed if he'd been offered a position at Harvard. "I think you're right."

"Dad!" Eli cried.

"You did express an interest. No getting around that."

Eli's jaw tightened.

"So," Tamar continued, "because you're new to town and just moving in, I'll give you two weeks after school starts to finish it and hand it in. I'm sure your principal, Ms. Marie, will want your eight-page report to count as half this semester's American history grade."

"Eight pages!"

"Can't wait to read it."

She turned away and focused on Jack. "If you want to follow me over to the diner for the meeting, I'm leaving here at six-thirty."

"Thanks."

"You're welcome. You two get some rest, now, and I'll see you later. Good-bye, Eli."

"Good-bye, Tamar," he replied, sounding miserable.

She smiled and departed.

This time, Eli had nothing to say at all. He instead claimed one of the bedrooms, closed the door, and when Jack looked in on him fifteen minutes later, he was asleep. Jack watched for a few minutes, listened to the soft snores, and reclosed the door. He was pleased.

The rest of Bernadine's morning was spent at the Power Plant and was fairly routine. She told Lily about the newcomers, and how Eli had been put in his place by Tamar, then asked her to check with the construction crews about how soon the Jameses would be able to move into the house being built for them.

Lily walked into Bernadine's office twenty minutes later with the update. "There's still some electrical and plumbing to take care of, and the interior finishes need to be completed. So another week to ten days."

The house would be the newest addition to their small subdivision and was going up next door to the home shared by Lily and Devon.

"Okay, good. So did Rocky call you about the food she wants to send back to the grocery suppliers?"

"Not yet. I'm going to have lunch there this afternoon with Trent. I'll ask her about it, if I get a chance."

"Were you friends with her in high school?"

"No, didn't know her that well. She was a couple years behind us if I remember right. I do know she was Old Man Dancer's daughter, though. He owned the garage where Trent and his buds used to hang and fix their cars."

"Okay. Get with her when you can."

"Will do."

After Lily's departure, Bernadine sat back and wondered if maybe she'd misread Rocky yesterday. She could've sworn the woman was holding some type of grudge, but Lily didn't seem to know much about her, other than her parentage. Interesting, she thought.

Also interesting was the talk she'd had earlier with Trent about yesterday's video clip featuring Cletus's wedding. According to Trent, Sheriff Dalton had the matter well in hand. He'd made contact with the Texas authorities, and hoped to have the two fugitives extradited back to Kansas as soon as they were picked up. It pleased Bernadine to learn that Genevieve had been the one to drop the dime on Riley. With any luck, it would be the first of many daggers Genevieve would get to use to puncture Riley's no-good hide before the sheriff threw him in the pokey, and a pork manufacturer turned Cletus into hot links.

Going back to her laptop, she checked out tonight's town meeting agenda. She wanted to see if Lily or Trent had added anything new. It didn't appear so, which meant that naming the school continued to be the most important item. The ribbon-cutting ceremony was scheduled for Saturday morning and everyone was hoping they'd have something to call the place by the time this evening's meeting ended. When she first came to live in Henry Adams it took her a while to stop shaking her head each time she saw the words *Dog and Cow* on the faded, listing sign above the diner's door. She couldn't believe someone would actually name an establishment that, but after getting to know the owner, she understood. Malachi's explanation of how the name came to be was tied to his having been a county veterinarian, with dogs and cows making up the bulk of his animal clientele. Add to that the fact that he'd been very heavy into alcohol back then, and you had everything you needed to know. Over time, Bernadine had come to enjoy the frivolity in the name, and in the man, but she had no intentions of letting Malachi July anywhere near the school-naming process.

She turned her attention back to the screen on her laptop. A few minutes later a soft knock on her opened door made her turn to see Sheila Payne standing there.

"Morning, Sheila. Come on in. You want coffee?"

"No thank you," she said, entering fully. "Mind if I talk to you for a few minutes?"

"No. What about?"

She took a seat. "I need to go away for a little while and sort some things out."

Bernadine viewed her silently before asking, "Are you and the colonel having problems?"

"In a way, but it isn't anything that can't be fixed."

"It isn't Preston, is it?"

"No. Definitely not. He's one of the reasons I need to do this so that I can be the best mother to him that I can be."

"Then as his advocate, you need to tell me what's going on."

So Sheila told her everything, from the affair to her melancholy to the conclusions she'd drawn last night while lying in bed. "I just want to take some time off to think."

"How long?"

"A month. Six weeks. No more."

"As a foster parent, that's a good chunk of time, Sheila."

"I know, so my question is, will Preston have to be placed elsewhere if I do go? I think of him as my son now, Bernadine. I don't want to lose him."

"Have you talked to your husband?"

"I wanted to talk to you about Preston's status first."

"And you don't want a divorce."

"I don't. I just want some time with me. That's all."

Bernadine didn't think it an unreasonable request and was pleased that Sheila's first concern was the effect on Preston. Bernadine's biggest concern lay with how the colonel and the Brain would do without Sheila there as the buffer. "Do you think they'll be okay without you around to referee?" The two males seemed to tolerate each other, but there'd been very little real bonding that she could see.

"They're getting along better, I suppose, but if we're planning on being a family, the father and son need to be on the same page. My leaving may help facilitate that. Barrett's faults aside, he is a fine molder of young men."

Bernadine considered that. She worried about Preston though. All the town's foster children had issues of one sort or another but Preston had opened himself up the least. She was aware that much of it had to with the fear of being disappointed. Kids like him kept their hearts closed because they were weary of all the broken promises. "Do you know where you want to go?"

"A nuns' house outside of Chicago."

That surprised her. She thought maybe a friend's house, an old girlfriend's, but a nunnery?

"Visitors are allowed to retreat there and I think it will be perfect for what I need to do."

"Okay. Discuss it with your husband and make sure you reassure Preston. I'll talk with them both as well."

Sheila nodded. "Thanks, Bernadine."

"You're welcome. Let me know if and when you plan on leaving."

"Okay."

Sheila departed and Bernadine was left to ponder their conversation. The colonel's adultery wasn't that shocking, but she was surprised by Sheila's plan of action because Sheila had never shown much spunk. Henry Adams had more than its share of strong women, and if you didn't speak up you could get blown over by all the sound and fury. Sheila was nice and dependable, even cracked a joke every now and again, but she rarely spoke up. Bernadine supposed that came from having grown up in a military family, where according to Sheila one was seen and not heard. Bernadine wasn't sure if a trip to a nunnery would help any of that, but she'd give Sheila her full support.

CHAPTER
9

Over at the Dog, Rocky and her staff had just caught their breath from the morning's mad rush and were now making preparations for the lunch crowd. The new Dog and Cow was a hundred times busier than the old place and the need for someone to help her with the cooking was a given. One of the students on the waitstaff had volunteered to pitch in with breakfast, and proceeded to wow Rocky with his skillet skills and efficient handling of the orders. She was so impressed she planned to hire him but wanted Mal to meet him first. He was one of Florene's classmates. His name was Matt Burke.

"I'm eighteen, the youngest of three," he explained as they all sat in Mal's office. "Been working at my parents' restaurant up in Decatur County all my life, and I love to cook."

He went on to tell them of his goal to own his own five-star restaurant one day. "We don't have anything that's even two-star around here. That Italian place over in Franklin was the closest to a nice place to eat, but they closed right after Christmas."

Rocky's initial impression was that she liked him. She could hear the passion in his voice when he spoke about owning his own restaurant, and she liked his smile even though it was easy to see he was nervous as hell. She gave Malachi an approving nod before asking the young man, "Do you prefer Mathew or Matt?"

"I prefer Siz. It's short for Sizzle."

She and Mal stared.

"It's what my family's always called me. My mom says when I was real little she'd have me in the kitchen in a high chair when she fired up the grills and skillets in the morning. Soon as they got hot enough and started to sizzle, I'd clap my hands and imitate the sound." He gave them an example and they all grinned.

"How old were you?" Mal asked laughing.

"According to her, about a year. Been Sizzle ever since."

"Great name for a cook," Rocky told him.

"Gonna be an even greater name for a chef," he boasted self-confidently.

Mal grinned. "I like your style, Chef Siz. Would you like to be Rocky's right-hand man? Job is yours if you want it."

"Yeah! Thank you! Would you mind if I took a couple Saturday evenings off a month?"

"To do what?" Rocky asked curiously.

"I manage a band."

"A band?" Mal asked dubiously. "What kind of band?"

"Jazz and blues mostly."

Mal lit up with delight. "You're lying."

He grinned. "No sir. It's called Kansas Bloody Kansas."

"Kansas Bloody Kansas?" Rocky echoed, skepticism written all over her face.

"Yes, ma'am. Has to do with Kansas and the fight for slavery back in the day. We thought it'd be a cool name."

She and Mal shared a look. *Lord.*

They spent the next few minutes talking salary and other employment items like hours, holiday pay, and such, and when they were done, Siz shook their hands and hurried back to the kitchen.

"Nice young man," Mal said once they were alone.

"I like him."

"So, how's it feel to be back?"

"I hit the floor running, so haven't had time to think about it. Love the new place, like I said before. Real busy this morning."

"Yeah. Lots more folks around to feed these days. No complaints from the populace about the service or the food this morning though, far as I know. Folks complained long and hard the week Florene was here."

"I had a few people stop and thank me for coming back. It felt good."

"Well, add my name to the list. Couldn't be happier having you here."

"Thanks. I need to get to the kitchen. Lunch calls."

"Let me know if you need more help. Got a stack of résumés from the culinary school you can go through."

"Good to know." She gave him a smile and left him alone.

* * *

Lily walked into the D&C for lunch and looked around the crowded, noise-filled diner for Trent's face. The jukebox was rocking "Flashlight" by George Clinton and his mother ship maniacs, and she unconsciously moved to the rhythm of the familiar tune as her eyes continued the search. She spotted him waving at her from a spot in the back. She gave him a nod, then threaded her way past crowded booths, tables, and wait people carrying trays loaded down with plates of food.

"Hey you."

She gave him a quick kiss on the lips. "Hey back. How'd the morning go?"

"No problems, so let's not jinx me by talking work. Look at all these people."

"I know. The D&C is back."

"I even saw some people from Franklin in here earlier. Word must have gotten around that Rocky's back."

"Bernadine wanted me to talk to her about sending back some food. Not sure I remember what Rocky looks like, so if you see her would you point her out?"

He studied her for a moment.

"What?"

"You don't remember her?"

"Nope. She was, what, a sophomore our senior year? Senior girls don't pay attention to sophomores unless they're hitting on their boyfriend, and I didn't come to Henry Adams until high school, so I didn't go way back with her like maybe you did." She immediately turned her attention to the menu printed out on yellow paper. "What am I going to have?"

He thought about that. He supposed she was right and turned his attention to the menu as well.

Waitress Kelly took their orders, and after her departure, he and Lily sat back and enjoyed the hustle and bustle
and each other's company.

Trent was surprised to see Rocky coming their way
bearing a loaded-down tray. Although he and Rocky had
ended their intimate relationship, he was still a bit appre-
hensive that her meeting Lily might go sideways.

"Hey Trent," Rocky said, placing a plate holding his
order of fries and a big BLT in front him.

"Hey Rock. How are you?"

"Busy. Real busy. And how are you, Lily? Been a long
time." Lily's plate of salad was set down in front of her.

"Doing fine, Rocky. It has been a while."

Rocky set down their two glasses of iced tea and added
two straws. On the jukebox, Gladys Knight was singing
"If I Was Your Woman" over the raised voices of the noisy
crowd. "Anything else I can get for you two?"

"I'm good," Trent replied.

"I think I am too," Lily added, then said to her, "Bernadine said there was food in the freezers you wanted sent
back?"

"Yeah, some of the stuff Florene ordered I'm not going
to use."

"E-mail me a list, or bring it by my office, and I'll see if I
can't sweet-talk the suppliers into taking it back or making
an exchange."

"Sounds good. I'll start on it tonight after we close."

"Okay."

"Well, if you two are all set, I'll see you later."

As she made her way back toward the kitchen, Lily

forked up some salad and asked the tea-drinking Trent, "So, how long were you two bed buddies?"

Trent spit tea across the table and coughed until he thought his eyeballs might burst. His fit was noticed by the people sitting nearby, and so Bing came over and slapped Trent on the back a few times. "You okay? You know we don't allow dying in the Dog."

Trent gave him a look that drew a smile from the old farmer, who then went back to his seat.

Trent turned his attention back to Lily and finally said in a strangled-sounding voice, "That was so wrong, Lily Fontaine." He wiped at his mouth with his napkin.

She offered him a smile and waited.

He eyed her. "On and off about six years."

She shrugged. "Fine. That was before we hooked up again, so I have no problem with it."

"That the truth?"

"You still have a thing for her?"

"No."

"Then we're good."

"Can I eat now?"

"Bon appétit."

He grabbed the bottle of ketchup and doused his fries.

"I love you, Trenton."

"Tell it to the marines."

He looked up, met her eyes, and they both laughed.

Meanwhile, over at the Paynes' house, Sheila was dragging suitcases out of the closet while her marine colonel husband looked on with disapproval. "Where are you going, again?"

Sheila pulled another suitcase out of the closet and replied, "Chicago. I'm taking a vacation."

"We just returned from vacation."

"That was yours. This one will be mine. I'll be leaving in the morning."

"Do you want a divorce?"

"No."

"Then you are coming back?"

"Of course." She set the largest suitcase on the bed and unzipped the sides and top so that it would open. Inside were two Florida postcards purchased during the reunion but never used. She set them aside on the bed. "Unless you prefer that I don't."

His arms were tightly folded. "I prefer that you do."

She searched his eyes. There was so much in her heart that she longed to say about all the things she wanted them to be, do, and share, but instead she said to him, "I talked with Bernadine and she sees no reason for this to affect Preston's status with us."

Just as she said that, Preston appeared in the doorway. He studied the suitcases and then Sheila. He asked coldly, "You pulling those out for me, right?"

"No, Preston," Sheila said softly. "I'm going on a vacation, that's all."

"You two getting a divorce?"

Barrett glared, "Not your business."

"The hell it's not," Preston countered. "If you two split, I get screwed again!"

Sheila gasped. "Preston!"

He snapped his mouth shut, then mumbled, "Sorry,"

and left. The slam of his bedroom door shook the house.

"He needs to show more respect, Sheila."

"Like the respect you showed me with that whore?"

Barrett's eyes widened.

"Yes, Barrett, I said *whore*. Shall I say it again?"

He stared at her as if he'd never seen her before.

"Go talk to Preston. I need to figure out what I'm going to be taking."

Preston was seated on the edge of his bed when a knock sounded on his closed door. "Come in." Seeing the colonel didn't help his sullen mood. "I suppose you want an apology?"

Barrett was still reeling from Sheila's temper.

Preston stared suspiciously at the look on the colonel's face. "What's wrong with you?"

"She just said the word *whore*." His face was filled with both wonder and confusion.

"To you?"

"Yeah."

"Why'd she call you a whore?"

"Not me. Marti," he offered, only half aware that he'd answered aloud.

"That the nurse at the reunion?"

That got Barrett's full attention. "How'd you know?"

"The way she was all over you, Goofy could've figured that out."

He went stock-still.

"You cheated on Mrs. Payne with a woman who still wears a Jheri curl? I didn't know they let you do crack in the marines."

Barrett paused, stared, and then, unable to help himself, laughed. "They don't, but you couldn't tell it by me, huh?"

"She's hurting bad, isn't she?"

Barrett sobered and nodded. "I think so."

"That why she's going away?"

Another nod.

"Did you ask her to stay?"

That tack had never occurred to him. "No."

"Man." Preston found that messed up, but he kept it to himself. "So, how long she gonna be gone?"

"A month, maybe six weeks."

Six weeks! Preston sighed. "You want me to move over to Amari's till she gets back?"

"Why?"

"So you don't have to put up with me."

"You think I just put up with you?"

Unsure how to answer, Preston shrugged and replied, "We get along sometimes, but not like Amari and his dad."

"I see." And for maybe the first time, Barrett saw Preston for what he truly was—a boy in search of a father. Barrett hadn't had much of one either. The only affection Lamont Payne ever showed his wife and son, Barrett, involved beating them down with his fists. "I told you about my dad."

"Yeah."

"So it's not like I have a good example to draw from."

"I know." Preston had had his share of beatings in his life so he understood where the colonel was coming from, but he kept that to himself too.

As they both mined their thoughts, there was silence for a long moment until finally Barrett said, "If you want to move to Amari's, that's up to you, but I'd prefer you stay here."

Preston eyed him suspiciously. "Why?"

"I can't learn to be a good dad if my son's living next door."

Preston wasn't sure how to take that either. "You saying that just because you're supposed to?"

"Preston, we may not know each other real well, but you know I don't say anything just because I'm supposed to."

"Right." Preston looked away.

"So, what do you think? Shall we try it?"

"Being son and dad?" Preston kept his excitement masked.

"Yes."

He shrugged, saying emotionlessly, "Sure. Why not?"

"Such enthusiasm."

"Never done this before. Don't want to invest in something that might not pay off."

Barrett studied him. "I see."

"It's the truth."

"Appreciate that. But you are willing to try?"

"Yeah, if you are."

"May not be easy."

"I know. Especially with you being kind of a hard-ass."

Barrett smiled. "And proud of it. Still want to try?"

Preston nodded.

Barrett stuck out his fist, and he and Preston bumped knuckles to seal their pact. "*Semper fi.*"

"What's it mean?"

"Always faithful. Be it to country, the corps, or family."

Preston thought that over. He liked the sentiment, and although his life had never had any *Semper* or *fi*, he tapped his knuckles to the colonel's again, and echoed, *"Semper fi."*

Outside in the hall, the eavesdropping Sheila smiled and quietly tiptoed back to her room.

Her men were going to be all right.

CHAPTER
10

As Preston and Amari rode their bikes out to Tamar's later that afternoon, Preston told him about Mrs. Payne's vacation and about the pact he'd made with the colonel.

"So you believe him about wanting to be father and son?" Amari asked.

"I guess. He sounded pretty for real but I'm trying not to get caught up on that hope thing, you know."

"I feel you. Be great if it worked out, then we can all do stuff together. Me and my dad, and you and your dad."

Preston, struggling with the exertion of the riding, nodded.

Seeing the difficulty his friend was having, Amari said, "Let's stop a minute, man. Need to catch my breath."

The ride from where they lived to where Tamar lived was a little over a mile. The unpaved gravel road hadn't been graded by the county recently, so traveling was rough on both bike and rider. In truth, Amari could have made the trip in half the time had he been alone, but Preston was with him, and because of his asthma, they had to go slow.

"I know you're stopping because of me," Preston wheezed. He dug into his pocket for his inhaler and took a quick puff.

"It's okay. You're getting better. Last summer you couldn't ride at all, remember?"

Preston nodded and welcomed the relief brought on by the inhaler's medication a few minutes later. Once he felt able, he said, "Thanks, man."

"Don't want you dying on me. Who'd I hang with? Devon? Crystal?"

Preston grinned.

So for the next few minutes, they sat in the grass, took in the silence and sunshine, and watched the breeze rippling through the fields of wheat lining the road.

"Who'd've ever thought we'd end up here," Preston mused aloud.

"I know. It's cool though. No crackheads, no sirens, no only getting peeks at the sky because of all the houses and buildings. Never knew the sky was so big."

"Yeah. You see places like this on TV and say, no way would you live there, but this ain't bad."

Amari agreed. "You think you could live here the rest of your life?"

"Only if Ms. Bernadine builds a college with a physics lab."

"Or a NASCAR track."

A big hawk circled lazily above them and the boys charted the flight with their eyes.

As it moved away and out of sight, Amari said, "Had a

dream about a hawk. It was riding shotgun in a car I was driving."

"Where were you going?"

"No clue."

"I had a foster mother who swore by her dreams. Even had one of those dream books where you look up stuff so you know what three-digit number to play."

"Seen those. No place to play a three-digit around here though."

"Nope."

Amari assessed Preston's physical condition to see if they could resume their ride. "You ready?"

Preston nodded and both boys picked up their bikes.

"Let me know if you need to stop again, okay?"

"I will. And Amari?"

"Yeah?"

"Thanks for not dogging me out about my asthma."

"No problem. We're family, man. We're supposed to look out for each other."

When they reached Tamar's place, she was seated on the porch in her rocker, reading and listening to her iPod. Lily had given her the popular music device last winter as a birthday gift, and with the help of Preston's laptop, she'd loaded it with everything from Aretha to ZZ Hill. Upon seeing them, she closed her book, removed her headphones, and stood.

For Amari, Tamar's height had to be one of her most intimidating features. She was six-foot-two, and standing next to her was like being towered over by a silver-haired tree. "Hey, Tamar. We came to see the old pictures, if you don't mind."

"Sure don't. Come on in."

She got the albums and they all took a seat on the sofa in her living room. Amari never tired of looking at the pictures of old Henry Adams. He liked the sepia-colored images of the dusty old streets filled with horse-drawn wagons and the buildings that no longer existed, like the Sutton Mercantile and the Liberian Lady Saloon. He also enjoyed studying the somber faces of the stiffly posed men with their thick mustaches and old-fashioned suits. "How come none of them ever smiled?"

"Photography was relatively new back then and people posed like they did when having their portraits painted. You ever seen a smiling portrait of anybody in the museums we've visited?"

Amari couldn't say that he had. He carefully turned the pages of the album to the next set of pics. They looked like they'd been taken during some kind of celebration. One showed a crowd of men and women lining the old Main Street. They were wearing fancier old-fashioned clothing and a few people were even smiling. There were flags hanging from some of the buildings in the pictures' background. Beside one of them someone from the past had written in swirly handwriting, *August First. 1882.*

Amari turned another page and studied the pictures. One showed a group of soldiers marching down Main Street. All the uniformed men were playing musical instruments, mostly horns.

Preston asked, "These pictures of some kind of parade?"

Tamar nodded. "It's the August First parade. 1882."

"What was so special about August First?" Amari asked. "Is that the day Henry Adams was founded?"

"No. On August 1, 1834, Great Britain ended slavery in the British West Indies. Free Black folks in America celebrated the date because it gave them hope that slavery would soon be abolished in the U.S. too."

"Ah," the boys said.

"Back then our people didn't celebrate the Fourth of July. Didn't make sense when the country had three million of us enslaved, so they did it up on August First instead."

"I didn't know that," Preston said, sounding impressed.

"So what kind of stuff did they do?" Amari asked. "Did they barbecue, shoot fireworks, what?"

"Good question. Be something for you and Preston to look up."

"Aw, Tamar. Come on. Why is it that every time we talk to you, we wind up having to look up something?"

"Because that's my job. Do you want to be a July or not?"

He sighed audibly. "Yes."

"I don't." Preston countered. "I got enough issues with the colonel."

She ignored that. "This is part of the town's heritage. Its history can only survive if someone's around to tell the stories. You're going to be the youngest July, Amari, so keeping the history alive falls on you now."

Amari felt glum for a moment, and then an idea came to him that made him sit up and smile. "That project you said I had to do for Henry Adams. Can it be an August First parade?"

Tamar stilled. Realizing she might have inadvertently stepped into her own trap, she said warily, "I suppose."

Preston looked at Amari. "You want to throw a parade?"

"Yeah. She said do something memorable. When was the last time Henry Adams had a parade, Tamar?"

She thought back. "Forty years, maybe."

"Perfect. We're going to have us an August First parade, and it's going to be off the chain."

Preston looked confused. "But you don't know anything about throwing a parade."

"But I bet we can find out how on the Internet."

"True," Preston allowed.

"Will you help?" Amari asked him.

"Sure."

"Then we're good."

Amari closed the photo album and stood. "Thanks, Tamar. You were right about the old pictures giving me some ideas."

Tamar wasn't sure if the town would thank her. Knowing Amari, some kind of disaster was undoubtedly waiting in the wings. "Make sure you get your dad's and Ms. Bernadine's permission."

Preston agreed. "Yeah. We may need permits or something."

"And horses, and bands," Amari added excitedly.

Tamar's mouth dropped.

Amari continued thinking out loud. "You think the colonel could get the Blue Angels to fly over, Brain?"

Preston blinked with surprise but before he could fit thoughts to words, Amari urged, "Come on, man. Let's get back. We've got work to do."

Tamar followed them outside. As she watched them ride off with Amari still spouting ideas, she stood on the porch and wondered why she felt as if she'd just unleashed the biblical whirlwind.

The town triumvirate, Bernadine, Lily, and Trent, were in Bernadine's office putting together the final agenda for the town meeting when they were interrupted by an excited-looking Amari and a closed-faced Preston. Bernadine had no idea why warning bells were suddenly clanging in her head, but she asked calmly, "What can we do for you, gentlemen?"

"I want to have a parade," Amari announced.

For all three adults, the world stopped.

Trent was almost afraid to ask. "What kind of parade?"

"August First parade."

Trent knew about the history of August First, but what— "Okay, start at the beginning."

So Amari did, recounting the visit to Tamar, the history tied to the date, and the idea he'd gotten from the old picture album.

"I think that is a great idea," Lily said, impressed. "Be a good way to bring folks together as a community."

Bernadine had to admit she agreed. Up until then she'd never heard of August First or its significance, but she wasn't sure about Amari being in charge. "How much might this cost?"

He shrugged.

"Then I'd like for you and Preston to put together a proposal. Estimate what you think the price tag could be and let us look at it. Who knows, this might become an annual event again."

Amari didn't want the adults involved because he was certain they'd take all the credit. "But this is my project. Tamar already approved it."

Trent asked, "Did she say she was going to pay for it?"

He looked down at his sneaks. "No."

"Then where does that leave us?" Trent asked.

"With me bringing you a proposal," Amari murmured.

Bernadine tried to lift his spirits. "It's a fantastic idea, Amari, and since this is your baby, you get to carry it, but you need some oversight."

Amari looked to Preston for a definition of *oversight*.

"Somebody to look over your shoulder so we don't wind up back in court."

"Oh."

Bernadine wondered what they'd do without Preston.

Trent said, "It is a great idea, Amari. Great idea."

"Thanks."

Preston had a question. "When do you want to see the proposal?"

"Does a week from today sound reasonable?" Bernadine asked.

Both boys agreed.

"Okay then," Amari said. "We're gonna go get started."

After their departure, the three adults shared a long look.

Trent cracked, "Going to be an interesting summer."

The women nodded agreement and they all went back to work.

Leo Brown stood in front of his office windows and looked out at the comings and goings of the small town. Driving past the window were more pickup trucks than you could shake a stick at, and although the citizenry was friendly, he'd yet to see anyone who looked like him. He had no idea what Bernadine saw in this part of the country because try as he might, he didn't get it. As far as he could tell, there was absolutely nothing to do for recreation except bowling. The secretary sent over to work for him by the temp agency said that for entertainment, the folks she knew went to Wal-Mart. Obviously that was good for the corporate chain's bottom line, but for Leo it meant being bored to death. He'd been sent there to oversee a new geological survey project on behalf of the company and he wasn't sure he'd be able to survive being there the estimated six weeks needed to complete the project.

He was also having a heck of a time coming up with a plan to win Bernadine back. Although she'd made it crystal-clear she wanted no parts of him, he was betting she didn't mean it, not for real anyway. He imagined she was still a bit hurt over his adultery and he couldn't blame her, but if he was willing to come begging, she should be willing to at least give his request for a second chance a fair hearing. After all it wasn't like she was getting any younger. Woman her age needed a man, and not one like the country bumpkins he'd met at the Henry Adams diner. Leo hadn't even bothered asking their names because it hadn't mattered to him one way or the other. His money and status set him apart from people like them and he had the chauffeur to prove it. The thought of money gave him pause. Maybe he could buy his way back into her heart. He knew she had plenty of her own—hadn't she gotten the bulk of it from him? But what could he buy her that she'd want or didn't already have? He walked to the door and stepped out into the outer office where the temp, named Cathy, had her desk.

"Cathy?"

She smoothly put down her nail file. "Name's Carol, Mr. Brown."

"That's right. Sorry. Let me ask you a question. If you could have a man buy you anything in the whole world, what would it be?"

She studied him for a moment. "Is this man my husband or a boyfriend?"

He didn't know he needed to be specific. "Any man."

"Well, if it's my husband, I'd want a new washing machine. Spin cycle is shot and it takes the dryer—"

"Your boyfriend," he stated, holding on to his patience.

"A new truck. I saw one at the dealer's last week that was candy apple red and so sweet—"

"Never mind."

He walked back into his office and closed the door. There was no way Bernadine would drive a pickup. She had way too much class for that. He'd just have to keep thinking.

A few minutes later, there was a knock followed by Carol's voice. "Local paper was just delivered, Mr. Brown. You want to take a look at it?"

"Bring it in."

It took him all of ten minutes to peruse the two-section edition, but something in the local happenings column caught his attention. It was a notice for the Henry Adams monthly town meeting. The brief announcement gave the date as that day and the place as the diner. Leo made a decision to attend. He'd wanted to know what Bernadine saw in this backwoods place. By going to the meeting maybe he could find out. She'd probably pitch a fit, but he didn't care.

Bleary from sleep and too much traveling, Eli James sat on the side of the bed in his boxers and tried to remember where he was and how he'd gotten there. When it all came rushing back, he groaned. He'd hoped this had been nothing more than a bad dream but it was worse; it was his life. He'd traveled halfway across the country so his dad could work in Little Town on the Prairie, and the two of them could live next door to a witch woman. That she'd put a spell on him was the only explanation he could come up with as to why he'd let her run over him the way he had, and kept him from telling her what he really thought, and where she could stick the report she expected him to do, which he had no intention of doing. He could care less if he flunked American history. The town was such a backward-ass place, the one-room schoolhouse probably didn't even have history books. *What the hell am I doing here?* he wailed inside. Why did life keep picking on him? His world fell apart when his mom died. All he'd wanted was for her to live. He missed her so much sometimes he cried at night. And now, it was just him and the Professor. The two of them had never been really close. Jack hadn't coached Little League or taken him bowling or done any of the other stuff his friends' dads were known to do. Now, with Mom gone, he wanted to get all fatherly, and Eli wasn't feeling it because why should he? Jack taught night classes every semester so no matter what after-school activities Eli participated in, he hadn't been there; not for the team sports Eli loved to play, any of the art competitions to applaud him for being the best high school sculptor in the state, not for anything; ever.

He ran his long fingers through his sleep-tousled, jet black hair and put his face in his hands. He couldn't wait to be eighteen so he could move out, take charge of his own life, and leave his dad and this stupid town behind.

Mal walked into the diner's kitchen and found Rocky and Siz going through the freezers. Because of the town meeting they weren't going to be open for dinner but he'd asked Rocky to provide some munchies. "You two figure out what we're eating for the meeting?"

"Siz wants to do an appetizer buffet. Were it left up to me, we'd just fry up a bunch of chicken wings and call it a day, but I'm going to let him teach me some of the things he's been learning in class and we'll see if this old cook can learn some new tricks."

Siz came out of the big walk-in freezer with two large, frost-covered bags. "You're not old, Ms. Rock."

"Compared to you, I'm Methuselah's wife."

"Who?"

She and Mal shared a grin.

"Never mind," she said to Siz. "What's in the bag?"

"Chicken drummies. There's a bunch of other stuff we can use too. But we're going to keep what we're making a secret."

"We are?" she asked skeptically.

Mal speared him with a look. "Don't do a Florene on me now, son. Hate to have to fire you your first day out."

"I'd hate it too, so don't worry. I just want everybody to be surprised by the food and the presentation. That's all. It's gonna be awesome. Promise."

"I'm holding you to that."

Rocky could see Mal's continued skepticism but she'd be there to haul Siz back if he went overboard, so she wasn't worried.

Clay Dobbs walked in, and after greeting Rocky and Mal, and nodding to the young man he didn't know, he said to Mal, "Just got a call from Marie. Their plane just landed."

"Okay, but meet Siz first."

Clay looked confused. "Who?"

Mal made the introductions.

Once they were done with the formalities, Siz asked Clay, "Anybody ever tell you you look like Julian Bond, sir?"

Clay cocked his head at the question. "What do you know about Julian Bond?"

"Well, he was the communications director for the Student Nonviolent Coordinating Committee, and in 1966 was denied his duly elected seat in the Georgia legislature because he opposed the war in Vietnam. I'm taking a humanities class on the sixties, and we're studying him and some of the other young African-American leaders like Bobby Seale and Stokely Carmichael."

Humor twinkling in her eyes, Rocky asked, "You didn't accept this job just so we could help you pass your class, did you?"

Siz smiled. "No, ma'am, but he does look like Julian Bond."

Mal said, "You should have seen him when he had all

his hair. He and Julian could've passed for twins. Now both of them are old."

"Shut up," Clay said, laughing. "Like you're not."

Clay turned back to Siz. "You're going to be a better cook than that other one, right?"

"I hope so, sir."

"Then we'll keep hope alive."

Mal shook his head, "Let's go. Rock, if anybody calls looking for me, Clay and I are heading to the airport to pick up Genevieve and Marie. We'll be back in time for the meeting."

"Okay. Drive safe."

After their exit, she turned to Siz. "Okay, Emeril, what are we cooking?"

For the drive to the airport, Clay was behind the wheel of his big green Chevy Suburban because Mal's old Ford couldn't seat four. They talked a bit about everything and nothing while on the way, until finally Clay asked, "You think the police are ever going to catch Riley?"

"Who knows. I'd've bet even money Dalton would've run him down by now."

"Me too. Can't imagine where he and that hog could be hiding out."

"Apparently with that redhead woman on the video."

"She's got to be crazy as he is to be marrying two hogs."

"I know. So, what are you going to do about Genevieve?"

"Nothing."

"Why not?"

"She's married, Mal. You and I had this discussion

when Riley first took off. Not messing around with another man's wife."

"You're not getting any younger."

"Morals don't age."

Mal sighed and turned his attention to the view passing by his window. He and Clay had been friends since second grade. They'd graduated high school together, ran the ladies together, and survived Nam together even though the carnage and death took its toll. Once home Clay turned inward and became more introspective while Mal sought refuge from the nightmares in drink and young women, the only two things that made him feel alive. "Okay, since you don't want to discuss Genny, what do you think about Siz? He manages a jazz band."

"Liked him. Seems a lot better choice than that Florene."

"Mr. Ed would have been a better choice than Florene. Glad Bernadine agreed with me."

"Speaking of Bernadine. Anything new on her ex?"

"Not that I've heard. She did tell me she wasn't taking him back."

"Good."

"Exactly. All I need is competition."

Clay grinned. "I told you this wasn't going to be easy."

"Yeah, yeah."

"Dealing with a grown woman's a lot more complicated than those coeds you're used to."

"I know. I know. But answer me this. How can you be so wise with my love life and so clueless with your own?"

"Shut up."

Mal smiled and settled in for the rest of the ride.

Clay made the turn that took them onto the airport property and he and Malachi scanned the faces of the few people standing outside the terminal. "Do you see them anywhere?"

"Not yet."

A few seconds later, Mal pointed. "There they are. Why's Genny in a wheelchair?"

"God. I hope she didn't have a stroke." Clay steered the truck to the curb and he and Mal got out.

"What happened to Genny?"

Marie shot a disapproving look at Genevieve over the rims of her black rhinestone cat eye glasses and drawled, "Too many Kamikazes."

Both men stiffened. "What!"

Genevieve reprimanded them in a weak voice, "Stop shouting. My head's hurting bad enough as it is."

Clay knelt down. "Are you okay?"

"No. Marie tried to tell me to go slow, but I wouldn't listen."

Marie took her cue. "Also told her not to chase Kamikazes with Hurricanes. Didn't listen to that either."

Clay's eyes widened. He studied Genevieve's pale face and slumped shoulders. "Since when did you start drinking?"

"When I saw Riley and that woman and those damn hogs. If that was your husband, you'd drink too. Should've married you, Clay. Probably had those babies I wanted by now."

Clay's mouth hit the sidewalk.

Mal and Marie shared a look.

Marie said, "I think she may be a little bit drunk still. Let's get her home."

Clay was staring at Genevieve, transfixed.

Mal called to him, "Hey, you. Pick up your teeth. Time to go."

Clay visibly shook himself before straightening to his full height. He got behind the wheelchair and pushed the eyes-closed Genevieve toward the truck. Marie and Mal grabbed the handles on the rolling suitcase and fell in behind them.

Marie sighed. "You know Mama's going to blame all this on me."

Mal cracked, "And well she should. You've been Satan's handmaiden since kindergarten."

She punched him in the shoulder. Hard.

"Hey!" he exclaimed, rubbing the throbbing spot, which earned a grin from Marie.

Once they were inside the truck and had their seat belts fastened, Clay drove toward home.

Marie was right. After she put Genevieve to bed, she came downstairs intent upon grabbing her car keys. Although she was dead on her feet from being dragged all over Vegas by Genny last night, she didn't want to miss the meeting due to start in less than an hour. According to Mal, the new teacher she hired for the school had arrived earlier today with his son. She was as anxious to meet them as she was to know what the name of the school was going to be. "Mama, are you ready?"

"Yep. How's Gen?"

Marie entered the front room. Her ninety-year-old mother, Agnes, was at the door, pocketbook on her wrist.

"She's asleep."

"Do you think she'll be all right here alone?"

"I think so."

"Okay then."

They left the house and got into Marie's old Pontiac. As she drove out to the road and toward town, her mother said, "You shouldn't have gotten her drunk like that, Marie."

"I didn't get her drunk, Mama. She saw Riley and that pig on the TV and she flipped out."

"Still."

The disapproval in the tone was hard to miss. "Still, what?"

"You should never have taken her to Vegas."

"It was her suggestion, remember?"

"I do, but you could have said, no."

"She's a grown woman, Mama."

"She's not used to the vices like you are, Marie. You should have been more vigilant."

"Mama, I didn't come home to argue with you. Okay?"

"Fine." She turned away in a huff.

Marie gritted her teeth. "Mama, I'm sixty years old. When are you going to let go of the past?"

"I'm not in the past."

"Yeah, you are. I admit, I was wild back then, but I'm no longer seventeen, pregnant, and a disgrace to the hallowed Jefferson name."

"Stop being disrespectful."

Marie sighed audibly. "How about we not talk about this. Sorry I brought it up."

Marie turned full attention to her driving but she was equal parts hurt and angry. Appearances meant everything to Agnes Jefferson, and for her only daughter to have gone away to college only to return home pregnant had been so devastating and shaming that all these many years later, the incident still resonated. Admittedly, Marie had been a wild teen; drinking, smoking, running with the proverbial wrong crowd because she'd found the strict tenets of small-town life so stifling, rebellion became a way to breathe. When she earned the college scholarship that gave her a ticket out, she'd grabbed it with both hands. Six months later she was pregnant. The father of her unborn child, a young graduate student, told her he had no intentions of divorcing his wife or claiming the baby, and that Marie was on her own. She'd cried for days. Faced with no other choice she returned home. Having to confess the situation to her mother was the hardest thing she'd ever had to do, and having to listen to the recriminations, devastating. The year was 1966 and in those days it was unheard of for a young unmarried woman of her age to keep her illegitimate baby, so Agnes drove her to a home for wayward girls in Topeka where Marie gave birth. She never even got to hold the baby boy—the nuns said it was better that way. Now, almost a half century later, the ache in her heart remained. She'd managed to fill much of the void by becoming a teacher, a profession she dearly loved, but she prayed for that child every night. Still.

CHAPTER
11

Before heading over to the town meeting, Bernadine swung by home to check on Crystal. They'd texted each other a few times over the course of the day and even though Crys assured her things were okay, she needed to see with her own eyes.

She found her in the kitchen making pancakes.

"Hey. You want some?"

"No thanks. There's supposed to be food at the meeting, but put the leftover batter in the fridge for me, please, just in case."

She nodded.

Crystal's quiet demeanor tugged at Bernadine's heart. "How you doing?"

"Okay, I guess, but this is so stupid. I barely knew her, so why am I feeling like this?"

"Because she was still your mom, and when she passed, your dream of getting back with her was taken too."

Crystal appeared to think that over. "I guess so." After a

few moments, she said, "I didn't know it was going to hurt like this."

"The sharp parts will fade over time."

"How long did it take you when your mother died?"

Bernadine thought back on that painful, life-changing episode. "A while. I don't think you ever get over it, but you do get through it. Does that make sense?"

"Yeah. In a way."

Having dealt with her own grief, Bernadine knew there was no rushing it out the door. "People heal in their own time and in their own way. So if you don't feel like doing anything for the next few days, it's okay. Folks will understand."

As Crystal's watery eyes held hers, Bernadine saw something in them that gave her pause. Not sure what it might be, she asked gently, "Anything else you want to talk about?"

"Yeah. Are you really going to keep me?"

Bernadine studied the face she'd come to love. "Forever and ever, amen." In fact, Bernadine was ready to begin adoption proceedings to make Crystal her own, but she didn't think now was the proper time to broach the subject. She wanted to wait until she finished her grieving. "You okay with forever and ever, amen?"

The soft smile temporarily masked the sadness. "Yeah."

"Good."

"Oh, forgot to tell you. Preston said the colonel and Mrs. Payne are having issues, and he's real worried. He made me promise not to say anything, but I thought you needed to know. He's really sad."

Although Bernadine had been alerted to the situation by Sheila, she was surprised to hear Preston had opened himself, and to Crystal of all people. "He just offered up how he was feeling? That's not like Preston."

"I know, surprised me too, but he was looking all beat down so I made him talk to me."

That was surprising as well. *Crystal as counselor?* "May I ask what you told him?"

"Not much. Mostly, I just listened. He thanked me, though. Made me feel like I was all mature and stuff."

"I'm glad you were there for him, Crys."

"Told him not to make it a habit, though."

The dry humor made Bernadine chuckle.

Crystal grinned in response before saying, "You should get going. Tamar'll be all up in your grill if you're late for the meeting."

"True." But before departing, she walked over and held out her arms for a hug. Crystal stepped into the breach and let herself be enfolded and held on tight in return. Bernadine had no words to offer, just love, so she kissed her brow, squeezed her one more time for good measure, and left the house for the meeting.

When Bernadine pulled into the D&C's parking lot, all the trucks filling the spaces made her wonder if more than just the meeting was going on inside. Upon entering she thought that must be the reason, because the place was in full party mode. On the new jukebox, the Ohio Players were belting out "Fire," over the sounds of laughter and raised voices. The fragrant smells of food cooking permeated the air. She glanced around approvingly at the people milling about with piled-high plates in hand. She spotted Malachi seated at one of the round tables slapping dominoes and talking smack. Seeing him made her think about their picnic date. In the back of her mind she really wasn't sure if agreeing to it had been the right thing to do, but she left her second thoughts alone for the time being and resumed checking out the faces in the crowd.

All of the foster parents were in attendance, as were the kids. In one of the back booths Amari and Preston had their heads together over an opened laptop. She hoped they were working on their proposal, but with those two one could never tell.

"Evening, Ms. Brown."

She turned to see Rocky coming up behind her. "Hey there. Looks like everyone's having a good time, and I don't see anybody sending their plates back to the kitchen."

"Which is a good thing."

"A very good thing."

"You can give most of the credit to my new assistant. His name's Matt Burke, but he calls himself Siz. Short for Sizzle."

Bernadine stared.

Rocky chuckled, "I'll tell you about it one day when we both have some time. Anyway, he's from the culinary college and tonight's menu is all his doing."

"Can I meet him?"

"He's in the back still cooking up a storm right now, but Mal's going to introduce him during the meeting."

Bernadine saw Lily waving her over to the table she was sharing with Devon, Zoey, and the Garlands. She waved back and asked Rocky, "Did you and Lily get a chance to talk about that food you wanted to return?"

"Sure did. I should have that inventory list to her some-time tomorrow."

"Okay, I'm going to go grab me a plate and a seat. Thanks so much for all this."

"You're welcome. I'll see you later."

Slowly making her way through the crowded diner, Bernadine spoke to those she knew, like Clay, Agnes, and Marie, and those she didn't, like a married couple who introduced themselves as the Clarks. According to them they once lived in Henry Adams, were presently residing in nearby Franklin, but were considering moving back so that their two daughters could take advantage of the new school. After telling them how pleased she was to meet them, she moved on. She was also pleased to see Jack and Eli sitting with Tamar, although she wasn't sure Eli found the arrangement pleasing.

She then stopped and talked for a minute with Bing Shepard, who was sharing a booth with some of his old bud-dies from the Black Farmers Association. The newly elected president of the United States had recently announced a plan that might finally settle the Black farmers' long-standing grievances against the U.S. Department of Agriculture for its well-documented discriminatory and predatory lending practices. Before Bernadine left for vacation, Bing had asked if she knew a lawyer who might represent the cases of the local farmers. She'd been given a name that afternoon.

She handed him a sticky note with the name and phone number written on it, and said over the din, "Call her to-morrow. She's very good and will look after you all."

"Thanks." Bing pocketed the note.

"Oh, and she's willing to do it pro bono. Her grandfather lost his land to the USDA back in the eighties. Let me know how it goes."

"Will do."

Glad that she'd been able to help, Bernadine finally took her seat. She was just about to get up and head to the buffet table when she saw Leo enter the diner.

"What the heck is he doing here?" she asked crossly.

"Who?" Roni asked, looking around.

"My ex."

Lily saw Leo and she stared with surprise. "What do you think he wants?"

"A big fat, restraining order."

"Well don't make a scene," Roni cautioned. "That might be just what he's wanting you to do."

"What's an ex?" Devon asked.

Lily said, "Someone you were married to but not married to now."

"Oh."

He and Zoey shared a glance.

"Just ignore him, Bernadine," Lily suggested. "If he gets stupid, Sheriff Dalton is just a phone call away."

Roni nodded agreement. "Go get something to eat, girl. We'll keep an eye on him."

Reg chuckled at all the intrigue and said to Devon, "Glad I'm not an ex."

Devon replied, "Me too."

By the time Trent walked over and shut down the jukebox so the meeting could get started, Bernadine had forgotten all about Leo because she was too busy wondering just how much Siz would charge her to cook for her exclusively and forever. She absolutely loved the little shrimp and spinach stuffed filo tarts. The meatballs were fabulous, as were the Asian spiced drummies. Sizzle, or whatever he called himself, *could burn* as they used to say back in the day.

"Okay," Trent called out. "Let's get this show on the road. Dad. You wanted to go first."

Malachi stood. "As you all know, Rocky Dancer is back with us."

Cheers greeted that and folks began chanting her name.

She came out of the kitchen with a wide grin on her face and stepped up beside Malachi. The cheering and chanting soared even higher until finally Trent had to get out his gavel and calm everybody down.

"It's good to be home," she said once the roar subsided. "But I want you to meet the young man responsible for tonight's meal. His name is Siz."

He came out of the kitchen, and the noisy cheers and chanting of his name greeted his arrival too. He stood there red-faced but smiling, and then did an elaborate bow.

Rocky held up her hands. "Okay, y'all. Quiet. Now, with Siz on board, we're going to be trying some new things. He's got a lot of good ideas about us eating healthier, but not with stuff you can't pronounce."

"We're holding you to that!" someone shouted.

Laughs followed that.

Rocky said, "Again, thanks for all the love. If you need anything just come on back."

She and Siz waved and headed off to their domain.

Next on the agenda was Amari, of all people. Bernadine and Lily stared, puzzled.

Lily asked quietly, "Did you put him on the agenda?"

Bernadine shook her head.

Amari walked up to the front of the room and said, "I need everybody to put August First on their calendars. We're having a parade."

"Will it have police cars?" Bing called out loudly.

The room erupted with laughter.

Amari grinned. "Hope not."

Tamar's voice followed loudly with "Better not."

More laughter.

"I don't have all the details worked out yet, and Ms. Bernadine and my dad have to see a proposal, but I'm trying to be a real July, and Tamar said I had to do something to honor the Dusters. Back in the day, they had parades on August First, so I want us to have one too."

The room grew quiet the moment he said he was trying to become a real July. Bernadine looked around the diner and saw the quiet pride in Tamar's face mirrored in Trent's and Malachi's as well. Amari's quest for family meant something to them. Apparently it meant something to everyone else too, because one by one folks got to their feet and applauded him and his plan to revitalize part of Henry Adams's grand past. Amari's young face beamed. He might have had half the town hauled before a judge, and lord knew how this whole parade idea would turn out, but from the construction workers, to the Julys, to Bernadine, Amari was loved.

"Oh, and anybody who wants to be in the parade just see me and Preston after the meeting." He went back to his seat.

The next business item also hadn't been on the official agenda. Trent called up Devon. Seeing him in his suit and clip-on tie always drew smiles, and that evening was no exception.

"I'm having church on Sunday at Ms. Roni's house," he told the assemblage. "Zoey's playing the piano and Ms. Roni is going to sing. You are all invited." Turning back to Trent, he said, "Thank you, Mr. Trent."

"You're welcome, Devon."

Devon walked back to his seat. Zoey patted him on the back and the meeting continued with the Mayor's Report.

Trent gave an update on the ongoing construction projects, and then reminded everyone that the Power Plant and the rec center were the town's designated tornado shelters. From spring through late summer, Kansas was right smack-dab in the middle of Tornado Alley, where the deadly twisters often sprang to life in the blink of an eye. Bernadine had yet to experience such destructive weather and she prayed neither she nor the town would be subjected to it any time soon.

Finally, the main event. The naming of the school.

Trent said, "Floor's open for nominations."

Murmurs filled the room as people debated the pros and cons of their personal choices.

Agnes Jefferson stood and said in a strong voice, "I nominate the name Cara Lee Jefferson."

Trent nodded and wrote it down.

Everyone knew Cara Jefferson had been the town's schoolteacher during Henry Adams's golden age back in the 1880s. She was also one of Agnes's ancestors. Her innovative teaching methods and tireless devotion laid the foundation for the schools that followed.

Bernadine scanned faces for reactions to the nomination. No one looked particularly gung-ho, but she did see a few thoughtful nods of agreement.

"Anyone else?" Trent asked.

Tamar called out, "Olivia July."

Bernadine saw the disapproving look Agnes shot her old friend Tamar and the way Tamar rolled her eyes in response. Bernadine hoped this didn't turn into an ancestral catfight.

Malachi stood up and announced, "No disrespect to the Ancestors, but I want to nominate somebody who's living. Somebody whose dedication to this town has been proven, and has given her life's blood to this place and its kids. I nominate the name: the Marie Jefferson Academy."

All hell broke loose. People jumped to their feet applauding, whistling and cheering. Marie dropped her head into her hands and her shoulders shook as she cried. Bernadine noticed that Agnes didn't appear to be totally down with the choice but she did applaud. However, Tamar was on her feet clapping wildly.

Trent said, "I think we just named the school. Get up here, Ms. Marie."

Marie Jefferson walked across the diner accompanied by thundering, roof-raising applause. The kids were cheering loudly as well. As she stood now at Trent's side, Marie's smile was as wide as the moon, and tears streamed down her cheeks. "Thank you," she choked out. "Thank you. I thought Mal was talking about Bernadine."

Laughter greeted that, and Mal shouted, "Wrong!"

Bernadine had been wrong too in not wanting Mal to be party to the school's naming because of what he'd named the diner. If the truth be told, since moving to Henry Adams, she'd been wrong on numerous occasions about Malachi July, the man, so she just added this latest instance to her growing list. Naming the school after Marie was a wonderful choice. Last summer at Marie's sixtieth birthday party Bernadine had been impressed by the many former students who'd either flown in or drove in to be a part of the festivities. The affection and respect shown to the teacher that day was something Bernadine would always remember.

And so it was official. The students of Henry Adams would be attending the Marie Jefferson Academy. Trent asked Marie, "Do you have anything you want to say?"

"I do. Would Jack James and his son please stand up."

Jack got to his feet. Eli followed grudgingly.

Marie said, "Jack is our new teacher."

He was greeted with enthusiastic applause. He blushed a bit and gave each part of the room a nod of thanks.

Trent said to him, "Welcome to Henry Adams. Everybody make sure you go over and introduce yourselves, make them feel like family."

Trent looked to Marie. "Anything else?"

Wiping her tears away, she shook her head.

Trent brought the gavel down. "Meeting adjourned!"

The jukebox was cranked up again. Shorty Long began wailing "Function at the Junction," and everyone mobbed Marie to offer congratulations. A pleased Malachi looked across the diner at the smiling Bernadine and acknowledged her with a wink. The atmosphere inside the diner felt like the old days. Folks were dancing, eating, and en-joying themselves. Not only had they named the school, but the new Dog and Cow was hosting its first celebration, and that made Malachi July one happy man, indeed.

Bernadine could see Leo across the room seated alone, apparently taking it all in. Again, she wondered what he hoped to accomplish being there. When his eyes met hers he dipped his head in greeting. She rolled her eyes. It was a free country, she supposed, and she couldn't ban him from a public place just because of who he was, but she didn't have to be happy about his presence, and she wasn't.

Jack James was impressed and amazed by the outpouring he was receiving. People from all over the diner were lining up to greet him, and he'd never seen anything like this in his life. He doubted he'd remember half the names but he didn't think it mattered, they all just seemed intent upon letting him know how glad they were to meet him and his son.

Eli didn't know what to make of all the goings-on either, so he tapped his dad on the shoulder and said, "I'm going outside to get some air. I'll be back."

Before he could reach the door, he was stopped re-peatedly by a thousand people it seemed like, all of whom wanted to shake his hand and tell him their names. He didn't have to turn around and look to know that Tamar was watching so he made nice.

Once outside he blew out a breath and looked around. Not that there was anything to see. It was dark, and the cold night air made him almost want to head back inside. Kansas wasn't anything like southern California weather-wise. One more thing for him to adjust to, he thought bitterly.

The door behind him opened, bringing with it the sounds of another old school tune playing on the jukebox, and two kids.

"Hey," the shorter one said. "Name's Amari. This is Preston."

"Hey," Preston echoed.

"Hey," Eli replied disinterestedly.

"Welcome to town."

"Some town."

Preston asked, "Where you from?"

"South L.A."

"You really from there, or just somebody claiming, like the suburban kids back home always claiming to be from Detroit?" Amari asked, his voice skeptical.

Eli stared. "What's it matter to you?"

"It doesn't really, but you're either perping or you're real."

Eli was busted, but couldn't figure out how the kid knew the truth. "You from Detroit?"

"Born and raised."

Eli looked at Preston, who responded, "Milwaukee."

"What in the world are you doing in Kansas?"

Amari answered by saying, "This is where we live now."

"How do you stand it?"

For a moment neither of the kids said anything, then Preston said, "It's not that bad. Tamar's ice cream alone is worth the price of admission."

He turned to them, "And what's the deal on her? Is she some kind of witch?"

"No, but she can make you think she's one if you get

on her bad side. Last thing you want to do is wake up the dragon."

"Tell me about it."

"Look," Amari said, "We didn't come out here to bother you, or get all up in your business, but you look like you got some issues. If we can help or you have any questions, let us know. We'll be around."

"Yeah," Eli replied.

They went back inside.

Eli looked up at the moon and after a few shivering moments alone, followed the kids back inside.

Smokey Robinson and the Miracles were crooning "Ooo, Baby Baby," and some people like Lily and Trent were coupled up slow dancing. Standing by the kitchen door and watching them were Malachi and Rocky.

"No offense to you, Rock, but they make a nice couple."

"Yeah, they do."

"You handling it okay?"

Rocky knew she could tell him the truth about her feelings, they'd been friends and neighbors for as long as she'd been alive. "On one level I am. I mean, we did break things off when I got married, but when I got back here yesterday, a part of me was thinking maybe we could hook up again and he'd finally admit I was the one. But guess not."

Mal nodded understandingly.

"I hated her back in high school."

"Really? Why?"

"What was there not to. She was the Fabulous Fontaine. Perfect grade point. President of the National Honor

Society. Wore all the right clothes. Held the state record for girls' hurdles in track, and she was Trent's girlfriend."

"I didn't know you had issues with Lily."

"Yeah, well, and you know what the worst part is?"

"No, what?"

"Talking to her today, I don't even think she remembers me."

Mal couldn't hide his smile. "Nothing like hating on somebody who doesn't know you're alive."

"Correct. So, I'm done. Gonna move on with my life. Preferably without any more male attachments."

"You'll find someone worthy one day."

"Don't want anybody. I'm through with men, present company excluded."

"Aw come on, Rock. Don't be so hard on us."

"I'm not kidding, Mal. First it took me most of my life to find somebody to marry and we know how that turned out, and did I tell you why I came back?"

"No."

"Was asked to leave the truck program because I had to bust the instructor in the head with a wrench."

"What?"

"He kept thinking my boobs were his personal property. Kept trying to touch me. Warned him off the first time, but when he grabbed me again, I let him have it. Sent him to the emergency room. Twenty-five stitches and a cracked skull."

Mal chuckled. "Good for you."

"Yeah well, there were plenty of witnesses to his harassment so the school offered me a big fat settlement so I wouldn't sue. May sue them anyway once I stop being mad."

The song was over and they both watched Lily and Trent smiling at each other like two people in love. In response to the applause, Lily and Trent bowed, and the next song up was Charlie Wilson and the Gap Band singing the hip-shaking "Gotta get up early in the morning to find me another lover . . ."

But Mal was focused on Leo, who appeared to be making his way over to Marie. "What the hell is he doing here?"

"Who?"

"Bernadine's ex. See the man talking to Marie?"

She did.

"I'll see you later." And he went off to investigate.

Leo waited until most of the crowd had drifted away from Marie Jefferson before making his approach. He wanted to congratulate her on her new honor and to see if she was really as pretty up close as she appeared to be from where he'd been sitting across the room. "Ms. Jefferson?"

Marie looked away from the hilarious sight of Bing Shepard doing the bump with the wife of one of his farmer buddies. "Yes."

"Name's Leo Brown. Just wanted to congratulate you on your honor."

"Why thank you. Have we met before?"

"No. I'm visiting."

"Leo is my ex husband," Bernadine said, suddenly appearing at Marie's side.

"Oh, really?" Marie said, looking from Bernadine to Leo.

Mal walked up. "He bothering you, Marie?"

She drawled, "Hard to tell since the man's barely had time to say more than a few words."

Bernadine wasn't sure whether she was being chastised but it sure felt that way, so she glared at Leo and said, "Excuse me for butting in."

"No problem," Marie replied.

Bernadine departed but Mal stayed put.

Marie said quietly, "Mal?"

"Yeah?"

"Bye."

His lips tightened, but after giving Leo a sharp look, he made himself scarce.

Leo said, "Pretty protective."

"Yeah they are. So, Leo Brown, what can I do for you?"

"Would you have dinner with me?"

Marie studied him for a moment. "Are you trying to make Bernadine jealous?"

"No. I'd just like your company and maybe get to know you."

"Why?"

"I just would."

She assessed him a bit longer, then made her decision. "Okay. I'll bite. When?"

He shrugged. "I don't know. Tomorrow?"

"That's fine. Here. Seven. Dutch."

He grinned. "Gotcha."

"Oh, and Leo. If this is about you trying to stir something up with Bernadine, I'll have Malachi dump you in a manure pit. You got me?"

"Yes, ma'am."

"See you tomorrow."

He nodded.

As the exuberant Leo made his way across the crowded diner and over to the exit, more than a few pairs of eyes followed his departure closely, but he paid them no mind. He had a date with Marie Jefferson and he'd be back tomorrow, seven o'clock sharp.

CHAPTER
12

In the dream, Amari and the hawk were driving again. The GPS said they were still traveling west. It was dark this time, so he couldn't see the landscape, but the convertible's top was down, the music thumping, and the moon was fat and bright. Suddenly, a tall, old, dark-skinned woman appeared in his headlights. She was standing in the center of the road. He hit the brakes. When the car stopped, the hawk let out a loud call, raised its wings, then flew out and came to rest gently on her shoulder. The woman stroked the hawk's head and fed it a strip of meat. They appeared to talk for a moment, though Amari couldn't hear what they were saying. She was wearing a long brown skirt. It had brightly colored symbols all over it and it brushed her bare feet. Her blouse was brown too, and on her head she wore a strange-looking, red head wrap that had a bunch of feathers sticking out of it.

Next thing he knew she and the hawk were in the seat beside him.

"Hello, young July," she said. Her smile looked familiar but he couldn't place it.

"Hi. Who are you?"

"I'm called Tamar."

"You don't look like Tamar."

Another smile curved her lips. "Drive on young July and all will be well."

Amari had no idea what that meant but he put the car into gear and continued the drive into the night.

Amari came down to breakfast that next morning and found his dad watching over a skillet of bacon on the stove, and the O.G. at the table reading a newspaper.

"Morning," Amari said as he took a seat.

"Morning," both men replied.

Amari said to Mal. "Thought you'd be over at the Dog this morning."

"Nope. Now that Rocky's back. I can go back to my gentleman's life of leisure. Just teasing. I'm going over later."

Trent rolled his eyes and asked Amari, "Sleep well?" He walked over to the table and set down a plate filled with fragrant strips of the now done bacon.

"Had this really weird dream."

Mal leaned his paper down. "Scare you?"

Amari shook his head. "No, it had this old lady in it, and this hawk. Had a dream about the hawk before, but the lady was new. She said her name was Tamar. She didn't look like herself though. Called me young July."

He saw Mal and Trent share a silent look.

"What?" he asked.

Trent was scrambling eggs. "Did she say anything else?"

"Just gave me her name and then told me all would be well."

Mal smiled. "Wow."

"What?" Amari asked urgently. "Do you know who she is?"

Trent brought a bowl of fat yellow scrambled eggs to the table, then took a seat. "Sounds like the first Tamar."

"Who?"

"Our Tamar's great grandmother."

Amari's mouth dropped. "Her name was Tamar too?"

Mal put some of the eggs on his plate, "Yep. Legend has it, she used to walk in the dreams of her children."

"That's crazy."

Trent said. "Nope. Make sure you tell our Tamar about her."

"Why?"

"Because far as I know, Old Tamar has never talked to her."

"Is it going to make her mad?"

Mal answered. "Hope not. Pass the pepper, would you?"

Amari complied, all the while wondering where he could get a dream book so he could figure out what this all might mean.

After breakfast, Amari went next door to hook up with Preston and found him home alone. "Where's the colonel and Mrs. Payne?"

"Airport. She's flying to Chicago today."

"You didn't want to go?"

"No. I mean I did, but figured they didn't need me

standing around watching." Preston took in Amari's subdued manner and asked, "What's up? You look pensive."

"Pensive?"

"Like you got something on your mind."

"Yeah. Had a dream last night. The hawk was back, and he had an old lady with him that dad says has been dead for probably a hundred years."

"Whoa."

Amari told him about the dream, and the woman who called herself Tamar, then what Trent said about her.

"Freddy Krueger showed up in people's dreams too. Remember him?"

"I know, but it wasn't like that, at least not this time."

"You're creeping me out, so how about we finish up the proposal for the parade?"

"Sounds good."

They got out the paper they had everything written on. "Doesn't look like it's gonna cost Ms. Bernadine anything," Preston said. "We may have to pay for those flag things you wanted, but just to have a bunch of people march down Main Street shouldn't cost much."

"Did you ask the colonel about the Blue Angels?"

"No."

"Why not?"

"Because he's too busy right now dealing with Mrs. Payne."

"But you are going to ask him, right?"

Preston hesitated.

"Come on, man. Tell him this is the kinda stuff dads are supposed to do."

Preston wasn't so sure about that, but nodded. "Okay. I'll ask."

"Good. Now, who signed up to be in the parade after the meeting last night?"

Preston surveyed the list. "Mr. Bing and the Black Farmers. Your O.G., Mr. Dobbs and the Buffalo Soldiers. Tamar said to add the Historical Society, and Zoey and Devon."

"Zoey and Devon? What are they going to do?"

"They just want to be in the parade."

"Okay. I guess that's okay. We're off to a good start, but I want the parade to be bigger than that. With that little list it'll last all of maybe ten minutes."

"I know. Tamar has some of the old newspapers the college preserved for her. Remember she showed them to us last summer?"

Amari did.

"Maybe one of them has an article on the old parades and we can see what kinds of things they did and we can look online and see what other cities did in theirs."

"That's why you're the Brain. I never would've thought of that."

Preston beamed.

"So let's take our proposal over to Ms. Bernadine and Dad and they can look it over."

"Good idea but I can't go. The colonel wants me to stay here until he gets back."

"Why?"

Preston shrugged. "Said it had to do with safety. Doesn't want me leaving the house if no parents are here."

"What, he thinks you're gonna get hurt or maybe kidnapped or something?"

"I don't know. I think it may have to do with the dad thing he's learning how to do."

"Oh. That's okay then, I guess."

"Yeah. I'll humor him."

"I have my phone with me, so text me when he gets back."

"No problem."

While Eli slept in, Jack James was outside seated in one of the lawn chairs that had mysteriously shown up this morning. He assumed Tamar had provided them and he was grateful. It gave him the opportunity to sit in the silence and sunshine and think back on last night. He was still marveling over the meeting and the warmth he'd been shown. He'd been a bit worried about being accepted because of his race, but that didn't appear to be a problem. He and Ms. Marie would be getting together later so he could get a look at the new school. She told him that many of the items like desks and tables and chairs had already arrived and that there would be a community effort to get everything moved in after the ribbon cutting on Saturday. As far as he knew there was just a handful of students ranging in age from seven to fifteen, sixteen if he counted Eli. *Eli*. Thoughts of his troubled son weighed heavily. All he wanted for his son was peace but Eli didn't seem to want it for himself. The therapist who'd treated Eli for depression said he was stuck on Eva's death because he didn't want to move forward in life without her. Both Jack and the therapist agreed that moving forward was essential, though, otherwise he'd never heal. Jack understood Eli's anger at being uprooted from his friends, but for the past few months he'd been drifting into new relationships with people more bent on drinking and stealing than anything else, and Jack's worry for him was part of the impetus for leaving California. He wanted to take him away from an environment he found not only dangerous physically but dangerous to both Eli's spirit and future as well. Eli was a gifted sculptor but hadn't touched clay since his mother died. Although Jack wasn't an artist it seemed to him that bottling up a gift that way couldn't be good. No, he and Eli had never been as close as some fathers and sons, mainly because Jack had been raised in a home where academic achievement was the only thing celebrated, so he had no idea how to coach Little League or how to fish. He couldn't fix a bicycle chain or tell you whether a baseball glove was worn on the right hand or on the left. What he did know was that he'd been blessed with a wonderful, talented son who had his mother's eyes, and no idea that his father loved him, nor did he seem to care.

But the peace Jack wanted for his son was the peace he wanted for himself. He was battling not only a broken heart, but also a guilt that said that maybe they'd hadn't tried every avenue in the search for a cure. Eva worked in a bookstore and he was a college professor. Neither's health insurance plan had been the best, so all the experimental drugs and therapies the doctors wanted to try hadn't been covered, so for the last year and a half of her life, he'd worked from sunup to sundown, teaching more classes than he'd ever done in the past in order to amass the money needed to pay for her drugs and her care. He knew Eli felt as if he'd neglected him, but Eva had been the love of Jack's life and he'd been hell-bent on doing whatever it took, if it meant she'd live to grow old with him, but she hadn't.

And now here he sat in the peace and quiet of the plains in a tiny town called Henry Adams. He could very well have wound up teaching anywhere; he'd just wanted to leave California because losing her hurt so much it was hard for him to breathe, let alone go to work every day and face the bright young faces of his students who had their entire lives ahead of them. In the end, he'd resented them, their freshness, their optimism, their dreams. The day he buried his wife, the world stopped, and all Jack could hope for was that one day soon, the Good Lord would take pity on him and his son and help them find a way to get it started again.

Seated at the kitchen table, Preston heard the garage door close and looked up from the Stephen Hawking book he was reading. The colonel entered the kitchen minutes later. One of the things Preston had learned early on as a foster kid was how to read the moods of the adults in his life, especially the drunks and the ones who liked to beat on kids. Both kinds were dangerous and could take a kid's life if the kid wasn't careful. That wasn't the situation he was in presently with the Paynes, but the colonel always wore such a poker face, Preston found him hard to read. Like now for example, Preston couldn't tell if the colonel was sad or glad that Mrs. Payne was gone. "Everything okay?"

"Yes. Her flight was on schedule and she should be flying out about thirty minutes from now."

"When will she get to Chicago?"

"It's a short flight, so probably early afternoon. She said she'd call when she arrived."

Preston was pleased to hear that. He liked Mrs. Payne a lot and would want to know that she was okay.

"Anything special you want to do today?" he was asked.

"Like what?"

"I don't know. Like father and son?"

Preston thought for a moment. "Can we just sit here and talk?"

"Sure."

He took a seat on the other side of the kitchen table and asked, "What shall we talk about?"

"Do you think you can call somebody and get the Blue Angels to fly over for the parade?"

Barrett paused and stared with confusion. "Parade? What parade?"

"Oh that's right, you and Mrs. Payne weren't at the meeting last night. Amari's going to have an August First parade. He's in charge and I'm helping."

Barrett was skeptical about Amari's ability to be in charge of anything. "Do Ms. Brown and Trent know about this?"

"Yes, sir."

"Why the first of August?"

"It's a special day in African-American history." Preston went on to explain why the date was celebrated and added some of the information he'd found online that day. "Back in the day there used to be a lot of August First parades and rallies all over the country. Do you know where New Bedford, Massachusetts, is?"

"Can't say that I do."

"Me either, but in 1849 seven thousand people came to an August First anti-slavery rally there. Another town in Ohio, I forget the name, had two thousand people, both Black people and White people."

"So Henry Adams used to have these parades and rallies too?"

"Yes. Tamar had some pictures from the one in 1882."

"Very interesting. Who's going to be in ours?"

"So far we have only a few marchers." Preston recited the list of names and organizations who'd signed up so far.

"I didn't know Malachi and Clay were in a Buffalo Soldiers Memorial Unit," Barrett said. "I'll have to ask them about becoming a member. The Ninth and Tenth Cavalry paved the way for military men like myself, but why the Blue Angels?"

"I think Amari thinks they'll make the parade really tight. Ms. Bernadine said that if the parade turns out good, we might have one every year. So, do you think we can get them?"

"They set their schedules a couple of years in advance, I'm pretty sure."

"Which means they're probably going to be someplace else on August First."

"Probably."

He sighed disappointedly. "Okay. I'll let Amari know when I talk to him."

"But maybe we can get them to come next year or the year after that."

Preston brightened. "That works."

Barrett did have a connection to the precision flying team and planned to make a few calls, but he kept that to himself for now. If things worked out, the boys would be surprised, and if not, they wouldn't be disappointed. "Is there anything else I can help with?"

"Not sure right now, but would you really help out?"

"Didn't I just say that?"

"Oh, yeah, you did. Sorry."

Barrett sighed. "Preston, one of the things I want you to know about me is that if say something, believe that I'm saying it honestly, because what comes out of a man's mouth should be truth. Maybe it's because I'm military or was raised in the military." The moment he said that, memories of his affair arose and called him hypocrite. The insight was sobering.

"What was that like?"

"What was what like?"

"Being raised in the military."

Barrett had just boasted of his honesty, and now, in order to back that up and not be hypocritical again, he had to speak of things he'd rather not. "Being truthful about this kind of stuff may be the hardest thing I have to learn about being a good parent."

"Appreciate that. If you don't want to talk about it, it's okay."

Barrett smiled wistfully. "Thanks, but I'm fine. Growing up in the military was hard. Every time we had to move to a different base that meant starting over in a new school, making new friends, adjusting to new neighbors, officers, teachers."

"Sounds like foster care."

Barrett went still and studied Preston's solemn eyes. "Never thought about it in quite that way before."

"Plus, you had a dad who beat on you and your mom. Sounds a lot like foster care."

"So you do understand."

"Totally."

Barrett viewed the young man across the table and realized Sheila had been right. Coming to Henry Adams was about changing lives, but not just Preston's. Barrett's personal paradigms were shifting too.

They talked for a long while about Barrett's many deployments and Preston's many foster homes.

Preston asked, "You know about the fire I set, right?"

"Yes. A copy of the police report was in the paperwork we received on you from Ms. Brown, but it didn't say why you did it."

"Because the foster mother wouldn't buy me an inhaler."

"You're kidding?"

"Wish I was. She didn't care. All she wanted was that monthly check and getting me an inhaler was a hassle, she said."

Barrett was appalled.

Preston smiled ruefully as he stared unseeingly at the wall. "I had a real bad asthma attack one afternoon, but had to wait for her to come back from getting her nails done before she would take me to emergency. Then she spent the whole ride there and back time telling me I didn't need an inhaler and dogging me about my weight."

"Did you tell your worker about her?"

"Yeah, but no clue what happened. She's probably still

fostering, though. Not enough good families open their doors to kids like me, or Crystal and Amari, so the state has to put up with the crappy ones that do it strictly for the cash."

"That's unbelievable."

There was silence for a long moment as Preston thought back on that portion of his life. He turned back and whispered through the emotion filling his throat and heart. "I was going to die there, Colonel. I had to set the fire to make the state move me to another home."

"I'm not judging you, son. Not at all. You did what you felt you had to do."

Preston wiped at his wet eyes. "Damn, I'm crying. Hate that."

"It's okay," Barrett said fondly.

The two of them looked into each other's eyes for a moment, and Barrett said, "Thanks for talking to me, Preston. This was a good idea."

"I think so too."

"I know a little more about you."

"Same here."

Barrett reached across the table and held his fist out. Preston did the same and placed his fist against his dad's.

"*Semper fi*," Barrett pledged softly.

"*Semper fi*," Preston echoed.

At the Power Plant, Bernadine, Lily, and Trent read over the parade proposal while Amari sat in a chair and looked on.

Trent asked him, "Are you planning on selling food?"

"Yeah. I'm going to talk to the O.G. and Ms. Rocky, and Tamar and her girls too."

"What about bathrooms?"

Amari stared, confused.

Bernadine said, "Honey, folks are going to need to use the facilities. Are you going to open up your bathroom at home?"

"No," he declared as if he found the idea crazy.

Lily grinned. "Stop by my office, Amari, and we'll talk to the construction crews and find out where they get their Porta Pottis. Should be easy enough."

Bernadine asked, "How many people do you think will be coming?"

Amari shrugged. "Maybe just the folks around here."

"So, say a hundred?"

"I guess."

Amari realized she was thinking of stuff he hadn't, and now understood the need for oversight. "Anything else you think I need to put in the mix?"

The adults looked to each other but no one had anything else to add, at least for the moment.

Trent said, "Something else is bound to come up, so we'll let you know."

Bernadine said, "Again, this is a great idea, Amari. You and Preston might want to print up some flyers explaining the history behind August First, so that folks will understand why it was celebrated."

Amari liked the sound of that. "Okay, so the parade is good to go?"

Trent nodded. "Good to go, but keep us in the loop, okay?"

"We will."

Trent asked, "So where are you off to now?"

"The Dog to talk to O.G., then make a quick run out to see Ms. Genevieve, and then home."

"Why are you going to see Genevieve?"

"Think I figured out a way to thank her for all her help with my reading."

"That's nice, just remember to check in when you get home."

Amari nodded.

"And be careful," Trent added.

"I will. "

Once Amari was gone, Trent asked, "How much do you want to bet that we're not going to be kept in the loop?"

"Depends on how much you want to lose," Lily replied.

Bernadine cracked, "All I ask is that we don't wind up back in court."

Riley Curry didn't want to wind up back in court either, which was why he, Cletus, and Chocolate were on the move. It had taken them a lot longer than he'd anticipated to drive across the state from near Abilene where they began to the Texas-Louisiana border, mainly because he'd traveled the back roads in an effort to avoid the big interstates where Texas Rangers might be on the lookout. What with having to stop at fast food places three, four, sometimes five times a day to feed the hogs, he felt like he'd been driving for weeks, and lord knew, he was tired of driving.

"I'm too old for this," he muttered.

He was also too old to go to jail, he reminded himself, so he quit his grumbling and turned his mind back to the drive.

He'd decided on Florida. Although he'd never been there, he knew they had good weather. His mind drifted to Eustasia, but not wanting to think about the pain she was probably in, he settled his thoughts instead on Genevieve. He still held her responsible for this whole mess. If she hadn't left him, none of this would have happened. He knew it wasn't right to be so uncharitable, but he hoped she was worried sick about him.

Genevieve wasn't worried at all. In fact, she swept into Bernadine's office shortly after Amari's departure, took a seat, and announced, "I need a lawyer, Bernadine."

"What kind?"

"One who handles divorces. I'm divorcing Riley, and his hog."

Bernadine hid her smile. "Let me make a few calls."

A short while later, Bernadine had a name and a number.

Genevieve took the information, thanked Bernadine, and swept out with such force, Bernadine was surprised the papers on her desk weren't blowing around. Genevieve had gone from doormat to damn mad since seeing Riley and the hog wedding on TV, and all Bernadine could do was applaud.

On the heels of her departure, Trent stuck his head in Bernadine's door. "What's up with Genevieve? She stormed by me just now like she was on her way to give somebody hell."

"She is. Riley. She wanted a name of a divorce lawyer."

"To be expected I guess."

"Yep. So, what can I do for you?"

"Need to talk to you." When he quietly closed the door behind him, Bernadine's eyebrow rose. "Must be something serious if you're closing the door."

"I don't want Lily to hear. Do you have anything planned that you may need her for, say, the last weekend of the month?"

Bernadine checked the calendar on her phone. "Doesn't look like it. Why?"

"I want to take her away for a long weekend."

"Well, now. Stepping up your game, are you?"

He chuckled. "You sound like Amari."

"Where are you going?"

"Thinking maybe we'd drive down to Topeka. Have some dinner, maybe catch a movie."

"Topeka," she echoed doubtfully.

"Sure. You got something against our state's capital?"

"Of course not, but this is going to be your first overnight, right? Not that I'm keeping track of your business."

"Well, yeah,"

"And you want to take girlfriend to Topeka."

"You have a better idea?"

"Yep. How's San Francisco sound?"

"Real good, but we can't drive there and back in a weekend."

"No, but you can fly."

"Last-minute tickets will cost me an arm and a leg."

"You don't need tickets. I have a jet, remember?"

He stared.

"And I have a place on the Bay where you can stay, and a driver I keep on retainer who knows the city and will take you anywhere you want to go. I'll even spring for dinner."

The look of sheer wonder on his face made her smile.

"But—"

"But what? You'd prefer Topeka?"

"I can't fly around in your jet."

"Why not? Obviously you don't know how much you and Lily mean to me. In the last year, you've worked your butts off for this town. Sending you to San Francisco is only a small token of my appreciation. And besides, you all being in love is too cute."

He dropped his head and grinned.

"So? Deal?"

"Why do I try and argue with you? Yeah. Deal."

"Excellent. You and Lily figure out when you want to go and I'll take it from there."

"I don't know what to say, except thanks."

"No thanks needed. It's my way of thanking you. Just make sure I'm invited to the wedding."

"Now you're really sounding like Amari."

"Great minds think alike."

"You're one of a kind, Bernadine."

"I am that. Now, go get your plans together and let me know."

He gave her a nod and departed.

Bernadine sat back and smiled. Trent and Lily had been given a second chance at love and she was honored to be able to play a part in making sure they got it right this time. She'd told Amari that he and the kids had been given a second helping of life too, and it appeared second

chances were going around. Sheila Payne was eyeing a
second chance, as was Genevieve in deciding to serve Riley
with divorce papers. Roni Garland had taken her second
chance by reclaiming her place in the music world. Even
the Dog and Cow had taken on a second life. She knew that
something had to be in the air for Leo to show up out of
the blue begging for another chance, but more importantly,
what in the world had he been up to talking to Marie last
night? She hoped it had been nothing more than pleasant
conversation, even though Marie made it plain she hadn't
needed Bernadine's help. Thoughts of Marie and Leo aside,
she moved on to the town's newest residents: Jack and Eli
James; talk about a second chance. Her first impressions
were that they really needed a dose. And they'd come to
the perfect place; hadn't Henry Adams offered her a second
helping as well?

Her thoughts drifted to Malachi. Lord knew the man
moved her, but a part of her deemed it much easier to just
keep saying no to his pursuit of her affections. Why do
something hard like opening herself up to him, when it
was far easier to maintain the status quo? She had a full
life. She had Crystal, her friends, her Bottom Women sisters, and Henry Adams. Why risk messing up the balance
by bringing a man into the mix? Her picnic with him was
tomorrow evening and she was half tempted to cancel, but
if Sheila Payne, Genevieve Curry, and Roni Garland could
make the decision to dive off the high board back into the
pool of life, why couldn't she? Surely she had more fortitude
than Sheila and Genevieve combined, at least on the surface, but inside? The jury seemed to be still out. She sighed.

Since meeting Malachi, she'd all but convinced herself that because she was Superwoman she didn't need a new man in her life, but in reality, even Superman needed Lois Lane. That being said, she decided not to find an excuse to cancel the date with him. Instead, she'd let God drive and see what happened.

CHAPTER
13

Sitting in his office at the D&C, Malachi was thinking about their date too, but not because he was afraid of the unknown. His worry lay in the differences in their circumstances. Although Bernadine had never been one to flaunt her money in a way that shamed folks, what business had he even thinking he could make her happy? He was a small-town boy and had just enough money to get by. He'd lived in Henry Adams his entire life and had only been gone for an extended period of time on two occasions; the first being when Uncle Sam drafted him for Nam, and the second when he'd been forced to work in the Oklahoma oil fields after the county confiscated his vet's license for being so drunk he'd given Cletus a tranquilizer instead of the antibiotic the hog needed, knocking Riley's pet out for nearly a week.

Bernadine, on the other hand, had traveled all over the world and seen places he'd probably never have the opportunity to. Yet he was stubborn enough to think he could make her happy but then again, maybe he was suffering from delusions of grandeur. He'd seen her ex. Leo Brown probably wore gold drawers. A man like that could buy her anything in the world. All Mal could offer her was a smile, someone to talk to when times got hard, and a shoulder when she needed it. Like everyone else in town, he knew that hers was the hand that turned the world, and he'd witnessed how tired it made her sometimes. He also knew from personal experience that the way things looked on the outside didn't always mirror what was going on inside and that's what concerned him about her. Granted, she had Crystal, but he didn't see Crys opting to live out the remainder of her life in Henry Adams just so Bernadine wouldn't be alone in her old age. Bernadine also had Lily, but if Trent had anything to do with it, Lily would be his wife probably before the year was out.

One of the most important things Mal learned while in recovery from being a 24/7 drunk was that you shouldn't measure life by what you do or what you have materially. All that truly mattered were the relationships you have with the people in your life. Bernadine Brown was a pretty high-powered force of nature, and he wasn't sure if he could explain why he wanted to be in her life in a way that wouldn't make her go off on him, but he cared enough about her to risk trying. For sure, she didn't think she needed anyone, but he was convinced that she did.

"You okay, O.G.?"

Mal swung his chair around to the door to see Amari standing there. "Yeah. Why?"

"You were staring off into space looking pensive."

Amusement sparkled in Mal's eyes. "What do you know about the word *pensive*?"

"Learned it from Brain. He said it means you got something on your mind."

"I do, but nothing to be worried about. What brings you by?"

"Been thinking about Ms. Genevieve."

"Again? Don't you have enough on your mind right now with this parade and your quest without adding Genny to the mix?"

"Yeah, but I still want to do something nice for her, somebody should, and I owe her for helping me learn to read. Thinking about asking her to the movies on Saturday night."

"The movies? Like a date?"

He shrugged. "Not really, but I guess."

"You planning on proposing too?"

Amari looked at him like he'd been smoking crack. "No. I just want her to know I appreciate her."

Mal couldn't wait to see Clay's face when he told him Amari was moving in on his woman.

"So, do you think it's a good idea?"

"Young gun, I think it's a great idea. Shows you got heart."

"Thanks.

"You're not planning on driving over and picking her up, are you?"

"No, sir."

"Good answer. Genevieve doesn't drive, so you'll have to figure that out too."

"Maybe I can get Ms. Marie to drive her into town, or have Dad pick her up."

"Sounds like a plan."

"Thanks, O.G. Knew I could count on you to help me think it out."

"That's all you needed?"

"Yep."

"Okay. See you later."

After he made his exit, Mal shook his head and made a mental note to sit beside Clay at the movies on Saturday night. He didn't want to miss a minute of this.

Because Preston was at home with the colonel, it didn't take all day for Amari to pedal out to the Jefferson's place where Ms. Genevieve was staying. When he got to the house and saw Tamar sitting on the porch with Ms. Agnes, he almost turned the bike around and hightailed it out of there, but figured he'd only have to explain to Tamar later why he ran, so he parked his bike by the porch and took in a deep breath. "Hey, Ms. Agnes. Hey, Tamar. Is Ms. Genevieve here?"

"Yes, she is," Agnes said. "I'll get her." She walked to the screen door and disappeared inside.

"How are you, Tamar?"

"Fine. You?"

"Had a dream last night about a hawk, and a woman Dad and O.G. said was the Old Tamar."

She stilled. "Really. Tell me about it."

Once he finished the tale, he added, "O.G. said she's never talked to you as far as he knew, and you might be mad. Hope you're not."

"I'm not, but it does make me curious. Do you know anything about your parents?"

"Nope. Why?"

"Just wondering. How about we talk about this next weekend when we do your quest."

"Sure. I was wondering when it would be."

Ms. Agnes returned. Behind her were Marie and Genevieve, who peered curiously at Amari for a moment before asking, "You wanted to see me about something, Amari?"

"Yes, ma'am, but, um, can we talk privately?"

"Why sure. Come on inside."

The eyes of the other women made Amari very self-conscious as he climbed the steps to the porch, so he avoided looking at them directly when he followed her into the house.

"Now, what is it?" she asked kindly.

"I've been trying to think of a way to say thank you for helping me with my reading, so I'd like to take you to the movies on Saturday."

Her smile was a mixture of surprise and delight. "The movies?"

"Yes, ma'am."

"Oh my goodness. What are we going to see?"

"Well, the kids' part is *Transformer*. It's about a race of robots who look like cars and planes and—"

"I've heard of it but not seen it. And what's the second feature?"

"I'm not sure."

"Doesn't matter," she replied while holding her hand to her heart as if overwhelmed.

"So, are you saying, yes?" he asked, unsure.

"Yes, Amari, I am. You are so sweet to do this. Are we going Dutch?"

"Dutch?"

"That means I pay for my ticket and popcorn, and you pay for yours."

"No. I'm paying. I have some money saved up from my allowance."

"Are you sure? I can pay my own way if necessary."

"I'm sure."

"Thank you, Amari." Her voice went soft and trembled a bit. "This is the nicest thing anyone has done for me in a very long time."

The tears in her eyes were making Amari's chest tighten up and want to cry too, so he decided it was time to go. "I know you don't drive, so can Ms. Marie bring you to the center?"

"I'll ask her, but don't worry, I'll get there even if I have to walk or ride a bike."

Her smile made Amari feel better. "Okay, well, I need to get back. I'll see you Saturday, Ms. Genevieve."

"I'll see you Saturday. You be careful riding home."

"I will."

They both walked back out to the porch. Amari said his good-byes, retrieved his bike, and pedaled off.

Marie asked, "What was that all about?"

"I have a date."

Tamar asked, "A date?"

"With whom?" Agnes wanted to know.

"With that gallant young man on the bicycle."

They all stared speechless.

"Think I'll go up to my room and pick out something special to wear."

Marie chuckled, "Lord. That boy. What are we going to do with him?"

"Make him family, is all I know to do."

"Remember you said that," Marie warned, smiling.

"I will."

A short while later, Tamar left the Jefferson place to head home, and as she walked, Amari was on her mind. Admittedly, she was a bit jealous that the Old Tamar had seen fit to visit him when she'd never done the same for her own namesake. Tamar knew the boy was special, but not so much so that he'd be blessed by the clan matriarch. The Julys rarely spoke to folks outside the family about the mystical Tamar, mainly because people thought the Julys were either crazy or kidding, or both. But they weren't. Stories of her power and wisdom had been passed down through time just like the July name. Those who didn't believe would never be convinced, so the Julys didn't bother. The family *knew* and therefore had no need to explain it to others. And now Amari *knew* too. That was mind-boggling to Tamar. The Old Tamar had never been known to walk in the dreams of anyone outside the family, and it made her wonder if that meant that lovable little car thief was already family. Lord. She had a lot of questions but no answers. She'd have to talk to Trent. Maybe he could find a way to trace Amari's birth family to determine if there was a link.

Since Bernadine Brown came to Henry Adams all kinds of odd circumstances had been occurring. Who knew that

Colonel Payne was not only Black Seminole like the Julys but was a descendant of Deputy Sheriff Dixon Wildhorse, an old friend of Neil July? Who knew that mute Zoey would turn out to be a musical prodigy, and strangest of all, that Malachi would stop chasing after women young enough to call him grandpa. Bernadine Brown had been responsible for many a blessing since buying up the town, and they were still rippling across lives like a stone skipping on water, and now even the Old Tamar had shown up. Tamar couldn't wait to see what happened next.

Eli had no interest in seeing the new school, so he left his dad there for the meet-up with Ms. Jefferson while he walked down to road to the diner. Being from southern California he rarely walked anywhere and was surprised at how odd it felt at first. A horn blew suddenly, startling him. Looking over he saw a green pickup slow down, just enough for the driver, a man, to wave and call out, "Hey Eli."

Eli started to ignore him but when Tamar's disapproving face floated across his mind's eye, he raised his hand and called back, "Hey!"

The truck moved on and Eli shook his head. *Hicksville.*

There were no sidewalks connecting the school to the area near the diner so he was walking on the edge of a dusty road. He passed piles of rubble that may or may not have been buildings and houses at one time interspersed with stretches of wide open plains. A few more pickups passed him, each honking a greeting. In California you didn't honk at strangers, but he guessed the folks around here didn't consider one another that, or him either apparently.

He walked past a boarded-up movie theater. It was in almost as bad shape as the piles of bricks and stone, yet it was still standing. His artist's eyes took in the detailing on the roof and in the old brick and stone façade and guessed it had probably been quite grand once. He saw the words *Henry Adams Hotel* chiseled in ornate letters in the stone above the tired-looking movie marquee and realized the building had been repurposed, which made him wonder when the town had been large enough to need a hotel. It was easy to see by the emptiness around him that it hadn't been in the recent past, but he found the nineteenth-century architecture interesting.

The next person to call his name was the kid Amari. He was riding his bike in the direction Eli was walking. Pedaling beside Amari was the other kid, Preston.

"You going to the Dog?" Amari asked.

Eli nodded.

"We'll save you a seat."

"Okay, thanks." In reality Eli wanted to tell them to get lost but they were the closest people to his age that he'd met so far, and at that point he would've kept company with anyone who knew the difference between Beyonce and Lady Gaga and under the age of thirty.

When he finally got to the Dog, he walked in and saw Amari and Preston talking to a girl sitting in one of the booths. The boys waved him over.

As he approached he heard Amari say to the girl, "Sorry about your mom's passing."

"Me too," Preston added solemnly.

"Thanks," she replied, then looked up at him. "And you are?"

"Eli James. My dad and I just moved here. He's the new teacher." Eli had no idea how old she might be because the heavy makeup and the gold weave made a determination difficult.

"I'm Crystal. Sit if you want."

Eli took a seat but Amari and Preston acted as if they weren't sure the invitation included them so they hesitated for a moment until she said, "You too."

Because they'd arrived after the breakfast rush and before lunch the place was empty except for Rocky and Siz, whom he'd been introduced to last night, and the waitstaff eating lunch at the back of the diner. Mr. July came out of the kitchen carrying a tray holding a burger and fries and set the plate down in front of Crystal, along with a tall glass filled with Pepsi and ice.

"Thanks, Mr. July."

"No problem. Hey, young guns. You all hungry?"

Eli and Amari nodded, but Preston had his attention glued on something or someone else. Mr. July waved a hand in front of the kid's face. "Preston. Do you want to eat?"

He jumped. "Oh, yes, sir."

Eli saw Amari grin.

"What can I get you?"

They all ordered duplicates of what Crystal was having and July walked back to the kitchen.

Eli asked Preston, "Who are you staring at?"

Amari answered, "Rocky."

Crystal said, "I met her earlier. She seems nice but she's way too old for you, Preston, so forget about it."

"She's still pretty."

Crystal rolled her eyes and checked out her plate. "I know I'm supposed to be polite and wait until you all get your food, but my fries will be cold by then, so . . ." She grabbed the ketchup bottle on the table and hit them up. "How old are you, Eli?"

"Sixteen." He found himself wondering what a girl with gold hair and so much makeup was doing living here. She looked more L.A. than Kansas. "How old are you?"

She eyed him over her big fat burger for a long moment. "I'll be sixteen in September."

"You grow up here?"

"No. I was born in Cleveland. Moved here last summer."

"Do you like it?"

"I suppose. How about you?"

"Not at all."

"Why not?"

Her direct questioning reminded him a bit of Tamar. He shrugged. "Not my kind of lifestyle."

"Not a lot to do here, that's for sure, but it's okay. We have fun sometimes."

"Doing what?"

"Nothing big, but we do. What's your dad like?"

"He's okay I guess, as long as you're not his kid."

"What's that supposed to mean?" Preston asked.

"He's real nice to his students but could care less about me."

Crystal studied him. "So you all don't get along?"

"No. Can't wait to turn eighteen so I can move out."

"He beat on you?"

"No," he replied as if the question was stupid.

"He ever starve you?"

"No."

Amari asked, "He ever hold your hand on a hot iron until you told the truth?"

"What?"

Amari held up his right hand to show the puckered skin on his palm.

"Damn, Amari," Crystal said quietly."You never mentioned that before."

"I know, but hey, it healed up pretty good for not being taken to the doctor afterward."

A puzzled Eli looked between them and received a cool smile from Preston, who said, "We're all foster kids, Eli. Your dad is probably a thousand times better than the dads we had. Not that I ever knew mine."

"Or mine," Crystal and Amari said in unison.

Mr. July returned with their food, and after his departure they started in on their meals.

Eli was still stuck on the last conversation. "So, you're all here as part of some kind of experiment?"

"Sort of," Crystal said, and took a few minutes to tell them how they'd come to be in Henry Adams. "Ms. Bernadine is one of the richest women in the world."

Amari took a bite and said around it. "She's got this really sweet all-white jet."

"And she owns this whole town," Preston added.

Eli was half thinking he was being punked, but they all

seemed to be telling the story so seamlessly. "So how many kids in all live here?"

Crystal said, "Just five. The three of us, and Devon and Zoey. Zoey is mute. She was homeless and got attacked by rats after her mother died and hasn't said a word since."

"My mom died about two years ago."

"Mine died day before yesterday."

Silence filled the table for a moment, then Crystal asked, "How's your dad dealing with it?"

Eli shrugged. "Okay, I guess. We don't talk a lot."

"Why not?" Crystal asked, "Ms. Bernadine and I talked for a long time. She's been helping me deal."

"All my dad's been doing is getting on my case."

"About what?"

"My grades. Me sleeping over with my friends instead of coming home, and everything else seems like. He really blew up when he had to come get me from the police station last month."

"Why'd you get picked up?"

"Friends and I stole a car."

Amari put down his burger and asked, "What kind?"

"A Taurus, I think it was. We were just riding around. The owner didn't even press charges so I don't know why he was so mad."

"You stole a Taurus?" Amari echoed skeptically.

"Yeah," Eli replied proudly. "Had it most of the night too."

"Why didn't you just take a minivan? How lame are your friends?"

Crystal chuckled softly and Preston smiled around the straw in his mouth.

Eli didn't get it. "What are you talking about?"

"I'm talking about standards, dog. Zoey and Devon could steal a Taurus."

"I suppose you're going to lie and say you stole what, a Ferrari?"

"No, I'm not going to lie and say I stole *a* Ferrari. Going to tell the truth and say I stole *three*."

"You're lying."

Amari threw up his hands.

Crystal was still chuckling.

Preston said, "Eli, meet Amari 'Flash' Steele, Detroit's most wanted car thief. They called him Flash because that's how fast he could steal a car."

Crystal added, "When we flew to Detroit in Ms. Bernadine's jet to pick him up to come live here, boyfriend was in handcuffs and leg irons for trying to steal a Viper while he was with the police, at the airport."

Eli stared. "How old are you?"

"Eleven. Be twelve next month."

Once again, Eli thought he was being punked but the kids seemed dead serious.

Amari added. "And been to juvie three times."

Eli stared again.

Crystal offered some advice, "You should probably eat before your fries get cold."

The stunned Eli looked around at their amused faces, then began eating again.

The kids held on to their booth throughout the hectic lunch hour, talking and ordering ice cream for dessert.

As the lunch crowd came and went and the diner began to quiet once more, July came over and said, "Need help in the kitchen, buckaroos."

The Henry Adams teens groaned silently but after a second or two got up to follow him into the kitchen. Eli didn't move.

July said, "I'm talking to you too."

"I'm not working in the kitchen."

"Yeah, you are," he countered. "Around here, everybody pitches in when needed and you are now part of that everybody, so come on."

Eli blew out a breath to show he wasn't pleased, but he got up too.

Jack was touring the new Marie Jefferson Academy with Ms. Jefferson and Ms. Brown, and he was blown away by the place. He'd been expecting a small humble school, not this top-of-the-line, million-dollar beauty. In addition to the classrooms there was a media center with wall-mounted plasma monitors, science labs, art facilities, a woodworking shop, and an Olympic-sized, in-ground swimming pool.

Marie was saying as they turned a corner into another hallway, "It's all on one level and partially below ground because of the tornado risk. That's how we lost the old school."

"All this for six students?"

Bernadine said, "We're planning for the future so we built it to hold about one hundred, but for now, you and the students will have plenty of room."

"So will it be operating as a one-room school, or do you want the children separated in different rooms by grade, which to me seems a waste of space, time, and energy."

Marie told him, "This is your school, Jack. Your call."

They continued down a hall and past a kiva with a stage. The room was filled with workers fine-tuning the audio system.

"Jack, Marie tells me that in addition to your college teaching credentials, you have a K–12 certification with an emphasis on the math and the sciences?"

He nodded.

"Good, because Preston wants to grow up to be Dr. Neil deGrasse Tyson."

"The African-American astrophysicist?"

"That's him," Marie replied, enjoying the surprise on his face. "And since I can barely spell *astrophysicist*, he'll be all yours."

"Wow."

Marie chuckled, "Wow is right. Preston is by far the brightest student I've ever had the pleasure of knowing and teaching, and I've been in the classroom a long time."

Jack looked around at the sparkling new equipment in the second science classroom. "When I interviewed with you, Ms. Jefferson, you said this was a small rural district so I expected a small rural school. I don't mean to be nosy or rude, but how did you all pay for all this?"

Bernadine said simply, "I wrote a check."

He stared with wide eyes.

Bernadine glanced at her watch. It was eleven-twenty.

"How about I call over to the diner, see if we can get some lunch delivered, and you can hear the story."

Still mute, he nodded.

While Jack turned to Marie with wonder all over his face and received an answering pat on the shoulder and an understanding smile, Bernadine stepped outside the classroom for a moment and dialed up the diner.

Malachi answered the phone. "This is the Dog and Cow. Mal speaking."

"Hey," Bernadine said.

"You're sounding awfully good this afternoon, Ms. Brown."

"And you need to stop all this flirting," she warned him playfully in response.

"And here I was just getting started. What can I do for you?"

"Is it possible to have some lunch delivered to the school for Jack, Marie, and myself? I know it's late."

"For you, it's never too late. What would you like?"

"Hold on." She went back in to take their orders, then returned to the call.

Mal listened to the selections before saying, "I'll have this down to you quick as I can."

"Thanks, Mal."

"You're welcome, pretty lady."

Bernadine ended the call and sighed. Realizing she was acting like a girl in high school, she shook off the remnants of what his voice did to her each and every time, and stepped back into the room to rejoin the others.

CHAPTER
14

To Bernadine's surprise, Rocky delivered the lunch.

"I just needed out of that kitchen for a while," she explained. "Here you go." The box in her arms held sandwiches, salads, and drinks.

"Thanks, Rock," Marie told her as she searched for the corned beef on rye she'd ordered.

Rocky, with her brickhouse stature and beautiful face, was accustomed to men staring, so she didn't pay much attention to Jack's muted interest. "Are we all set here?" she asked.

Bernadine handed out the last of the food. "Looks that way. Thanks so much. Have you decided whether you want the trailer or not?"

"Yes. I do. Okay if I move my stuff in this weekend?"

"Yep. Let me know if you need any help."

"Will do, but I think I can manage. Should I let Tamar know?"

"Might be best."

Jack found the conversation quite interesting and so said to Rocky, "Sorry to butt in, but are you moving into the other trailer on Tamar's land?"

"Looks that way."

"Welcome to the neighborhood."

Rocky gave him a noncommittal "Thanks," before turning back to Bernadine and Marie. "Gotta go. I'll see you all later."

She shot Jack a quick glance and made her exit.

"Tough lady," Jack said.

"She's earned it," Marie replied.

Jack waited for her to say more but when she didn't, it piqued his curiosity. What was Rocky's story? But he didn't ask. He was new here, and it was going to be a while before he earned his way into learning the town's secrets, and he was okay with that.

His thoughts of Rocky were set aside as they ate lunch and he listened to the story of Henry Adams's revival as he'd been promised by Bernadine. When she finished the tale he found himself staring and speechless once again. "That must've been some kind of serious divorce settlement if you were able to buy an entire town."

"And have plenty left over for all the trimmings," she responded with a twinkle in her eye.

"So, how much larger do you envision the town becoming?"

She shrugged. "No idea, but if we start to lose the closeness, it'll be time to pack up the bulldozers and call it a day."

Marie nodded her agreement. "This is a very special place, Jack. I told you the history on the phone. We want to pass that legacy down just as it was passed down to us. Can't do that if we don't know our neighbors."

"True. I grew up in Boston. Town that big, it's impossible to know everyone."

"Here, we can," Marie said. "And we'd like to keep it that way."

Jack had no idea if he could thrive in such a simple isolated environment but after all the upheaval in his life, simple and isolated was something he was willing to try.

"Any other questions for me?" Bernadine asked as she gathered up her lunch trash and placed it the large bag the sandwiches had arrived in. "I need to get back to my office."

"Which is where?" he asked.

"Power Plant. When you go out, turn right. Red, round building. You can't miss it. Town administrative offices are there. Stop by later today or tomorrow at the latest, so that Lily can get your payroll info plugged into the system. School starts next week, and after dealing with the Big Three—Crystal, Amari, and Preston—you'll definitely want to be paid."

His smile met hers. "Thanks for everything, Ms. Brown."

"Call me Bernadine, and your house should be ready in about ten days. Feel free to go over and take a peek. You'll be next door to the Paynes."

Jack was still blown away by the fact that he and Eli were being given a brand-new house as part of his salary, for free. If this was a dream he sure didn't want to wake up.

"Okay," Bernadine said as she shouldered her purse. "I'm outta here. Jack, thanks for signing on. You're going to like it here."

"I'm hoping to."

With a wave, she was gone, and he and Marie began their plans for the school's upcoming semester.

An hour later, when Jack finally drove away from the school, his head was spinning from everything he'd seen, heard, and talked about with Marie, but it was a happy spin. He was actually looking forward to teaching again. At the moment, he wanted to drive over and check out the house, but decided to go and get Eli first, so that he could see the place too.

He found him inside the diner drying pots and pans in the kitchen along with Amari, Preston, and a teenage young lady he assumed to be Crystal, one of the students he hadn't met. To say Jack was surprised to see Eli working was an understatement, but that Eli looked angry was not surprising.

As soon as he saw Jack he said angrily, "You want to tell these people that there are child labor laws in the real world."

Before Jack could counter that a little honest work didn't constitute child endangerment, Rocky walked in.

"Hope you don't mind that I put him to work. The wait-staff has been busting their butts since I took over, and a few of them missed class today, so I gave them the afternoon off. I didn't need permission to turn those three into kitchen help," she explained, indicating Crystal and the boys. "But I suppose I should have asked you about Oscar the Grouch over there."

"Quit calling me that."

Rocky just smiled. "Kid's got a real loving attitude."

"Tell me about it. How much longer will you need him?"

She glanced around at the small mountain of pots and pans still waiting to be dried and put away. "Another half hour."

Crystal cracked, "Be less if he'd stop whining and start drying."

Jack liked Crystal instantly. He asked Rocky. "Is there any coffee?"

"Dad, get me out of here!"

Amari snapped. "Dog, shut up. Tired of you complaining."

"Make me," he grumbled. "If you think you can."

Crystal shook her head, "Tamar's going to love you."

"They've already met," Jack related.

"How'd that go?" Amari asked.

"Tamar, one. Eli, zero."

Preston swung his dish towel inside a big roaster. "Glad I missed that."

"Me too," Amari tossed back.

Eli's lips tightened further but he kept drying.

Rocky said to Jack, "Go get a seat and I'll bring your coffee."

"Thanks."

While waiting for his coffee to arrive, Jack mused on this decidedly different place called Henry Adams. Unlike in the popular culture of TV and movies, kids didn't rule here—adults did, and it made him feel as if his tireless and sometimes thankless campaign to make Eli do the right thing in life wasn't in vain. He'd be supported here, he thought, as would Eli. According to Bernadine, all the children in town had spent time in foster care, yet here, out in the middle of nowhere, they were living in paradise, surrounded by adults dedicated to the proposition that they be loved—unconditionally. Eli could use that, as well.

"Here's your coffee."

Rocky's voice and presence broke into his thoughts. "Thanks. Um, since we're going to be neighbors, I'd like to formally introduce myself, Jack James."

"Rocky Dancer."

"Pleased to meet you."

"Same here."

"Will you have dinner with me sometime?" Jack had no idea that was going to come out of his mouth, but now that it had, he cursed himself and waited for a reply.

Arms crossed, coffee carafe in hand, she looked him over for a moment and asked, "That your standard line for women you just met?"

"Well—uh, no. Look, I had no idea I was going to say that to you. It just sort of escaped, somehow."

"Escaped?"

"Yeah." He wanted to climb under the table.

"Thanks for the invite but I think not."

"Didn't mean to offend you."

"I'm not offended. I'm just not interested. Can I get you anything to go with the coffee while you wait?"

"No. I'm fine. Thanks."

"Okay. I'll send Oscar out when he's finished."

"Appreciate it."

Wondering if he should look down to see if his head was rolling around on the floor, Jack smiled and brought the rim of the cup to his lips.

* * *

The work in the kitchen was finally completed, and to compensate them, Rocky gave Amari, Crystal, and Preston ten dollars each.

Eli got five. Confused, he looked at the bill, then at Rocky. "You give me five and them ten?"

"You did half the work. The rest of the time you were either whining or slowing around so much the other members in your crew had to take up your slack. Half the work, half the cash."

He tossed the bill onto a table. "Keep it," and he strode out.

Rocky let him go and said to the others. "I really appreciated your help in here. Thanks a lot."

Sounding annoyed, Crystal asked, "What is up with him? Everybody's got issues, but he's just rude."

Rocky shrugged. "I know. Let's make sure it's not contagious."

They gave her a smile.

Preston said, "Usually when we're volunteered for stuff like this nobody ever pays us, so thanks a lot."

"Yeah," the other two echoed.

"My daddy always said, an honest day's work, an honest wage."

Amari asked, "You think you can teach that to Tamar?"

They all laughed.

"See you later," Rocky said.

They nodded and departed.

As they walked back into the main dining room, they

spotted the angry Eli sitting silently in a booth waiting for his dad to finish his coffee.

Ignoring him, Amari said to Crystal, "Did Ms. Bernadine tell you about the parade?"

"Yeah."

"I think I may need your help. That okay?"

"Depends on what you want me to do."

So he told her about the flags he wanted her to make.

"Sounds easy, but where are you going to hang them? We don't have a bunch of buildings on Main Street anymore like back in the day."

"We can put them on the school, the rec center, and here maybe?"

"It's your parade. I'll do some drawings and you can take a look at them, how's that?"

"That's good."

"I'll work on them when I get home."

"Thanks, Crystal."

Eli's dad came over and asked Preston, "You live with the Paynes, right?"

"Yes. Do you want to talk to them?"

"No. Ms. Brown said Eli and I will be living next door to you, and I wanted to get a quick look at the house, but I don't know where it is."

"I'm on my way home, so you can follow me and Amari in your car if you want."

"I'd like that. Thank you."

Crystal had a better idea. "Why don't you just give me a ride home, Mr. James? That way you'll get there faster. Me and Ms. Bernadine live right across the street from him."

"That would make it faster, but Amari, where do you live?"

"Next door to Preston."

"So we're going to be neighbors. I like that. How do you feel about the teacher living so close by?"

Amari broke it down as always, "Do we have a choice?"

He laughed. "Let's roll."

They trooped toward the exit with the sullen Eli bringing up the rear. The kids waved to Rocky standing at the cash register (Eli didn't), before stepping outside into the sunshine and fresh air but Jack stopped. "How much do I owe you for the coffee?"

Rocky looked up. "Nothing. Coffee at the Dog's always been free."

"Good to know." He knew he should move on, but he couldn't quite seem to make himself comply.

She waited and when he didn't say anything else, "Is there something else?"

"Yeah. I'm going to ask you again."

"I know."

He smiled.

She didn't.

Grinning, he left.

Rocky growled like a frustrated tigress and slammed the cash drawer closed with a force that shook the machine and counter.

"What the heck's the matter with you?" Mal asked, coming out of his office.

"Nothing."

"Oh, just exercising your lungs?"

She nodded tersely.

"Next time do it outside, or post a sign. You give a poor brother a heart attack."

"Sorry."

"Uh-huh."

He left and Rocky wanted to kick something. She was not going to be attracted to another man! She was not! Especially not one she'd only met today! Firm in that belief, she headed back to the kitchen but swore she heard the Ancestors laughing.

Riley was driving across the state of Louisiana and his gas was getting low. He knew he should stop and fill up, but Chocolate had been wailing and acting up since yesterday, and he wasn't sure what might happen if he did. He guessed she was homesick and missing Eustasia and wanted to go back to Texas. He knew this might happen, which was why he'd told Cletus bringing her along was a bad idea. She'd been so distressed this morning that when Riley stopped at McDonald's, she'd refused to eat her fast food breakfast sandwich; even tried to bite him, which was not like her at all. Mercy, he was in a heap of trouble. He had a mad hog in the bed of his truck, the police were after them, and by now Eustasia was probably home and fit to be tied. Nothing he could do but keep driving, so he did.

A few more miles down the road the needle on the gas gauge was hovering at empty so he pulled off the interstate to find a station. When got out to go inside and pay, both hogs put up a fuss, so on the way out he bought them a couple of snack cakes, in hopes the treat would satisfy them until he came up with a plan for their next meal. He was hungry too, but it was just about dinnertime and all the fast food places would be filled no matter where he went, so they'd have to wait and eat later because the less people saw them the better.

In the end, it didn't matter. As soon as Riley turned back onto the interstate, he could see Chocolate in the mirror trying to climb out of the bed. The sight scared him so badly that he swerved and didn't see the Louisiana Highway Patrol sitting on the side of the road until it was too late. He sideswiped the cruiser like a drunk driver at three in the morning. The roof's light began to spin, the siren wailed, and Riley Curry's Great American Adventure was done.

Leo was in the back seat of his limo being driven to Henry Adams for his date with Marie Jefferson. He'd been thinking about her nonstop since their conversation yesterday and he felt happier than he had in years. He couldn't put his finger on why, though. No amount of speculation had given him an answer. He was admittedly nervous; he hadn't had an evening with a woman old enough to know Aretha Franklin from Gladys Knight since Bernadine left him. His ex had been on his mind too. The way Marie had politely encouraged her and July to butt out last night had shown him that the teacher was a woman of confidence. He doubted Bernadine would mind her own business, however, but he hoped Marie would give him the opportunity to show her who he was in his life now, as opposed to who he'd been when he and Bernadine split. And no, he no longer wanted Bernadine back, because coming to Henry

Adams had offered him something he hadn't expected. For a man who'd been bemoaning his life seemingly just the other day, he felt rejuvenated. Last night's town meeting had surprised him. The sense of community, the common bonds the residents shared had touched him in a way that was also unexplainable. The little boy who'd invited everyone to church on Sunday and the other kid who'd given the announcement about the parade made him want to be a part of things too. After leaving town last night, he'd gone back to his hotel room and Googled Henry Adams on his laptop and the information the search engine turned up was astounding. The place was as historic as Williamsburg, but tied to the history of African Americans. He had no idea all-Black townships like Henry Adams had ever existed, let alone that he'd come across one alive and well in the twenty-first century. Its second chance at life was being funded and spearheaded by his ex-wife, and he envied her that benevolence because she was making a difference, not only in dollars but in commitment. Bernadine had always wanted children but during the early years of their marriage he'd keep putting her off because he thought himself too busy. By the time he realized it was too late to start a family, it really was.

Now, according to the CNN reports, Bernadine was a foster parent to a teenage girl Leo had yet to meet. He wondered if Marie had any children. Having no answer, he turned his eyes to the scenery moving by his window.

Moments later, they rolled past a hitchhiker holding a cardboard sign with the words *Henry Adams* written on it in big letters.

"Jason! Stop!" he called out to the driver.

Jason complied. "What's the problem, sir?"

"That guy we just passed is going to Henry Adams. Give him a ride."

"You sure?"

"Yep. He might be one of the residents."

"Okay," Jason replied skeptically and got out.

A moment later, Jason pulled open Leo's door and a Black man he didn't remember seeing at the meeting last night stuck his head inside and said, "Sure appreciate this."

"You're welcome. What's your name?"

"Otis. Otis Miller."

"You live in Henry Adams?"

"No, sir, but I'm hoping to find some work there. Unemployed right now."

"You wanted by the law?"

The man shook his head. "No sir."

"Take a seat up by my driver."

"Thanks a lot."

So Otis Miller aka Ray Chambers settled into the seat next to the driver and smiled to himself as the limo eased back onto the road and continued the journey to Henry Adams. So far, all the luck he'd needed to get to his daughter had fallen into place and the horizon looked bright. He'd ditched Anita's BMW back in the parking lot of a bar in Topeka, then hitched a ride with a trucker named Randy who spent the long haul across the state boring Ray with the details of his home-based poodle-breeding business. While he talked, Ray nodded in the appropriate places and noted the miles and miles of fields lining the highway dotted here and there with weary-looking, pay-by-the-hour motels, more Wal-Marts and small strip malls.

After Randy dropped him off at the closest exit to Henry Adams, he set out on foot. Now he was in a big black limo and he couldn't think of a more appropriate way for a player to ride into town.

CHAPTER
15

Bernadine got up Friday morning and made a pledge to herself that she wouldn't worry about that evening's impending date with Malachi. With all the work waiting on her desk, she figured she'd have no problem keeping the vow.

But when her workday began with a call from Malachi, it effectively shot her pledge to pieces.

"Morning," he said to her.

"Morning," she said with a soft voice and a smile. "How are you?"

"Wanting to see you, but until that happens, called to give you a heads-up."

"On what?"

"Man came into the Dog last night looking for a job, says he's an unemployed autoworker. Seems honest enough, but I'm having Sheriff Dalton run a warrant check just to make sure he's on the up-and-up. If he passes, think I'm going to offer him a job sweeping floors here."

"That's nice. Maybe he can do double duty as the school custodian, until we hire someone."

"I'll see if he's interested. Can't think why he wouldn't be though. Says he's looking for any work he can find."

"Is he local?"

"No. Michigan."

"How in the world did he get here?"

"Said he's been hitchhiking across the country, but got here courtesy of your ex. Leo picked him up."

"Was Leo on his way to town?"

"Yeah. He had dinner here with Marie last night."

"Excuse me?"

"I didn't stutter."

Bernadine sighed. "Lord. Okay. Thanks for letting me know, although Marie made it real clear she didn't want my opinion."

"Then don't give it."

"But he's—"

He cut her off gently. "Marie's grown, Bernadine. She can handle herself. Unless of course you want Leo back in your life."

"No."

"Then let this be."

She didn't respond.

"Bernadine?"

"I'm still here," she said glumly.

"I'll let you know what Dalton turns up on Miller. You haven't forgotten about our picnic tonight, have you?"

"No."

"Then stop pouting."

"I'm not pouting."

"Sure you are. I can hear it in your voice."

She smiled. "You're good for me, Malachi July."

"Been trying to tell you that since the first day we met. Glad you're starting to figure that out."

"Modest too."

"I'm a July. What can I say."

"Are all the July men swellheaded?"

"Yes, ma'am. Confidence is in our genes."

She laughed. "I have work in my genes and I need to get cracking."

"Okay. I'll see you later."

"Counting on it." And he ended the call.

Bernadine sat at her desk smiling for quite some time. He was good for her, she decided, and turned her attention to her laptop.

Preston and Amari hooked up after breakfast and sat on Preston's porch to talk about the parade. Preston's Internet search for other activities had turned up an interesting list that included everything from choir competitions to pet races.

"Pet races?" Amari asked.

"Yeah, people bring their pets and they race."

"That sounds fun."

"It does, but it wouldn't be fair to race their dogs against bunnies though."

"Yeah, but we could have a separate race for dogs."

Before Preston could respond, Amari said, "Or we could have one of those dog obstacle course contests they have on Animal Planet."

"I don't know about that. What would we have to do to have one of those?"

Amari shrugged. "Let's look it up."

Preston made a note.

"You think Ms. Roni would like to be in charge of the choir competition?"

Preston shrugged. "We could ask her. She'd probably know more about that kind of thing than us."

"Okay, write that on our list too."

"What else?"

Amari thought back, "I saw a bike parade one time where all the kids decorated their bikes and rode down the street. I remember it because I didn't have a bike."

"Been there."

"You want to have one for the little kids?"

"Yeah." And he put that on the list, as well.

"So, what did your dad say about the Blue Angels?"

"That they make their schedule years in advance."

"Oh."

"I know, but he said he'd see if maybe we could get on the schedule for next year or the one after that."

Amari was disappointed but glad that Preston had at least asked. "So, how's it going between you two?"

"Not bad. We've been watching DVDs, and he's teaching me to play chess. I miss Mrs. Payne though. Six weeks is starting to be an eternity."

"What do you think of Mr. James?"

"Too early to tell, but he seemed okay."

"Eli can go back where he came from."

"True dat. I wanted to smack him upside the head with a pot yesterday."

"I know. Appreciated the way Rocky called him out though."

"Tell me about it. He didn't look happy at all."

"Like he was going to do something about it. He's in Henry Adams. He'd better ask somebody."

Preston grinned and they went back to work.

All Eli wanted to ask was how to get the heck out of Dodge. He'd been in town only two days but felt like he'd been hating the place for a lifetime. His dad had driven into town to do something at the school, but Eli had passed on accompanying him. Belatedly he realized that might not have been such a great decision because now he was stuck at the trailer with no way to leave.

He'd also decided that he hated the other kids. They didn't seem to mind being turned into forced labor yesterday at the diner, but he did and he'd let that Rocky and Malachi know. Apparently Amari and the rest were too scared to express themselves, but he wasn't. Rocky tried to play him by giving him that lousy five dollars but she'd probably never had a kid toss her money back in her face because she didn't say a word to him when he walked out. The adults needed to recognize that he was different from their little robotic foster kids and wasn't going to play along with this crap. He was sixteen years old, from California, and he could think for himself.

Out of nowhere, his mom's smiling face floated across his mind's eye and the pain in his heart swelled. He missed her so much. He thought back on the stuff they used to do together and how she'd laugh, then he was at the funeral again standing next to his father. Next Eli knew he was crying and the tears were streaming down his cheeks. He wiped them away angrily, and when he looked up, there stood Tamar.

Without asking his permission, she took a seat on the step below him, and for a moment, the breeze rustling through the grasses was the only sound. Finally, quietly, she said to him, "You have to let go, Eli,"

"Of what?" She was the last person he wanted to talk to.

She seemed unaffected by the belligerence in his voice. "Your anger over whatever it is."

"What do you know about me?"

"Not much, really. Other than that you're mad as hell about something, and it's trying to eat you up inside."

"Why do you care?"

"Because you're one of mine, now."

"You're not my mom!" he snapped bitterly. "And you never will be."

She looked up at him. "I know, so how about you tell me about her."

Eli went back into his mind and the hurt got worse."She was funny and smart. She played catch with me, rode bikes with me, helped me with my homework, even though she was as bad at math as I was." The memory evoked a small smile even as he dragged his palms over his wet eyes.

"How long has she been gone?"

"Two years this September."

"That's not a very long time for a grieving son. You loved her a lot."

He nodded. "I miss her so much. So much."

"She misses you too, I'm sure."

"Do you think the dead can see us?"

"Some people say yes, others, no. Me, I'm in the first group."

He went quiet for a moment.

She asked, "So, let's say I'm right. What do you think your mom sees when she sees you now?"

"A pretty messed-up kid."

"Maybe, but I'm a real big believer in things happening for a reason, and I think you and your dad were sent here by God, the Spirit, maybe even your mom."

"Why?"

"To heal, find happiness again, start a new life. In my world love never dies, and even after death we are watched over and guided."

Eli looked out over the plains and wondered if what she was telling him was true.

"Eli, I'm not asking you to believe what I believe, but think about it when you get a chance. In the meantime, I'm making pancakes. You want some?"

As if a veil had been lifted, Eli saw the kindness in the piercing black eyes, something he'd never noticed before, so he nodded slowly. "Yeah."

"Then come on. You're going to have to help with the dishes when we're done, though."

"You don't have a dishwasher?"

"Don't need one. I have you all."

That truth garnered a smile and a shake of his head but he stood up and followed.

Back at the Power Plant, Bernadine ended a phone call and sat back in her chair. She'd just touched base with the Illinois mortuary holding Nikki's body to see if contact had been made with her family. The woman on the phone assured her that it had, but apparently no one in Nikki's family wanted to take on the expense or the task of a funeral, so a disappointed Bernadine gave the mortuary permission to bury Nikki at her expense. Because Crystal had no interest in attending a service, there would be none. The mortuary told Bernadine to pick out a headstone from their Web site and they'd order it upon receipt of her check. She sighed. No one, not even a crack addict, deserved such an ignominious end. The thought occurred to her then that maybe she could have Nikki's remains interred in a cemetery near town. That would at least make Bernadine feel better. She'd find a pastor to say a few words, and if Crys didn't want to go, Bernadine would stand at the graveside alone. Feeling the rightness in that, she picked up the phone, made a few more calls, and this time when she was done, she felt better.

Lily walked in and upon seeing Bernadine's sad face, asked, "You okay?"

"Yeah, I am." She gave Lily an update on what she'd been told about Nikki's family, and the decision she'd made in response.

"You did the right thing."

"I think so too."

"You're good at the heart stuff, you know."

"Am I?"

"Yep. Take the trip you're giving me and Trent to San Francisco, for example."

"He told you about that, did he?"

"Yes, he did." Lily walked over and kissed her on the cheek. "You're the bomb."

Bernadine grinned. "Got to keep you satisfied. Can't have you moving away looking for another job."

"Don't worry. With perks like these, you'll have to pry me out of here."

"Good to know. So when are you leaving?"

They discussed the dates they'd picked out, and that Lily's son Davis would be coming to visit for a week in July.

"Can't wait to meet him," Bernadine replied happily.

"I'd asked Devon earlier in the week if there was something special he wanted to do and he told me this morning he wanted to meet his big brother. Just talked to Davis, and he's tickled to death."

"Does he need a plane ticket?"

"No, Bernadine. He's making good money designing software. He can pay his own way."

"Just asking."

Lily chuckled. "You're something."

They were interrupted by the entrance of Sheriff Dalton.

Bernadine looked at the serious set of his weathered features and asked, "What's happened?"

"Riley and Cletus were apprehended by the Louisiana Highway Patrol."

"Finally."

"Yeah. They had that Texas lady's hog with them too."

"The one in the wedding video?"

He nodded. "Prosecutor will start extradition procedures soon as she can. They have to make arrangement to haul the hogs back too."

"Lord," Bernadine whispered. "Is the woman in the video going to press charges, you think?"

He shrugged. "Not sure. I was told she'd been contacted."

"Have you told Genevieve?"

"Stopped there first. She just smiled." He smiled as well. "Also, did a check on the new man, Otis Miller. He came back clean. Told Malachi."

Bernadine was glad to hear that. "Good."

"Gotta head back. Wanted you all to know about Riley. You ladies have a nice day." He touched his hat and exited.

'Well," Lily said. "Good news."

"Very good."

"And now that that's resolved, you can concentrate on your date tonight with Malachi."

Bernadine went still. "This isn't a date."

Lily crossed her arms. "What are you calling it?"

"Not sure, but it's not a date."

"You know you're pitiful, right?"

"Yeah."

"Just so you know. Have a good time."

"Thanks."

Bernadine was having trouble deciding what to wear. Malachi had specifically said, casual. As she looked through her vast walk-in closet she wondered if that meant no jewelry. Deciding he couldn't possibly have meant that, she ran her fingers down the labels on the seventy-five neatly stacked shoe boxes in her search for the navy blue snakeskin boots she'd picked up in Barcelona last week. She paused. Had it really been only last week? She'd returned home on Sunday night, but after all that had transpired since then, she felt as if a month had passed. And now here she stood making herself crazy by trying to dress to please a man instead of herself. Reason number one hundred and twenty-five why she didn't need a new man in her life.

"What are you doing, Ms. Bernadine?"

She looked out of the doorway to see Crystal standing there.

"Trying to find something casual to wear."

"Why?"

"Malachi has invited me to a picnic." She made her decision and grabbed a hanger with a pair of black jeans folded meticulously over it, and another hanger holding a long-sleeved, navy twinset with little rhinestones on the neck and cuffs.

"You're going on a date with the O.G.? Sweet."

"It's not a date."

"Who else is going? Trent and Lily?"

"No. Just us."

"Hate to tell you, but that's a date."

Bernadine moved past Crystal and laid the clothes on the bed.

"And if the O.G. wants to get his freak on, make sure he uses protection."

"Crystal!" Bernadine turned, stunned.

"I'm not playing. Nikki died of AIDS. You think she got

it eating at Mickey D's? I know about this stuff. You have any turpentine?"

"What? Why?"

"Old guys give you worms, so you're supposed to drink a glass of turpentine afterward before you go to sleep."

Bernadine didn't know whether to laugh or fall out in a faint. Surely teenagers didn't believe that, but apparently they did because she was talking to one. "If you drink turpentine you won't have to worry about worms, baby."

"That's what I mean."

"No, Crys. Turpentine will kill you."

"So will the worms. I always made the guy use protection and I stayed away from the geezers."

Bernadine cocked her head. "You're sexually active?"

"I used to be."

Bernadine responded with a whisper. "You're only fifteen."

"I was twelve the first time. Didn't like it."

Bernadine was speechless, but she supposed she shouldn't be surprised. Crystal had been trying to make it on her own since she was seven years old. Being raised in foster care had probably taken away most of her physical innocence a long time ago.

Crys asked, "Is this something maybe you and I should talk about?"

"I think so, yeah. Just so you'll have the right information."

"How about after your date?"

Bernadine nodded. "But it's not a date."

"Whatever you say, Ms. Bernadine. I'll get out of here so you can get ready."

"Crys?"

"Yes, ma'am?"

"I'm not mad at you or anything because of what you just told me."

"I know. You're not like that."

She exited and closed the door quietly behind her.

Bernadine stood in the silence and stared at the door for a very long time. Finally shaking herself free, she dressed.

Crystal walked outside and sat on the porch. One of the things she liked about Ms. Bernadine was that she could talk to her about just about anything, or at least so far. She looked across the street and saw Eli and his father checking on the progress of their new house. Although she'd only been around the new teacher one time, he seemed okay, but Eli was a mess. Yesterday when they were drying the pots at the Dog, she thought Preston was going to take a pot upside his head. And the way Eli acted with Rocky? Not only was he a mess, he was a disrespectful mess. She watched Colonel Payne step outside and walk over to where Eli and his dad were standing. She hoped he didn't talk smack to the colonel because that wouldn't be a good idea.

She saw Eli look over at her on the porch. He said something to his dad, and to Crystal's displeasure started across the street. *Now what?*

When he reached the foot of her steps, she asked, "What do you want?"

"To talk to you."

"About what?"

He looked off into nothingness in a way that reminded her of Preston. *Not again.*

He asked her finally, "Are you mad about your mom dying?"

"Yeah."

"You don't act like it."

"Is that what's wrong with you? You're mad because you lost your mom?"

"I guess. Yeah. So why aren't you acting mad?"

"I don't know. It hurts a lot, but it doesn't make me mad at everybody. It's nobody's fault that she died of AIDS."

"AIDS?"

"That's what I said, and being mad? So what. It's not going to make her be alive again. I deal with it best I can. Talking to Ms. Bernadine helped a lot though."

"That's what you said yesterday."

"It's the truth. Maybe you should talk to your dad."

"I told you, we're not close."

"Preston and the colonel are trying to learn how to be father and son. Maybe you and your dad can too."

"I don't know." He paused and didn't say anything for a few seconds, then looked up at her on the porch. "Tamar said she believes that when people die, they still look out for us."

"You talked to Tamar?" she asked with surprise. "When?"

"This morning."

"Bet you didn't talk to her the way you've been talking to everybody else since you got here."

"No, I didn't."

"Tamar's tough, but when she's not working you to death, or all up in your grill because you screwed up, she can be okay."

"Found that out. Do you think she's right about being looked after?"

She shrugged. "No idea, but she knows a lot of stuff. All I know is that acting like a jerk makes people think you're a jerk, so you might want to change channels. Folks don't play that around here."

"Yeah, I noticed." He then asked, "Do you really like it here?"

"Beats being on the street, and I got a family here. Never had a real one before, so it's pretty sweet being the big sister. Amari and Preston can be real annoying sometimes, but I know that if push comes to shove, they've got my back, just like I got theirs. As long as it's not every day."

He smiled at that. "Thanks, Crystal. Thanks for listening."

"You're welcome, but like I told Preston, 'Don't make it a habit.' People keep coming to me for advice, I'm going to have to start charging."

"Gotcha."

"Eli?"

"Yeah?"

"Welcome to the family."

He searched her face for a moment, then said, "Thanks."

"Now, go home and talk to your dad."

"Yes, Crystal."

As he left and crossed the street, she had to admit that he was kind of cute, for a White boy.

CHAPTER
16

H e's here, Ms. Bernadine."

"Thanks, Crys. Tell him I'll be right down."

Dressed in her black jeans, twinset, and matching snakeskin boots, Bernadine look one last look at her gorgeous self in the mirror and was pleased. Makeup was tight, hair was laid, and the gold around her neck, just the right touch. Ready, at least physically, she grabbed her black leather jacket and her tote and headed down to meet him.

He was seated on the sofa in the living room but rose to his feet at her approach. "You look good."

"Thanks."

She noted that he did too, in his light blue denim shirt, string tie, clean jeans, and polished cowboy boots. She glanced over to see Crys watching them with a knowing grin, and prayed she wasn't about to be subjected to another round of teenager dating advice.

However, all Crystal had to say was "Have a good time, you two."

"We will," he replied with his eyes riveted on Bernadine's.

His gaze was so intense she took in a deep breath to try and slow down her pounding heart.

He smiled and offered her his arm.

Wondering what in the world she'd been thinking to have agreed to this, she swallowed, took his arm, and let him escort her to the door.

Outside, he handed her into the passenger side of the freshly washed, old Ford truck, and as he closed her door and moved around to get in on the driver's side, Bernadine couldn't remember ever being so nervous. Crystal was on the porch watching. Roni was on her porch watching; Lily too. She wanted to yell at them to get back inside, but knew that would only make people think she'd lost her mind, so instead, she did her best to ignore them and their smiles and fought to draw in more calming breaths.

Once he was settled, he looked over at her from his seat behind the wheel and asked, "Ready?"

She nodded.

"We're going to a picnic, not a hanging."

"Would you just drive please?"

"Yes, ma'am."

He started the engine and after waving to the onlookers headed the truck away from the subdivision.

Saxophonist Grover Washington was on the CD player. The familiar strains of "Winelight" gave her something to hold on to instead of obsessing over the unknown. She was a wreck inside, a total and complete wreck, mainly because—a date at her age! And with Malachi July, aka the

Playboy of the Western Plains, of all people. The only man she'd ever been with in her whole life was Leo.

"Comfortable? I can turn up the heat if you're cold."

"No, I'm fine thanks."

"Music okay?"

She nodded.

When he didn't look away, she asked, "What?"

"Just checking you out. Wondering why you look so nervous."

"I'm not nervous."

"Uh-huh."

"I'm not." When he didn't respond, she asked, "Where are we going?"

"Thought maybe the creek on the edge of Tamar's land. There's a picnic table that's out there year round. And I have the food in the bed."

"Good."

She remained silent for the rest of the ride but couldn't help taking peeks at him as he drove. There was no denying that he was a good-looking man. The hands on the steering wheel were strong and sure and for someone sixty years old he was in great shape, so why was she so hesitant about accepting his company? Much of it had to do with being gun-shy after her divorce and knowing that Malachi had in the past preferred his women young and thin. She, of course, was neither.

When they arrived at the creek, it was nearly quarter of eight and the sun was dying fast. Dusk-fed shadows were creeping over the open land, and she wondered again at the sense of this. In a few minutes it was going to be too dark to eat outside.

"Guess I should have planned this for later in the summer," he said as if reading her mind. "Getting pretty dark."

When he looked her way, she replied amusedly, "You think?"

He grinned. "We'll just sit in the truck. Let me get the food."

A few moments later he was back, picnic basket in hand. Trying to open the lid and remove the food and plates within the small confines of the front seat was comical. His elbow kept accidentally hitting the horn, and the initial blast scared the heck out of them. More maneuvering resulted in more blasts, reducing them both to fits of laughter.

He noted, "We keep this up and Tamar's going to drive down here wanting to know what's going on."

A chuckling Bernadine took the small plate he handed her. It was filled with Sizzle's now-famous spinach tarts and some tasty little meatballs. On the side were sliced apples accompanied by a great tasting ranch-flavored dip, a bowtie pasta salad, and some still warm cheese biscuits.

"This looks fabulous."

"Much better than the bologna sandwiches and potato salad I'd suggested."

Her plate balanced on her hand, she laughed. "I had more than my share of bologna growing up."

"Me too, but I still love it."

"You do?"

"Sure. Nothing better than a late-night fried bologna sandwich."

"Haven't had one of those in years."

"Come by one night and I'll make you one."

The thought intrigued parts of herself as she wondered how spending a late night with him might be, but other parts were just plain scared to death. "I'll keep that in mind." The food was wonderful. "If you ever decide to get rid of Siz, he can come work for me."

"He's good, isn't he?"

"Absolutely."

Their gazes met. In the silence that rose and filled the truck, she took a bold leap and asked, "What are we doing here, Malachi?"

"Talking about bologna sandwiches."

"Be serious. You know what I mean."

He shrugged. "Hoping maybe we can come to closure on a few things."

"Such as?"

"My wanting to spend more time with you."

She had no idea why his confession left her so heady; he'd made it clear from the first time they met that he was interested, but to hear it put in plain words . . .

"Cat got your tongue?" he asked quietly.

"A little bit."

"I'll wait."

He'd always had the ability to make her smile from the first time they met too. "I'm so used to doing things my way, I'm not sure I can handle a man telling me how to run my life."

"Who said anything about running your life? No way in the world I want that job. Too hard, too involved, and way too much work. I just want to be the person you kick back with; hang with. The one you can call day or night when you need to talk. The brother who takes you on picnics in an old pickup truck and lets you be Bernadine Brown, the woman, as opposed to Bernadine Brown, She's Got the Whole World in Her Hands."

That made her laugh.

"Besides, I got my own life to work on, and that's more than enough for this former drunk to handle."

She'd learned about his battle with alcohol last summer. At the time his candor had surprised her. Now he'd surprised her again with his take on how he wanted to fit into her life, and she found the approach both novel and tempting. "So if I say yes, then what?"

"We have a good time. I'll be yours exclusively and you'll be mine.

"Sounds simple enough."

"No sense in making it complicated."

She agreed. The last thing she needed was "complicated." Presently, her life had more tangents than a geometry class. What she needed was quiet and drama-free.

"So?" he asked quietly.

"A girl would have to be crazy to turn down an offer like that."

Humor curved his mustached lips. "And we know you aren't that."

"Not most of the time anyway." She looked over at the man who'd been wooing her in spite of her protestations since the day they were first introduced to each other by Tamar, and knew what she wanted to say. "My answer is yes."

"All righty, now," he said, sounding pleased. "Houston, we have ignition."

Their smiles met and Bernadine sensed the rightness of her decision melt away all the stress she'd been carrying since he'd invited her to this decidedly unique get-together.

"Then I propose we seal our bargain with a slice of Rocky's famous apple pie."

"And I second that."

As they ate, she asked a question she'd been wanting an answer to for some time. "What made you decide to be a veterinarian?"

"Found a young hawk with a broken wing. Didn't know a thing about caring for it, but I took it home and did my best."

"How old were you?"

"About Amari's age."

"So what happened?"

"It died, of course."

"I thought you were going to tell me that you healed it and it flew away."

"No, that's television. This was real life, but it made me want to learn how to doctor a bird if I ran across one again. I went to vet school, minored in raptors, but there's not much call for that out here if you're trying to make a living, so I ended up treating farm stock instead."

"Raptors are?"

"Birds of prey. Hawks. Falcons. When I was fourteen, I tried to talk Tamar into buying me one for Christmas, but you can pretty much imagine how that went."

She could. "Were you eventually able to get one on your own?"

"No. Between finishing school, being sent to Nam, and coming back married to Satan Alcohol . . ." His voice trailed off as if no further explanation was needed. He added, "Besides, training a bird like that is a full-time job."

"How much do they cost?"

He looked over to her face in the darkness. "Why?"

She shrugged. "Just curious."

"Uh-huh," he said skeptically, turning his attention back to the last of his pie. "I know you, Bernadine. Do not buy me a raptor."

"Who said anything about that?" she asked innocently.

"You didn't have to. Promise me, now."

"Can't do that. Suppose they're on sale the next time I'm in Neiman Marcus?"

He laughed. "Crazy woman."

"I'm just saying."

"No raptors."

"I heard you."

"I know, but why does that scare me to death?"

Smiling, she didn't say another word.

When dessert was done, they gathered up the plates and silverware and placed everything back in the basket.

"I should get you home," he said. "You have a lot to do in the morning."

"I know." The school opening was scheduled for tomorrow, but she didn't want the evening to end. "Can we do this again?"

"Anytime you like."

Silence rose up between them and their eyes met in the dark. When he leaned over and kissed her gently, it felt natural and right. As the kiss deepened, they drew each other closer, and the soul-filling emotion Bernadine had been so reluctant to embrace took hold. Finally, reluctantly, he eased away. She was left with her eyes closed and her heart racing. "You're a very good kisser, Mal July."

"That's in my genes too."

She chuckled softly. "Start the truck."

So he did.

When they arrived at her house, the porch light was on. Lights were on inside the other homes in the subdivision too, but as far as she could tell, neither Roni nor Lily were standing on their porches trying to be nosy. He got out and came around to hand her down. Once she was on terra firma again, he held on to her hand and walked her up the steps and to the door.

"I had a good time, Mal." And she really did. His holding her hand felt good too.

"Thanks for going." He gifted her with one last lingering kiss that left her shimmering. "See you in the morning. Night, baby girl."

"Night, Mal."

After leaving her on the porch, he drove away and Bernadine watched until the taillights of the old Ford disappeared into the night.

Inside, she found Crystal curled up on the couch watching a cooking show. "Did you have a good time?"

"I did."

"Did he kiss you?"

Bernadine cut her a look.

Crystal smiled. "Just kidding."

Bernadine took up a seat beside her, all the while thinking about Mal and his bone-melting kisses. "Anything happen while I was gone?"

"Nope. Just been plain old boring Henry Adams, but while you were getting dressed for your not-a-date . . ." She grinned. Bernadine grinned back, and Crystal continued, "Eli came over."

"What did he want?"

"To talk. I told him I'm going to start charging people for all this advice."

She chuckled. "What kind of advice did he need?"

"He had more of a question at first. Wanted to know if I was mad about Nikki passing. I told him I was, and that's when I figured that he was all angry and stuff because his mom had passed too."

"I was wondering if that had something to do with his bad attitude."

"It does, but he's taking it out on people and I told him that dissing everybody just made him a jerk."

"How'd he react to that?"

"After I broke it down like that he seemed okay with it. Not that I really cared because it was the truth."

Bernadine wondered if Crystal knew how special she was.

"Then I told him how much it helped me to have you to talk to about my feelings and stuff, and that he might try talking to his dad."

"Great advice. Do you think you got through to him?"

She shrugged. "Who knows, but at least he wasn't acting like a jerk. Said he had talked to Tamar some and I guess she made him feel better. He said she told him that when the people we love die, they can still watch us and guide us from heaven. Do you think that's true?"

"I don't know, but I like it."

"Me too."

Bernadine then told her about the decision she'd made surrounding Nikki's interment. Crystal twisted around so she could see Bernadine's face.

"You'd go to the burial all by yourself?"

"Yeah. Somebody should be there when she's lowered into the ground."

Crystal was silent for a few moments. "I'll go too, then."

"You sure? I'm okay going alone."

"I know, but if you can go, I can too. She was my mom."

"Thanks, Crys." She gave her a hug. "Nikki's spirit will probably like having you there." Bernadine turned her loose. "I'll let you know when everything's arranged."

"Okay, but what kind of family doesn't want to be bothered burying their own blood?"

"I don't know. Maybe they have their reasons."

"I didn't want to go because I thought it would just make me sadder, but you're right. She shouldn't be alone."

Bernadine leaned over and kissed her on the forehead. "You are a sweetheart."

She brightened. "Trying to learn from you."

"You get an A for this lesson."

"Thanks."

"I'm heading to bed. Are you going to the ribbon cutting for the school in the morning?"

"Yep. I still feel down but being in the house by myself only makes it worse. Seeing Amari and Preston today made me feel better, which is pretty wack, but hey?" and she shrugged.

"Then how about we go to the Dog for breakfast first."

"You just want to see the O.G., don't you?"

"No, I want to see a plate with breakfast."

"Whatever you say."

Bernadine yanked gently on one of Crystal's Crayola yellow braids. "I'll see you in the morning."

"Night, Ms. Bernadine."

"Night, baby."

Mal decided he'd had a real good evening with Bernadine and was looking forward to more. The kisses weren't bad either. When he walked into his small apartment attached to the back of the D&C, Otis Miller was chilling in the living room on a mattress on the floor.

"How'd your picnic go?"

"Real good. You doing okay?"

"Yep. Just watching the ball game. Cards are up by two. Seventh inning."

"You have dinner?"

"Ms. Rocky let me eat at the diner. Told me I could have three squares a day on her until I get my check. She told me about the school thing in the morning too. Thought I'd go check it out, if there's time after I'm done with breakfast cleanup."

"Good. You can meet Ms. Brown. She'll be paying your salary over at the school."

"This the lady you went out with tonight?"

"Yeah."

"You all tight?"

"Getting there."

"I wish you luck, then."

Mal grinned. "Thanks."

"By the way, thanks for all this. That truck driver sure knew what he was talking about when he dropped me off and told me to look for work here. He said you all were good people."

"Glad we could help you out. I'm going to put this leftover food in the fridge. Help yourself if you want. Plenty of pie left."

"Might just do that. Thanks."

After storing the remaining food, Mal walked back in and said, "I'll see you in the morning, man."

"Okay. Good night."

Ray heard July's door close and he grinned. He was sitting real pretty at the moment. Tomorrow, if everything worked out, he'd get to meet Bernadine Brown. He wondered what she looked like, not that it mattered. She could look like a toad's butt if the money was long and green. He wasn't worried about July having a previous claim either. If he decided to pursue her romantically, country boy July wouldn't stand a chance against the game of an ex-pimp like himself. Now he'd settle for just meeting her. After that, he'd lay low, check out the landscape, and go from there.

CHAPTER
17

On Saturday morning, Bernadine and Crystal drove over to the Dog. The place was bustling. On the jukebox, Undisputed Truth was warning anyone who'd listen about the dangers of backstabbing "Smiling Faces," and Bernadine moved unconsciously to the beat while she and Crystal waited to be seated.

Crystal said, "Looks like everybody had the same idea."

Bernadine agreed. Trent and Amari were sharing a booth with Preston and the colonel. Lily and Devon were eating with the Garlands and Zoey. In the back she spotted Tamar sitting with Agnes, Genevieve, Eli and his dad, and in the booth behind them, Leo and Marie. Bernadine was not happy. Granted she didn't want Leo back in her life, and yes, Marie was a grown woman capable of deciding on her own who she wanted to be with. But Leo! Bernadine didn't understand that, or why Leo was sniffing around. Surely he wasn't trying to make her jealous, but if he was intent upon making her angry, he was doing a fine job.

She saw Malachi weaving his way expertly through the packed place with a coffee carafe in his hand, pausing here and there to freshen people's brew. Memories rose of last night and she smiled inwardly while wondering how soon they could get together again.

The hostess Kelly hurried over. "Sorry to keep you waiting. We're short on staff, so I'm hostess and doing tables. This way please."

As they followed her to the now empty booth in front of Trent and his party, Kelly looked back and asked Crystal, "How old are you?"

"Be sixteen soon."

"If you want to make some money waitressing, we could sure use you."

Bernadine watched Crystal consider that. They took their seats, and Kelly left to bring coffee.

"What do you think of me working?"

"As long as it doesn't interfere with your schoolwork, I don't have a problem with it."

Crystal paused for a moment to wave to Zoey across the room. "Be nice to have my own cash when we go shopping."

"I like the sound of that."

She smiled. "No. Sometimes, I want to buy stuff for you, but I don't have any money. I have my allowance, but not money I made on my own."

"That's sweet."

Kelly returned with coffee. They gave her their breakfast orders and continued their conversation.

Behind them, Barrett Payne was looking skeptical at

the idea Trent had just proposed. Edwin Starr was on the jukebox growling his way through "War!"

"Isn't that more of a woman's thing?" Payne asked.

Trent shrugged a bit. "I suppose, but that doesn't mean we can't put our own spin on it."

"A fathers' support group?"

An enthusiastic Amari broke into the conversation. "Yeah. You could all have tee shirts with your names on the back and on the front it would say . . ." He paused to think for a moment and then, nodding his head rhythmically, said, "Dads Incorporated."

A surprised Trent declared, "I like that, Amari."

"Yeah," Preston said. "Dads Inc. I like it too."

Amari added, "You all could meet, have a good time, and learn how to be good dads together."

Trent chuckled. "Guess we have a name."

"I guess." Barrett's skepticism could still be heard. He glanced over at Preston, who turned away to the window, but not before Barrett saw the disappointment in his eyes. Realizing belatedly that as far as Preston was concerned, he'd screwed up by not being more open to the idea, he tried to make amends, "How about we ask Garland too? And from what I've been hearing from Preston about Eli, Jack could probably use a cold one and a pat on the back once a week as well. So let's include him, if he's willing."

Seeing the way Preston smiled in response touched Barrett inside in a place that seemed to want the boy's approval. He didn't know what to call it, but he knew it was there.

Trent nodded. "We have a deal."

Malachi brought Bernadine and Crystal their plates. Walking with him was a thinly built, dark-skinned man she didn't know.

Mal set down their food, saying, "Bernadine, want you and Crystal to meet Otis Miller. He's working here at the Dog, and Crys, he'll be working at the school too."

"Nice to meet you," Bernadine said pleasantly. She'd been looking forward to being introduced.

Crystal said, "Pleased to meet you."

He gave them a nod. "Nice meeting you ladies too."

Bernadine had a strong feeling that she'd seen him before. "You look familiar. Have we met?"

"I don't think so, ma'am. I'd remember a classy lady like yourself. People used to tell me I favored Ike Turner, though. Maybe that's it."

Bernadine searched his features. "Maybe."

She glanced over at Crystal, who replied, "Not to be disrespectful or anything, but I know I've never seen him before."

He smiled.

Bernadine shook herself free of the sensation. "Sorry if I embarrassed you."

"No problem, ma'am. Let me get back to work. Again, nice meeting you all. Enjoy your meal."

As he walked away, Bernadine still had the feeling that she knew Otis Miller from somewhere, but she let it go, thanked Mal, and she and Crystal picked up their forks.

Ray went back into the kitchen and began rinsing the dirty plates for their trip to the dishwasher. So now he knew what his pigeon looked like. She was a big girl.

That made it easier because all of the heavyset women he'd charmed in the past had been insecure because of their size, and therefore open to any kind of affection they could find. Bernadine Brown probably fit that same category, seeing as how she was with Malachi July. She wasn't bad to look at though, which also made the job easier. Nothing worse than having to do the do with an ugly woman. As for Crystal, her Goldilocks-looking weave was even worse in person, but she favored Nikki so much, the only thing missing was a crack pipe in her hand. That she didn't know Ray from Adam was a big plus; he wouldn't have to worry about her messing up his plans. However, since he didn't see a girl like her being happy way out here in the middle of nowhere, maybe she'd be willing to help him with the fleecing in exchange for a cut. Right now, anything was possible. He just had to play his cards slow and right.

The ribbon cutting drew most of the town's core residents, along with dignitaries and visitors from Franklin and many of Marie's former students from places like Kansas City, Topeka, and St. Louis. Bernadine noticed that Leo hadn't left her side and that Marie was actually introducing him to people. Mind-boggling. She wanted to march over there and toss him out into the street. Seeing as how the street in front of the school was filled with people, and that causing a ruckus would get her tossed into the street by Tamar et al. for ruining the event, she took a deep breath and tried to put Leo out of her mind. It was hard. "Okay, everybody, I think we're ready to begin."

Folks began to quiet, and when she had their attention, Bernadine said into the mic, "Would all the Henry Adams students, Mayor Trent July, Marie Jefferson, and Mr. James please join me here."

She was standing in front of the school's steps and the crowd was spread out around her. Some of the attendees were taking pictures with cell phones and digital cameras. Others like Lily were holding video cams. Bernadine spotted the CNN crew in the back filming as unobtrusively as they could with all the equipment mounded around them. They were shooting yet another installment on the town's progress and she didn't mind. Their reports had generated quite a bit of interest over the past year from corporations wanting to do sponsorships and high-tech firms wanting to use Henry Adams to test out everything from wind turbines to the plant-based solar cells that were on the roof of the new school.

The people she'd requested came forward, and once they were all assembled, she handed the mic to Trent. He began by welcoming everybody, then talked about the significance of the day. "A school defines a community and this new school represents part of the phoenix the Henry Adams community has become. I know the Dusters are proud of this building, our students, teacher, and the woman this school will be named for. Let's cut the ribbon."

A long blue ribbon stretched across the steps and anchored on each side to an idle orange backhoe. Bernadine handed each participant a pair of kiddie scissors and on Trent's count of three, they all made cuts.

Wild applause followed, and the kids smiled widely. Lily moved in closer so she could get a shot of the kids with their scissors in one hand and their other hand holding high their piece of ribbon.

The reception followed. Siz had outdone himself. The huge buffet inside the cafeteria had everything from crab cakes to fancy asparagus to nachos and a large variety of desserts and fruit.

Bernadine worked the crowd, pausing here and there to say hello, then made the mistake of greeting Franklin's mayor, an elderly old snake named Riggins. Since his election last fall, he'd been pestering her with his ideas on how Henry Adams and Franklin could work together to uplift the region. Everything he proposed would either cost Franklin no money or her plenty, or be of more benefit to Franklin alone, like the pitch he was making to her now about folding the new Henry Adams school into Franklin's aging school district.

"Of course," he said with a mouthful of shrimp, "with Henry Adams only having six students our school board would naturally oversee curriculum and dispense the budget."

Bernadine was so outdone she almost asked him if he thought she was crazy, but instead she said quietly and distinctly, "No." And moved on.

On the other side of the cafeteria she found Trent standing with Colonel Payne, Amari, and Preston. All had piled-high plates.

Bernadine said, "Nice short speech, Trent."

"Thanks, I didn't think folks were here to hear me."

Amari asked, "Dad, do you know those people Ms. Marie is talking to?"

They all looked over.

Trent said, "That's the Clarks. They live in Franklin. I went to school with the dad before he married Colleen, his wife."

Preston asked, "The girls their daughters?"

"Yeah. Leah, the one in the green dress, is the oldest. The younger one is Tiffany Adele."

Amari said, "She has two names?"

"Apparently. Her parents have always called her by both."

"That's wack. She sounds like a store in the mall."

Bernadine choked on a piece of fruit.

Trent chuckled. "I heard they're thinking of moving back here."

When Bernadine could breathe and speak again, she gave Amari a sideways glance, then added, "They said something similar to me the night we had the town meeting."

Barrett said, "The oldest looks about your age, Preston."

He shrugged. "I don't like girls."

Bernadine asked, "Why not?"

"Because they don't like me."

"Ah." Bernadine said, noting another issue Preston had in his makeup "They're pretty girls, though."

Amari said, "Yep. I'm going to go say hi. Want to come, Preston?"

"Only if one of them knows who Dr. Neil deGrasse Tyson is."

"Okay, I'll go see."

"Amari, no!" Preston cried.

But he was already gone.

Amari walked over. "Excuse me."

Leah turned and looked him up and down.

"My name's Amari. Just came over to ask you something."

Her younger sister stepped away from the conversation her parents were having and checked out Amari too.

"What's the question?" Leah asked. She was a tall girl. Long hair. Brown skin. Skeptical eyes behind her glasses.

"Do you know who Dr. Neil deGrasse Tyson is?"

"Yes! Why?"

"My friend over there, his name is Preston. The Dr. Tyson guy is his hero."

Leah's eyes lit up with interest. "He is? Where's your friend?"

Amari pointed him out. "See the kid in the red shirt?"

Leah checked out Preston and turned away.

"What's wrong?" Amari asked.

"Why are all the smart boys short and overweight?"

Amari's mouth dropped. "Hey. Don't be dissing my boy. You're not exactly Beyonce."

Tiffany Adele snapped, "Don't you talk about my sister, ghetto boy."

Amari checked his temper. "Okay, that's it. Forget I even came over here."

"Don't worry, we will," Tiffany Adele said haughtily and glared.

Amari walked away from them, grumbling, "Good thing I don't cuss anymore."

When he returned, Trent looked at his face and asked, "You get shot down, ace?"

"Forget them girls. Bunch of stuck-up snooties."

Bernadine looked over at the girls now talking with each other. "Really?"

"Yep, Ms. Store in the Mall called me ghetto boy, and the other one said Preston was short and overweight."

Bernadine cocked her head. "Excuse me?"

Preston said, "Told you."

Amari said, "Ms. Bernadine, if they move here, I'm telling Mr. James, do not put them in the classroom with me or Preston. Can we be excused? I need some air."

"I'll come with you," Preston said. "Will you all call us when it's time to move stuff?"

"Sure," Trent responded. "That okay with you, Barrett?"

The colonel was shooting daggers across the room at the stuck-up snooties, "Of course."

When the boys left, Barrett asked, "So what's the deal on this family? The girls sound pretty mean."

"They take after their mother. Colleen's been a witch since grammar school. Gary got shotgunned into marrying her."

"Was she pregnant?" Bernadine whispered.

"Told everybody she was. He married her to do the right thing, but she wasn't really pregnant, or at least that was the rumor."

"And they want to move here?" Barrett asked skeptically.

"Yep. Colleen's father was the first Black man with a car dealership in this part of the county. Pretty big time. Raised her like she was a princess. Next time you see Rocky, say Colleen's name and watch her head spin around on her neck."

Bernadine laughed. "What happened?"

"Fight. Eighth grade. When the dust settled Colleen was on the ground, and so were her two front teeth."

"Oh my goodness," Bernadine exclaimed.

Trent said, "Can't imagine why she'd want to move

back. After the fight, her parents moved to Franklin and enrolled her in a private school. Colleen hated the kids here and the feeling was mutual."

Barrett said, "I know kids can be cruel, but talking about Preston's weight is not going to endear those girls to me."

"Nor me," Bernadine declared testily. "Had to deal with skinny little hussies like that all my life."

Trent and the colonel were taken aback by the heat in her voice.

Seeing their reaction, she placed her hand against the gold framing her neck and feigned surprise. "I'm sorry, did I say that out loud?"

They chuckled.

"Okay. Thanks for the 411, Trent. Needed to know that. Going back to mingling now."

And she moved on. The crew from CNN had asked to speak with her for a moment, so she searched the crowded cafeteria until she spotted them. Wanting to dispose of her plate first, she made her way over to one of the trash cans and saw Otis Miller removing the now filled trash bag inside.

When she walked up, he held out his hand. "I'll take that, Ms. Brown."

"Thanks." She headed off to meet the CNN people. She still had the feeling she knew Otis Miller from somewhere, but so far hadn't figured it out.

Outside, Amari was picking at the food left on his plate and still grumbling about the Clark girls.

Preston, sunk in his own bad mood, said, "Just forget about them."

"Hard to do because there goes one now."

Preston turned to see Leah Clark coming out of the school door.

They assumed she was heading to the parking lot to retrieve something from the family's car, or on another mission that in no way involved them, but they were wrong.

She walked over to where they were sitting on the steps and stopped directly in front of Preston. "I came to apologize for what I said about you in there."

"Huh?" was all he could say.

"People have called me a tall, four-eyed geek, and it really hurts, so I'm sorry if I hurt your feelings."

Amari asked, "You mean that, or you just here because somebody made you come apologize?"

"I came on my own. If we move here, I don't want people thinking I'm like my mom."

Both Preston and Amari raised an eyebrow.

Preston asked first, "What's wrong with your mom?"

"Crazy. Sometimes crazier. Depends on the day. Do you really know who Dr. Tyson is?"

"Yeah. Be dumb to lie about something like that."

"Do you like physics?"

"Want to study it at MIT eventually."

"Me too. What theory?"

"String."

"I like string too, but I'm more into the magnetic fields of coronas and sunspots."

Preston's mouth dropped.

Next thing Amari knew they were talking a language as foreign-sounding to his ears as Russian. Every now and then he caught a few familiar words like *particles* and *gravity* but what or who was a *planke*, and was *hadron* really a word?

He hadn't seen Preston so animated, ever, and the girl looked happy too. When they started using rocks to scratch math equations in the dirt, Amari knew it was time for him to go. "I'll see you all later."

Preston looked up, gave him a quick nod, and immediately went back to the equations. They were now talking about some guy named Stephen Hawking.

As Amari reached the door Colonel Payne was stepping outside.

"Where's Preston?" he asked.

"Over there with Leah. She came out to apologize for dissing him, and now they're doing math equations in the dirt."

"Math equations?"

"Yeah. She's a brain too. They're talking about strings or something. Not sure what kind, but Preston's real happy though."

The colonel smiled. "That's good.

"Yeah. He finally has somebody to kick it with and talk about all that deep stuff in his brain. He tries it with me sometimes, but remember I'm the one who just learned how to read, so most of the time I don't have a clue, even when he calls himself breaking it down for me."

"So you won't be mad if he spends time with her, if she and her family move here?"

"Unless it's 24/7, nope. Frees me up to be at the garage with my dad and help him work on his cars, which is what I like to do."

"You and your dad get along real well, don't you?"

"We're working things out."

"How do you think Preston and I are doing?"

"Wouldn't you and Preston know better than me?"

The colonel smiled. "Yeah. Guess you're right. I came out to get you two because they're getting ready to start the move."

Amari turned and yelled, "Yo, Brain. Time to move."

"Okay," he called back. "Be there in a minute."

Amari said, "I'll see you inside."

He went in, but the colonel stood outside and watched Preston and the Clark girl going at it with their rocks. He could see the happiness on the boy's face as he wrote in the dirt, and all Barrett Payne could say to himself was *Wow*.

As he waited for them to finish up, he took Amari's suggestion and quizzed himself about the relationship he and Preston were trying to build. If he was being truthful, his answer would be a tentative okay. They'd been talking more as of late, played chess every night before going to bed, and Preston seemed to be much more relaxed around him. Barrett was more relaxed as well, and learning that he enjoyed the boy's company, but like Amari, when Preston began talking physics, something he was very passionate about, Barrett didn't have a clue. He should have asked Amari for the details about how the mind melding of Preston and Leah came about, but it didn't really matter. Preston looked to be in heaven, and Barrett wished Sheila was around to witness his gleeful transformation. Her face floated across his mind's eye. The place where she was staying didn't allow phones so he wondered how she was doing.

She'd been gone only a few days but it felt like weeks. He hoped the transformation she was seeking for herself materialized so she could come home. He was certain she was going to be pleased by the progress he and Preston were making as a unit, and when she learned he'd joined a fathers' support group of all things she was going to fall over. In the past he never would have admitted this so readily, but just as in Florida during the reunion when he'd spent those nights in bed alone, he missed her big time.

As people hauled books and chairs and tables and dry erase boards into the building, Bernadine, carrying a large potted plant, knew she could have easily hired a crew of workers to handle getting everything in place, but having the locals do it had been Marie's idea. She wanted the day to be a collective memory and Bernadine agreed. The school belonged to the community and this was a novel way for everyone to take ownership.

She saw Amari and Preston carrying in the pumps, filters, and some of the other equipment needed to get the big wall-sized aquarium in the main hallway up and running. Trent and Jack were maneuvering a flatbed dolly stacked with chairs, followed by one Otis Miller was pushing. Zoey and Devon and Eli were helping Crystal set up the art room. Tamar and her crew were in the media center stacking the shelves with the hundreds of educational DVDs Marie had ordered. Roni was in the kiva-shaped auditorium hitting keys on the piano to make sure it was well tuned, while her husband was down the hall opening boxes in the room that would serve as the in-school clinic. Even Leo got into the act. She saw him dragging a huge Sam's Club bag filled with paper towels and toilet paper for the bathrooms. When he saw her, he winked. She rolled her eyes and kept walking. The old axiom "Many hands make for light work" was definitely in play because by mid-afternoon, they were done.

Bernadine was tired. She'd started the week in Barcelona and now six days later, she was sitting in a chair in the hallway of the new school, saying good-bye to everyone who'd pitched in to help. Most would be back in town later to take in the movies at the rec center, but she planned to pass. All she wanted to do was go home and kick back. The weekly Saturday evening gathering would have to do without her this time around.

However, when Mal called her at home and asked if she wanted to go, her answer was yes.

Later that afternoon, with help from Otis, Siz, Clay, and Bing, Rocky moved into her trailer on Tamar's land. She'd never seen a double-wide so spacious, and she was thankful for the blessing courtesy of Bernadine Brown.

When they were done, Otis said, "You're all set now, Ms. Rock."

"Thanks. You've been a great help."

"Just trying to give some payback for everybody being so nice to me."

Clay said to Rocky, "Bing and I are going to head home. If you need anything just call."

She gave her two old friends a kiss on the cheek. "You're the best."

Siz had driven over in his own car. He left with a wave, so Clay asked Otis, "You need a ride back to the Dog?"

"I do."

"Then come on. We'll take you."

After they departed, a weary Rocky plopped down onto one of the plush couches that had come with the place. She hadn't had a moment's rest since returning from Boston, but now she had a sanctuary to retreat to and planned to enjoy it.

She was unloading a box of books onto one of the book-shelves when she heard a knock on the door. "Come on in," she called.

In walked Jack James.

She paused.

"Hi. Came by to welcome you to the neighborhood and to see if you needed help with anything."

"Thanks, but I'm good."

"Sure?"

"Positive."

Silence rose.

"Um," he began. "Tamar mentioned the movies tonight at the rec. Would you like to go?"

"No. I'm going to finish unpacking and then relax."

"Okay. Well, just wanted to say hey."

"Appreciate that."

"See you around."

She nodded.

He left.

Rocky went back to unloading the books, determined not to think about Jack James, but it was difficult.

CHAPTER 18

A mari and Trent were standing together in front of the big bathroom mirror. Amari checked out his reflection dressed up in its fancy attire and asked in a glum tone, "Why do I have to wear a suit?"

Also in a suit, Trent draped his tie around the collar of his crisp blue shirt "Because when you take a special lady to a special event you dress like it."

"Suppose she's wearing jeans? Then I'm going to look stupid."

"Knowing Ms. Genevieve she won't be wearing jeans. Now grab your tie, and let me show you how to do this."

Amari put the tie around the collar of his new white shirt. "Why couldn't we get some of those clip-on ties?"

"Because one, they're tacky, and two, being able to tie a tie is a part of being a man. Not to mention, it's one of those things a father passes down to his son. My dad taught me. Now I'm teaching you. One day you'll teach your son."

"I'm not having a son."

"Probably not, but your wife will. Just do what I do. I'll go slow."

It took them a few minutes, but in the end, Amari succeeded.

"Looking good," Trent said approvingly.

Amari checked himself out and ran his hand lightly over the fresh haircut his dad had given him earlier. He was so accustomed to seeing himself in tees and jeans it took him a minute to recognize himself, but he had to admit he did look good.

"So, what do you think?"

"It's okay. As long as I don't have to do this every day, I'm good."

"You look great. Let's get our coats and we'll be ready to roll."

Downstairs, Trent swung by the fridge.

"What's this?" Amari asked, looking down at the transparent plastic container Trent handed to him after they got in the truck.

Trent started the engine and backed the truck down the driveway. "Corsage."

"Looks like a flower."

"It is a flower. Ladies wear them on their wrists."

"You giving this to Ms. Lily?"

"Nope. You're giving it to Ms. Genevieve."

"Dad!" he cried. "Why I gotta give her flowers too?"

Trent tried to hide his smile as best he could. "Because, Amari, that's what men do."

"But I'm still a kid."

"Think of it as practice for the future. You'll thank your old dad for this one day."

Amari slumped back into his seat. "If you say so."

Trent didn't hide his smile that time.

With a big tub of no-salt, no-butter popcorn in her lap, Bernadine sat beside Mal and watched the rec center's media room fill with the evening's moviegoers. The Garlands and Zoey came in. Seeing her, they waved and took seats up front. Crystal, who seemed to have taken Eli under her wing, came in with him and his dad. Crys waved to Bernadine and she waved back. Bernadine was very surprised to see the colonel and Preston in the crowd. She couldn't remember ever seeing the retired marine at the movies before but she supposed he was trying to do his best by his foster son now that Sheila was gone.

Amari and Genevieve came in. "Oh my goodness," she breathed. "Amari has on a suit."

Genevieve was all decked out in a lovely blue dress, pearls around her neck and a beautiful pink and white orchid on her wrist.

"Boy does look good, doesn't he?" Mal responded with a grin.

"He's going to be a heartbreaker one day."

Everyone in the room turned to see them. Mal could see Clay standing and staring. Clay swung questioning eyes to Mal, who simply smiled. Clay dropped back down into his seat. Mal laughed inwardly.

"I didn't know they were dating," Bernadine joked.

"He's been trying to come up with a way to pay her

back for helping him with his reading, and this was his solution."

"That is so sweet."

"He's got a big heart. Runs in the family."

She gave him a look that he met with a smile and a wink.

Still bowled over by the handsome Amari, Bernadine watched as he and Genevieve took seats. They were soon joined by Trent and Lily, also dressed up, and Devon, who apparently planned to wear suit and a clip-on tie every day for the rest of his little life. Seeing him gave rise to the worries she'd been harboring all week about the church service he was going to hold in the morning. She knew everyone who was able would show up to give him support, but suppose he couldn't really preach? Suppose he was terrible? Last thing she wanted was for him to be a flop. There was no way to know how it would turn out, however, so she decided to let the angst go; tomorrow would come soon enough.

Another kind of angst grabbed her when Leo came in with Marie. He was politely handing her to a seat. They both had tubs of popcorn and drinks. The smile they shared made Bernadine unconsciously grind her teeth.

"Who are you glaring at?" Mal asked, then when he looked over and spotted Leo and Marie, he said, "Thought you were going to let that go?"

"I'm trying, but I just don't want to see Marie hurt."

"Not your concern, now."

"I know."

A few seconds later, the houselights went down. The

opening score for the blockbuster adventure *Transformers* began and Bernadine turned her attention to the movie.

During intermission, Bernadine made a quick trip to the ladies' room; as she was leaving, Marie was coming in. "Hey, Marie," Bernadine called, hoping the greeting didn't sound too false.

It did.

Marie asked, "Can we talk a minute?"

"Sure."

Since they were by the building's front door, Marie stepped outside and a wary Bernadine followed.

Marie looked out at the night for a few seconds, then asked quietly, "When are you going to stop tearing up your face every time you see me and Leo together?"

Caught off guard and, yes, shamed, Bernadine asked, "Is it that obvious?"

"Stevie Wonder could see it."

She offered a chagrined smile. "I'm sorry, Marie. I just don't want you hurt."

"Didn't we have this discussion before?"

"Yeah, but—"

"No buts, Bernadine Brown. I know you think Leo is the scum of the earth, and if I was in your shoes I'd probably feel the same way, but I'm not you. And I'm not inferring that he'll treat me better because I'm better than you, but can you let me have a bit of fun and attention? If he turns out to be someone I don't want to be with, I'm okay with that, but at least let me find out."

Bernadine sighed. "You're absolutely right."

"Thank you."

She looked Marie in the eye. "I'll get it together. I promise."

"I'm holding you to that. Now, let's go back in."

Feeling like she'd been in the principal's office, Bernadine led them back inside. When she returned to her seat it was dark and Mal leaned over and whispered, "Was just about to go looking for you. Did something happen?"

She whispered back, "I was outside being read by Marie."

He tried to see her face in the dark. "You okay?"

"No, but I will be."

He reached over and gently squeezed her hand. She could've kissed him for the small but needed show of support.

Amari had a good time with Ms. Genevieve. When it came time to go home, she gave him a big hug and left with Ms. Marie and her new boyfriend.

"You did a good thing, son," his dad told him as they drove home.

"I did, didn't I," he replied, grinning. He felt good.

Marie wasn't feeling so good. Her mother, Agnes, had ridden over to the rec with Tamar, but was going home in the limo, along with Marie, Leo, and Genevieve. Marie could tell she had to something to say. "What's the matter, Mama?"

"Nothing."

But Marie could see the way she was glaring at Leo and how uncomfortable he appeared as a result. "If you have something to say, just say it. You're as bad as Bernadine."

"Bernadine has a right to be mad. Isn't he her philandering ex-husband?"

Leo's lips tightened and he came to his own defense. "Yes, ma'am, I am, but—"

"You got no business being with him, Marie."

Marie sighed. She glanced Genevieve's way and received a look of sympathy. "I'm sixty years old, Mama."

"So you keep pointing out, but you're acting like a teenager in heat, just like last time."

Genevieve gasped and scolded, "Agnes, that is not right."

"It's the truth. What if Bernadine gets mad and fires her? She can, you know. She owns the whole town."

Leo said, "Bernadine would never do that."

"Bet you never thought she'd divorce your cheating behind either, did you?"

Marie was so angry and humiliated, all she could do was stare out at the darkness and hope Leo didn't see the tears in her eyes.

He could. He had no idea what the old harpy was referring to about Marie's past but he could see how devastated the words left her and it angered him. It was obvious that Marie needed to be extricated from what appeared to be on the surface a difficult situation, and he knew just the man for the job. As for Agnes, she could go to hell.

Mal and Bernadine were sitting in his truck out in front of her house. Even though she'd enjoyed the movie, she was still brooding over her encounter with Marie.

Mal sensed that, so he said, "Weatherman is forecasting a good breeze tomorrow. Want to go fly some kites after church?"

She turned his way and stared. "Kites?"

"Sure. You ever flown one before?"

"No."

"Nothing like it. Real good way to shake off the stress."

She'd never heard of such a thing, and wondered what this crazy, wonderful man would come up with next.

"Yes? No?"

"Yes," she said with a laugh. "But you'll have to show me how."

"Be happy to. How's two o'clock sound?"

"Sounds good."

Later, while lying in bed, Bernadine replayed her run-in with Marie and decided she needed to grow up and stop acting like somebody in middle school. But she was conflicted. Large parts of herself were still angry and humiliated by Leo's adulterous behavior, while other parts wanted to know how dare he find someone new.

She hadn't minded him hooking up with his ex-wives, Thing Two and Thing Three, because neither of them could compete with her in spirit or intelligence. Marie, however, was Bernadine's equal, and she was having a hard time with that. *Am I just jealous?* She was certain that she wasn't and decided it was more of her not wanting him to find love again and certainly not with a woman from Bernadine's own backyard, but it was out of her control. She'd been talking the talk about being over Leo and moving on with her life but she hadn't walked the walk. Now she would.

Marie had made it quite clear that she didn't need or want Bernadine's input, so it was time for her to put away wanting to blow up Leo every time she saw him and act like the grown woman she was supposed to be. As she noted earlier, this was life, not middle school.

The next morning Amari, like everyone else, was at Zoey's house for Devon's church service. So many people showed up that they wound up caravanning over to the school to use the new auditorium. None of Amari's past foster parents had been churchgoing folks so he didn't know a lot about the whole organized religion thing but even he knew Devon rocked the house. The usually timid kid Amari had nicknamed Creflo Jr. was transformed on the stage. He was shouting and pointing and quoting the Bible. At one point he got so into it he shouted at the audience, "Who in here knows the Lord!"

The adults looked blown away. He and Preston shared grins.

"Even if you don't know Him," Devon exclaimed walking back and forth across the stage, "He knows you! He makes the crooked road straight, the lame walk, and the blind see the light."

His voice rose in volume and resonated. "He'll hide you from the darkness under the pinion of His wings, and you shall not be afraid. Hallelujah!"

People were shouting and yelling. For another thirty minutes, Devon spread the Word.

Amari looked over at Ms. Bernadine. She was all dressed up and wearing a big fancy hat. She had tears in her eyes.

Ms. Lily had her hand in the air and was crying too. All over the auditorium people were on their feet and Devon was working it.

"Can you feel His presence? Do you need His Presence? Don't matter if you don't know Him! He knows you! Can I get an *amen*?"

The responding *amens* filled the air.

Then Ms. Roni walked onto the stage. Zoey began pounding the keys like she'd been playing gospel all her life, and Roni lifted her beautiful voice and sang "Oh, Mary Don't You Weep."

By the time she got halfway through the old standard, the adults in the audience were swaying, keeping the beat with their claps, and singing along. "Oh, Mary don't you weep. Tell Martha not to moan."

Zoey's small face was a study in concentration as she accompanied Mama Roni, and she didn't miss a change or a note.

Amari had never heard the song before, but he got so caught up in the electricity in the air that even he was singing the chorus by the time the song ended, "Oh, Mary don't you weep. Tell Martha not to mooannn."

When Roni ended, her performance was greeted with thunderous applause. Teary-eyed, she took a bow, then extended her hand to acknowledge Zoey. Zoey stood, face beaming, and bowed too.

Devon walked back to the center of the stage. Everyone quieted, and he said in the small, polite voice they were all more familiar with, "Thank you for coming to my church. I'll see you next week."

If any of the adults had had any doubts about Devon's abilities, there were none now. As Amari followed his dad up the aisle and toward the exit, he heard Ms. Bernadine exclaim to anybody who'd listen, "That boy can preach!"

Just as promised, Mal showed up at two o'clock to take Bernadine kite flying. They drove out to the creek, then left the truck.

"Perfect weather," he called out over the wind.

Bernadine begged to differ. The wind was whipping her hair like it didn't care how much time she'd spent making it look good.

He reached into the Ford's bed and after moving some stuff around, handed her a cheap plastic kite with a spindle of string attached. Batman was in the center of it and she laughed. "Batman? Isn't this more Devon's style?"

"True, but it was either that or SpongeBob."

The wind was whipping the edges of her Batman kite so she held it and the spindle close to her body to keep it from being carried away. With her other hand she pushed her blowing hair out of her face. "What are you flying? Spider-Man?"

"Nope. This."

He lifted out a large red dragon, complete with teeth and scales. Unlike Batman, it wasn't made of plastic but of fine gauged paper.

"Aw. I want one of those."

He shook his head negatively. "Once you can fly Batman without losing it, we'll talk."

As they walked out onto the open prairie, he gave her some basic instructions.

She said, surprised, "You mean I don't have to run up and down like a crazy woman to get it in the air?"

"No. For now, just give it a short line of string out and let Batman decide which way it wants to go."

So she did that. She unrolled just enough string for it to rise a foot or so above her head and shoulder and suddenly felt the kite pull sharply.

"Give it some string. Slowly now."

Following instructions, she let out more string and then more, and suddenly the kite was airborne and soaring.

"It's flying!" Filled with excitement, she let out more string in response to the kite's wishes. "I never knew this was so easy!"

"Keep your eye on it."

"This is fun!' she called over the wind.

He grinned, walked a few feet away, and put his dragon in the air. Soon it was flying too.

Bernadine looked over. "Why does yours have more than one string?"

"So it can do this."

As she watched, he tugged on the strings and made the dragon dance. The head and tail bobbed up and down as if it were alive.

"Oh my goodness!" She turned her attention back to Batman, which by then was so high up it was just a small triangular shape in the sky. "I want one of those."

"Just don't cross your line with mine."

She took a few steps to her left and gave her kite the rest of the string. Suddenly she was holding an empty spindle. "Mal! My string's gone!" Batman was flying away like Superman and she had no way to bring him back.

"Aw baby, I'm sorry. I forgot that sometimes those dollar store kites don't attach the string to the spindles."

"Shoot!" She pouted. Batman was halfway to Gotham by then.

He chuckled.

The kite was soon out of sight. "Not funny."

"I'm sorry. Here, come fly the dragon."

She stood in front of him and he very carefully handed her the lead string but kept his arms around her so that his hands could guide hers.

"Keep it even. Don't let the head dip down or he'll crash."

Bernadine concentrated but it was difficult with him standing so close that she could smell his cologne. She turned her head and looked back. "You smell good."

He kissed her. "Keep your eyes on the prize, missy. I paid three hundred dollars for that kite."

The power of the kiss made her sway a bit but she fought it off. Smiling, she kept her eyes on the dragon in the sky.

They flew the dragon until her arms tired, then she ducked out from under Mal and let him reel the beautiful kite in.

Driving home, he asked, "Did you have a good time?"

"That was marvelous. When can we do it again?"

"Whenever you like."

Bernadine couldn't remember having so much fun. All

it had taken was a cheap piece of plastic and a line of string. "I'm getting a better kite, though."

"My apologies again."

"It's okay. I had a good time."

On Monday morning school started. Trent considered it a blessing because it was now Jack's job to answer Amari's 24/7 questions, at least until the end of each school day. Trent loved being Amari's dad and he wouldn't change his decision to foster him for the world. He also didn't mind being mayor, most days. However, both jobs took up a lot of time, leaving him just bits and pieces to do the other thing he loved, restoring cars.

By all rights, he should be at work handling things needing his attention like approving the final blueprints for Roni's studio and her husband's clinic. But now that the kids were back in school, he looked upon the resumption as the beginning of his vacation, so he called the Power Plant and told Lily he was taking a vacation day.

He was in the garage with Black Beauty, the old Chrysler New Yorker Malachi had handed down to Trent his junior year in high school. After graduation he'd totaled it during an ice storm. Beat up and banged up, it had sat under wraps in storage until last summer, but now, it was fully restored and gorgeous.

As he slowly circled the body checking out the new paint job and how it looked outfitted with new chrome wheels and door hardware, he reminisced on high school and driving around with Lily Fontaine riding shotgun. They'd made a lot of memories; some never to be revealed, but they'd had more fun than two kids playing in a pool on a hot day. Back then, he'd loved the car almost as much as he had her and it was ironic that his relationship with Lily and the car had both shared the same fate—totaled.

Now the three of them could be together again, and who better to share the first ride than the Fabulous Fontaine, the nickname she'd earned during her high school track days. He picked up his phone and got her on the line. "What are you doing?"

"Working, unlike you."

He grinned. "I'm working too, and to prove it, I'll be there in a few minutes. Got something I want to show you."

"What is it?"

"I'll call you when I get there."

"Trenton—"

"Bye, Fontaine." He ended the call.

When Lily got the call that Trent had arrived and was outside, she walked out to meet him. The sight of him leaning against the beautifully restored car stopped her in her tracks. "Oh my," she whispered, hands over her mouth.

"Like it?" he asked, arms crossed, looking all of seventeen again.

"Trenton, she's beautiful." Finally able to power herself forward, she moved closer. Memories flooded her and she looked at him with awe. "You told me she'd been totaled."

"She was, but I took the wraps off last summer and started restoring her. "

"We had some times in this car."

"Oh yeah."

Lily circled the vehicle silently, her eyes darting and lingering. She peeked through the window. "You put in a CD player."

"Yep, redid all the wiring. She may be a classic on the outside but inside she's twenty-first century."

"Doesn't that affect the value?"

"It would if she were for sale, but she's not."

"You're going to keep her?"

"Yep. With us back together, we need our car."

She stopped and met his eyes. Emotion filled her. "That's so sweet."

"Want to test her out?"

"Right now?" She felt seventeen all over again as well.

"That's why I'm here."

She nodded excitedly. "Let me call the Boss Lady first."

Once that was accomplished, Trent opened Beauty's door, his beauty got in, and off they went.

"You know you're not going back to work today."

She laughed. "Yep. Told Bernadine exactly that when I talked to her."

They grinned. She cuddled up against his side and he draped his arm around her possessively. As the Temptations sang "My Girl" on the CD, neither Trent nor Lily could imagine life being any better.

At lunchtime, the kids left the classroom and trooped outside to eat. The beautiful May day was a harbinger of the summer to come and the sun's warmth felt good. Preston and Amari were discussing their parade plans and the response of Mr. James to the project.

Preston said, "Mr. James giving us extra credit for doing this is great."

"Yeah," Amari said distantly.

"What's the matter?"

"Worried about this Spirit Quest thing this weekend."

"When do you leave?"

"Friday after school."

"Do you know where Tamar's taking you?"

"No." Amari sighed. "It's not so much the where, but the what if I don't get a sign?"

"Your dad already said it won't matter."

"But it'll matter to me." Amari wanted to be a July in every way. Sure the original Tamar had come to him in a dream, but everybody in the July family had been given a sign and he wouldn't feel complete without one of his own.

"It'll be okay, man. You'll see."

Amari hoped he was right.

Crystal and Eli came over and sat next to them.

"Hey," she said, and pulled a drawing pad out of the big purple tote she carried to school instead of a backpack. "Are these sketches okay for your flags?"

Amari looked at the drawings. There were four flags. One per page.

Crystal continued, "I talked to Tamar and she looked through the old pictures and gave me the ideas. One's the American flag of course, and that one is Liberia and this one, Haiti. Why the Dusters had flags for them, I don't know."

Amari said to Preston, "Add that to your list. We need to know the answer because you know somebody's going to ask."

"Check."

"Now this last one," she said, turning the page to the final sketch, "is the original Henry Adams township flag. Not sure about the colors, so I had to guess."

The flag was blue, and in the center was a golden sun with rays leading to the four corners. One ray had a plow, one a set of chains, the third corner had a silhouette of a family, and the last one had what appeared to be an open Bible.

Eli said to Crystal, "You did these sketches?"

"Yes. Haven't you been listening?"

"These are fresh."

"Thanks."

"I didn't know you could draw."

"Why do you think I was the one setting up the art room Saturday morning?"

He shrugged. "I don't know."

She rolled her eyes and turned her attention back to Amari. "So are these okay?"

"Perfect. Thank you. I owe you big time."

"Not necessary. I owed you anyway for that ride in the O.G.'s truck last summer."

"True."

"So we're even now, correct?"

"Correct."

"Okay. I'm going to have Ms. Lily see if she can find somebody to do these on silkscreen and that way if we want to use the flags again, we can."

Preston said, "Great idea, Crystal."

"That's why I'm the best."

Mr. James appeared by the door and waved them back

inside, so the four kids gathered up their things and walked back to the building.

"I sculpt, you know," Eli told her on the way.

"As in clay?"

"Yeah."

"You any good?"

"Good enough to win a bunch of awards back at my other school."

"Did you bring any of your pieces with you when you moved here?"

"No, broke everything after my mom died."

She stared aghast. "Why?"

"Seemed like a good idea at the time."

She sighed and shook her head. She knew from talking with Ms. Bernadine that people grieved differently, but she couldn't imagine destroying her art.

He said, "Pretty dumb, huh?"

"That's up to you."

He decided that it had been.

On the ride home with his dad after school, Eli asked, "Did you know Crystal was an artist?"

"Marie Jefferson included it in her profile, yeah."

"She's good too." He told him about the flags for the parade.

"I'm looking forward to seeing them. I'm pretty impressed by Amari too. Not many kids his age willingly take on a project like this."

"So you knew he was a car thief too?"

"Yep."

"This town is a different kind of place."

"What do you mean?"

"Everybody sticks together."

"Noticed that."

"You don't think that's different?"

"I do. Different and wonderful at the same time."

Eli thought that over. "I don't feel so Goth anymore."

"You've been through a lot, feeling dark inside's pretty normal. Been feeling pretty Goth myself. Being here's been good though."

"You know, this is probably the longest, nonyelling conversation we've had since Mom died."

"True." And it was.

"Crystal told me that Preston and his dad are trying to learn how to be father and son. Think maybe we could do that?"

Jack could feel water forming in his eyes, emotion filling his throat, "You want to?"

"Yeah."

"What should we do to start?"

"Think you could order me some clay?"

"Yeah, son. Just let me know what kind and we'll jump online soon as we get home."

"Thanks."

"You're welcome."

As they continued the drive Eli lapsed into silence but for Jack it was okay. He sent up a prayer and a thank-you to Eva for directing them to this wonderful place, because he knew she had.

*   *   *

On her breakneck drive across the Pelican State, Eustasia Pennymaker received two speeding tickets, each a hundred miles apart courtesy of Louisiana Highway Patrol, but she didn't care. She had enough money to pay a dozen tickets so she kept the Hummer rolling at ninety as she and the big truck behind her trailering a large hog carrier burned up the road to fetch Chocolate and bring her home. She'd hired a lawyer for Riley, but had no intentions of getting involved any deeper. All she wanted was to make sure her baby was okay and head back to Texas.

However, when she got to the small town where they were all being held, she took one look at Riley languishing in the cell in his orange jumpsuit, and her heart melted. "Hey, Riley," she said.

His face brightened. "Hi, Stasia." Then he turned glum again. "Sorry about taking Chocolate, but Cletus wouldn't leave without her. You know how he is."

"I do. They treating you okay here?"

"Well as can be expected, I guess. How are you?"

"Better now that I've seen Chocolate and know she's all right."

"I suppose by now you know all about why Cletus and I were running from the police and what happened back up in Kansas."

"Yes, but I'd like to hear your side."

So he gave her his side, and mostly told the truth. He left out the parts about why Genevieve left him and Cletus running roughshod over him and the house. "Cletus was just protecting us. He sat on Prell out of self-defense."

"Hogs can be that way."

"I didn't think the county would believe me and would put Cletus down, so we hotfooted it out of there."

"And then you met me in the parking lot that day."

"Yep. And you and Chocolate were so nice to us. Sorry I had to lie to you and run off without telling you good-bye like I did."

"I understand why you thought you had to."

"Thanks for the lawyer too. Court's gonna appoint me a new one once the extradition papers get signed and I'm sent back. Been nice knowing you, Stasia."

"Hold up, pardner. You're not getting rid of me that quickly. I'm going to hire the best defense team since O.J. and we're going to get you and Cletus out of this mess."

Riley stared, "You mean that?"

"Have I ever said anything I didn't back up?"

"But Stasia, why?"

"Because you're my man, Riley Curry, and a woman always stands by her man. Once this is all settled, we're going to plan another wedding, but this time, it'll be me and you."

It occurred to Riley that he'd never mentioned a word to her about Genevieve. "Got something else you need to know."

She didn't let him finish. "About your wife, Genevieve? I know all about her. Divorcing her shouldn't be hard."

"Divorce? I was raised Catholic, Stasia. I don't know if I can do that to Genevieve."

"Apparently, Genevieve isn't Catholic. I talked to the prosecutor's office up in Graham County. Genevieve's already filed for divorce."

"What! Why that ungrateful—"

"Let's just forget about her for now. We need to concentrate on seeing if my legals can get you out on bond. If not, I'll meet you in Graham County and be there until this ends."

"You sure?"

"Positive."

He smiled. "I feel a lot better knowing you're in this with me."

"Wouldn't have it any other way."

Ray got paid Friday morning, and after lunch he and Siz headed over to Franklin to cash their checks. Once that was accomplished they got back in Siz's rust bucket and Ray asked, "Do you know if there's a flower shop around here?"

"There's one on Main. Who are you buying flowers for?"

"Ms. Brown and Ms. Rock."

"You trying to hit on them?"

"Not that it's any of your business but I just want to show them my appreciation."

"You know Ms. Brown is Mr. July's lady, right?"

"Don't mean I can't buy her flowers."

"No, but I don't want you to get it twisted."

"You just drive and stay out of grown folks' business."

Siz shook his head and drove back to Henry Adams.

"Drop me at the Power Plant," Ray told him. "I'll walk back to the Dog."

Siz let him out and Ray went inside.

Although he'd been in town only a few days, he'd decided it was time to test the waters. If he couldn't get Brown to bite on his charms, he'd get to her through Crystal. From what he'd seen of their relationship, the two seemed very close. His question was how many dollars did that closeness equate to. Ray had no morals, and if he had to snatch Crystal in order to get paid, so be it.

"Ms. Brown?"

Bernadine looked up from her desk. "Hey, Otis. How are you?"

"Doing good. Just wanted to give you these."

Her mouth dropped. Taking the wrapped roses, she studied them for a moment before turning her attention on him. "They're lovely. What did I do to deserve them?"

"My way of saying thanks for helping me get back on my feet. Got some for Rocky too. Do you like them?"

"I do." She set them on her desk. "I'm going to put these in a vase ASAP."

"You know, you're a real classy lady. Never met anybody like you before. Sure would like to get to know you better."

He watched her eyes evaluate him for a moment before asking with a smile, "Are you hitting on me, Otis?"

He gave her his famous grin. "Trying to."

"That's so sweet, but I'm in a real good relationship with your boss. I am flattered though."

"Okay. I recognize no when I hear it."

"No hard feelings?"

"None."

"Good, because I understand you're doing a great job over at the Dog and at the school. Even though you've only been here a few days, I'm hoping you'll stay and become a member of the community."

"I'm thinking about it. I like it here. Kinda slow, though."

"I agree, but once you get used to it, it's not that bad."

"Gonna take your word for it." He paused and checked her out in her suit and gold. "Sure I don't have a chance with you?"

She laughed. "Go back to work, Otis. Thanks for the beautiful roses."

"Can't fault a man for trying. You have a good day, Ms. Brown."

"You too."

Walking back to the Dog, Ray had to give it to her. She'd handled him like the class act that she was. She hadn't gotten offended or cussed him out for trying to hit on her, but he got the sense that she would trust him a little bit more after this, so that was good. Now, to work on Crystal.

Mal swung by Bernadine's office to make sure they were still on for dinner that evening. The roses on her desk were impossible to miss. "Where'd you get the roses?"

"From Otis of all people. Aren't they gorgeous."

"Why's he giving you flowers?"

She studied his face for a moment. "Just to say thanks for the job and helping him out. He did try and hit on me but that was beside the point."

"Hit on you?"

"It was harmless. I wasn't offended, and he was very sweet about it when I told him I was in a committed relationship with you."

"I'm going to kick his ass."

"No, you are not."

"Yes, I am."

"No, you are not. What will that prove?"

"That Otis needs to get his own woman."

"You're jealous?" she asked, sounding surprised.

"Damn straight."

He saw her trying to hide her smile as she said, "He gave Rocky roses too. You going to kick his behind twice now that you know that? He was just saying thanks, Mal."

"Yeah, right. I'll be talking to him."

"This is not anything for you to be all bent out of shape about. He's been doing a nice job and I don't need you going Neanderthal over a bunch of roses."

Mal stared off.

"Stop tripping. The only man I care about is you."

He met her eyes.

"Promise," she added, then sighed. "Didn't know you were the jealous type."

"I didn't either. Never felt this way about a woman before, Bernadine, and frankly, it's scaring me to death."

She chuckled. "Why's that?"

"Not used to thinking about a woman all day, wanting to see that woman all day. Not usually in that deep. If she doesn't call, fine. If she kicks me to the curb for someone else, I'm okay with it because another one will come along, but you, you're different. You got me going in circles. Remember that old Friends of Distinction tune?"

"I do."

"That's me," and he sang the chorus, "Round and round and round."

"Nice voice."

He nodded, then said seriously, "I guess what I'm saying is that I want what we have going between us to work out."

"As do I, Mal, so you have nothing to fear from the town handyman."

He sighed. "Pretty silly, huh?"

"I think it's kinda cute. Never had a man get all worked up over me this way."

"Well, I'm worked up in more ways than one. Just so you'll know."

"Noted," she said. "We're not going there just yet, but we'll revisit the subject at the appropriate time."

Both of their faces shone with the affection they felt for each other. "So are we still on for dinner tonight?" she asked.

"Yeah, call me when you get home."

"I will, and Mal?"

"Yeah?"

"Thanks for letting me know how much you care."

"No problem."

Mal left the Power Plant and went directly back to the Dog. He found Otis at the apartment.

"What's wrong?"

"You bought my lady flowers."

"Yeah. Just a thank-you. Nothing more."

"Next time, use words."

"Hey, I'm sorry. Didn't know you were going to trip."

"Now you do. Don't do it again."

"Damn. You that insecure?"

Mal's jaw tightened. "What's that supposed to mean?"

"Hey, if you and Ms. Brown are as tight as you say you are, a bunch of flowers from me shouldn't make you flip out."

"I'm not flipping out. I'm just letting you know what time it is."

"Okay, okay."

"Soon as Jack moves into his house, you're outta here. You can live in the trailer next to Rocky."

"The flowers were just a thank-you, man. That's all."

"I heard you the first time. Just make sure you heard me. Stay away from Bernadine."

"Okay."

Mal slammed the door on his way out.

As the reverberation faded away, Ray smiled. Who knew that playing Satan in July's Garden of Eden would be so much fun.

Mal was still fuming as he drove away and headed out to Clay and Bing's to check on their sick milk cow. He knew he was way over the top on this roses thing with Otis but he couldn't seem to help himself. Bernadine Brown had him turned inside out. If he thought he was in uncharted territory last summer when he first began having feelings for her, he was so far off the map now, he might as well have been circling Saturn. This was a mess. Up until that afternoon, he would have said he didn't have a jealous bone in his body. Liar. He wanted to smack Otis into next week for even looking at Bernadine, let alone buying her roses. He fought to remember whether he'd taken his blood pressure meds that morning. Being with her was going to give him a heart attack.

After school, Trent drove Amari to Tamar's. As they parked and then walked around to the back of the truck to remove the tent, hatchet, and an overnight bag holding his toiletries and changes of clothing, Amari began feeling anxious.

Trent knew his foster son well enough to sense his moods and so asked, "You okay?"

"Yeah. Just not sure how this is going to go."

"It's going to be fun."

Amari wasn't so sure but he kept the doubts to himself. "What time are you picking me up?"

"Tamar will bring you home."

"Oh."

Trent gave his thin shoulders a quick squeeze. "You'll be okay, but do something for me and keep an eye on her. She thinks she walks on water but those feet of hers will be eighty-six come December. Don't let her do too much."

It never occurred to Amari that someone would have to look out for Tamar. She was bigger than life in his eyes. "Okay, Dad."

"Did you charge your phone like I asked?"

"Yep."

"Good, in case of an emergency you can get in touch. But remember, you're not allowed to be on the phone for any other reason while you're doing this though. No texting Preston in the middle of the night. Understood?"

"Understood."

Tamar stepped out onto the porch. "Hey there, Amari. Are you ready?"

"Yes, ma'am."

"Good. Got all your stuff?"

"I think so."

"Then load it in Olivia's bed." Olivia was Tamar's pickup. Once the transfer was made, she said, "Tell your dad good-bye, then come on in the house."

Amari looked up at Trent. "Feel like I'm getting ready to be shipped off with the army."

Trent pulled him close for one last hug. "See you Sunday. Take care of Tamar."

"I will."

Amari watched him drive away, and only afterward did he climb the steps and enter the house.

"You're looking kinda down, Amari."

"Just not sure what this is going to be like."

"You're not supposed to. If we knew how everything in life was going to turn out beforehand, our existence would be pretty boring, don't you think?"

"I guess."

"Life is an adventure, and you can't stop living it just because you don't know what's coming next or what's waiting around the corner. The Dusters didn't know what they were getting themselves into by moving West, but if they hadn't taken a chance there'd be no Henry Adams, and you and your dad would never have met."

"Never thought about it like that."

"That's what some of this weekend is going to be about, thinking about stuff."

He smiled, and when she smiled back, Amari felt himself relax a bit.

"You grab that cooler and I'll carry this water."

He looked at the cut-off cardboard box that held the plastic wrapped bottles. "How about I take the cooler out and then come back for the water."

"Your dad tell you not to let me do too much?"

"Yeah."

"I appreciate that. Shows he cares, but I can handle this. You get the cooler."

Amari found the cooler to be very heavy.

"What's in here?" he groaned as the weight of it tested the strength in his young arms.

"Bit of this and that."

"This and that need to lose some weight."

Taking very short steps he managed to get the cooler out to the porch, but how to get it down the steps and over to Olivia and then into the bed of the truck wasn't going to be easy. He looked at the cooler and then through the screened door to see if she could see him. Hoping she couldn't, he quickly lifted the lid to see what was inside and found it filled with rocks! "Tamar!"

"Yes?"

He looked up to see her standing over him.

"Why do you have all these rocks in here?"

"Your first test."

"Huh?"

"You passed the first part. Now, can you get the cooler to the truck?" She set down the box bottom filled with the bottles of water and took a seat on the porch's old sofa.

"We can't leave until you get this done, and remember, you have a tent to raise when we get where we're going. Nothing worse than trying to raise a tent in the dark."

Amari looked at his watch. He still had a few hours before then. Turning his attention back to his task, he asked, "Did O.G. and my dad have to do this too?"

"Yep. One was better than the other, but both wound up taking so much time they had to put their tents up at night."

He looked down at the cooler again, trying to figure out the riddle. "Can I use something to move it with?"

"Sure. The biggest part of their problem was they never opened the cooler though."

He studied the cooler again and repeated to himself what she said. *They never opened the cooler.* He repeated it again, and then again. And then epiphany. "Oh hell!" he said, mad at himself. Seeing the censure in her eyes, he apologized for the cussing. "Sorry."

"Figured it out?"

"Yeah. If I unload the rocks I can carry the cooler to the truck. Then I carry the rocks to the cooler until it's full again."

"Very good. Now we can get going."

"We're not taking the cooler?"

"Nothing we can do with a cooler filled with rocks, Amari."

Carrying the water, she walked by him and down the steps. "You coming?"

He looked at her in shock then down at the cooler. Since she obviously had said all she intended to about the cooler, he hustled to catch up because he wouldn't put it past her to leave without him.

With Tamar driving at the upper limits of the speedometer as she always did, they reached their destination in a short time, so short a time that Amari knew where he was. It was July land where he and his dad had gone fishing and hunting over the school break. The old picnic table he and his dad had eaten at was still there.

"I didn't know we were coming here."

She drove a bit farther and stopped the truck a short walk from the creek. "Where'd you think we were going?"

He shrugged. "I don't know, someplace scary and far away."

Her smile was soft. "Sometimes what's waiting around life's corner is the familiar."

He nodded and felt silly for having worried all week. "I get it, now."

" 'Getting it' is part of the reason we're out here."

"What's the other part?"

"To have some fun."

"Really?"

"Yes. So raise the tent and we'll get started."

Easier said than done. Although he'd practiced putting up the tent under his dad's watchful eye every day after school, and had even managed to do it alone by week's end, now, for reasons unknown, nothing went right; not putting in the poles, or tying the guide ropes to the stakes that anchored the tent to the ground. Everything that could go wrong did, and when he was done, forty minutes later, the tent was up, sort of, but to his dismay there were two extra metal poles lying on the ground waiting to be used.

Biting back his frustration, he tried again. Another forty minutes. Only this time there was one pole left over, and the prospect of having to tackle it again made him want to cuss. Loud. He was tired, he'd cut his finger on the metal, and he was hungry. He glanced over at Tamar sitting serenely on the picnic table and asked, "Can we eat? I'm hungry. I'll put this up after."

"Always secure your shelter, first. Tent, then food."

"But Tamar," he whined, then snapped his mouth shut. Whining wouldn't get the job done, but he was so frustrated, hot tears were stinging his eyes. He wiped them away quickly, praying she didn't see.

She did. "Amari?" she asked gently.

"Yeah," he responded with muted anger as he snatched the stakes and guide ropes out of the ground so that he could take the lopsided tent down again.

"Do you remember what I asked you the first time we talked about this quest?"

He took a deep breath and quickly wiped away more unshed tears. "Yes. You asked me if I could put up a tent."

"And what was your answer?"

"No."

"So?"

When she didn't say more, he waited, and when she still didn't say anything, he asked testily, "So? What?"

No response. The sun was getting lower in the sky. He studied her for a few more moments, then epiphany time again. "This is another test, isn't it?"

"Is it?"

"Yeah, it is."

"What do you think it relates to?"

He looked at the messed-up tent and then back at her seated on the old picnic table. "I don't know."

"Think about it, Amari. If you can't raise the tent alone, fine, but that means we sleep in the bags under the stars. Been doing it all my life. You, however, are a city boy."

Amari hadn't minded sleeping on the streets of Detroit in the summertime. Only thing you had to worry about were the vampire crackheads and the crazy homeless, and them he could deal with, but out here on the plains, there were coyotes and snakes and big-ass bugs. He preferred to sleep inside the tent, but he was going to have to sleep outdoors, if he didn't get some help. The word *help* resonated and brought him up short. He had it. He hoped. "Can I ask you to help me?"

She smiled. "Of course."

"But will you, is the big question."

"Won't know unless you do."

"Tamar, will you please help me put up this tent?"

"Certainly, but first, what's the lesson here?"

He thought for a few moments, then said questioningly, "If you need help, ask somebody?"

"Exactly. Sometimes we think we're the only person we need in life, and folks wind up giving themselves heart attacks or worrying themselves right into a hospital bed when all they had to do was ask the person maybe sitting on the picnic table right in front of them. Women sometimes think only men have that problem but we ladies can be just as guilty."

He understood and so told her, "I get this one too."

"Good. Now, pull those stakes out of the ground and let's get this joker up before it's too dark to see each other."

As he went about it, he asked, "Did my dad or the O.G. have trouble with their tents too?"

"Nope. They're country boys, they'd been raising tents all their lives."

Amari was disappointed. "Oh."

Tamar smiled inwardly and began taking the tent apart.

In town, Mal and Trent were out on Trent's deck enjoying the warm night and a couple of cold ones. Trent had a beer; his dad a Pepsi.

Trent asked, "How do you think our boy is doing out there with Tamar?"

"I don't know. Because of where and how he grew up he's smarter than we were, but dumber in a lot of ways too. I'm sure he'll do fine though."

"I remember my weekend and how anxious I was the first night. Did she make you carry the cooler?"

"Did she? By the time I got that thing in the truck, I wanted to run her over with the truck."

"Me too. Have you ever figured out what it was about?"

"Nope, and she never volunteered anything, of course. All I knew was I had to put that sucker in the truck and take it out when we got back."

"Me too. What was inside, do you know?"

"Nope. Too scared of her to crack it open and see."

"Ditto. Maybe he'll be the first one to figure it out, and he can tell us."

"She'll probably swear him to secrecy."

They shared smiles.

"I asked him to keep an eye on her. I don't want her pushing herself. She still thinks she's sixty."

"Sometimes, twenty-five."

Trent sipped his beer. "That too." He looked off into the night for a moment. "I can't imagine life without her."

"You probably won't have to. Knowing her, she'll outlive us both."

"Wouldn't that be something?"

"Wouldn't I be pissed?"

Trent laughed. "Not nice."

"I know, just kidding. I love her madly. May she live forever."

They clinked cans and went back to enjoying the silence of the night.

Lying in his sleeping bag inside the tent, Amari looked over at Tamar lying in hers nearby. "Why do you do this?" he asked her.

"You mean this Spirit Quest?"

"Yeah."

"One, it's tradition, and two, it lets me spend some time alone with my kids."

That surprised him.

"Parents watch their children and grandchildren grow up from tiny babies, and when the kids get to be about the age that you are now, their relationship with their mothers or whoever's raising them changes. They no longer need you for every little thing anymore, they start developing strong friendships, discover girls, music, sports, and the older they get the less of them you have to yourself. So this was my way of letting go, for me. It's like having the last dance before the doors close on the club."

"You used to go to clubs?"

Her responding chuckle barely ruffled the silence. "Yes, Amari. I haven't always been eighty-five."

This was definitely not the Tamar Amari thought he knew, but being with her made him feel special. Honored.

"But since I am eighty-five, I need my beauty rest. I'll see you in the morning. Night, Amari."

"Night, Tamar, and thanks for bringing me."

"You're welcome."

Saturday morning when Amari opened his eyes inside the sun-dappled interior of the tent, it took him a couple of minutes to figure out where he was. When his memories filled him in, he immediately turned to the spot where Tamar had been sleeping but saw only her sleeping bag. Thinking he might be late for whatever she had planned for the morning, he got up quickly, pulled on his jeans and sneaks, and made his way outside.

"Morning," she called.

Glad to see her smiling, which he hoped meant he wasn't in trouble for just getting up, he called back, "Morning."

The air was alive with smell of the bacon she was frying in a skillet atop a small black grill.

"Grab a bottle of water and go down to the creek. You can brush your teeth and take care of whatever you need to take care of," she said. "Breakfast will be ready by the time you get back."

Amari, like most urban kids, was a bit hesitant to go off alone, even knowing Tamar was just a shout away, but he did as he was told.

The creek wasn't very wide by nature's standards, nor by Amari's, who'd grown up in Detroit and was therefore familiar with the city's river that separated it from its Canadian neighbors in Windsor, Ontario, but it was for sure deep enough to drown in for a kid who couldn't swim, and he was one of those. Still, he was curious about the water and what was in it, so he carefully made his way down to the bank. A big white-tail doe and her spotted fawn were drinking on the other side and the sight stopped him in his tracks. He knew to stand still so as not to scare them and he did so until after they'd had their fill and bounded away. He and his dad hadn't seen deer when they were fishing so he thought seeing them now was cool. And the fact that there were no hunters around to shoot at the mom and her baby made it perfect. On the water's surface a big brown duck led a line of six fuzzy ducklings on a morning trip. Watching them gliding along made him smile. The way the mother was leading them made him think about the way Tamar was leading him. Tamar the mama duck. Amari the duckling. He wondered if the mama duck had a cooler filled with rocks. Deciding he'd better get going, Amari brushed his teeth, took care of what he needed to take care of, then climbed the bank to rejoin Tamar.

For the rest of the day they did a whole lot of nothing, but as she'd promised it was a fun-filled nothing. They walked and looked at the grasses growing, caught crickets that Tamar said they'd need to fish with later, and stretched out in the grass and searched the clouds overhead for faces and shapes. Amari spotted one that he swore looked like Crystal and her weave, and Tamar laughed until tears formed in her eyes.

The whole while she talked to him about Seminole history: the thirty-year war the Black and Native members of the tribe waged against the United States government for their land and freedom; the forced removal of all the tribes to Indian Territory—which later became the state of Oklahoma; the Long Walk led by Wild Cat and the Black Seminole chief John Horse; and the present-day court battle between the Native Blood Seminoles and the Black members of the tribe over who should be able to file a claim to receive a share of the millions of dollars due to the tribe by the government.

She taught him some of the old songs that had been handed down. Some were traditional Seminole songs sung in words and a language that sounded foreign to his ears. Other songs were Texas trail songs taught to Tamar by her outlaw aunt Teresa July Nance, who'd grown up in a Black Seminole township on the Texas Mexican border before she and her brothers started robbing trains and stagecoaches.

"Aunt T was tough," Tamar told him. "But she was funny, smart, and loved her family. You would have liked her. She would have liked you too."

"You think so?"

"Yep. You have a lot of her qualities, especially the family part."

"That's because I never had one until I found you guys."

"And we've been waiting many years for you to find us."

He saw a hawk circling above and it made him think about his dreams. "So have we seen my sign yet?"

They were walking back to the picnic table after having spent most of the morning just wandering and talking.

"I don't know, have you seen anything memorable?"

He told her about the deer and the ducks.

She shook her head. "It will be something more powerful than that. We'll just keep waiting on the Spirits. We have until tomorrow morning."

Amari was trying to be patient, but the longer they went without seeing anything, the more worried he became.

When they reached the picnic table, Tamar said, "One of the things Aunt Teresa was famous for was her fishing."

"She was good at it?"

"The best and she didn't use a line and a hook."

Amari's brow wrinkled with confusion. "What did she use?"

"Her hands."

He stopped. "No. I don't believe that."

"Believe it. And if haven't lost my touch, I'll show you."

So a few minutes later they were down by the creek. She cautioned him to be very quiet, and they took off their shoes. She waited while he rolled up his jeans and they waded out. She reached into the pockets of her robes and took out some of the crickets they'd found earlier and cast them onto the waters. Scared to even breathe lest he make a sound, Amari watched and waited. Soon he could see three fish swimming in the clear cold water down by his legs. Tamar put a cautionary finger to her lips and put a few more crickets in her hand. She didn't release them until her hand was under water. The fish, so busy eating crickets, totally ignored it. She waited a few silent moments more and then struck. A blink of an eye later, she had a fat, flopping trout caught in both hands. The other fish scattered of course but with her furious prize tightly secured, she and the whooping Amari waded back to the bank in triumph.

"That was awesome, Tamar! Awesome!" He'd never seen anything like it before in his life. "Can I try? Will you video me with my phone in case I get one? Preston is not going to believe this."

Her eyes were lit with amusement. "Sure, but let me gut this fish first."

She sat on the bank and used the large blade of her pocket knife to get the fish ready for the skillet. Once she was finished, she washed it out in the creek and walked the short distance back up to their campsite to store it for later in one of the real coolers they'd brought along. When she returned, he showed her how to work the phone. In exchange, she handed him the last of the crickets.

Flush with anticipation and nervous excitement, Amari quietly waded back into the creek. The water had felt very cold the first time, but now he barely noticed. As he carefully made his way he could feel the rocks on the creek bottom against the soles of his feet but he didn't pay that any mind either.

He kept walking until the surface lapped around his knees. Then he stopped. Looking back at Tamar, he saw that she had the phone raised and focused. She gave him a thumbs-up. He grinned, then taking in a deep breath, concentrated on making himself stand perfectly still. When he could hear nothing but the breeze and the silence of nature he mimicked Tamar's motions of earlier and very slowly bent and placed a few of the crickets in the water. Employing the same smooth motions he straightened. Soon, the fish arrived. Sleek and silvery, the trout, only two this time, swam around his legs and then glided in between. While they snacked on the crickets, Amari soundlessly bent over again. This time, he slipped his gently closed hand beneath the water's clear surface, and after a few long seconds slowly opened it. The crickets began scrambling and his eyes widened as he noticed a trout even larger than the one Tamar caught silently appear. Watching it for a few breathless seconds, he waited until it swam past. When it opened its mouth to snag a cricket, he grabbed and caught it! Fumbling to hold on while the fish twisted and bucked, he quickly put it against his chest and held on tight. "Tamar! I got it!"

Filming and grinning, she called back, "I see ya! Good job!"

He'd just made it back to shore when a loud angry caw filled the air. Amari turned and was knocked flat by something flying and big. The fish went sailing, he saw feathers and a curved beak and claws, heard wings beating, all as he put his arms up to defend himself. A sharp pain brushed his forearm and he cried out in pain and surprise. Next he knew he was on his butt and less than a foot away from the largest hawk he'd ever seen. Its dark eyes were riveted on him and its big clawed foot was holding his struggling trout flat against the ground.

Above him, he heard Tamar say quietly, "Don't move, son."

Amari couldn't have moved if he'd wanted to. The hawk's stare had him pinned much like the trout. He could feel a strange warmth on his arm but he didn't dare move to check out whatever it was.

The bird screamed at him and Amari jumped back. The bird was big. Had Amari been standing, the raptor's head and powerful feathered shoulders would have reached past his knees. The face was outlined with white dots making it resemble an owl. The chest was brown up high, but below, the feathers were lighter with spots.

The wicked-looking claw was still holding down the fish, which by now was moving only slightly. Amari drew in a shuddering breath and the bird slowly cocked its brown head one way and then the other. It screamed at him again, then lifted its wings and took flight with Amari's fish in tow.

Amari watched its powerful wings moving up and down as it moved away over the creek and was soon gone from sight. He fell back against the bank. His heart was pounding so fast he thought it was going to burst out his chest.

Tamar hurried down the bank. "You okay?"

Amari wasn't sure. He finally checked out his arm. There was a ton of blood running from his elbow and down to his wrist. As soon as he saw it, the gash began to hurt like heck. "Ow!" He grabbed it as the pain increased.

"Let me see." She looked and her lips tightened with worry. "Come on, let's wash this off and get you home to

Doc Garland. No telling where that hawk's claws have been. Looks like you may need stitches."

His arm was on fire. He stumbled up but he didn't want to go home, at least not just yet. "But what about my sign?"

She chuckled and shook her head. "Where have you been for the last ten minutes? Do the Spirits have to knock you in the head?"

His jaw dropped. "That was it? That hawk?"

"Come on. I'll send your dad or Malachi out here later to bring everything home."

"That was my sign!"

"Yes, it was."

Even though his arm felt like it was being cooked over a pile of white-hot charcoal, he grinned.

Doc Garland, Trent, and Malachi were waiting at Tamar's when she and Amari drove up. They hustled him into the kitchen, and while Doc Garland looked at the wound, Amari excitedly told them how he'd gotten the gash.

"Dad, you should have seen how big it was!"

Reggie Garland said, "Hold still, Amari."

Tamar had been right, he did need stitches, eight of them in fact. It wasn't the most fun thing Amari'd ever had done to him, but he was so blown away by the experience it temporarily overrode the pain.

When the doc was done, he gave Amari something to take for the pain and then gave the rest of the pills to Trent to give to Amari later. Once he was patched and the wound wrapped, they gathered around his phone to look at the video Tamar had taken of the encounter.

Mal said with surprise, "That's a female northern harrier, Amari."

"She took my fish too."

Mal grinned. "Usually they go after field mice, smaller birds, and the occasional frog. She probably had a nest nearby with babies to feed. You gave her a great lunch."

"I caught it for my own lunch," he groused, still disappointed over losing the trout.

Trent brushed an affectionate hand over Amari's short cut hair, "You'll get another chance."

Doc Garland cautioned Amari to take it easy for the next few days and gave Trent some last-minute instructions. After a wave good-bye he and his doctor bag departed.

Trent asked his son, "Ready to head home?"

"Yeah."

Mal said, "That was quite an adventure, young gun."

"It was!" And a second later he was back into the story, telling them how the hawk screamed at him and how big the talons looked and everything else he could remember.

Tamar grinned. "Amari?"

"Yes?"

"Go home."

He dropped his head. When he raised it again he was smiling. He walked over to Tamar and gave her the biggest hug he'd ever given anyone in his life. "Thank you," he whispered.

"You're welcome, young July."

He looked up and she winked.

"I'll give you a call tomorrow to check on you," she assured him. "And remember what Doc Garland said. Rest."

On the ride home with his dad, Amari replayed the weekend in his mind and how eye-opening it had been to be with Tamar. "I see why you and the O.G. love Tamar so much."

"Do you?"

"Yeah. She's awesome."

"I think so too. You two have a good time, I take it?"

"We had a great time. Up until this weekend, I was scared of her. I didn't know who she really was, like underneath, you know?"

"And now you do?"

"Yeah. Did you know she used to go to clubs?"

Trent smiled.

Amari finally stopped talking because the pain meds were starting to kick in. As he placed his head against the window of the truck and drifted off to sleep, there was something he belatedly realized—the hawk at the creek was the same hawk from his dreams.

CHAPTER 20

Things in Henry Adams settled down pretty much for the remainder of the month of May. On the eighteenth, there was a town-wide celebration at the Dog to honor Amari's twelfth birthday. Siz made him a huge cake that looked like a red sports car and Bernadine, who never did anything by half, hired a fireworks company to treat them all to an hour-long show to top off the celebration.

Spring's warmth finally came to stay, and as always happens, the state of Kansas was treated to a series of tornadoes that ripped through the plains, leaving destruction and sometimes death in their wake. Henry Adams and the other small towns in Graham County found themselves under their own share of tornado warnings from the National Weather Service, and during the week of Amari's birthday, the residents spent three consecutive nights underground in the shelter at the rec center.

Watching the devastation on the Weather Channel

in the days that followed, Bernadine sent up thanks that Henry Adams had so far been spared.

The first official meeting of Dads Inc. took place the next day. Trent, Jack, Reg, and Barrett grabbed a booth at the back of the Dog. When their food came, they all dove in, but Barrett had a question. "What makes a woman up and decide she needs a vacation from her marriage?"

Most of them knew Sheila had taken off, and for a moment, no one answered.

Reg said finally, "Not getting what she needs at home is my guess."

"What do you mean?" Barrett said, sounding offended. "I give her everything she wants, clothing, food on the table, a car."

Jack said, "I think Reg is talking about emotionally, man. That touchy-feely stuff women seem to thrive on."

Trent raised his glass of iced Pepsi in agreement. "Have to play with them, man. Find that soft place inside that most men don't want to go and go there."

Reg tossed in, "Give her a back rub when she's tired. Sit her on your lap and talk to her. It doesn't even have to be anything serious. For them, it's about the closeness."

"And flowers. Just because," Jack said. "It doesn't have to be a birthday or an anniversary. Women love that. Says you're thinking about them."

Reg added sagely, "But don't do like one of my boys who only brought flowers when he'd been out cheating."

"That's cold," Trent said.

"Tell me about it. Of course his wife figured it out. I think they can smell when you're messing around."

Barrett looked down at his plate.

"Anyway," Reg continued. "She busted him, set the flowers on fire along with his new Benz, then divorced his dumb behind."

Rocky walked up. "What are you all doing? Plotting to take over the world?"

Trent said, "We wish. No, this is the first official meeting of Dads Incorporated."

Rocky echoed skeptically, "Dads Incorporated."

"We thought getting together would help us survive our kids."

They all laughed and raised their glasses.

Reg said, "And compare notes in hopes we'll be better dads."

"I like that," she replied, sounding impressed. "I had a great dad, and any man trying to raise the bar on fatherhood gets my vote."

Jack sipped his drink but his eyes never left her.

"Okay, I'll let you all get back to it. If you need anything, let me know."

When she walked away Jack's eyes trailed her.

"Jack?" Trent said, then again, "Jack!"

Jack shook himself free. "Sorry. If I ever decide to jump back in the pool, it's going to be with her."

Trent stared, then laughed. "You jump in the pool with her, she'll put you in a headlock and hold you down until you drown."

Everyone laughed.

"I'd be willing to risk it," Jack responded.

Trent looked at him, really looked at him, and declared, "You're serious, aren't you?"

"As a heart attack. The minute I laid eyes on her, I knew."

Trent asked, "Are you crazy?"

"Maybe. Probably."

Trent found the confession unbelievable. "Okay, man. I'm wishing you luck."

Reg chuckled. "If this is the kind of stuff we're going to be talking about, I'll be here every meeting."

Male laughter rang out and they raised their glasses.

Amari spent the remaining month of June going to school, and with Preston's assistance working on the details for the August First parade. Things were coming together. Church choirs from as far away as Abilene had signed up and sent in their entrance fees. The frats and sororities at KU in Lawrence who rarely got a chance to publicly strut their stuff had agreed to participate in the step show. Lily had found a printer to turn Crystal's sketches into silkscreen flags and when they were shipped back, Rocky and Mal displayed them on the walls of the Dog where they'd grace the place until the parade.

Ray spent the month discreetly watching Crystal. Whenever he ran into her at the school or at the Dog, he spoke to her. He made it a point to interact with all the kids, so he wouldn't draw unnecessary suspicion, but she was the one he spoke to the most. Being the school custodian helped.

One afternoon the kids were all huddled up around the picnic table at lunch like always. He passed them on the riding mower when he saw Crystal waving at him. Taking off the earphones Ms. Marie insisted he wear to protect his hearing, he turned off the machine to hear what she wanted.

"Can you come here a minute, Mr. Otis?"

He walked over. "What's up?"

Crystal explained, "Tamar wants us to do a service project. We've been asking around for ideas. You have any?"

Amari said, "We swept out barns last time, this time we want to make some money."

He thought for a moment, "How about a car wash?"

They all looked at each other with excitement.

Preston said, "Now that's a money idea."

They jumped in and began planning.

Crystal said, "Mr. Otis, you are the best."

"I try," he said to them, and headed back to his mowing.

During the last week of June, Sheila Payne returned from her retreat, and Barrett and Preston met her at baggage claim. Her husband grabbed her and kissed her the way Bogart did Bergman in *Casablanca*; long and deep. When he turned her loose, she was so overcome it took a moment for her head to stop spinning and for her to catch her breath. "That's quite a welcome, Barrett," she whispered.

"Missed you."

She found that so surprising she was at a total loss for words. Turning to Preston, she smiled and opened her arms. He came eagerly and hugged her tight. For the first time in her life, Sheila felt herself brimming with a mother's love. Savoring it, she placed a long kiss on the top of his head. "How are you?"

"Doing good. Good to see you again."

"Good to be back. Have you been giving the colonel courting lessons?"

Preston grinned. "Yeah," he kidded. "Me and Amari both."

Sheila met the eyes of her husband, and the warmth in them let her know that something in his makeup had changed during her absence and she felt buoyed. "Well, you and Amari seem to have done a great job."

"We try. Let's get your bags and go home."

Her eyes still on her husband, she nodded. "Excellent idea."

They had dinner that evening, and to her surprise the men cooked.

The colonel grilled chicken for her and steaks for them, and Preston put together a pretty good-tasting potato salad.

"Where on earth did you learn to make potato salad, Preston?"

"Ms. Agnes and Tamar roped me and Amari into it one afternoon. Thought I'd try and impress you."

"You have. Chicken is wonderful too, Barrett."

After dinner, Preston cleaned up the kitchen, then walked out to the deck where the colonel and Mrs. Payne were sitting and talking. "I'm going to go hang with Amari for a while, if that's okay. You two probably want some private time."

Sheila nodded, "That's very perceptive of you, Preston. Thank you."

"No problem. I'll be back later."

Once he was gone, Sheila said, "He's getting taller."

"And has a girlfriend who speaks physics."

"Really?"

He told her about Leah Clark and how the teens met. He then caught her up on the happenings in town, from the parade, to Otis the new town handyman, to the new teacher Jack James, and everything in between. "I'm even in a fathers' support group."

Her eyes widened.

"Been learning a few things."

"Such as?"

"Can you step over here for a moment?"

Sheila got up and walked the short distance to his chair. When she reached his side, he placed gentle hands around her waist and guided her down onto his lap.

Dumbstruck, she looked up and asked, "Who are you and what have you done with my husband?"

He laughed and eased her back against his chest and, more importantly, his heart. "One of the things I've learned from Trent and the others is to be softer with you. Just trying to get in a little practice now that you're home."

She basked in the feel of his arms around her. Never ever had they done this before.

He used a finger to raise her chin so he could look into her eyes. "I want to apologize for disrespecting you the way I did with Marti. You deserved better."

"I appreciate that, Barrett."

"I'm going to do better by you, Sheila, I promise."

Sheila swore aliens had taken over his body, but she didn't care. She let him hold her and listened to the strong beat of his heart. "Henry Adams has been real good for us."

"Yes, it has. Did you get what you wanted out of the retreat?"

"I did. I got this, us. It's all I ever wanted."

"I love you, baby."

"I love you too."

That night after receiving a very passionate welcome home from her husband, Sheila lay in their bed in the dark with a big smile on her face. She looked over at Barrett, who was now asleep and snoring, and all she could say to herself was *Wow!*

CHAPTER
21

In San Francisco, Lily was also wowed. She felt like a rock star riding around with Trent in the back of their Bernadine-provided limo. This would be their last night, and that made her a bit sad, but she was determined to enjoy every last inch of the wonderful experience. "I could get real used to living like this."

Beside her, the formally dressed Trent drawled, "Until the bills start coming in."

She elbowed him playfully. "Always the practical Trenton July. Whatever do I see in you?"

He grinned. "You tell me?"

She looked up into his handsome face and said from her heart, "I see goodness, and kindness, and a man I'd like to be with forever and ever, amen."

He kissed her softly. "Flattery will get you everywhere."

The car stopped and a few minutes later the door was opened. The driver helped her step out in her very expensive high-heeled sandals, and she gracefully adjusted her silk wrap and waited for Trent to join her.

Like everything else the Boss Lady had hooked up during their stay, the restaurant they entered was elegant. The sharp-dressed maître d' welcomed them warmly and asked for their names. After confirming their reservations in the open book resting on a raised gold stand, he gracefully picked up two folio-sized menus and led them back. The dining room was not large, but Lily could see and smell money in the way the white-draped tables were set and in the faces and clothing of the other diners she and Trent passed.

When they reached their table, Trent stepped in front of the maître d' to help Lily with her chair and he stepped back with a knowing smile on his brown face.

Dinner was fabulous, the view they had of the Bay memorable enough to take to the grave, but when Trent stood, got down on one knee, Lily's hands flew to her mouth and she started to cry.

"Aw Fontaine, stop crying. Let me say this. You know this is my bad knee."

She grinned, wiped at her eyes, and nodded.

His stance had caught the attention of the other diners close by. They stopped eating and looked on with pleased interest.

"Will you marry me, Lily Flower?"

She nodded, then said through the emotions stacked up in her throat, "Yes."

She stood and he took the ring from his pocket and slipped it onto her finger.

The diners broke into applause and cheers.

"Forever?" he asked her softly.

"Forever," she replied with a whisper.

He pulled her back into his arms and then Lily really bawled.

Amari spent the weekend with Malachi.

"O.G. What does being a July mean to you?"

Mal thought about that. "Let's see. It means we try to carry ourselves with respect—something I didn't do when I was drinking."

Amari took in his grandfather's solemn face.

"I didn't. I was a disgrace, and you need to know that."

"Okay."

"It also means being proud of the fact that we Julys have something many other families don't."

"The history?"

"Bingo! Yep, the history. Of our family, this town. Most people these days can't even imagine what it feels like knowing you're walking down the same streets that your grandparents used. We see the same sunrise, travel down the same roads. Pretty special, I think."

"I do too."

"And, best of all, at least in my book. As Julys, we are the descendants of some of the baddest outlaws that ever robbed a train."

Amari grinned. "How bad were they?"

"So bad that their baby sister had wanted posters."

"Now, that's bad."

"You got that right."

Amari thought of something that made him uneasy. "They didn't kill a lot of people, did they?"

"No, not that I know, but they did steal a whole lot of gold."

"What did they do with it?"

"Most of it they sent back to the First Tamar in the little town down on the Mexican border where they all grew up, to help feed people."

"So that was good, right?"

"In their minds, yes. There was a lot of political stuff going on back then between the tribes and the government, and the Seminole scouts who worked with the U.S. Army, and in the end the tribe wound up with the short end of the stick, as usual, and the families were abandoned by the government."

"Why didn't they get jobs?"

"No jobs to get. They'd originally been hired to help the cavalry hunt down the other Native tribes still fighting to keep their land. Government promised to take care of their families and children."

"But they didn't?"

"Nope, so the July boys started robbing trains."

"Then they were sort of like that Robin Hood guy on that old movie we saw last month at the rec."

"In the world of Hollywood. Yeah."

"That's cool."

"So cool they all wound up doing time. Don't get it twisted now."

"I won't, but it's still cool."

Mal smiled around the sip he took from his can of cola.

Amari thought about the tale and asked, "Did any of the gold wind up here in Henry Adams?"

"Not sure, but there's an old legend that an outlaw friend, guy named Griffin Blake, did bury a sack of railroad gold out on the outskirts of town somewhere."

Amari's eyes widened. "Aw man, really?"

"I said legend."

"Anybody ever look for it?"

"Every kid who ever grew up here. Some adults too," he said, chuckling.

"Wow. Wait until I tell Preston."

Mal enjoyed Amari's abundant enthusiasm and planned to savor every minute the boy was in his life. "Have I ever officially welcomed you to the family?"

"No, not officially, no."

"Then let's do it now. Hold on a minute."

He went into his room and came out with a bottle of medicinal alcohol and some gauze pads.

Amari looked quizzically at the items, then warily upon seeing Malachi pull out his pocket knife. He watched him clean the long shiny edge with a bit of the alcohol and the gauze. After which Malachi pricked his finger with the tip of the knife. A tiny bit of blood rose to the surface of his weathered skin.

Mal looked up and said softly, "Give me your finger."

Amari swallowed but complied. His finger was gently pricked. When the small drop of blood appeared, Mal placed his finger against it and said, "My blood is yours and yours is mine. Forever."

Amari nodded. Now, it was official. He was a full July and it felt good.

When Lily returned home Sunday night around eight, the first person she wanted to show her ring to was Devon. He'd spent the weekend with the Garlands but she'd hired Crystal to bring him home Sunday evening, put him to sleep in his own bed, and watch over him until Lily got back.

"Did you have a good time?" Crystal asked as she gathered up the homework she'd been doing while watching TV.

"Yes we did. Is Devon asleep?"

"I don't think so. He was reading the Bible. I told him to come and get me when he was ready, so I could tuck him in, but he hasn't yet."

"Okay. Here's your money."

A pleased Crystal stuck the crisp twenty into the back pocket of her black jeans. Lily gave her a kiss on the cheek, and Crystal left for home.

Upstairs, Lily found Devon just putting away his Bible and when he glanced up and saw her standing in the doorway, his little face brightened. "Ms. Lily!"

He ran and jumped into her arms, and she hugged him like he was one of the most precious things in her life because he was. "I missed you, boo."

"I missed you too," he said, giving her a big kiss on the cheek. "Did you and Mr. Trent have a good time?"

"Yes we did."

He was wearing Batman pajamas and he smelled fresh from showering. She walked them over to his bed and sat on the edge with him in her lap. She asked, "Did you talk to Davis today on the computer?"

"Yep. He said he may not be able to come see us because of his work."

"Well, that's pretty disappointing news, huh?"

"Yeah."

"Maybe we can fly out and see him instead? What do you think?"

"I think that's good."

"Me too. So let me talk to him later on and we'll see if we can't make that come true."

He nodded.

She asked, "Did you have church this morning?"

"Yep and there were a lot of people. Some man there wanted to know if he could be my manager and put me on television. What's a manager?"

"In this case probably somebody who thinks he's going to make a whole lot of money. Did one of the adults talk to the man?"

"Ms. Roni. She told him to beat it."

Lily chuckled. "Good for her." Devon's fame was growing. She and the others knew that the leeches would probably be coming out from under their rocks, but the folks of Henry Adams were prepared to beat back all comers.

Devon continued their conversation by asking questions about her trip, what she had done and seen. After answering, she said, "Something very special happened too, and I want you to be the first to know."

"Even before Davis?"

"Even before Davis," she said, her heart full. "Lift up, let me get my purse."

He scrambled out of her lap and she retrieved her purse from the top of his dresser where she'd placed it upon entering his room. She'd taken the ring off before coming into the house to keep the sharp-eyed Miss Crystal from peeping her surprise. Now, with the curious Devon by her side, she took the blue velvet box out and opened it. The ring blazed in the light.

"Ooo. That's pretty."

She slipped it on her finger and they both admired it silently for a few moments until Devon asked, "Where'd you get it?"

"Mr. Trent gave it to me."

"Is it for your birthday?"

"Nope. It's an engagement ring, and that means he asked me to marry him, and I said yes."

His eyes grew big. "For real!"

The prominent Mississippi accent made her laugh. "Yeah, baby, for real."

"When?"

"Around Thanksgiving. What do you think about that?"

"Sweet."

Lily almost fell over laughing. When she recovered she hugged him. "So this means you and Amari are going to be brothers. Is that okay?"

Devon, his eyes still big with surprise, nodded. "Yeah."

They spent a few more minutes talking about the future

and then she tucked him in. She kissed his brow. "Thanks for coming into my life, Devon."

"You're welcome. Can me and Amari have a little brother?"

Lily began to cough violently.

He leaned up and slapped her on the back a couple of times. "Are you okay, Ms. Lily?"

After a few more coughs, she nodded. "Yeah. How about we talk about that later?"

He nodded and leaned back again. "I'm real happy, Ms. Lily."

"Me too, boo. Now you get to sleep. School in the morning."

"Okay."

They shared a final hug. Lily kissed him on the cheek, and after turning off his bedside Batman lamp, she slipped out.

Across the street, Amari was in his bed dressed in his pajamas and playing a video game when Trent broke the news about his engagement to Lily. Amari immediately jumped to his feet and began dancing on the mattress with joy. He made so much noise in fact that Malachi, who'd been hanging with Amari while Trent was in San Francisco, came upstairs to see what was going on.

"He's going to marry Ms. Lily!" Amari screamed excitedly when he saw Mal standing in the doorway.

"About time," Mal pointed out.

Trent gave him a look.

Mal took the hint. "Congrats, but guess I'll mosey on back downstairs."

Trent chuckled, "You do that."

A grinning Mal, glad to finally be able to call the Fabulous Fontaine daughter-in-law, left them alone to continue sharing Trent's happy news.

Back in the forties and fifties, there was a popular African-American singing group called the Inkspots. As those familiar with the group know, the lead singer performed with a ring on his finger that sported a rock the size of Georgia, and when he sang he'd flutter his fingers so everyone could see the big stone. One of their most popular tunes was "If I Didn't Care."

Lily remembered seeing their act on the old *Ed Sullivan Show*, so when she walked into work on Monday, she approached Bernadine's desk, fluttered her hand with the engagement ring beneath the Boss Lady's nose, and crooned, "If I didn't care . . ."

Bernadine's mouth dropped and she clamped a hand onto Lily's wrist. "He proposed?"

"Yes! And on one knee in the middle of that fancy restaurant!"

A happy Bernadine jumped to her feet and hugged her across the desk, "Congratulations! Oh, that is so wonderful. Let me see!"

They studied the beautiful princess-cut sparkler.

"Isn't it gorgeous?"

"Yes." And because Bernadine was an expert on such things she knew the ring had cost Trent a pretty penny. She also knew he could easily afford it on the residual payments he received for the mechanical devices he'd patented in his twenties, but as far as she knew, he'd never spent any of his wealth on anything that didn't apply to Amari or auto parts. "So, when's the big day?"

"Thanksgiving weekend at the Dog."

"I like that."

Lily looked at the woman she loved like a sister. "Thanks so much for the weekend. It was magical."

"I guess so if you come back engaged. Is he in his office?"

"Nope, had a meeting this morning over in Franklin. He'll be back this afternoon."

"I want to tell him he did good."

Lily looked down at her engagement ring. "Yes, he did."

Preston had a problem. There was tons of work left to do for the parade and he was tired of being the one responsible for doing it all. He and Amari were tight, but he felt like he was being played. Every time he turned around Amari was giving him something else to do. For example, somebody had to do something with all the checks sent in by the choirs. He and Amari hadn't realized they'd need a bank account to deposit them in and Amari wouldn't tell his dad or Ms. Bernadine about it so they could get one. He just kept telling Preston to take care of it but didn't seem to understand that he couldn't without bringing one of the adults into the picture, which Amari kept insisting they didn't need. It was stupid when you thought about it, but Amari wanted to run the show without oversight. Doing all the work, making calls, and writing stuff down was leaving him little time to read or text Leah Clark. They'd become pretty good friends since the day she apologized to him at the school opening, and he found he liked her a lot because they spoke the same language—science. She knew stuff girls like Crystal had never even heard of. He was hoping her family did move to town so she could start school with them in the fall. It would be awesome to be able to discuss stuff face to face. She wasn't sure they were going to move, though. Her parents were under some kind of money strain and no decisions had been made concerning their future, at least none that she knew about.

Something had to be done about the parade, though, so at lunch he tried to talk to Amari about it, but all Amari was interested in was telling everybody about his dad getting married to Ms. Lily and his Spirit Quest. After trying three times to change the conversation and being unsuccessful each time, Preston gave up.

At home that evening, the colonel must have sensed something wrong because he came up and knocked on his bedroom door. "Preston?"

"Come on in, Colonel."

He complied and stood in the doorway. "You okay?"

"Yeah, I guess so."

"Doesn't sound like it."

Preston looked his way. Feeling like he was going to burst if he didn't talk to someone, he asked, "Can I talk to you about something?"

"Sure."

So Preston told him about all the stuff that was going on and how he was feeling.

Barrett listened, and then asked, "How much work are you talking about exactly?"

Preston handed him the binders he used to keep everything organized, and Barrett looked through them. "You created all of these forms for the participants to fill out and send back?"

"Yes, and we got a bunch of checks that need to be dealt with, and of course, he wants me to handle it."

"This is very impressive, son."

"Thanks, but I feel like I'm working 24/7, and all Amari is doing is bragging about how tight 'his' parade is going to be."

Barrett leafed through the binders and paused a moment to look at the copies of all the letters that had been sent to organizations like area high school bands; two different Buffalo Soldier reenactment groups; the Black Farmers and Black Cattlemen; area historical societies; fire departments and police agencies; Boy Scout troops, Girl Scout troops; National Guard units. "All of these people are marching in the parade?"

"Yes, sir. Plus he wants to have one of those dog obstacle courses, but he won't call the sponsoring people back. Keeps telling me to do it."

"Preston, I am impressed."

"Thanks."

"So what do you think you should do? Have you tried talking to Amari about how you're feeling?"

"I can't get him to sit still long enough. Every time I try, he blows me off and gives me more stuff to work on."

"So, deep down inside, what does Preston want to do?"

"Preston wants to kick all of this to the curb, and Amari too."

Barrett understood his frustration. "Want me to talk to his dad?"

"No."

"You sure?"

"Yes, sir. I'll figure it out."

Barrett gave him a supportive pat on the back. "Keep me posted."

"I will, and Colonel?"

"Yes?"

"Thanks for wanting to help."

"No problem."

So the next day at school, Preston dropped all the binders on Amari's desk.

Amari looked at the binders and up at Preston. "What's this?"

"The parade stuff. I'm tired of doing all of the work while you run around orchestrating and taking all the credit. I tried talking to you about it, but you're not hearing me, so I quit."

Amari's eyes went wide. "But you can't. Come on, man!"

"I quit, Amari. Good luck with *your* parade." And he went to his seat and sat.

When Amari showed up at Trent's office after school, Trent took one look at his son's dejected demeanor and asked, "What's wrong, bud?"

"Preston quit."

"Quit what?"

"The parade company."

This was the first he'd heard that the two friends were having issues, although he sensed Preston was doing the lion's share of whatever they'd been doing, mainly because he hadn't seen Amari working on anything tied to the parade at home. "Did he have a reason?"

"Yeah, me." Amari wriggled out of his backpack and plopped down in one of the chairs. "Dad, I can't do this without him."

"Okay. Let's back up. Why're you the reason he quit? You and Preston are close as brothers."

"That's what I thought. He said he's doing most of the work and all I'm doing is orchestrating and taking the credit."

"Are you? And be truthful with yourself."

Amari sighed. "Yeah, he's right, but he's so much better at stuff than I am, you know?"

"No reason to treat him like a mule."

He sighed again. "I know, but somebody has to do the groundwork."

Trent shook his head at Amari trying to play victim. "Why isn't that somebody you? Preston signed on to help, that's all. This was supposed to be your baby."

"But Dad—"

Trent folded his arms. "Go ahead."

"It's like this. I know what I want the parade to look like, but I don't have time to be making phone calls and writing letters."

"Why not?"

"Because I had to make sure Crystal did the flags right. I have to talk to Nathan so he can give us a good rate on the airport pickups. I have to—"

"Nathan? Ms. Brown's driver? What airport pickups?"

"For the people who are flying in."

"What people?"

"People like the choirs for the choir competition, the Buffalo Soldiers. I got to talk to the hotel people in Franklin about room rates."

"What? Wait a minute, back up again. Start over. Better yet, how many people are you expecting?"

"Last count, two hundred so far."

"So far?"

"We're still waiting to hear from some of the other frats and sororities about the step show competition. There are at least three more choirs that have to send in their forms and money."

"Money?"

"Yeah. We're charging them a hundred dollars apiece entrance fee. I got to have at least five choirs sign up so I can pay out the five-hundred-dollar prize to the winner."

Trent stared. When he finally got his brain to move, he asked, "Does Bernadine know about any of this?"

He shook his head.

"Were you going to tell her, or me, or any of the adults?"

"Wanted you all to be surprised."

"I'm surprised all right. Tell you what. Do you have your paperwork?"

Amari fished the three binders out of his backpack and turned them over.

"All of this?"

"Yeah, Preston gave them to me when he quit."

Trent paged through and he was impressed. "Who made up all these application forms?"

"Preston."

"These letters too?"

"Yeah."

"No wonder he quit. Looks to me like you've been riding him hard and putting him up wet."

"But he's so much better at that kind of stuff."

"So you keep telling me." Trent saw a manila mailer stuck into the binder's front pocket. "What's this?"

Amari shrugged.

Trent looked inside and found checks made out to the August First Parade Company. "What are these for?"

"The choir thing, I think."

"You think?"

"Preston was supposed to handle it."

"Does he have a bank account?"

"No, but I told him to get one and . . ."

The look on Trent's face made his voice peter out.

Trent stood. "Let's go see Ms. Bernadine."

"Am I in trouble? I'm not going to have to paint Ms. Agnes's fence again, am I?"

"Just come with me."

All Bernadine had to see was the way Amari dragged into her office with his head down and the tight set of Trent's jaw for her to ask, "Okay. What's up."

Trent set the binders on her desk.

Amari sat in a chair to await his fate.

After she leafed slowly through the binders and heard Trent's explanation as to what it all meant, she gave Amari that look that he swore she'd learned from Tamar, then she called the Paynes.

When she ended the call, Amari said, "This is all my fault, Ms. Bernadine. Preston didn't do anything."

"Looks like he did plenty and he did it well."

That made him feel a bit better. Even though Preston was mad at him, Amari didn't want to be the cause of him getting in trouble.

The Paynes showed up a short while later. Bernadine then called in Lily and put Roni, who was in New York for a recording session, on the speakerphone. The adults with the help of the kids brainstormed what needed to be done. They discussed pretty much everything the parade needed. They felt they had to, seeing how things like bank accounts, travel arrangements, and everything else need adult oversight.

Lily and Sheila volunteered to help Amari and Preston with all the paperwork, and Roni readily agreed to help co-ordinate the choir completion. Trent and the colonel volunteered to help the boys contact the hotels and motels in Hays and Franklin to see what kind of room rates were available. Bernadine would help in the talks with Mal and Rocky about food and concessions. She also said she'd ask Otis to handle the cleanup crew because she could only imagine how much trash would be left behind after a parade and a full day of fun.

Once everything had been crossed off the list, everyone was confident the August First parade now stood a chance of being as tight as Amari had envisioned it to be, and they thanked God and the Ancestors that they'd learned about this potential debacle that day instead of the day before the parade.

Bernadine looked at the still solemn Amari and his equally solemn buddy. According to Trent the two boys had fallen out over this parade business, but she was sure they'd work it out. She had something to say to Preston, however. "Preston. Your hard work made it easy for us to pick up all this and run with it. Thank you."

He smiled shyly. "You're welcome."

Lily added, "And if you ever need a job before you become a big-time astrophysicist, I'll hire you as an office assistant in a minute."

That made him grin.

Bernadine turned to Amari. "Baby boy, you have vision coming out of your ears, but you can't put all the work on other people."

"I know that now."

Trent added pointedly, "And you need oversight."

For Amari there was that word again. "I understand." He looked over at Preston and said from the heart, "I'm sorry, man."

Preston nodded.

"We still friends?"

Preston extended his hand and they shared a grip. "Always."

Amari grinned.

Bernadine stood. "And with that, class is dismissed."

CHAPTER
22

Mal hadn't had much to say to Otis after their blowup over the roses, but Bernadine wanted him to talk to the man about heading up the cleanup crew for the parade, so Mal stopped him one afternoon just as Otis was preparing to take out the trash.

"Need to talk to you, Otis."

"About what?"

"The parade."

"Oh, thought maybe you were going to fire me."

"No. I only fire a man for not doing his job, and you've been on point with handling your business."

"Good to know."

Mal didn't like the man, at all. "The parade committee wants you to spearhead the cleanup crew if you would. Keep in mind part of that will be horses that me and the Buffalo Soldiers are going to be riding."

"That's okay. I'll do whatever you folks need to help out.

Sounds like this is going to be a big to-do, the way every-body's talking about it."

"Yeah it is. We'll pay you for the work, of course."

"Appreciate that."

"I'll have details later."

"Okay. And Mr. July. Hey, I'm sorry you and I got off on the wrong foot."

"It's okay," Mal lied, and went back inside.

Otis knew July didn't like him, and the last thing he wanted to do was stick around this sorry excuse for a town long enough to be in charge of sweeping up horseshit. First opportunity he got, he was blowing this pop stand and Crystal was going with him.

Over at the school, Jack dismissed class, and once the kids were gone, he sat at his desk and mused over life as it now stood. He'd landed in heaven. Not only did he have the full support of the parents and the community but he had a new house, and apparently a new relationship with his son. Things weren't perfect; he and Eli still got into it as all parents and teens tended to do, but the bitterness Eli had wrapped him-self in since Eva's death seemed to be dissipating. Jack, on the other hand, had become a proud member of Dads Inc., and had a black tee shirt with his name on it to prove it. Get-ting together with the some of the other fathers in town had helped him go from stranger to neighbor and he enjoyed their weekly Thursday evening get-togethers at the Dog and Cow.

"Can I talk to you for a minute?"

To his surprise and delight, Rocky stood in the door-way. He rose to his feet. "Sure, come on in. Grab a seat."

She didn't. "I wanted to talk to you about Eli and Crystal."

"Problems?"

"No, they asked if they could work at the Dog, but I wanted to see where they stand with their classes first."

Jack was confused. "Eli wants a job?"

"Freaked me out too, but I think he's just doing it to be around Crystal. She came to me first."

"Really?"

"Hey, he could do worse. If somebody could convince her to do something about that hair . . . never mind. What do you think?"

Sidetracked by her beauty, he asked, "You want my opinion on Crys's hair?"

"No, Jack. Her and Eli working. Stay focused here."

"First time you ever called me by my first name."

"It escaped."

He smiled.

She sorta did.

"They're both doing well in their classes," he told her. "So if you want to hire them, it's okay."

"Good to know. Thanks." For a moment she lingered, then turned and departed without another word.

Savoring the fading scent of her perfume, he sat back down and said to himself, *One step at a time.*

Everyone in town seemed to working on some aspect of the parade and there was a lot of hustle and bustle going on. Bernadine had Main Street paved. She didn't want their first parade to be held in the dust and dirt, and since the repaving project was already on the list of municipal improvements, she just had Trent and the construction guys move it up a year. It took them until the middle of the month to get it finished, but when it was, everybody said good-bye to the old rut-filled, pock-filled one, and hallelujah to the smooth, even-riding new one. Roni and Amari were talking to the choirs via Web cam and conference calls to put together the mass choir she wanted to sing as the last event Saturday night. They ran into problems with the big solo when a couple of soloists argued over who would be tapped for the role, but Amari hoped they'd act like the adults they were supposed to be and not kids when it came time for the performance. Sheila, who was pretty handy with a sewing machine, made vests for the men in town who were going to be marshals. She had Crystal sketch the flag design, then used the sewing machine and a laptop to turn the rendering into an appliqué that she applied to the back of the royal blue vests. Both Amari and Preston thought the vests were sharp.

The boys rode to Franklin with the colonel and Trent to check on room blocks for the visitors who would be staying overnight, and since business was slow, all the hotels and motels in the area gave them a great rate.

In the midst of all this, Bernadine also finalized the final arrangements for Nikki's burial, and on a rainy, stormy July day, she and Crystal drove over to the cemetery in Franklin and stood by her gravesite as one of the town's pastors spoke the words and the workers lowered the casket into the ground.

Henry Adams school went year round but there were extended breaks throughout. The current semester that began last May in conjunction with the opening of the new school would end at the end of July, and Crystal couldn't wait. She was really enjoying her waitress job at the Dog and would be able to work full-time just as soon as the school semester ended. She wouldn't have to go back to school until mid-September and she'd already picked out the clothes she wanted to order online with all her extra cash.

She and Eli usually worked the same shifts, but he and his dad had gone to Hays right after school to check out some new clay he wanted to get. She was glad he was getting back into his art; this new Eli was a lot better to be around than the old one.

Crystal entered the Dog, and after tying back her braids and washing her hands and doing the rest of the prep routine that she'd been trained to do by Rocky, she gave Siz a wave and went out to the diner floor. Kelly, the hostess, pointed out a family that had just arrived in the section Crystal was covering, so she hustled over to greet them and take their order.

"Hi," she said with a smile. "My name's Crystal and I'll be your server. Can I start you off with drinks? We have Pepsi products." And she verbally went down the list of beverage offerings.

Only then did Crystal realize that the family, a man and woman with two daughters, looked sort of familiar. "Weren't you all at the school opening?"

The mother, wearing a fancy suit that looked way out of place for the diner and the time of day, looked Crystal up and down and said haughtily, "Yes. We're the Clarks."

"Okay. Nice to meet you. What can I get you?"

"You can get a hairnet."

"Huh?"

"How much rayon is in those nasty little braids?"

Crystal's eyes widened and her heart began beating real fast.

One of the daughters, the little one, snickered. The older daughter shook her head and turned away as if it might make her invisible. The husband glared at his wife, but was ignored.

The woman didn't even look up from her menu. "Go! Get a hairnet. No one wants that mess in their food. Better yet, send us another server."

Her husband said warningly, "Colleen."

"Don't Colleen me. And you want my girls to move here with all these ghetto kids? Not on your life, Gary."

She then looked up at Crystal. "Are you deaf?"

By now the other handful of people in the restaurant were staring. Crystal could feel hot tears of shame and anger burning her eyes. "I'll get you another server," she whispered.

By the time she reached the kitchen, she was in tears and so mad she wanted to go back and slap the taste out of Colleen Clark's mouth. Instead, she snatched off her apron.

Rocky walked in and upon seeing her face asked with alarm, "What happened? Why are you crying?"

"I quit," she choked out, and started for the door that led from the kitchen to outside.

Rocky very gently grabbed her hand. "What happened, Crys?"

"Go ask that witch at table seven. I'm going home."

Crystal blew out of the door.

Rocky and Siz shared a concerned look. Then Kelly came in angrily. Having heard everything, she explained to them what happened and what had been said to Crystal.

Rocky was not happy. "Are these people regulars?"

"Not sure, but it's the first time I've seen them in here."

"Okay. I'll talk to the woman."

So Rocky walked out to the floor and upon seeing Colleen and Gary Clark and their girls at table seven, she said to herself: *Oh hell, no!*

Hiding her anger behind a fake smile, she went over to the table. "Colleen, I hear you insulted one of my servers."

Colleen looked up.

Rocky saw fear flash in Colleen's eyes before she hid it behind a show of disdain.

"I was insulted by that hair of hers."

"Do you remember the fight we had in eighth grade?"

"I don't know what you're talking about."

"Sure you do, and you're reminded of it every night when you take that front partial out of your mouth before you go to sleep."

The daughters stared.

Colleen asked huffily, "Are you the replacement server?"

"No, Miss Witch, I'm the manager."

Rocky glanced over at Gary. "Hey, Gare."

"Hey Rock. Heard you were back. Good to see you."

"You too. Mind if I take care of this?"

"Nope. Be my guest. She wouldn't listen to me."

"Thanks."

And then, in front of God and everybody watching, Rocky reached down, grabbed Colleen by her fancy suit, and snatched her up out of the seat so that Colleen would be sure to hear every word. "Don't you ever insult one of my employees again."

"Get your hands off me before I sue you!"

Rocky tossed Colleen back into the seat and before she could threaten Rocky again, Rocky picked up a pitcher of ice water from the nearest table and slowly poured the freezing cold contents over Colleen's head.

She screamed.

Tiffany Adele cried, "Dad, do something!"

He shrugged. "Your mother's on her own."

Leah tried very hard not to let anyone see how much this pleased her.

Sputtering, Colleen jumped to her feet, but everyone noticed that she didn't throw a punch. They guessed Miss Witch knew better, having already lost two teeth to Rocky the last time they came to blows.

"I will sue you!"

"Go for it." Rocky said to her before turning her back on Colleen so she could speak to Gary. "You and your girls are welcome to come back anytime. Not her, so get her out of here if you would."

"Got it. Thanks, Rock."

"No problem."

And Rocky walked away.

*   *   *

Thanks to the good folks of Henry Adams, Ray had been able to buy a car today with the money he'd been making. The Taurus wasn't new by any means but it rolled and it was his—well, Otis Miller's. Having wheels gave him options and a quick way out of town, so he was ready to make his move. He was tired of playing handyman and everything that went with it. Once he got his payoff he'd head for California, and Henry Adams could kiss his ass.

All that was left to do was getting Crystal alone. He figured his best bet would be to offer to drive her home and then go from there. He knew her work schedule and that she often walked to and from home. Another plus was that she and the rest of the hicks trusted him.

As he drove down the newly paved but deserted Main Street on his way back to the Dog, he spotted Crystal walking toward him. She was alone.

Crystal was crying and stomping mad as she walked down Main Street toward home. She knew her hair needed to be done, and she was planning to tell Ms. Bernadine to help her get it fixed, but that woman back there didn't know her! And then to talk to her like she was a piece of gum on the bottom of her shoe! She was so mad she could hardly see.

"Hey, Crystal. You okay?"

She wiped at the tears running down her face and looked over to see Mr. Otis in a car that had slowed beside her. "No." He'd never been anything but polite to her, unlike that Clark heifer.

"What's wrong?"

"Just got into an argument with a woman at the Dog. I'll be okay."

"You don't look like it. Hop in and I'll take you home."
Walking over, she pulled open the door and got in.

Over at the Power Plant, Bernadine looked through the mail
Trent had just brought in from his daily afternoon run to the
Franklin post office. Most of the envelopes looked to be town-
related, some of it addressed to the parade company, but there
was one addressed to her that was handwritten. Seeing the
return address was a J. Hurley in Cleveland, Ohio, she opened
it and took out the folded lined paper inside and read:

Dear Ms. Brown.

You don't know me, but my name is Jean Hurley
and I'm Nikki Taylor's sister and Crystal's aunt. The
prison gave me your name and address because
of my being worried about you being contacted
by Crystal's daddy, Ray. I hear he's been sniffing
around trying to find you because he heard you had
a lot of money. He's a no good lowlife. If he shows
up call the police. I'm sending you his picture so
that you'll know what he looks like.

Best Wishes, Jean.

P.S. Thanks for what you're doing for my niece and
for burying Nikki. I didn't have the money.

Bernadine looked in the bottom of the envelope and
found the picture. It showed a smiling, young, and healthy

Nikki. She was wearing a slinky dress and had a party hat on her head that made Bernadine think the pic had been taken at a New Year's Eve party. Crystal's resemblance to her mother was well shown. Bernadine then turned her attention to the man with his arm around Nikki's waist and her heart stopped. "Oh my lord," she whispered. Now she knew why she thought Otis Miller looked so familiar. As with all children, Crystal favored her mother and her father, and it was her face that Bernadine had seen in his. Terrified, she grabbed her phone, hit Crystal on her speed dial, and while she waited for the call to go through, she yelled for Trent and Lily.

"Hey, Mr. Otis, you missed the turnoff," Crystal said, a bit confused. "My house is back there."

"I know."

"Are you going to turn around?"

"Nope."

Crystal started to get anxious but tried to stay cool. "Then let me out. I'll walk."

"Nope."

"Let me out! Now!"

He didn't respond.

She opened her purse to get her ringing phone, but he snatched it away and tossed it in the backseat.

Then she was scared. "Where are you taking me?"

"Don't worry about it."

"Let me out!" She fumbled with the handle on the door, attempting to get it to open, but the lock controls were on his door.

He looked her way and smiled. "You might as well as just chill. You ain't going nowhere."

Crystal grabbed the steering wheel. The car swerved. He cursed and backhanded her so hard she fell back against the seat and saw stars.

He yelled, "Do that again and I'll kick your ass! You hear me?"

He righted the car and after giving her a frigid look, kept driving.

A terrified Crystal put her hand over her mouth and sobbed silently.

Bernadine was also terrified. Crystal wasn't answering her phone. According to Rocky, Crystal had left the Dog around four o'clock, but it was now seven and no one had seen her. Otis Miller aka Ray Chambers had taken the day off to see about a car he wanted to buy down in Hays but was supposed to be back in time to start his evening shift at five. No one had seen him either. She'd notified Sheriff Dalton and he in turn notified law enforcement in the surrounding areas, but officially they couldn't classify Crystal as a missing person until forty-eight hours had passed.

It was maddening.

But the residents of Henry Adams were too worried to wait for the police to officially get involved. They were all fairly certain Crystal hadn't taken off on her own, so everyone who was able was out searching the roads, the fields, abandoned farms and silos, and any other place they could think of where Ray Chambers might have gone to ground.

Bernadine drove around too. It was getting dark and her fears were rising. Where had he taken her and for what purpose? Sheriff Dalton kept reminding them that there was no concrete evidence that Ray had taken Crystal—after all, Crys had tried to run away before—but Bernadine knew in her gut that he had her, and she was going to move heaven and earth if need be to get her daughter back home.

It was past midnight when her BlackBerry sounded. The caller ID identified the caller as Crystal and Bernadine quickly answered with equal parts worry and relief.

"Hey honey. Where are you?" Bernadine could see concern on the faces of the crowd of people in her office.

"I can't tell you," Crystal responded in a voice that sounded like she was crying.

Bernadine's heart cried in response. "Are you hurt?"

"No. He says if you bring him a hundred grand, he'll let me go."

"Can I talk to him please."

"He just wants me to talk."

"Okay. Getting the money is not a problem, but I need to know where to take it."

The phone on Crys's end sounded as if it went to mute.

Her voice came back on a few minutes later. "He says he'll call you back, and that if you call the FBI or anybody like that, he's going to kill me."

Bernadine shivered. "Okay, I won't call the FBI. Tell him I'll get the money together and he can let me know where he wants me to bring it."

"Okay, Ms. Bernadine."

"Stay strong, sweetheart. I'll get you back home as soon—"

The line went dead.

Bernadine took in a deep breath and after fighting off her tears, she let her anger have its head and made another call.

Lily asked, "Are you calling a bank?"

"No. The FBI. Ray Chambers can kiss my behind. A hundred grand. Lowlife doesn't have a clue how much she's worth to me."

Mal nodded. "That's my girl."

The next morning dawned gray and humid. The Weather Channel was predicting severe storms for later in the day, but Bernadine didn't pay the announcer much mind. She clicked off the flat screen and focused her attention on the FBI agents setting up their equipment in her office.

Harris, the female agent, said, "If your daughter calls again before the phone company calls back with the location of her last transmission, we need you to keep her talking for as long as you can."

Bernadine nodded. She felt like a member of the walking dead. She was so worried about Crystal that sleeping had been out of the question. She and the rest of her extended family had been up all night waiting for Crystal to call again.

The agents had shown up about two hours ago. They reassured her that they'd find Crystal and she prayed they'd be able to keep their word. Rocky and Siz had sent over enough food to feed the army waiting for word, but no one but the agents seemed to have much of an appetite. Marie had had Jack cancel school. The kids were all at the rec center under the watchful eye of Tamar, Bing, and Clay, and the three were armed.

Crystal didn't call again until noon; by then the phone company had pinpointed the location of her first call, but when the team of agents had descended on the motel in a strip mall off Highway 183 south of Hays, the room was empty.

"How are you, baby?" Bernadine asked, trying not to let the worry seep into her voice. "Tell him I have the money."

A note from Agent Harris was slipped to her, and it read, "She's on different phone. Keep her talking."

Bernadine nodded at the agent. "Did you hear me? I have the money."

Ray was suddenly on the line. "I hear you. Bring the money to the Fort Larned Historical Site. Make sure you come by yourself and be here in two hours. I'd hate for you to take Crystal home in pieces just because you were late."

And the call ended.

She looked over at the agents and they shook their heads. "The new phone threw us off. It's one of those pay-as-you-go kind. Harder to trace. Her phone, the one she used the first time, is apparently turned off."

"So now what?"

"We send you to the meet and hope he's there."

So she made some calls. A courier with the money would be arriving via helicopter within the hour, but twenty minutes later, Bernadine's pilot, Katie Skye, called.

"Ms. Brown, we have a real problem. The courier can't get here because of the storm, and we can't fly out to pick him up for the same reason."

Mal, who had been monitoring the weather down near the drop area with his laptop, called out with alarm. "A tornado is moving through the Fort Larned area, right now!"

Gasps were heard and Bernadine's hand went to her mouth. She thought she might be sick. There was no way to get to Crystal now. She could only imagine how scared her daughter must be, and with storm on top of them, there was a possibility that Bernadine might never see her alive again. She ended the call to Katie without saying good-bye and prayed.

CHAPTER
23

Crystal was sitting in the car with the man she knew as Otis Miler and she hated him now. Her face was achy and swollen from the backhand he'd given her yesterday and she was hungry. "I need to eat."

"You need to shut the hell up. She'll feed you after she gives me the money, and I'm gone." Ray was nervous. He'd never done anything like this before. All kinds of things could go wrong before he got the money.

"You're gonna go to jail. The people in town gave you a job and everything and this is how you pay everybody back?"

"I told you to shut up!" He didn't need to hear no morality speeches.

The anger in his voice made Crys think twice about saying anything more. She focused instead on the sky. It was getting dark, real dark, and leaves were blowing around. She and Otis were sitting on the side of the road near the entrance to Fort Larned. Cars were passing by but they were all moving fast as if they were trying to get away from something. "There's a big storm coming. That's a wall cloud and wall clouds bring tornadoes."

"What are you, the Weather Channel?" he asked sarcastically.

"No, but I've lived here long enough to know that when the sky looks like that," and she pointed to the ominous green hue, "it's time to go to the basement."

"Yeah right."

But she noticed he was starting to glance up at the sky now.

"We need to get out and take shelter," she told him excitedly. "Maybe they have one inside."

The wind was whipping now. Cloud to ground lightning flashed in and out of the black clouds and the responding thunder boomed angrily. The area around them was so dark the passing cars now had on their lights.

Knowing all hell was about to break loose, she frantically pulled on her door handle. "Open the door, fool! You want us to die!"

The car was beginning to rock from the rising force of the wind. Airborne debris was swirling around like a scene from *The Wizard of Oz*.

She screamed at him, *"Open the damn door!"*

An airborne trash can slammed into the hood and then flew on. They both flinched at the impact and the now alarmed Ray hit the switch on the lock. Crystal was out in a flash. The wind was so strong it stole her breath and tried to force her to her knees, but she knew she had to get to the ditch behind the car. It was her only hope. She bent low and fought with each step. Her ears began to pop from the change in pressure. Stuff was blowing around her, smacking her in the face and body with dirt and twigs and gravel from the road's shoulder. Each step felt like it was taking her a million years but she kept going. The thunder and lightning strikes were so loud and so close, she could feel the ground shake. Rain was now coming down so hard it was horizontal, making it next to impossible to see. The wind was screaming and the force of it knocked her down. On her knees, she crawled and cried. She couldn't see the ditch, Ray, or anything else. Her entire world was owned by the raging storm. Suddenly she felt herself roll into a depression in the ground. Lying flat, she placed her hands over her head, closed her eyes, and prayed not to die.

The howl intensified until the wind blowing over sounded like a train. Suddenly she felt something hit her back, hard. It hurt so bad, she screamed, but the wind was louder. She wanted the pain to stop but instead it got worse, and then everything went black.

When Crystal opened her eyes, she felt really sleepy, but then she saw Ms. Bernadine standing beside her and she had tears in her eyes. Crystal wondered if she was dead and seeing her foster mother from heaven. "Am I dead?"

"No, baby, you're in the Hays hospital."

"What happened?"

"You were almost a tornado snack."

Crys grinned, or at least she thought she did. She was so tired she could barely keep her eyes open. "Am I okay?"

"You have some broken bones and some bumps and bruises, but looks like you're going to be okay."

She nodded.

"Go on back to sleep. I'll be here the next time you wake up."

"Okay," Crys murmured. She felt Ms. Bernadine kiss her cheek and she drifted back into the void.

Tears in her eyes, Bernadine stepped outside the room and told the assembled crowd of Henry Adams residents, "She's awake."

People clapped, cried, and everyone said thanks to the Lord for this much-needed blessing.

Bernadine hurried off to alert the nurses. What she hadn't told Crystal was that she'd been in coma for the past three days and everyone had been worried sick. Her injuries had been caused by the car rolling over on her. She had a broken collarbone and a broken right arm. She'd also sustained a major concussion, and the nurses had to shave her head in order for the doctor to stitch up the gash that had caused it. So it was finally good-bye to the gold weave, but Bernadine took no joy in it because of how it had come about.

Mal had been with her every moment of every day while she sat at Crystal's bedside. She knew that had it been necessary she would have been able to handle the vigil alone, but having him with her made the long wait more bearable.

When Bernadine returned with the doctors and nurses, they went in to check Crystal's vitals. Bernadine stood outside the door and wiped at more happy tears.

Amari, Preston, and Eli walked over to her. "Can we see her?" Preston asked. The boys' faces were lined with concern.

"Let's let the doctors finish up first."

They'd been at the hospital the whole time as well. Roni was home with Zoey and Devon and was being kept up to date by phone. Reg was the town's liaison with the doctors, and Bernadine was grateful that he'd been there to break down the medical lingo into plain English so she'd understand just what Crystal was up against.

The doctor and one of the nurses stepped out to talk with Bernadine, and while they were consulting, the three boys slipped into the room.

The nurse inside looked up at their entrance. She was checking all the machines and tubing Crystal was hooked up to. "You boys family?"

Amari answered for them. "Yes, ma'am. She's our sister. We just wanted to see her."

The lady looked at Eli. "She your sister too?"

"Yes, ma'am."

She smiled softly. "Come on over, but you can only stay a minute."

Without her makeup and with her head shaved, Crystal was almost unrecognizable. She appeared younger and more vulnerable. Amari thought her head looked like the head of the ducklings he'd seen on his Spirit Quest but he was happy to see her breathing. Preston too. To their surprise Eli bent down and kissed her cheek. Amari's and Preston's eyes went wide.

He saw their faces. "What?"

They both shook their heads in unison. "Nothing."

Preston said, "She'd never let him do that if she was awake."

"True," Amari said softly, willing her to open her eyes and look at him so he'd know for sure that she was okay, but she didn't.

"Okay gentlemen," the nurse said. "You'll have to go now."

Preston surprised Amari by doing an Eli and kissing Crystal on the cheek. It made his heart tight to see the tears standing in Preston's eyes even though he tried to wipe them away before anyone could see.

Amari kissed her cheek too, and whispered, "Hurry up and get well, Crystal. We love you."

When they stepped outside, their parents said it was time to head home. On the way out they waved to Ms. Bernadine, who was talking to Ms. Marie and Leo Brown, who'd just showed up.

"How's she doing?" Marie asked with concern.

"She's finally awake."

"Thank God," Marie said. "Everyone has been so worried. We've all been praying."

"And it helped, so thank you."

Leo asked, "Does she need anything, Bernadine? If we have to fly in an orthopedic surgeon or fly her somewhere to get more help, just let me know. I'll help with the costs."

Bernadine looked at the concern in his eyes. "You really mean that, don't you?"

"Of course."

Marie said, "I'm going to join the others, so you two can talk."

When she was gone, Leo said, "This has to do with Crystal, not you and me, so if there's anything I can provide, it's yours. I know how much she means to you, Bernadine."

She was touched. "Thanks, Leo."

"And I meant what I said, I don't care how much it costs."

For the first time in years, Bernadine was able to look him in the eyes and not want to feed him rat poison. "So it's going to be you and Marie?"

"I'm hoping. We're taking it a day at a time. She wants to go slow and I respect that."

"She's a very special lady."

"Yes, she is, but so are you. I'm sorry for what happened."

"So am I, but we've both moved on."

"Thanks to this town. Pretty good place you all have here."

"We think so."

"I may move in."

Bernadine went still. "Really?"

"That going to bother you?"

"I don't think so."

"Throw my millions in with yours, there's no telling what can be accomplished."

"True. Just don't be mad when I send you the bill."

"I promise I'll pay whatever it is with a smile."

She held out her hand.

He grasped hers. "To second chances."

"Let the church say amen."

As Bernadine walked with him over to where the rest of her friends were waiting, she felt as if a huge weight had been lifted from her soul.

*　*　*

Crystal came home a week later. Now, propped up in her own bed, her right shoulder and arm in a cast, she asked Bernadine, "So what happened to Mr. Otis?"

"Killed in the storm."

What Bernadine didn't say was that the authorities had found him five miles away from where Crystal had been found by the National Guard. The storm had evidently swept him up and then thrown him down so that he landed face up and impaled on the wide jagged points of a large picket fence. All in all, a terrible end to a terrible man. Bernadine had also been waiting for Crystal to come home before telling her the truth about Otis Miller's true identity.

"I need to tell you something else, Crys."

"What?"

"About who Otis Miller really was."

"Who was he?"

So Bernadine began.

The morning of August First dawned sunny and bright. After the near tragedy with Crystal, who was still laid up, the residents of Henry Adams were looking forward to having some fun. Amari and Trent shared a quick breakfast at home, then jumped in the truck and headed to the parade staging area set up in the field across the street from the Dog.

On the drive, Amari said, "I think it's going to be a good day, Dad."

"You think so?"

"I do."

"Then let's have a good time."

When they reached the field, marshals Jack and Eli were already at their posts and wearing the official blue and gold vests Sheila had designed.

"Morning," Trent called out as he drove past them to find a place to park.

"Dad, look!" Amari said excitedly. "Some of the bands."

It was 7:00 a.m. Parade participants had been asked to assemble no later than eight for the ten o'clock start. Three school buses were parked at the edge of the field. Kids in shorts and tees, their instruments in hand, were milling about.

"Looks like a parade to me," Trent replied.

Trent parked, and as they got out, they were greeted by Malachi, wearing a sleeveless tee and the blue pants of his Tenth Cavalry uniform.

"Morning, you two."

"Hey, O.G.," Amari called. "You look like a real soldier." Amari could see the other members of the troop a few feet away. They were laughing, talking, and getting their horses ready for the ride down Main Street.

"Gotta come correct," Mal told him proudly. "The legacy of the Ninth and Tenth demands it. Everything from our saddles to our caps are as authentic as we could make them. We'll put our coats on when the parade starts."

Amari knew from his class work tied to the history of the parade that the Black men of the Ninth and Tenth Cavalry patrolled the western United States from the U.S. Canadian border to the Rio Grande. The soldiers were the only law in a lot of areas that had no law back then.

"Come on and let me introduce you to my guys."

Amari shook a bunch of hands and received lots of thanks for coming up with the idea for the parade.

Moments later, Lily and Ms. Bernadine rode up on individual golf carts. Preston was on the cart with Lily, and Amari would be riding with Ms. Bernadine. He got in, waved good-bye to his dad, and headed off to get things under way.

By nine thirty everyone was lined up and Amari, carrying a clipboard, was seriously beginning to question whether this parade had been a good idea. First of all, the kids who were marching in the pet parade had everything from geese to goats, both of which kept trying to mix it up with the horses. After a goose charged the horses for the third time, causing the horses to rear and almost throw their riders, Amari threatened to kick the goose's owner out of the parade if the bird wasn't controlled. The goose's name was Gus, but Mal said his name was going to be *cooked* if it charged his horse one more time.

The goat, named Buster, apparently didn't like dogs and kept trying to butt any canine that made the mistake of coming close. Buster's owner, a ten-year-old girl from Hays, had to borrow a leash from one of the dog people in order to keep Buster at her side. Even then, Buster was dragging her all over the place. Her teenage brother stepped in and took hold of the leash and Buster was no longer able to terrorize, but Amari vowed to keep an eye on him. He ran a weary hand over his fresh haircut and hoped Preston was having better luck with the humans on his end.

He wasn't. The choirs were supposed to march in back-to-back each singing a different song. However, two of the choirs were singing the same song and an argument broke out over which choir was going to change. Neither wanted to, so he, Roni, and Lily came up with a compromise that put one of choirs at the front of the parade line and the other at the end.

Farther down the line the frats were talking smack to each other and wanted to fight. One of Sheriff Dalton's deputies had to step in on that one and threatened to take everybody to jail if they didn't start acting like they had some sense.

Bernadine was dealing with the local politicians. They too were jockeying for what they thought would be the best positioning. The plan had been to have them march in between the three bands, but they wanted to be first. They soon found out that this was her town's parade and she gave them the option of getting with the program or watching the parade on the sidelines with their constituents. They got with the program.

By the time ten o'clock rolled around the adult parade coordinators were searching for over-the-counter pain relief to ease their throbbing headaches, and Amari and Preston were looking for ice cream.

However, the parade went off without a hitch. The choirs rocked, the bands played, and the frats and sororities stepped.

The Black Farmers marched behind the Black Cattlemen's Association. They were trailed by Trent and the other fathers of Dads Inc. Mal and his Buffalo Soldiers rode proudly astride their mounts. Even the pets behaved—

although Gus's owner had to carry him, and Buster the goat strained at his leash the entire way.

Bernadine couldn't believe the number of spectators. They lined Main Street from the Dog to the Power Plant, waving and cheering. Television crews from all over the state had turned out in force, and the marshals ran out of the flyers that had been printed up to explain the history behind the celebration.

The final choir marched by but their voices were suddenly drowned out by the thundering roar of jet engines. Everyone looked up. Sleek blue fighters were rolling and diving and streaking low across the sky. The Blue Angels had arrived.

Preston and Amari began jumping up and down and screaming with joy. The jets stayed only a few minutes but it was more than long enough to knock the socks off everyone in attendance. They disappeared as quickly as they'd appeared, but the resulting buzz in the crowd was enormous.

Preston made his way to the colonel and ran and leapt into his arms. The grinning colonel enjoyed the moment. "How was that?"

"That was so cool! Aw man! Thank you!"

"You're welcome."

"I gotta get back to work."

"Go, go. We'll hook up later."

Preston hurried off to judge the pet races, and the smiling colonel watched him until he was swallowed up by the crowd.

The pet races turned out to be another questionable

idea, Amari decided. The first race, which had some cats and hamsters, turned out to be a mistake when a couple of the hamsters were chased down by the felines and sent to hamster heaven.

The second race had some of the bigger animals, like Buster the goat, Gus the goose, and a couple of hogs named Mutt and Jeff. Most of the dogs had opted to compete in the obstacle course set up on the other side of the field and were over there minding their own business.

As the second race began, things went okay until Buster the goat saw the dogs on the course and charged off in that direction. The other animals followed, and before anyone could react, the goat and his buddies were causing havoc. Dogs rose to the challenge, barking and charging back. People ran. The course's gates and chutes were knocked over as the big hogs, Mutt and Jeff, powered their way through. One lady fell and broke her ankle trying to get out of the way. An ambulance had to be called to take her to the hospital. It roared up with lights flashing, and Preston and Amari got an earful from the sponsors of the obstacle course over who was going to pay for the damage.

By the time the choirs sang at seven that evening, neither Amari nor Preston wanted to hear the word *parade* ever again, because even the choirs acted up. The feud between the soloists that Roni thought she'd taken care of broke wide. The woman she'd designated as the soloist began to sing but out of the back row came another voice. The one who'd lost was singing the solo too. As everyone looked on in shock, it became clear why the second singer hadn't been tapped. Soloist number one had way better pipes. In the end, someone nudged singer number two off the edge of the riser and she landed on the ground in the dark.

A fabulous fireworks display would end the celebration, and as it began a tired and glum Amari and Preston came over and sat down on the ground next to Bernadine, who was watching the show from her golf cart. "What's wrong?" she asked.

"This was a disaster."

"No it wasn't. Everyone had such a good time all they've been asking is are we going to do this again next year. They liked the food, the parade, the history exhibit, and the fun."

Both boys stared.

"Really?" Amari asked.

"Yep."

By the light of the fireworks Amari and Preston looked at each other with surprise.

Lily drove up.

Bernadine asked her, "So how many lawsuits are we looking at?"

"Eight, so far. The lady with the broken ankle, the people who owned the hamsters, the obstacle course sponsors, and the woman in the choir who wound up in the dirt."

"Total damages?"

"Give or take, fifteen, twenty thousand."

"Do me a favor. Once everything is all totaled, send the bill to Leo."

Lily laughed. "You're kidding?"

"Nope. He wants to help out, so we'll let him."

"Okay," Lily said. "I'm going to go watch the rest of the show with Devon and the Garlands. I'll see you in the morning. And Amari and Preston. Good job."

They were still stunned.

Bernadine said gently, "You two were looking at this from what went wrong, but the people who came looked at it from what went right. So like Lily said, good job. The Dog's closed, but tomorrow, the ice cream's on me."

They grinned.

"Now shoo. Go find your families and enjoy the rest of the show."

To her surprise, they gave her a kiss on the cheek and ran off into the dark.

Of course they were going to have to rethink the pet races if they did indeed decide to throw this again next year, she told herself, but all in all the August First celebration had been a great success.

She looked up at the fireworks display exploding against the night and sent up a thanks for all her blessings. Yes, there were still things to be resolved. Zoey still hadn't spoken. Riley and Cletus were now back in Kansas, and rumor had it there was going to be a big trial. Marie and Leo were still seeing each other, and she had no idea how that was going to turn out. And was Jack James really sweet on Rocky, as Lily swore he was? Bernadine didn't know what to make of that, but having lived in Henry Adams for a full year now, she knew that anything was bound to happen in the little town she'd purchased on eBay, so she didn't worry. Everything would be resolved in its own time.

Looking up, she saw Malachi walk out of the darkness and head her way. When he reached her side, they shared a smile and he gave her shoulders a tender squeeze. She scooted over to make room for him on the golf cart. He draped an arm over her and together they watched the fireworks fill the sky.

That night, Amari dreamed he was driving again, but then he realized he wasn't driving. He was actually flying on the back of a big hawk. He could feel the wind in his face and the bird's powerful wings pumping up and down. This time there were two suns. The one behind him from the other dreams had almost set, but a new sun was rising bright in front of him. He knew where he was going now. Home. Happy, he shouted with joy, and the hawk turned its head and looked back at him. The face was Tamar's. His Tamar. She winked, turned her head back around, and they flew on toward the brightly rising sun.

A+

AUTHOR
INSIGHTS,
EXTRAS &
MORE...

FROM
**BEVERLY
JENKINS**
AND
AVON A

Book Club Questions

1. Forgiveness and personal growth are two of the themes threaded through *A Second Helping*. Discuss these themes and the character(s) who exemplify them best.

2. Who got the most out of Amari's Spirit Quest, Amari or Tamar? Explain your choice.

3. What does Eustasia Pennymaker see in Riley Curry that would make her support him in spite of what she knows about him?

4. Will Bernadine continue to open her feelings to Malachi? If yes, why? If not, why not? And what role might Leo play in Bernadine's future relationship with Mal?

5. Two new characters were added to the mix. Discuss Jack and Eli James and the impact of Henry Adams and its residents on them.

6. Crystal says Eli was kind of cute. Would you like to see a relationship blossom between them? Or do you think it will never happen?

7. How has Lily and Trent's relationship evolved since *Bring on the Blessings*? Will Lily's organized and no-nonsense ways clash with Trent's laid-back attitude once they are married?

8. Discuss the difference in Preston's character from *Bring on the Blessings* to *A Second Helping*. Has there been a change? If so, what do you think are the causes?

9. One of the themes of *A Second Helping* deals with personal growth. List and discuss the characters this theme applies to.

10. Do you think Devon has a true gift for the Word? Will he change his focus as he gets older?

11. Does the Dog and Cow need a new name now that it has been rebuilt? If yes, what might it be called?

12. What do you hope to see if there is a third book in this series?

Dear Readers,

I hope you enjoyed *A Second Helping*. Looking in on the folks of Henry Adams, Kansas, was a treat. Per the title, this is our second visit to the small, all-Black township I created in 1994 for my first published novel, *Night Song*. Like Henry Adams, *Night Song* has been given its own second chance. It's back in print and I thank my publisher, HarperCollins, for the blessing.

Bring on the Blessings, the initial book in this series, generated a host of congratulatory mail and e-mails. Thanks to all the readers who contacted me. A special thanks to all the foster parents and adoptive parents who took time out of their busy days to let me know how much they loved the story and the many ways in which *Bring on the Blessings* mirrored the experiences of them and their kids. I urge them to stay the course. I also urge anyone who may have been moved by Bernadine's dream to reach out and share your gifts with a child in need. It will change your life. I promise.

This series has brought many new readers to the Beverly Jenkins table and I welcome you with open arms. I hope the modern-day stories of Henry Adams will pique your interest enough to look into my historical titles and learn more about the Jefferson and July ancestors and the establishment of the real Black townships founded in the wake of the Great Exodus of 1879. African-Americans have a rich history in this country and I am honored to be one of the *griots* telling our story.

Until next time,
B

Greg Anthony

BEVERLY JENKINS has received numerous awards, including three Waldenbooks Bestsellers Awards, two Career Achievement Awards from *Romantic Times* magazine, and a Golden Pen Award from the Black Writer's Guild. In 1999, Ms. Jenkins was voted one of the Top Fifty Favorite African-American Writers of the Twentieth Century by AABLC, the nation's largest online African-American book club. To read more about Beverly visit her website at *www.beverlyjenkins.net*.

Beverly Jenkins

BOOKS BY BEVERLY JENKINS

BRING ON THE BLESSINGS

ISBN 978-0-06-168840-9 (paperback)
The town of Henry Adams is falling apart.
Bernadine Brown is a woman with money to spend,
and she has some ideas about how the town should
be run. But will the townspeople be willing to shake
up their comfortable lives to save their home?

"*Bring on the Blessings* is a tasty reading confection
that you'll savor long after the story ends."
—Angela Benson, *Essence* bestselling author of
Up Pops the Devil and *The Amen Sisters*

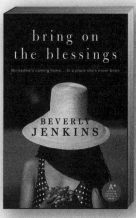

A SECOND HELPING
A Blessings Novel

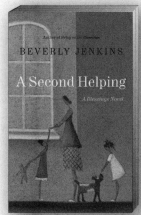

ISBN 978-0-06-154781-2 (paperback)
A lot has changed in Henry Adams since Bernadine
Brown saved the historic community from
bankruptcy. Now she's turning her attention to
revive the diner that was the town's former bustling
hub and meeting grounds. But life in Henry Adams
gets even more interesting when her ex-husband
comes crawling into town and stirs up trouble.

TOPAZ
A Novel

ISBN 978-0-06-117304-2 (paperback)
Kate Love is an ambitious reporter on the trail of
a mastermind swindler, Rupert Samuels, in 1884.
But when her investigation leads her into danger,
she is saved by Dix Wildhorse, a daring knight her
father sent to rescue her. Determined to hold on
to her independence, Kate challenges him at every
turn—but can't deny the growing passion
between their unlikely pairing.